# M.T. FORGOTTEN

Glory Peak

A Novel

Kevin Casanova Abrams

Editing, interior design, and distribution by Bublish
Published by Oso House Mercantile

ISBN: 978-1-64704-891-4 (hardcover)
ISBN: 978-1-64704-955-3 (paperback)
ISBN: 978-1-64704-956-0 (eBook)

For my parents, and their parents, and their parents before them,
but mostly for my parents.

And my uncle, who taught me to look at the moon and jump in the water.

# PART 1

*Oh-Sah-Cha-Me*

I know, now, yes, I know, that our sun
will soon catch up to the path of our days.

—As translated from the Le'Echuwanna
"Song of the Thousand and Two Moons"

## PRESENT DAY

Clover opened her window and stuck her head into the cold mountain air. Jade Ridge, Miner's Gasp, Pike's Pickled Pepper Peak; below her sat the entire mountain range that made up the Farangotta valley. It was still white winter, and as she inhaled, she could smell that it was going to be a long one, extending into April, maybe even May. That meant she wouldn't be able to harvest the morels or wood ears till June. That meant she would have plenty of time for *the other things*.

*The other things* she was thinking about waited for her in her downstairs office. Taking the form of banker's boxes and moldy trunks, she had not looked at them in years. Last, she did, they did not reveal much, just sterile information on the people who came before her. Of course, she knew their faces, so well she could trace them by memory and did, on occasion, with her finger in imaginary sand. Supposedly she had her mother's curls and her father's near perfect dentition. But when she asked those who spoke of how she looked like her parents if they were happy, there was silence.

And *the other things* spoke nothing of whether it even mattered to them to be happy.

# CHAPTER 1

**FEBRUARY 9, 1988**

T uesday, officially, the most pointless day of the week. So pointless, in fact, that Tuesday's mother refused to acknowledge Tuesday's existence. Life was not for changing on Tuesday; it was for getting to Wednesday, then Thursday, then Friday, when, thankfully, the weekend could start. Because on weekends, life could be for changing.

At least, that was what Annabelle Macklemore thought. Which, of course, contradicted what she was about to do because today, on Tuesday, February 9, 1988, she was going to end her marriage.

This was a very un-Annabelle thing to do. Annabelle, like all the women on her mother's side, was that tenacious, never-quit type of human who, at times, wondered if being relentlessly persistent was coded straight into her DNA. Thinking back, she realized she may have never quit anything— but then again, she had never been married. And after watching the buck stumble through the woods for the past five years, a bullet lodged in its neck, Annabelle realized it was time to put it out of its misery. So, that morning, as the sun cleared the Spotted Horn Range and feathered the Farangotta Valley pink, she and her husband, Bobby Mac, were going to administer their marriage the death shot.

Based on their history, this was a peculiar place to sign their divorce papers. When Bobby and Annabelle first started their life in the Farangotta, it was here, on this trail, which wound like leather up the peak called Miner's Gasp, they detailed their future. And it was on this trail they talked of underwear empires, braising turkeys, and what color sandstone they should use to finish their fireplace. But even though these hikes beamed with promise, at night, when they retreated into the hold of their alpaca-lined bed, they knew the future they honed with each step would one day disappear like a snowflake in June.

Bobby Mac was privy to this knowledge before Annabelle. Annabelle, in her dogged persistence, believed every plan and every discussion was a further rendering of their future. She was, by all accounts, a doer, and when a doer discussed something, that was the first guarantee of a doer doing. Bobby Mac, on the other hand, was a yayer. Yaying left, yaying right, yaying in a way that always ensured whatever they talked about would never happen. With the exception of their divorce. It was the one thing Bobby did not yay at, and it was even Bobby who suggested they meet at 6 a.m. on a Tuesday, at Prescott Loop, to sign their papers.

Spotting Bobby Mac appear on the horizon, Annabelle was relieved to see him walking her way. Watching his gait, the gait she knew so well she could use it as a metronome, she wondered if someone who had never seen it before would register it as peculiar. Each step started on his heel, and as he swung his off leg forward, he would then roll onto the ball of his foot like he was about to take a layup. And then, just when it looked like he would find air, his other heel would fall, and the up-and-down motion would continue trading sides like a piston.

Somehow, Bobby was still capable of this walk on snow. And one of the magnificent things about witnessing it was that it came with the fairylike suggestion that he made no sound or left no footprint. Watching him trudge toward her, Annabelle couldn't help but smile. Because as tough as it was to live with, she knew never to underestimate the value of a fairy.

When Bobby finally did arrive in front of her, she got a sense of how labored his walk was. His face was covered in sweat, his eyes red and swollen. *B-Mac must be cold*, she thought, because the alternative could only be that he'd been crying. And that would be unimaginable. Maybe on a Sunday, after a Seattle Seahawks loss, or even a Thursday, after a death in the family—but crying on a Tuesday, without a death in the family, *no, that would be impossible*.

Looking at her, Bobby breathed heavy. Catching his breath, he finally said, "So do you wanna do a quick Miner's Gasp?"

Annabelle was uncertain they needed to log that much altitude. But when Bobby raised his arm to present lead position, she instinctively said, "Okay, sure," and took a tentative step.

The problem with Miner's Gasp was it took the form of a maze of switchbacks that zigzagged up the steepest mountain in the Farangotta. For someone not familiar with altitude or trail climbing, the hike would be a series of jabs to the lungs and thighs. But the reward, especially for those who liked to reach back and look for the dig, was the greatest possible view of the valley.

Halfway through the climb, it was apparent Bobby was not prepared to reach back and dig. He was off—a wobbling top struggling to hold its spin. Concerned, Annabelle tried her best not to pry, but after Bobby almost tumbled after a simple step, she could not help but ask, "Bobby, are you drunk?"

Righting himself, Bobby spun toward Annabelle. The sweat on his face had now thickened and reflected what looked like the entire morning sun. Just as Annabelle was about to regret her question, Bobby flashed a snow-white grin and answered, "Yes, Belle, I'm fucking hammered."

Annabelle let out a quiet chuckle then brushed one of her curls off her face. "Listen," she said, "I've got an idea—why don't we hold off on this and just take Wobble Trail to the Boneyard and talk there? With the fresh snow, I'm sure it'll look pretty spectacular."

Huffing, Bobby nodded in agreement, then gathered his balance and started the ascent toward the southern ridge of the Boneyard. As they reached the top of the ridge, the promise of Annabelle's words came into view. Below them, a fresh field of snow unfurled over the Guinness Plain and dotting through the expanse of white were pines and redwoods with limbs raised in what seemed a celebration of morning light.

"Holy shit!" Bobby exclaimed through labored breaths.

"Right?" Annabelle said and stopped next to him.

Startled by her proximity, Bobby took a step toward the valley side. Unsure what to do next, he bent over and began foraging for something.

"Let me see if I can find something to sit on. I-I brought pens," he stuttered. "And I-I've got some other papers. They're for Clover and shouldn't take too much time."

Annabelle watched as Bobby shuffled about. Hoping to make eye contact, she sent a stare toward him. It didn't land. Instead, she just watched as his scurrying became squirrel-like. Exasperated, Annabelle sighed. "Bobby, it's okay. I can stand."

"I know. It's just that I don't want you to get wet or anything. I'm sure there's some bark or—"

"Bobby, don't worry about it. It's okay."

"I know, I know . . . but I just want this to go, you know . . . Just let me find you a log or something . . ."

"Bobby! Stop!"

Bobby stood straight and spun toward Annabelle. Watching him, backlit by the sun, Annabelle wondered if it was even him anymore or just an outline and shadow. As he took a step toward her, a tear rolled down his cheek in the streaking morning sun. Yes—the regular Tuesday sun.

"I'm sorry. It's just that . . ." Bobby stopped. His lips trembled; his knees trembled; his voice trembled. Not knowing what was gonna happen next, Annabelle tracked his hand as it reached toward her, his fingers spread open and twitching. Staring at it, she wondered if she should let it pull her into his neck and the cold of his jacket. Shifting her gaze to his face, she finally found his eyes. They were wide, watery, big enough to climb into. Studying them, she couldn't help but let a smile creak from her lips.

Extending her hand, Annabelle watched as Bobby lifted his fairylike feet off the snow. About to touch his hand, Annabelle then watched Bobby's fairylike feet float back onto the snow. But this time, despite their fairylike nature, they fell through the snow. Through all the snow—in front, behind, and around him.

Lunging forward, Annabelle tried to grab him, but it was too late. They were falling, arms punching up and down against gravity which had taken over. And before Annabelle could realize they had stepped into a crevasse or fathom how long the fall might take, all she could do was watch, stargazed, as she, Bobby, and a cascading flurry of white were lost to darkness.

# CHAPTER 2

**FEBRUARY 9, 1988**

When Bobby woke, three things came to mind. First, he was medical-grade sober. Second, his face hurt, brutally, as if someone loofahed it with a swatch of broken glass. And third, he was hot—like stuck-in-the-Sahara-Desert hot. This was more of a surprise, given he was lying in an enclosed snow cave the size of a Chevy van at the bottom of a two-hundred-foot crevasse. Unsure if bones were broken or chipped, he clenched his fists when a fourth thing came to mind—

"Annabelle! Annabelle?"

His scream ricocheted off the snowpack. When it finally died, Bobby heard, faint, in the distance, a whisper.

"Bobby, please stop screaming. I'm okay."

"Thank God . . . Thank fucking God!" he said. Slapping his hands together, he scanned the walls for the origin of Annabelle's voice. "Can you hear me? Like, can you tell where I am?"

"Yeah, I think so," came back, muffled.

Tracking the voice, Bobby turned left at a wall of snowpack. "Belle, can you move? I mean, I can. It's sorta . . . it's crazy. It's like I fell into some air pocket or something. I got about four or five feet above me and..."

"B, but can you just do me a favor? Can you please stay focused? I need you to . . . we need to work on getting me out of here because I don't have a lotta room here."

"Like, how much, a closet?"

"Less. So, I think it's best if I cool it on the talking."

Pulling his ankles from the snow, Bobby rolled onto fours and looked at the snowpack hiding Annabelle's voice. "Umm, okay. Well, how 'bout you kick your foot so I can track the sound?"

Bobby heard Annabelle grunt on the other side of the snowpack. Then he heard Annabelle say, "I . . . I think I can get to one of the pens in my pocket. I'll scratch the snow with it."

"Okay, perfect!" Bobby responded.

In the past, he'd been accused of being a poor listener, but Bobby knew that had nothing to do with his sense of hearing. His ears were good, and he knew he could navigate any type of snow. Suddenly, Bobby felt this plan had possibility.

Annabelle thought this plan had possibility, too. So, she pulled the pen from her jacket and dug it into the snow above her. As she moved the pen steady, the sound soon became hypnotic, allowing her breath to settle into a heavy rise and fall. Lulled by the warm tease of a meditative state, seconds blurred to minutes, and minutes crept toward the half-hour mark. Eventually, each one of her microbreaths brought her down a deeper path, where her thoughts floated above her like clouds, clouds that drifted across yellow skies and morphed in shape from sausage patties to leprechauns, humpback whales to a smiling Boz Scaggs. Then, as the tapping of her pen all but stopped and she inched toward unconsciousness, Annabelle's clouds turned into one last thing—irises.

The irises in question were not from the flower section of her garden or the bouquets from her wedding, but instead belonged to the eyes of Gunther Wolfe. Arctic blue, a feather of gray taking them several degrees cooler, they circled wide black pupils and connected to a man whose greatest attribute was that he had no problem looking Annabelle in the eyes during sex. So much so, it almost became unbearable. And though he wasn't her husband, and though she did not love him, it was in that gaze that she felt something. And in 1988, despite the jabbing guilt of those moments, Annabelle needed to feel something.

At times she wondered if Gunther needed the same. She watched him after sex. Usually asleep on his side, a half-open mouth peeking out from under a snoring nose. Based on his breathing, she knew he was content, but what she really and always wanted to know was *what does he feel?*

She knew he hated being alone. This was evident every time she tried to leave, and he would offer her a taste of his latest batch of schnitzel. And it was evident every time he woke up when she shifted in bed and asked if she needed water or more oral pleasure. These were just surface reactions she knew, a panicked reflex to her inevitable departures. But still, they told her nothing of whether he thought about her when she was gone? When his morning started, which she knew began the same way every day at six fifteen, when his alarm would go off to the notes of the prog-rock band Metromania, then continue with a cold shower at six thirty, a bowl of muesli at 7:02, and finish at 7:33, when he would exit his front door for a five-mile run.

She knew all this because he told her the details of his mornings every time he saw her, the times only slightly shifting. She also knew he once was a documentary filmmaker, a high-ranking slalom skier, a born lefty who was trained to become right-handed by his grandmother Marianne. But she still didn't know how he really felt. Like if he thought about her during his morning shower, or tasted her with each spoonful of oats, or fantasized about chewing on her neck when he ran. And if, as her husband Bobby dug through the snow to find her, he would care when she did not show up at his house today. And whether he would care enough to look for her when she didn't. Maybe missing their appointment would force him to go into town to figure out where she was. He would have to lie to everyone, of course, masquerade his curiosity for her whereabouts with the pretense of some sort of business as to not alert anyone to the real reason he was looking for her. Which was that she missed their weekly sex session because she was trapped in a crevasse two hundred feet below Farmer's Ridge. Swearing she heard

Bobby grunting just inches away in the snowpack, Annabelle wondered if Gunther could even come up with a decent lie.

# CHAPTER 3

**FEBRUARY 9, 1988**

In a town as small as Fortooth Bend, it was a lot easier to spread a lie than come up with one. Founded in 1847, when Prescott S. Norville bought 714,000 acres of land from a tribe known throughout the Pacific Northwest as the Le'Echuwanna, which meant keepers of the bighorn sheep, Fortooth was one of those towns where reality was far more potent than myth. By streets and buildings alone, Fortooth resembled many mountain towns in the Pacific Northwest. Born from an iron mine that employed almost two thousand in the mid-1800s, its boom created a grid of Victorian homes with front porches, pitched gable roofs, dormer windows, and pine trims painted yellow and blue. There was a Main Street with three brick banks, four insurance companies, six bed-and-breakfasts, and a hardware store. Feeding the town were two steak houses—one specializing in certified Angus beef, the other elk—a Chinese restaurant that served pizza, a hot dog shop that served Mexican food, a diner known for its blueberry pancakes, and a chocolate shop known for its vanilla ice cream. And hovering above it all was the Glory Peak Ski Resort, adored by tourists and locals and about to be hallowed by *SKI* magazine as the greatest winter resort in the Americas.

But it was when the snow melted in spring and the land would once again become visible beneath swatches of chocolate-colored slush that the town revealed its true Fortoothiness. Grass would sprout neon over the valley, and ponderosa pines would fill the slopes. Then, sprinkled across everything, were the columbines, their petals so bright it was as if they dusted every ramp in the valley with a glaze of fire-engine red.

Still, the most notable thing that emerged during this time was the viperous rattlesnake for which the town was named. Possessing four long fangs, two on top and two jutting from its bottom jaw, it was known throughout the state as the "four-tooth." With colors that blended, watercolor-like, between green, red, and yellow, they were known to disappear into any summer field below the tree line. But their camouflage wasn't what most people would have expected. Instead of lying under a swatch of bark or leaves, they would raise their body upward like an arrow, its rattle wrapped around the base of a stem and head pointed, next to a flower at the sky—that was until a critter or, worse, a human came too close. Then it would choose which set of fangs to use and which extremity to strike. In the case of Phil Simmons, it chose his penis, and for thirty-three years since, the men of the Farangotta preferred to piss themselves rather than risk an April Fortooth strike.

Gunther Wolfe had resided in Fortooth for eight years before he saw his first Fortooth. It was seven years before he caught his first golden Lahontan cutthroat, a species of trout so rare it was required by law to plant a time-stamped flag at the exact location it was hooked. And as far as being invited to join the Le'Echuwanna bear dance, well, Gunther would not have enough time in two lives for that. Often passing the Le'Echuwanna Reservation on his way to town, he would wonder what this rumored ceremony looked like. But more often, he wondered why the Le'Echuwanna had such strong disdain for him. Next to feeling alone, feeling disliked was the most difficult emotion for Gunther to handle. To counter such aversions, he often showered his target with compliments and gifts. This did not work with the Le'Echuwanna, who refused to befriend him even after he presented them with a trunkful of alpaca sweaters.

Maneuvering his 1977 Volkswagen Iltis toward town, Gunther wondered if any of the Le'Echuwanna ever wore his sweaters. They took them from him, never said thank you, and never spoke to him again. But were they wearing them? Using them with glee in winter? Maybe he could go to their reservation under the guise of looking for Annabelle to see if any of them were wearing his undeniably warm and colorful garments. *Aargh, they would see through this miserable and transparent ruse*, he thought. Gunther knew he was a terrible liar and even worse manipulator, as the rash now forming around his neck proved.

But he did discover one thing on this drive, he was good at worrying. And since Annabelle had missed their meeting without a phone call, worrying was all he could do. Annabelle had never been late to or skipped an appointment before. If anything, she would either arrive early, or if plans had to change, she would call the night before—which did not happen. All this, combined with a collection of gray clouds moving steadily toward town, gave Gunther the gnawing feeling that something might be wrong. Like when he almost bought two hundred acres of land out by Punishment Lake from Earl DeRichard. "Deal of the century," Earl kept telling him, but Gunther sensed something was off. Not the price, which was decent but not a steal; it was the fact that Earl claimed he only wanted to do business with Gunther or not sell at all. Digging through the property's history, Gunther discovered that Earl didn't even own the parcel. He also discovered that Earl wasn't even Earl. He was Rudy Della Russo from Toms River, New Jersey, a fugitive hiding out from the IRS on embezzlement charges stemming from his dental supply company. Proud that he followed the question mark in his gut, Gunther took this experience as an example of his astute business intuition instead of what it really was—Earl/Rudy thinking Gunther was a putz.

Pulling onto US 421—or, as the locals called it, Yeehaw Pass—Gunther smiled at the memory of that victory. His car now heading toward town; his intuition began to tell him something different. Sure, Annabelle missed a meeting, but she had a family and life was unpredictable. Most likely she got stuck running some last-minute errands or was putting a fire out for Bobby Mac. Gunther was aware of Bobby Mac's capacity for causing chaos nd figured all he had to do was take a quick tour of town to find Annabelle's Subaru parked somewhere, biding time, to solve her disappearance.

Bearing right onto Main Street, Gunther watched the tourists walk hand in hand past the leaded glass storefronts. Her car nowhere in sight, he spun through a list of other places she could be—Diggity's getting a hot dog, oil change at Sven's, picking up vegetables from the Mountain Bean Co-op? None of these felt right until the slot machine of options landed on Glory Peak. Founded by none other than Annabelle's father-in-law, William Jefferson Macklemore, the World War II hero and reigning figurehead of the Farangotta Valley, Glory Peak was, per the brochures, "where heaven went to ski."

Turning left as Main Street dead-ended at the south end of town, Gunther hummed his way through a series of snowbanked S-turns. *Of course she was there*, he thought. *And what a treat it would be to see her at his favorite on-piste place to ski in the world.* Besides skiing, she was one of the few things in his life that made him feel something—specifically, the something he felt when he was twelve and saw his neighbor Hannah Spengler. *Bliss. Teeth itching bliss.*

Which was the opposite of the scene outside the Glory Peak offices. Usually, Bill's vintage red 1976 four-door Land Rover stood watch out front, flanked by the white GMC pickups that were the unspoken mascots of Glory Peak resort. On their doors, and darn near every available wall in town, was Glory Peak's bright-blue emblem: two white skis crossing in an *X* inside a navy-blue rectangle with the words Glory Peak above them. Gunther loved this emblem, even though it was a direct reference to the insignia of the US Army's 10th Mountain Division, the regiment who happened to be responsible for killing Gunther's grandfather on the slopes of the Po Valley on April 4, 1944. Bill had built his reputation by being a decorated hero in this advance, so it was quite possible Bill himself may have killed Gunther's grandfather. Regardless of the details, Gunther's grandfather was a Nazi, and if he did, by chance, end up on the end of Bill's bayonet, what an honor it was for his grandfather to be gutted by the man who brought "Glory" to America.

But instead of seeing Bill's red Land Rover outside the Glory Peak offices, Gunther saw four of Fortooth Bend's eleven police cars. Confused, Gunther parked behind one and watched a small posse of mountain staff run toward the offices. Next, above him, came the steady fan of a distant helicopter. Leaning forward to get a better look, Gunther watched the helicopter bank left past Glory Peak and head toward a storm forming in the distance.

*Avalanche*, Gunther thought. They averaged between seven and nine a year in the Farangotta, and with this year's record-setting snowfall and unpredictable rise in temperature, more avalanches than normal were expected.

Impressed by Bill's quick response, Gunther pulled the key from the ignition, opened his glove compartment, and grabbed a yellow scarf adorned with the outline of a wolf howling at the moon. He was about to exit his car and head toward the resort village when, through his windshield, he saw three more police officers and a fireman sprint toward the offices. In that quick moment, his intuition shifted back to worry, and instead of walking toward the resort village he walked toward the Glory Peak offices.

Opening the front door, he saw a makeshift command center taking effect. People paced the halls as police radios squeaked and hissed static. A deputy tacked a map of the valley to a wall in a glass conference room while the receptionist spoke into a phone cupped to her face.

Tapping his foot, Gunther scanned the office and wondered who to approach. As the receptionist lowered the phone and offered some eye contact, he decided to approach her. Landing at a brown formica counter that connected to her desk, Gunther smiled and unwound the scarf from his neck.

"Um, excuse me, ma'am, can you tell me what's going on?"

The receptionist rested the phone on her shoulder. "I'm sorry, but I am not at . . . It's a personal matter," came out in a whisper. She then nodded at someone behind Gunther and pointed right. Turning around, he saw a police officer walk towards a conference room. In his hands was a poster board with the pictures of Annabelle and Bobby Macklemore pasted to it.

Turning back toward the receptionist, Gunther began to shake. "Did something happen to Annabelle? She was supposed to . . ."

The receptionist pulled the receiver from her shoulder, then placed it on its cradle so quietly, one would think if any sound was released, the world would turn to smoke.

"Wait, you know something about Annabelle?" she asked.

"Of course, I do. I'm Gunther Wolfe, her real estate advisor. I mean . . . Yes, I . . . We are friends."

It took a moment for Gunther to notice the quiver of the receptionist's lips and a further moment to notice the water swelling at the base of her eyelids.

She then leaned forward and said, "Annabelle and Bobby Mac were lost this morning in an avalanche by Miner's Gasp."

Gunther recoiled as if she pointed a shotgun at his face.

"What, what, how . . . how do you know?"

"The police put it together when Clover never showed up to school."

# CHAPTER 4

**FEBRUARY 9, 1988**

C lover Dolores Macklemore loved mornings, a sentiment most people would not expect a four-year-old to have. Alert, she would wake with the sun, roll her body east, then take in the warm rays as they peeked through her bedroom windows. Next, she would listen for the sounds from her parents' bedroom as they woke. Sometimes, they would be made up of the slap of her dad's hand on the alarm, followed by the squeak of the mattress and his feet pittering to the bathroom. Sometimes, it was the slap of her mom's hand on the alarm, followed by the squeak of the mattress and her feet pattering to the bathroom. And sometimes, though not so much these days, it was the sound of her father's hand on the alarm, then a deep "nooooo," followed by a giggle from her mom. This giggle would, eventually, give way to several squeaks of the mattress and end with her mom praying to God and her dad releasing a wall-shaking "harrumph." Every time this happened, sure as dirt, Clover would be late to school and wouldn't see her father until dinner.

This morning, none of that happened. Clover woke, hoping to hear something from her parents' room, but before she could even roll over and feel the morning sun, her mother was opening the door and tip-toeing over to her bed. Pulling her arms from under her flannel sheets, Clover watched her mom sit down and look at her. Her hair was pulled back, a light trace of lipstick and mascara on her face.

"Morning, sweetie," Annabelle said as she smiled at Clover. Clover was still a bit crusty, her eyes slow to move, still somewhere closer to sleep than wake-up.

"I need you to do me a favor, okay? Your dad called, and he wants to meet me this morning, up by Miner's Gasp."

Clover listened, her hands rubbing her eyes. She liked going for hikes up there. Maybe this meant she would miss school today.

"But it's a big-person meeting," Annabelle continued. "So, I need for you to stay here for a little bit while I go visit with your dad."

Clover scrunched her face. She was not sure where this was going.

"Please don't be mad at me, sweetie. I know this is a grown-up thing to ask, but I'll be back in just a little bit. And I'll have Daddy, and we can get you some Swedish fish and spend the whole day together."

Clover stared back at her mom. This was not where she wanted the conversation to go. Yes, she wanted to see her dad; yes, she wanted Swedish fish; but no, she did not want to wait at home, alone.

Digging her eyes deeper into her mom, Clover scanned her from head to foot. She looked pretty. But also rubbed her scalp a bunch when she stared back. Clover did not want to make her sad. She looked sad a lot lately. Watching a hint of the morning sun wink in her mom's eyes, Clover rubbed her nose, and finally nodded yes.

"You're the best, pea." Annabelle grinned back, a set of relieved teeth. "Two hours tops."

Before Clover could nod yes again, her mother was up and walking toward the door. Pausing one last time, she looked at Clover. "You know I love you, pea?"

Of course, Clover knew that. Was there supposed to be another option? Sitting up against the wrought iron of her bed, Clover watched her mom turn and walk out of her room.

Now fully awake, Clover jumped out of bed and ran toward her east-facing windows. Through them, she watched her mom's white Subaru Outback speed down the driveway and sputter a trail of black. Confused, she began to tear up. *Why can't I come, too?* she thought. Actually, what she really thought was, *I WANT TO GO TOO.*

Angry, Clover ran to her bed, pulled the covers over her face, and kicked an imaginary outline of her mom. Soon, she was flushed and her screams turned to gasps for air. Air she welcomed when she pulled the covers back. Outside, the sun was spreading its gold over the valley, but the warmth of its rays ran cool in her room. What was she supposed to do? And then it hit her. Her mom did not love her.

When Clover's grandmother, Nanny A, showed up three hours later, she was shocked to see Clover on the sofa, elbows-deep in a mess of pillows and Pound Puppies. A jar of pickled habaneros in hand, Nanny A watched Clover jump from the pillows and sprint up the stairs. Confused, she followed a trail of raisins from the living room into the kitchen and placed the habaneros in the refrigerator.

Turning back to the chaos in the living room, Nanny A finally said, "Clover, what are you doing up there?"

Waiting for a response, Nanny A only heard the scramble of feet, and a wooden trunk slam shut.

"Clover, get down here now!" she followed.

Nanny A knew Clover would listen to her. And as Nanny A heard the trunk squeak open, she knew Clover would be downstairs soon. Waiting, she began to dismantle the pillow fort and redress the sofa. When the last pillow was placed, Clover sat on it.

"So?" she asked, trying to lock eyes with Clover. But Clover only looked at her feet and gripped her polka-dotted Pound Puppy. This was out of character, so Nanny A followed with, "You okay, pea? What's going on? Where's mom?"

Eyes still locked on her feet, Clover said nothing. Finally, after a three-sniffle pause, she said, "She's not home."

"What do you mean she's not home?"

"She left in Scooby. She said she'd come back."

Shaking her head, Nanny A placed her hands on her hips. *For fuck's sake . . .* Looking down at Clover, she squatted down to be at her eyeline.

"Listen, sweetie, this is important: Do you know what time it was when she left?"

Clover shook her head no, then placed the Pound Puppy on the sofa. "Can I have some more raisins?" she asked.

Eyeing the empty house, Nanny A started to tap her lip. "I've got a better idea—how about we go into town and get you some pancakes?"

Turning her Volvo 240 onto Yeehaw Pass, a million possibilities of Annabelle's whereabouts sped through Nanny A's head. *Morning hike? Possible, but she'd be back by now. Meeting with Gunther? No, not if it risked taking Clover to school late. It had to be Bobby Mac. That worthless juvenile sack of a husband.*

Squeezing the steering wheel, she mumbled about how she "should have sprung and got her that fucking mobile phone for Christmas," unaware, as she revved toward town, of the giant mass of clouds forming above her.

When they pulled into the parking lot of Lola's Diner, the mass of clouds began to shake down a confetti of white. Unimpressed by the large, feathery flakes, Clover's thoughts were locked on the mounds of blueberries and chocolate chips she was going to pour on her pancakes. Nanny A, on the other hand, was locked on finding Sheriff Dan Daley, who used Lola's as his unspoken office.

On entering, she saw him where she expected—in the back-left booth, negotiating a hot cup of coffee. Sprinting to a booth across from him, Clover began arranging the butter packets on the table in a giant letter *C*. As Nanny A approached Sheriff Dan, he smiled, took a big sip of coffee, then said, "Abigail, what a lovely surprise."

"Okay, okay, Dan, I don't want to make a scene here."

His smile still full, Dan put his mug down and looked at Abigail. "C'mon, I'd never do that in front of Clover. Sincerely, it is a nice surprise. How can I help you?"

Nervous, Nanny A slid into the booth and grabbed the fork from his table setting. "I found Clover at home running crazy in the house. She said Belle left this morning and hadn't come back."

"Really, by herself?" Sheriff Dan answered.

"Don't, Dan. She's a damn good mom."

"I know, I know. Well, maybe she had an errand to run. You know, get to the bank early or go see Bobby Mac?"

"Bobby Mac." Nanny A shook her head. "Of course, she went someplace with that piece of . . ." Nanny A paused and looked over at Clover, who was watching her. Turning back to Sheriff Dan, she leaned in and whispered, "Listen, I know her. There's no way she wouldn't have been back to Clover as soon as she could."

Thinking, Sheriff Dan Daley lifted his mug and took a sip. "Let me check in with the station."

Relieved, Nanny A grabbed his hand and mouthed a small "thank you." Sheriff Dan smiled when she touched his hand. Realizing she may have sent the wrong signal; she pulled her hand back and let him walk to his patrol car parked out front. For the moment, Nanny A felt calm. Sheriff Dan, surely, would sort this out. In a minute or two, he'd walk in, all smiles, and tell her Annabelle's Subaru got a flat tire a half mile away or something like that.

Smiling now, Nanny A slid into Clover's booth.

"Nanny, can I have some rasp-perry syrup?"

"Of course, sweetie. You get to eat whatever you want."

But just as Clover reached for the syrup jar, the diner door opened, and Sheriff Dan Daley ran inside. Studying the look on his face, Nanny A felt the hole already forming in her heart triple in size. Without a word, she got up and met him halfway.

"There was an avalanche at Miner's Gasp," he said. "Happened early this morning. It was reported about fifteen minutes ago." Breathless, Nanny A felt the hole grow big enough to swallow her ribs.

When they found Annabelle's car, it was half-buried in snow. Examining the surroundings, Nanny A knew any hope of finding footprints would be erased by the twenty-three inches of fresh powder accumulating around them. But sitting before them, beneath a dense squall of snowfall, stood one obvious suspect—Miner's Gasp. On its slopes, which led to an area locals referred to as the Boneyard, were splintered shards of trees and, at its base, swollen, irregular mounds of snowpack—both telltale signs of an avalanche. Looking at Sheriff Dan's face, she knew what had to happen next. But she also knew that Sheriff Dan would have to make the call because, as she once promised herself, no matter what happened, even if the world cracked in two and broke down into a rain of rock and sand, she would never, ever, in a billion light-years, reach out to William Jefferson Macklemore.

# CHAPTER 5

## A BACKSTORY

William Jefferson Macklemore loved the mountains. He also loved salt-cured trout, the feeling of his Hart skis as they carved through fresh powder, and his testicles. The trout, these days, got more attention than his skis, and the skis, these days, got more attention than his testicles—but it was his testicles that still had the greatest value. And candidly, it was because they worked so poorly. Because that meant for nearly forty-four years of his life, these poorly working testicles enabled Bill to have wonderful, passionate, irresponsible, unprotected sex.

Growing up in New York City, where the women were plentiful and came in a variety of flavors, this would have been an incredible talent to have. However, growing up in the Northern California town of Pine Knolls—a town with a population of three hundred and eleven, whose greatest renown was the Convent of Saint Paulinus de Nola—his testicles barely had an opportunity to perform, let alone perform poorly. Yes, there was masturbating—the mad, multiday, multihour, sometimes multiminute examples of it—but the women in Pine Knolls were raised under the watchful eyes of parents and nuns, so the time he would have spent romancing a sweetheart in the back seat of a Packard was instead spent on mastering other skills.

In Bill's case, the most important skill he mastered during this time was skiing. Eventually, this skill became so great, nothing in Northern California could challenge him. So, on a dare from his high school gym teacher, he enlisted in the army, specifically the 10th Mountain Division, which specialized in Arctic warfare. And it was then, when he was stationed in Italy during World War II, that his poorly performing testicles finally had their opportunity to shine. Like polished marble.

Truth be told, he could have been a glass-blowing monkey juggler, and he still wouldn't have had trouble bedding the Italian women who came his way. World War II was coming to an end, and Mussolini was on his way to being shot. A six-foot-two Allied soldier with a coif of blond hair, who glided on skis, ballet-like, through Italian snow, was as unstoppable as Axis surrender. Knowing this, Bill took advantage. And when he got back to the States and worked as a ski instructor at the Sun Valley Resort, Bill also took advantage. And during the eleven years he coached the US ski team, Bill especially took advantage. But when he accidentally stumbled into the town of Fortooth Bend and set his eyes on Suzanne Joanne Dempsey, for the first time in his adult life, Bill did not want to take advantage. He wanted to settle down.

Suzanne, however, did not.

At only twenty-two years old and fresh out of college with a fashion degree, she'd tasted enough of the real world to know she did not want to spend any more time in Fortooth. For her parents, a pair of first-generation Irish immigrants, Fortooth may have been the perfect place to in America to settle. They'd grown Danu's Candy, a modest confectionary they founded, into a soda shop, then a hardware and department store that anchored all retail in Fortooth. But Suzanne craved a different version of the entrepreneurial dream—a saltier, more bohemian one. Her plan was to move to London, the epicenter of swinging sixties fashion, and launch the most psychedelic miniskirt empire Europe had ever seen. Of course, her gentle, loving parents were supportive, as they were with any of Suzanne's whims. But their support came with stipulations. In this case, no money if she went to England but an above-average salary as head of shipping and receivables at Danu's if she stayed. That meant after six months, she would be able to save enough money for a one-way Pan Am ticket to Europe and start that Savile Row life.

The last thing she needed as she edged into her fifth month of savings was a six-foot-two skiing veteran with a coif of blond hair courting her in Fortooth Bend. But it happened and they happened. And one month after their wedding, for the first and last time in Bill's life, his poorly functioning testicles functioned.

Their marriage, however, did not.

It had promise, at first, as all new marriages do, but tension soon bled into their dewy mornings and lantern-lit nights. Mostly, this tension came from Suzanne's parents, who thought Bill's square-jawed entitlement smelled of gopher turds and turned milk. Concerned with his ability to find steady, interest-earning income for their daughter, they offered him a managerial position at Danu's. But Bill refused and instead spent his days selling ski lessons and mountaineering courses on the ranges of the Farangotta.

For a six-foot-two adventurer new to Fortooth, there was no better way to discover its scruffy beauty than by teaching mountaineering on its craggy rocks. Every perch provided a world of tectonic discovery as cliffs staggered here, hills swelled there, and a valley stitched it all together with the iridescent thread of glacier-blue runoff.

And above it all, wafting along its epic winds, were the smells. Millions of them. Trillions of them. Sage, iron, limestone tinged petrichor, marinating for centuries and mixing into the giant olfactory stew that could only be summed up as the Farangotta Valley. During these days of exploration, Bill would lie on the snow, somehow both warm and cold, and study every ingredient in this potpourri. Within two years, he became the preeminent guide in the valley, and it was accepted one year after that, no one, outside of the Le'Echuwanna, knew Jade Ridge, Mt. Forgotten, or the Sad Sack River better than William Jefferson Macklemore. So, even before his legacy as a ski impresario was born, a version of his legacy was turning and smiling somewhere in utero as Bill became known throughout Fortooth as Mudhook Bill.

The arrival of this nickname, of course, wore heavy on Suzanne. Not only did it come with the acceptance of Bill disappearing during the daytime, but it also came with the crankier acceptance of Bill overnighting in the bush. Coupled with Bill's insistence on reinvesting all his earnings into mountaineering gear, it soon became apparent to Suzanne's parents that their daughter would shortly be cooking by fire outside a military-grade tent they called home. Hoping to avoid that outcome, they presented the couple with an offer—or an ultimatum. They would give Suzanne 20 percent ownership of Danu's if Bill agreed to give up his outfitting business and manage the store. Excited by the possibility, Suzanne presented the offer to Bill one early August morning. Without conversation, Bill declined and added spelunking to his offerings.

This was a brutal shot of reality for Suzanne. She had a husband and now a son, Robert Butler Macklemore—who was almost two years old and soon to be nicknamed Bobby Mac—but she no longer had the support of her parents. Growing up, she never thought the narcotic buzz of love would take her down this road—one where decisions splintered family trees and fractured years of harmony and allegiance. And up until Bobby Mac's third birthday, it did. But on that afternoon, as she sat alone in her kitchen, with lit candles, a caramel cake, and Bill somewhere walking the backcountry, she realized she had given up too much—way too much. Bill, of course, did return, drunk on stories of the Sad Sack and its elk—but there was no comment on Bobby's birthday, and besides the erection he tried to place as they lay in bed, no comment of how much he missed Suzanne.

That night as Suzanne drifted to sleep, heartbroken for her parents, she resolved to approach them the following day. But under the windy cry of a half-winter moon, they passed in their sleep. And when the cashier discovered them the next morning, eyes still open, lying in separate beds, they were, as the coroner stated, two people "whose tickers had just done ticked enough." Suzanne, of course, was devastated, as was the town, which held a three-day wake. Bill, at a loss of what to do, asked if he could ski a torchlit procession down Mt. Forgotten in their honor. Touched by the gesture, Suzanne asked if he would carry Bobby Mac in his arms when he did.

Bill nodded yes, and holding Bobby Mac as he skied under the bronze glow of the torch, he, for the first time, understood why the locals named the peak Mt. Forgotten. Because as he drifted into the looping arcs of his

S-turns, he forgot about everything outside the moment and entered a conversation with just him, Bobby Mac, and the heavens. It was during this moment that Bill had two epiphanies. First, he would turn Mt. Forgotten into Glory Peak—a ski resort to rival Sun Valley—and second, Bobby Mac would one day lead this same procession for Bill. Inspired by this vision, Bill let out a ferocious yell that rattled through the valley. Cooking at a firepit on a nearby peak, a group of Le'Echuwanna stood and answered with a chorus of yelps and hoots. Soon, the howls of wolves and bass-heavy growls of bears layered into the refrain. These were all the answers Bill needed to wake early, walk to the Fortooth Savings and Loan, and secure the down payment to buy Mt. Forgotten.

The first two years of building Glory Peak could only be described as hell. Suzanne would tend to Bobby Mac, Bill would tend to the mountain, and the mountain would respond with stubborn swatches of stone and dirt. With just his first attempt to fell trees, Bill discovered they had much deeper roots than expected and instead of two months, it took him almost a year to clear Glory Peak's first ski run. Forty-six feet wide, it had a pitch of eleven degrees, a length of ninety-eight yards, and a ragged rope pull made from the motor of a 1948 Chevrolet Fleetline and rusty cable Bill found in the abandoned Plymouth Rock Quarry. Each day, as the locals drove past while Bill chopped down trees on the slope, they would wager on when the bank would call its paper. But Bill knew something the locals did not: the power of beer. And in an inspired effort to bring people to the slope, Bill offered any skier over the age of eighteen four free beers with each lift ticket. And to make sure people didn't just buy a ticket, drink their beers, and leave, Bill implemented two more rules: skis only on the slope and beer only served at the concession stand at the top of the hill. This way, if you wanted your free beer, you had to buy a ticket, put on some skis, and go to the top, then ski back down and go back up for your second, third, and fourth. Before long, all the locals were knee-deep in hefeweizen and powder, and Bill was elbow-deep in cash. Which allowed him to clear more timber and build the ski runs that would eclipse every other resort in North America.

Unfortunately, this meant most of Suzanne's days were spent alone. And like with most erosions of love, it came in small chips, then large cracks that spread like the branches of electric discharge across a glass pane. At first it was the "I'll be home for lunch" broken promise or the "I'll be home for dinner" broken promise, which rapidly devolved into the "I'll be free this weekend" broken promise. Suzanne could stomach these broken promises because, after all, he was building a business. But the stings that were too painful to endure were the ones that took place when they were alone. Like when she asked him about his day and he would mumble back one-word answers that barely made sense in the context of their conversation, or when she'd run her hand through his hair, and he would pull away to readjust it. Or worst of all, when she tried to make eye contact during dinner, and he would avoid her gaze and disappear into collections of receipts and menu designs.

Then, in 1967, two days after Bobby Mac turned seven, and one week after gas prices rose above thirty cents, Suzanne showed up at the just-opened Glory Peak corporate offices and presented Bill with divorce papers. Bill was not surprised; he was embarrassed, but not surprised. He had been craving freedom for years, but as the man who wed the local princess, he was afraid if he left her, the town would become too small for him—Glory Peak included. But it didn't, because at this point, Glory Peak was the town. Every aspect of it, somehow, connected to that blue-and-white logo and massive thrust of stone and dirt that hovered like a cracked pyramid over Fortooth.

The only exception was Danu's. On her parents' passing, Suzanne inherited the store, and after her divorce was finalized, she cleared its second-floor storage area and moved in. Bobby Mac came with her, riding ahead on his bicycle, and before the dust could be swept away, Suzanne made two promises: Bobby Mac would be treated as an adult, and she would never speak to Bill again.

Bill knew when Suzanne served the papers that she would never speak to him again. But he also knew she would be a wonderful mother. So, to make the experience as easy as possible, he submitted to her a three-page document outlining how they could co-parent. Suzanne countered with a single piece of paper. On it was a simple list of rules: "You can see Bobby Mac from eight a.m. to nine a.m. Monday through Friday, and Sundays from eight a.m. to eight p.m." Anxious to put his marriage behind him, Bill agreed, especially seeing as this was more time than he'd already spent with Bobby Mac.

It was under these terms that the first divorced-parent meeting between Bobby and Bill took place. They met at Lola's Diner, and it being a small town, and Bobby being a young adult of seven years, Suzanne felt it was safe for him to walk there by himself. Arriving as the morning crowd shuffled toward their morning duties, Bobby sat in a booth and watched as Lola and the waitstaff cleaned the aluminum-walled space. Seventeen minutes later, and fourteen minutes late, Bill arrived. A bead of sweat on his temple suggested maybe he ran there from a finance meeting or a construction review, but when Bobby saw Bill's six-foot-two frame shrink to five-foot-six, he knew it was as simple as he forgot. Never adept at honesty, Bill circled for an excuse.

"Uh, I-uh, I'm . . . sorry, bud, the morning has been . . ."

Bobby, not caring, just stared back at his father. Like his mother, his eyes were emerald-green saucers of sparkle that made it impossible to ignore any emotion they broadcasted. Over time, Bill trained himself to ignore Suzanne's eyes. However, this morning, staring into Bobby's, something in him suggested he needed to succumb to their humbling power.

"Ah, shit, Bobby. I don't know what to tell you," he continued. "I most likely am going to be bad at this. It's not that I don't love you or don't think you are the best thing on the planet. It's just . . . I don't know if I was made for this."

Bobby looked back at his father, his eyes channeling something Suzanne's could not—acceptance. Bobby was, after all, 50 percent Bill, and in that 50 percent, Bobby understood the inherent truth of what his father had just shared.

Looking at a chalkboard of specials on the wall, Bobby said, in a voice free of concern, "What's a burr-ree-e-too?"

Over the years, these morning meetups took on a variety of renderings. Some were in the front seat of Bill's heritage green Land Rover as he shared plans for Glory Peak's expansion. Others were on the back slopes of Glory Peak as he explained how he cleared terrain for expansion. Bill would chuckle as he explained these techniques because somewhere in the back of his mind, he knew Glory Peak would be known for this terrain. This rugged terrain that most resembled the growth of his hair. No longer the perfectly coifed rectangle of a man who once arrived in Fortooth, Bill was now a curly-haired rectangle of a man who let the untamed spirit of the Farangotta twist his man-do wild. And more than anything, he wanted the Farangotta to twist its wild through Bobby's man-do, too.

Because as Bill discovered over the years, children were divided into two factions: the child who would embrace the uncertain rush of adventure or the one who would avoid it with sweat-filled screams. And every winter Bill witnessed this truth as he watched them clip into skis and take their first step down his bunny hill. Inevitably, there would be at least one kid who retreated, snot greased and teary eyed, from the slopes. But every day, he would also witness a child take that faithful turn down a slope, unaware of the pain associated with the crack of a fibula or the burning scrape of a wipeout. Watching, he would beam as they discovered the shock of adrenaline that came with a downhill run and how it lit up their circuitry and turned them into glowing two-foot-tall nuclear explosions. These were the children he respected. The ones who chose the scruffy side of the adventure coin. The ones who chose courage.

Thankfully, Bobby was on the side that chose courage, and growing up, Bill proudly watched as he ran, jumped, flipped, and action verbed through any fear-based scenario that came his way. By the time he was fifteen, Bobby was the first person to traverse Fool's Domain, the first person to ski Asterisk's Face, and the first person to land a 360 off the Pope's Hat. As the rate of Bobby's first descents increased, so did the expansion of Glory Peak. Of course, this synchronicity did not fall blind on Bill. The first night he skied down Mt. Forgotten promised this. Bill reigning over the valley, his prince, one day, ready to inherit the mantle. A dream no doubt attainable, but for one thing—Bobby was made of something stronger and more resilient than Bill's fortified carbon. Something so elemental that all creatures—conscious, mobile, or microscopic—needed it to thrive. Because despite how much Bobby Mac carried Bill in him, he also carried another force: air.

By the time Bobby turned eighteen, the air side of his personality had begun to dominate his carbon side, and Bill was quick to recognize this change. Anxious to find blame, he attributed it to the adventuring Bobby did with the locals. Specifically, a stocky Le'Echuwannan with a long black mohawk ponytail named Snow Feather, who, instead of skiing, skated down the snow on a surfboard-shaped contraption he carved from a Sitka spruce. At first, Bill was in complete support of these adventures. He had watched Snow Feather grow up and considered him one of the greatest examples of wilding he ever saw. In some ways, even a greater example than Bobby. It was Snow Feather who suggested they try Asterisk's Face, and it was Snow Feather who taught Bobby how to land a 540 daffy. It was also Snow Feather who invited Bobby north to the Weeping Sky Fork, a thundering tributary off the Spoon Spoon River, and taught him to carve canoes and take them, torpedolike, through Weeping Sky's class V rapids.

Bobby would proudly recount these adventures to Bill, and in secret, Bill wished Snow Feather would invite him to these hidden Le'Echuwannan places. Places ol' Mudhook Bill would have spent weeks in his youth searching for. Hoping to maneuver his way into their adventures, Bill started inviting Snow Feather on his morning meets with Bobby. Together, they shared Pop-Tarts and warm steak burritos as Bill gave pointers on how to handle the backcountry. Most of these pointers Snow Feather found useless. Except for one. One that Bill shared on a frigid morning as they prepared to ski down the fractured glacier face of Puma's Paw.

That morning, after Bill tightened his boots in anticipation of stepping into his bindings, he unzipped his Spyder ski pants, removed his penis from his long johns, and sprayed his skis and bindings with urine. Watching the stream splash over the frozen components, Snow Feather was amazed to see how easy it was for Bill to slide into his skis. Smiling, Bill said, "Sometimes I also piss on the tips so they'll cut through the snow better."

Smiling back, Snow Feather looked down at his Sitka board, then back up at Bobby. In unison, they unzipped their pants and pissed on their gear. Watching the yellow sluice cut like acid through the ice on their bindings, Bill inhaled the sulfurous scent and gave them an emphatic, "Well done, gents!" Then, he looked down at their junk and noticed that while short, Snow Feather's penis had impressive girth, and Bobby's, while thin, had length and a perfect mushroom-shaped tip, courtesy of a circumcision Bill arranged for in Denver. *That pecker will fill out a condom nicely*, Bill thought and, looking at it, hoped Bobby would use it madly in his youth. But Bill's hope was quickly lost in the morning wind, extinguished by the percolating air building in Bobby.

For air in Fortooth was the main ingredient of puberty. There was something about its chemistry of lavenders, pine, and lion's mane that pulled every teen into its addictive grip. The Le'Echuwanna referred to this pull as the *Oh-sah-cha-me*, or the New Breath, and every year, as summer began to regress from view and orange began its creep over the valley, the Le'Echuwanna would celebrate this transition with a ceremony. This ceremony consisted of taking the teenagers of the tribe to Tear Cup Lake, where the Elder Elders would bathe them in its waters and thump on earthen drums. It was led by Lady Dog, a long-haired strap of muscle and bone, who would chant softly through a whistle in her teeth, "*Mi-esse, esse, ni-wanta tom yay. Mi-esse-esse ni-oh-wanta tom-nay.*" My breeze, my breeze is for all the leaves. My breeze, my breeze is for earth and trees.

Once the bathing element of the ceremony was complete, each participant would then walk to a pine tree where a ladder waited. Climbing it to a small platform affixed to its top, they would next undress and strap themselves to the bark with elk leather. For the next two days, they would wait and fast, exposed and vulnerable to the ever-shifting elements. It was during these moments that they learned how the invisible, uncontrollable universe of energy that floated around them in gusts felt but never seen was, in fact, part of each of them. Part of all of them. Part of everything. And to walk through life was to walk in complete accordance with the wind. Maybe at times touching it; maybe at times moving through it; maybe even, at times, being stopped by it—but always with the understanding that it was for you to flow through. Or around. Or against, until it changed its direction and mind, like air.

When Bill was told by the locals to have patience as Bobby Mac transitioned into his air self, all he could think was, *Air? You want me to listen to air? Well, screw that because nothing in life is built on air.* In Bill's mind, life was built on work, commitment, and intention, and the Bobby Mac he had come to admire was now becoming an airy Bobby Mac he could barely look at. Of course, he refused to blame Bobby Mac for this shift. That would mean Bill's DNA was somehow capable of weakness, which, of course, was impossible. Especially when he had Snow Feather and the Le'Echuwanna to blame.

As a result, it was no surprise Bill blamed Snow Feather for introducing Bobby to alcohol, even though it was Bobby who stole the bottle of grappa from Bill's liquor cabinet and brought it to Snow Feather's to try. And it was no surprise Bill blamed Snow Feather for introducing Bobby to weed, even though it was Bobby who approached Snow Feather's third cousin, He Who Eats Rabbit Tails, for a dime bag to try. What was a surprise to Bill was that Snow Feather was the person Bobby preferred to spend time with when discovering these things. Now, if Bill was lucky, Bobby would show up only ten minutes late for their morning meets, and if luck was out to breakfast, he wouldn't show up at all.

In a final attempt to lull Bobby from the cultlike effect of Snow Feather, Bill offered to let the two of them design the layout of the new mountain he was adding to Glory Peak. The locals called it the Tit—named, well, after the supple, raised mound of rock and dirt that sat nipple-like at the top of the peak. It was steep, stained pink from a layer of iron oxide, and Bobby and Snow Feather had spent many days logging tracks through its open terrain. So, they knew it well. They also knew that to preserve its unique recipe, they would recommend keeping it open and bowl-like. Not a fan of open ski runs, Bill was hesitant, but after Snow Feather suggested they could blast a portion off its south side to create an accessible drop-in, Bill acquiesced and approved the design.

Deciding to manage the blasting himself, Snow Feather showed up predawn on a late November Sunday to walk the ridge and pick the best place to bury the dynamite. Overwhelmed by the adventures to come, his mind was lost in thoughts of the new layout and how he soon would be able to treat the mountain like a playground, attacking every angle like a gymnast in tumble mode. The problem with being lost in thought was that he did not notice the morning's surprising warmth or how the warmth melted the snow cover and turned the base slushy and soft. Walking the area below the south side, Snow Feather was also blocked from the morning rays and did not see how they heated the snow. By the time he circled north, a large cornice hanging from the Tit was melting fast. Hearing the ice fastened to it squeal,

Snow Feather watched as the cornice fell from its position and exploded with a loud, watery thud.

The vibration from the collision quickly shocked through his legs as a giant gust of air followed, knocking him back with such force, he somersaulted backward down the Tit. Chasing him, and gaining in size, was a giant rush of snow—one that would soon be known as the first official avalanche on Glory Peak. Watching it barrel toward him, Snow Feather knew he would never have the chance to share with Bobby, or his unborn son—who was still nothing but a bean growing inside his girlfriend—how the avalanche punched him into unconsciousness. Or the chance to next share what the taste of air felt like when he emerged from the snow. Because Snow Feather never emerged.

His death crushed Bobby. But not as much as Bill's refusal to compensate Snow Feather's family or any of the Le'Echuwanna for the accident. Bill kept telling him how "it would set a bad precedent," and there would be no way he'd be able to "insure Glory Peak if he took responsibility." Already on the way to hating his father, this betrayal sent Bobby into orbit. When he did leave Fortooth three weeks later, it came to no one's surprise. Bobby's air had grown so hot, so strong, so determined, it extinguished all other matter inside him. And as much as Bill thought it was, his carbon was not more powerful, resilient, or indefatigable than air.

# CHAPTER 6

## FEBRUARY 9, 1988

As Bobby Mac clawed his way through the snow and ice toward Annabelle, he expected the worst. The tapping of her pen seemed to stop a lifetime ago, along with Annabelle's responses, and he knew in his gut there was a possibility he'd discover a corpse instead of his wife.

*I mean, what the hell happened?* he thought.

After a fuzzy replay, he concluded they must have fallen into a crevasse, which triggered some sort of avalanche that covered the crevasse. *I mean, who the hell falls into a fucking crevasse that gets covered by an avalanche? Well,* Bobby then thought, *yeah...*

To his surprise, as he continued pawing away at the ice and snow, he next began to laugh, a soprano cackle mixed with a staccato cough. The laughter was short-lived, however, given every breath was harder to take than the last—and at this point, he felt like he was sucking in oxygen through a hole the width of a coffee straw.

Looking down at his fingers, he saw nothing but red, their tips rubbed raw from digging through the ice crystals that were now shards of glass. His muscles were heavy, too, and moved as if submerged in petroleum jelly with thirty-pound dumbbells attached. He wondered if he had anything left, but then, as that last drop of adrenaline-filled desperation was about to leave his body, he saw it: the faint outline of a leather Salomon boot behind snowpack.

An explosion of nerves followed. Cupping his digits, Bobby created a mini shovel with his right hand and with three hard strikes, broke through the snow onto Annabelle's foot. He saw her shudder, and before she could gasp for air, Bobby pulled her through his burrow into the hollow where he'd landed.

Her fingers were frigid—nothing but tiny icicles extending from a slightly warmer palm—and her lips were painted a grayish blue. Three steps past panic, Bobby rubbed her hands and massaged her cheeks. Soon, the blue dissolved to pink and was soon followed by a long, cracked wheeze. In anticipation of her eyes creaking wide open, Bobby sat back and watched Annabelle wriggle awake.

"Belle? *Belle?*" Bobby whispered. Annabelle didn't respond. Looking at her limp body, Bobby could never have imagined she was lost in the hold of a hallucination, one that had her blasting through Atlantic waves on a Boston Whaler with a blurry Boz Scaggs at the helm.

"Goddamn it, Belle, you wake the hell up now!" Bobby screamed. With that cue, Annabelle lifted forward, breathed in, and released a weak cough.

"Yes! Fucking thank God, thank God!" Bobby followed. Ecstatic, he floundered about, looking for a pillow or blanket or anything for her to sit on. Annabelle, meanwhile, let the warm rush of air run through her lungs. Creaking forward she searched for the icy touch of the snowpack floor. Finding it, she dug in her numb nails and pulled herself into a cross-legged seat.

"Babe, babe, wait," Bobby pleaded.

Ignoring him, Annabelle pulled her legs close to her chest and said, "Jesus, Bobby, I'm fine!"

Bobby leaned back, the cave falling to silence. He was nervous now, his eyes searching for Annabelle's. She was looking at her feet and rocking back and forth. Then, after a violent shake that ended in a quick yawn, she raised her head and looked at him. In the swollen pink of her eyes, he saw something familiar—relief. It wasn't romantic relief, but it did measure somewhere near the wagging relief a dog felt when its owner walked through the door. After several breaths and several shudders, Annabelle broke the look.

"I cannot believe you landed in this place." Shaking her head, Annabelle released a chuckle. "Of course you landed in this place. I mean you're not even breathing heavy. . . You probably landed next to a Coors and roast beef sandwich for Christ's sake."

Bobby stuffed a fist into his pocket and pulled out two plastic bags. "No, but I got gorp. And some bison jerky."

Annabelle chuckled again. "Fucking gorp."

"What?" Bobby said. "You don't want some?"

Annabelle looked at the bag. M&M's, granola, raisins, chocolate chips, and peanuts molded into a smash of sugar and salt.

"I cannot believe you eat that."

"What? It's perfect for hikes."

"Hikes? It's Halloween candy."

Bobby looked at her, then down at the bag. "Fine, you don't have to—"

"Wait, wait," Annabelle interrupted. "I'll . . . Can I?"

Bobby nodded and opened the Ziploc. Annabelle reached in, pulled out almost the whole bag, and devoured it in one bite.

Bobby watched her chew, then watched the chewing stop, and turn into a smile. Looking up at him, she said, "Holy shit, that was incredible. I know you've got more, right? Tell me you got more, Bobby Mac."

Bobby smiled. Of course, he had more. Reaching into his jacket pocket, he pulled out three more bags. At their sight, Annabelle's eyes widened. Something was happening. Something, for the first time in what felt like years.

He and Annabelle were having a moment.

That was, until Annabelle made her next statement. "God, sometimes, I tell ya, Bobby, you are incredible. Except when you're being a complete idiot."

Bobby's eyes went flat. And then, as if by tribute, he placed the bags at Annabelle's feet and sat back against the curve of the snow cave. *Things were not always this way*, Bobby thought. *Belle*, he wanted to ask, *How the hell did things end up this way?*

∿

## APRIL 1981

In the early 1980s, Boulder, Colorado, was a place that colored many a hotspur's fantasy. Not only did it possess the remnants of a cowboy enclave, it was also a burgeoning city moseying its way toward becoming a college football powerhouse while it somehow still held tight to a faux-hippie aesthetic that covered its streets like a tie-dyed moss.

Nanny A was a large part of what triggered this shift. In 1964, eight months out of a divorce, with Annabelle just a hair from four years old, Nanny A began her doctorate studies at the University of Colorado Boulder. During that time, women's studies was finding its foothold in academia, and cultural studies was starting to be recognized as a viable tool in measuring social patterning within communities. When Nanny A decided to combine the two for her PhD, then continue her postgraduate teachings at CU Boulder, it was no surprise it came with the creation of a Women's Studies Department focusing on developing Indigenous communities.

Raised by her mother's emphatic aim to celebrate women as the societal power source, Annabelle cultivated an independence unique even to the manifest destiny of this western town. She dated a lot but rarely romanced—and most of what transpired on those dates took place with an unspoken agreement that once the deed was done, she would never be heard from again.

She was untethered, bound only by the scholastic expectations of being the daughter of an admired academic. And dutifully, when the time came, she pursued a BA in cultural anthropology at CU Boulder. So, when the summer of 1981 brought an opportunity to visit Ecuador to document Achuar matriarchs, all of Annabelle's ambitions directed her to the South American rainforest—and she almost made it there unencumbered. But one boring Sunday afternoon, while working part time as a waitress at The Sink, Bobby Mac strolled into Annabelle's untethered life.

It happened while she was hunched over a barstool looking through a Quechua dictionary. With Annabelle's back to the door, her manager had to inform her a table needed to be seated. Annoyed she had to pull away from learning the Quechua word for corn, she spun toward the restaurant's entrance, only to be immediately met with a blinding flash of light. At first, the light was painful and poked tiny rainbow holes in her retinas, but when it cleared and her diffused spread of RGB gave way to clarity, she discovered what blew her corneas to white- a bronze eagle-shaped belt buckle.

And then she saw the man attached to the belt buckle, and what appeared to be all eighteen feet, two inches of him. Somehow he seemed to be floating twelve feet off the ground and spreading a ten-thousand-watt floodlight of a smile that dwarfed the Bat Signal. Before she could even offer him a menu, he said, "Howdy-do, my name is Bobby Mac, and I'm looking for a burger, well done." At that moment, the lush saxophone coo of Gerry Rafferty's "Baker Street" started to play through the house speakers, and Annabelle knew in that moment she, too, was, well . . . done.

The courtship barely existed. It was more of an alliance, already in effect, with Bobby stepping into a relationship forged over millennia. Within a week, they were living together; within two weeks, it was decided he would accompany her to Ecuador; and within two months, they were rattling their way, in a four-seat Cessna, to a muddy airstrip hiding in a panoply of green along the Amazon River. Two days later, after a hike with burros old and angry, they were finally embraced by the tribe.

Annabelle loved their days during that time and unlike the alarm blaring mornings of college, these started with a different intention. At 4 a.m. she would rise with the tribe and drink a highly caffeinated tea made of the Wayusa plant. This tea would clear her bowels and free her spirit to meet with the tribe and discuss their dreams from the previous night. Her day would then be spent taking photos as the women harvested yucca from the fields and husked it into chewable pellets of maize. From these pellets, the women made *chicha*, a fermented beer-like drink that welcomed all visitors and lubricated the men of the tribe. Conversely, Bobby would sleep past the tea drinking ceremony but would wake just in time to trail the men as they went on their fishing trips. Following Annabelle's precise instructions, he would record their conversations on a Nagra reel-to-reel audio recorder and every afternoon when Bobby returned from fishing, she'd ask him to disappear with her into the forest to replay everything he'd witnessed.

At first, this recap came with the intention of deciding what to keep for her research, but over time, it became apparent each recap was just a story they framed for each other. Stories wrapped up with a giddy magic, which felt, at times, like a Harlequin romance novel colored by a kaleidoscope of green and green and green and red. Though Bobby was, by definition, her assistant, his support was something far greater, and he relished the opportunity to enhance everything she did. And she just relished him—how his sweat tasted at the end of the day, how his hair felt after a downpour of bullet-size rain, how the men of the village mimicked his walk through the jungle. That gait. Those long, bobbing-up-and-down steps that seemed to fall with the weight of the world but land with none of it. Watching him walk, it became apparent to those in the village that Bobby was something they had never seen. Or seen in human form. But they understood what he was. As they understood from the conversations the leaves had with the trees and the water had with the banks, that Bobby was, simply and elementally, air.

When their time in the village was coming to an end, it was met with the same refined understanding the Achuar used to approach life. Even though they had come to embrace the daily ritual of watching and being watched by Bobby and Annabelle, they were aware that one day, these exchanges would disappear like a sloth from the jungle floor. Playful, observing, respectful, the sloth would take an occasional trip down from the forest's canopy to settle its hairy ass on the moist ground. The initial belief as to why it did this was to relieve itself in a small hole dug with its hooklike claws. This, of course, had legitimacy, but only in a physical sense, because the Achuar had another theory—one that found roots in the idea that sloths possessed the reincarnated souls of their lost tribe. For the Achuar, a visit from a sloth was a visit from a relative, a friend, or even a lover—and with their departure came the reminder that the world was a place of memory, connection, appreciation, and transience.

As gratitude for this sloth-like reminder, on the last day of their stay, the Achuar allowed Bobby to not just watch, but partake in a hunt. Rising early for the first time, Bobby prepped with the men under moonlight, still hours before the sun crested the horizon and got lost in the thick canopy overhead. In the rainforest, it was difficult to see sunlight due to the incredible density of the vegetation, so the passage of time was measured by the chroma of the canopy's leaves. On hunts, it was imperative to leave before the leaves took on any hint of emerald. They needed to be the green of dark moss, barely any saturation, with only the faint touch of moonlight kissing them with color. The goal, of course, was to be in their hunting area before the animals woke. Wakings that would first come with the birds—the alarm clock of the jungle—squawking and flapping their wings. Then the howler monkeys, their deep guttural screams announcing to all creatures that day was on its way.

It was during these epic call-and-repeats of the howler monkeys the Achuar men were most active. Camouflaged by the screams, they would run through the forest and find their positions in anticipation of an attack. This morning, as they sprinted along the banks of the Río Toachi, Bobby understood their goal was ambitious. They wanted to find a white-lipped peccary—known in the North American Southwest as the javelina and known in lore as the skunk pig.

It was also, unfortunately, a mission filled with the expectation of failure. A skunk pig's skin was a layer of armor, part tree bark and part rotting leather. To kill it, you would have to not only get the dart past the thick wiring of its hair but also between the armor plates of its skin and into the nape of its neck, where the poison could absorb fast into its bloodstream. If the shot was missed, the skunk pig would squeal, setting off a relay of auditory signals that would effectively tell all creatures in the area to run and leave the Achuars without food for a month. But if done correctly, and if the dart somehow managed to hit the exact kill spot, the skunk pig would take the hit, spin in a drunken stupor, and release its spirit to the winds.

Bobby held on to the image of a spinning skunk pig as he settled into position at the base of a fallen Ficus. Its crown, once a prince standing among the top of the rainforest, had collapsed during a storm and created a gap in the canopy the size of a small ranch house. Through this gap, he could feel the rays of the sun, and hoping to absorb them, decided to lay along one of the large roots that buttressed the tree to take in one last breath of the forest.

Beneath him, just a finger reach from his dangling arm, was the flannel moth caterpillar undulating its hairy body across a fallen branch. Fully aware that if touched, its poisonous hairs would cause violent swelling and vomiting, Bobby rolled to his right and focused on a Brazilian wandering spider, which somehow wandered in from Peru. These spiders were alternately feared and worshipped by Achuar males. Feared because they possessed one of the most venomous bites in the jungle, worshipped because one of the many side effects of their bites was priapism, which resulted in erections that lasted for hours or, in the case of one remorseful shaman, days.

After briefly weighing the benefits of what a bite could do for his eventual wedding night, Bobby turned his gaze to his legs, where he noticed a line of bullet ants making their way toward his right knee. Aware that unlike the Brazilian wandering spider, no benefits of pleasure came with the bite of the bullet ant, Bobby tightened his buttocks, held his breath, and prayed they would get bored with the synthetic feel of his pants and climb back to the jungle floor. They did, which allowed Bobby to roll behind the tree's root and peer over its moss-covered top. They were gone now, all those curious crawlies, so now it was time for Bobby to admire the trees. All the magnificent trees which swayed or stood immovable, their bark holding the pulse of the rainforest. Inhaling, Bobby pulled in their scents, an earthy combination of damp wood and tar musk, a petrichor so rich he felt it grab him by the wrist and place him on winds that carried him through the forest on a roller coaster meant for leaves. Giggling, it took him almost three minutes to return to his body and when he did return, it was then that he saw it, standing just twenty feet from him, a skunk pig.

At first Bobby swore it saw him but quickly realized it was staring at a bush, dotted with ripe red fruit, by his feet. Then, he saw the pink stain that painted its lips and realized the skunk pig was chewing on a swatch of camu camu berries. Knowing the skunk pig would be hypnotized by the bitter taste of the fruit, Bobby realized this was an opportunity he needed to take swift advantage of. So, fighting the boil of adrenaline, he reached down for the blowgun by his feet—oblivious to a coral snake easing its way in ribbons through the moist fallen leaves.

Focused exclusively on the skunk pig's staccato chewing, Bobby raised the blowgun with molasses-like speed, unaware the coral snake had slithered its way through the front hole. Fully inside now, the snake stretched its arrow-shaped head forward and inched its vertebrae bone by bone down the blowgun's chamber. In most situations, Bobby would have noticed the added weight of the snake, but as the adrenaline bubbled through his body, he was too juiced to recognize that just a few inches from him, a coral snake was sliding its way toward his open mouth. The skunk pig was oblivious as well. Drunk on the camu camu berries, it had no clue of the trees, river, coral snake, or Bobby hovering around it. It was in heaven, until the sound of a dart sliding into a chamber clicked it out of its reverie. Turning right, it saw a six-foot barrel and an inhaling Bobby Mac aiming right at him.

Realizing his cover had been blown, Bobby inhaled, and . . . *pfffffft*, exhaled, sending the dart down the blowgun chamber, into the lunging coral snake, then sending the snake out of the blow gun and into the open mouth of the skunk pig.

Shocked by the stab of the dart and the snake now choking his throat, the skunk pig stumbled backward. Its windpipe now stuffed, it burped in silence and attempted, in crooked steps, to balance itself. But it couldn't. Finally resigning itself to the onset of the dart's poison, the skunk pig dropped its tongue and laid on its side in the shape of a letter C. By the time Bobby and the other hunters reached it, the coral snake lay rigid, a straight line through its swollen mouth. Amazed at what they saw, the Achuar thought Bobby had replaced the dart and used the snake as an arrow. Amazed at what he saw, Bobby decided never to eat pork again.

When the hunters returned with the body of the coral snake dangling from the skunk pig's mouth, the women of the village cried in disbelief. These cries, however, were not from the morbid sight of a dead skunk pig half swallowing a dead coral snake. It was because for Achuar women, coral snakes represented the fierce intoxication of the feminine spirit. To witness it swallowed by the skunk pig suggested there would be an imbalance in the world and that the male would overtake the female. Which meant the lush fertility of the rainforest would be lost to barrenness and the storms of masculine chaos.

As Annabelle and Bobby tried to sleep that night under an invisible moon, they wondered if they should have visited this unspoiled land. When they left the following morning, the answer was apparent in the avoidant eyes of the villagers. The shaman's first wife, now wary of Bobby, was the only one to offer any semblance of a goodbye, and as she did, she presented Annabelle with an amulet. It was made from the tusk of the skunk pig wrapped in the skin of the coral snake. Without Bobby seeing, Annabelle took it, hid it in her bandana, and placed it at the bottom of her fanny pack. That evening, when they returned to Quito, it was decided that instead of exploring the Sacred Valley, they would depart the following day for Colorado. Falling asleep, Annabelle's face resting on an alpaca blanket, she swore never to leave the United States again.

Now, lying in the strange hold of a snow cave, buried two hundred feet in a crevasse, Annabelle thought of all the places she didn't go. Madagascar, Seville, Oaxaca, sure, all possibly interesting places to visit. But what she saw forming in Kodachrome behind her eyes was a fleet of whale sharks cresting off the banks of Tanzania, sunrise turning the Zhangjiajie National Forest Park a rusty bronze, and the crabs rolling a fire engine red across Christmas Island. The world was big, unexpected, full of smells and colors, but now it was reduced to white, a waft of peppered jerky, and the salty vodka scent of Bobby's skin.

She looked at him across the snow cave, and like a child of six waiting for a compliment on the macaroni art he brought home from school, he looked back. She did not have patience for this look. In fact, she'd lost all patience for Bobby nine months, three weeks, four days, and approximately eleven hours earlier, when she'd learned he was having an affair with a college student who was spending her summer selling Chicago-style hot dogs at Diggity's on Main. But it wasn't the affair that had zapped her patience. At this point, she'd discovered no fewer than five of Bobby's flings and was deep into her own affair with Gunther. It was the possibility that maybe, somehow, Bobby would rob another young girl of a dream. Maybe a dream to travel the world. And that, in every form of the word, was unacceptable.

"God, I'm glad you are okay," Bobby said. "This would have been brutal if anything happened to you."

"Yeah," she responded, her gaze locked on her feet again—because even though she could not see it, she could feel that ten-thousand-watt smile forming on Bobby's face. Without shifting her look, she said, "This isn't a fucking date, Bobby. We gotta get out of here."

Bobby traded his impending smile for what was almost a frown.

"They'll come find us. I imagine the school would've contacted your mom to let her know Clove hadn't shown up. And they must've heard the avalanche—so putting two and two together will be pretty easy. We gotta just sit tight until they find the starting point and hope our tracks are still visible."

Annoyingly, he was right, and being right was one of the lures Annabelle had to ignore. This was easy to do when she did not have to spend time with Bobby. But now, there was not only time, there was also proximity. And conversation. And conversation was another lure Bobby employed to illustrate that in spite of the space cowboy aura he flashed for his fans, when he spoke of the tangible world, he was often, and annoyingly, right.

"Let's hope so," she countered. "I'm sure Mom is figuring this out. God, she is so going to use this against me for not letting her get me one of those mobiles."

"Yeah, well, I'm sure Dickface is on it too. And I'm sure he's using that five-star avalanche team he keeps yapping about to find us."

Annabelle leaned back and rested her head against the ice pack. It was cold, and she felt it through her hair, matted in forming icicles. Yes, there was Dickface, that horrendous dickface of a father-n-law she had to endure for the past seven years and as much as the notion of Dickface helping her ran acid in her heart, she found peace in knowing that no matter the situation, Dickface would utilize every resource he had to find Bobby and, by association, her.

And he did. Unbeknownst to Bobby and Annabelle, in the time that Gunther arrived at the Glory Peak offices to the time the helicopter took off toward Miner's Gasp, a brutal, unfathomable, wet, thick, and blinding snow front had come in. It was as if the heavens themselves decided to take all the dandruff it accrued over seven and a half billion years and dump it on the Farangotta Valley. By the time the rescue helicopter passed Glory Peak and tracked down Yeehaw Pass, visibility had gotten so bad the pilot could not make out the sky two feet in front of him. Then, as the weather further soured, a sudden gush hit the helicopter, turned its rudder useless, and forced it to yaw left. To avoid crashing into the foothills, the pilot opted to land and wobbled its skids onto the single yellow line of Yeehaw Pass.

Exiting the helicopter, the pilot realized visibility on the ground was worse than it was in the air. Arm over face, he stumbled to a Ford F-150 parked on the shoulder. Diesel fumed from its tailpipe as a hulking figure sat in the driver's seat, just visible through the snow on the windows. Rapidly, the figure motioned the pilot to get into the passenger seat, which he did. It took a beat for the pilot to wipe the snow off his face and collect his bearings and a longer beat to recognize in whose car he sat. It was that of Fred Robert Charles, or in the vernacular of the Le'Echewanna, *Me-e-tah Ho-say-osh*, or in the English translated vernacular of *Le'chu*, the native language of the Le'Echewanna, He Who Eats Rabbit Tails.

"What's wrong, cat got your balls?" He Who Eats asked, partly to break the silence and partly because he was fond of the saying.

"Excuse me?" the pilot responded, awed by the six-foot-five, three-hundred-pound frame sitting to his left.

"I said, cat got your balls, man? You're taking sips like it's costing silver. Drink the fuck up!" And with that followed the deep rumble of a laugh, one that started somewhere in a bass line and finished in the high-pitched cackle of a hyena. "You gotta drink up, brother. We are witnessing the *Pay-ah-eh-ah-poe*. It's gonna get pretty cosmic!"

The *Pay-ah-eh-ah-poe* was an unquestionable cornerstone of the Le'Echuwanna belief system. Part meteorological lightning bolt and part spiritual convergence, it was an occurrence admired for its ability to destroy and create. It was rare. So rare that it happened once in maybe every five lifetimes and was depended on by the Le'Echuwanna to equalize the forces juggling time and space. And though He Who Eats could not see through his snow-frosted windows, he knew something transcendental was happening.

"Fuck, I think I got a boner." He Who Eats laughed and turned toward the pilot, his eyes swirling a delirious clockwise. The pilot, now panicked, reached for the door handle. Looking at him, He Who Eats said, "Settle down, *kemo-wabi*. I don't mean I got a hard-on like I want to screw ya. I mean I got a hard-on like this is so crazy it's making my blood flow rivers and rains. I'm gushing, bro. This is history, this is fucking history!"

Three days later, when the snowstorm finally subsided, it was official—this *was* history. On final count, there was a snowfall of 187 inches. This covered all the roads, all the paths, all the hills, all the mountains, and all the footsteps in the Farangotta. By the time the search parties went back out to look for Bobby and Annabelle, all remnants of where they were, or could have been, were erased. To have found them would have been to find a raindrop in the ocean.

# PART 2

*He-Oh-Wah-He-Cha-Me*

Tapping Bird, you beaver's ass.
Why peck at the wood when you could use it to build your home?

—As translated from the Le'Echuwanna firethought sharings

# CHAPTER 7

## JANUARY 1998

In the ten years since the disappearance of Clover's parents, two things happened: everything and nothing at all. Now fourteen, she was taller than expected but still had her cocoa-blonde curls. She had learned to appreciate the flavor of pesto but still liked the simplicity of peanut butter. She enjoyed one-on-one time with her grandmother but still preferred being alone. And most important, she learned that despite the comic chemistry between Adam Sandler and Drew Barrymore in *The Wedding Singer*, the world was a caustic, unforgiving, and unpredictable place.

To escape this fact, Clover decided to spend her mornings in glide— specifically, in glide on a pair of 180 cm Kneissl Pentron 46 cross-country skis. Her routine was simple—and being the granddaughter of Nanny A, inflexible. Monday through Friday, without error, she was in her bindings at the base of Prescott Loop at 7:01 a.m., where she would then ski for one hour and meet Nanny A at the parking lot at 8:01 a.m. Sometimes, Clover would finish her run early and wait with her skis off for her grandmother to pick her up. But that depended on how fast she found her rhythm and form. Or how many times she stopped to stare at the snow-covered surroundings to wonder where her parents were hiding.

There had been a morning not long ago when she'd slid to a halt at the base of Prescott Loop, unable to tear her eyes away from the horrible and glorious view of Miner's Gasp. Pointing tall at the sky, it sat there, nothing but an eighteen-hundred-foot tombstone. Usually, the sight of it filled her with something she couldn't explain. Making her chest full and empty all at once and her heart a stone she could barely hold up behind her ribs.

But this time, it whispered to her. In windy words sounding like lullabies. Lullabies her mother or father once sang with warm whiskey breath. But then those lullabies were lost to noise, the noise of gasps and screams fighting and dying for air. It was these thoughts that knocked her over and left her gasping on the ground, somehow in spirit with her long-dead parents.

But the thoughts of her parents were not the only reason Clover trained at Miner's Gasp. There also was the possibility of seeing members of the Le'Echuwanna on their morning hunt. Some mornings she would see them, the limp body of a deer draped over a shoulder, another with a bow or rabbit in hand. Passing her, they never spoke, but they always made eye contact. Clover took comfort in this. She was not prone to human connection, but in the quiet of a winter morning, there was something welcoming in their unspoken glances. Something that said *we share the same air*.

Like on this January 8th training session. Which burned deep, thanks to a brutal windchill. It was during a particularly tough dig up a long hill that Clover felt the icicle stab of cold air in her lungs. Needing to bring her heart rate back to a manageable thump, Clover paused and held herself against a tree. When it subsided and she was able to focus again, she noticed a large bush fifty yards down the trail. Having never seen it before, Clover rubbed her eyes but clearing them did nothing. It just sat there, swaying in the wind, pine needles all atwitter. And then, the swaying stopped, the bush stood and revealed He Who Eats with the top of a pine tree strapped to his back. Quiet, he pulled a flask from his jacket, took a long swig, and rested it on the path. Then, like a grizzly in chase, fell on all fours and bolted into the forest.

When Clover got to the flask, she smelled the remnants of chocolate and cinnamon. It was mostly full, still hot, and provided the warm fuel she needed to finish her morning practice. Sliding back to the parking lot, Clover felt she could have skied ten more miles. Spotting Nanny A already parked, she slid the flask into her jacket, then her skis and boots into the back of the maroon Subaru.

As usual, Nanny A was nursing a cup of matcha. And as usual, she wanted to talk. Clover, however, just wanted to breathe into her cupped hands and watch the ponderosas blur by.

"You got finished five minutes early today," Nanny A started.

Looking at the clock on the dash, Clover saw it was 7:55 a.m. Smiling, she let a soft cough out. "It was good. Like I was just getting started."

"I just can't believe how good you are getting at this."

Clover looked at Nanny A. She was spinning the steering wheel with her palm and pretending to look over her shoulder as she turned onto Yeehaw Pass.

"You ever think about doing a race? I read there was one coming up next month, the day before Valentine's. I could register you."

Clover studied Nanny A. The car was pushing sixty now, and she was still trying her best to make it seem like she was not looking at Clover. Clover knew this tactic. Nanny A used it anytime she thought Clover would be sensitive to a discussion. Clover wondered why Nanny A would think this now—Clover was, after all, the one who initiated the daily workouts and enlisted her as driver.

"Don't you have to be eighteen to enter?" Clover asked.

"I think. But I could see if they would make an exception. All it would take is a question."

Clover watched Nanny A reach for her matcha steaming in the cupholder. Finally, Nanny A turned right and made eye contact.

"Why don't you just think on it, okay?" she said.

Clover nodded. She had been thinking on it. Every day. It was a 10K; she could easily handle that. And it wouldn't be till mid-February, so she would have four more weeks to train. And she'd always had a weird affection for February. Short, underappreciated February. February, somehow, reminded her of her schoolmate Jimmy Harriman. He was all teeth, a foot shorter than anyone else in her grade, and always sat alone at lunch. Watching Nanny A sip her matcha and hum Cat Stevens, Clover remembered the day she decided to make Jimmy her new friend. He was sitting in the cafeteria, frown covered, and picking his way through a muenster and bologna sandwich. Clover remembered how watching him there, alone at that big round table she felt such a tear in her skin, she had to find a seat next to him. Then how, just twenty minutes later, they were palm-deep in Clover's gorp and talking about the frustrations of the Capri-Sun's straw. Soon after, they were friends, and soon after, Jimmy found a smile. For some reason, Clover felt she could find a way to do the same thing for February. So, she decided to partake in her first race in sad, short, little February.

✳

The day of the race, Clover was up before the sun. Alone in her basement, she spent her prerace morning with a bar of ski wax and a rusty file that once belonged to her father. She was sharpening her skis and losing herself in the soothing sound of the file scraping its way along the edges. It was melodic, a long tenor drone that sprinkled fiberglass dust in spirals toward the ground, each speck swaying in unexpected directions like drunk snowflakes.

Next came the wax. Cold from the winter morn, she initially had trouble opening the thin circular can. When she finally did, its smell kicked back a taste of Bazooka bubble gum. Taking a small swab, she sniffed it, then massaged it into the bottom of her skis. This was her favorite part of tuning her skis, when she could feel her fingers slide over the grain and account for every infinitesimal bump and groove of their base. Later, when she skied, she would imagine the roll of each groove against the snow and be able reduce each step and glide to such micro-moments that she could feel every molecule of fiberglass pass over every molecule of snow. This was one of the reasons she was pulled to the sport, the feeling that, despite her speed, when she was cross-country skiing, nothing around or inside her moved faster than a drip of syrup.

The drive to the event was surprisingly quiet. Nanny A did not force conversation, and outside of putting a CD of Nusrat Fateh Ali Khan on, disappeared into the driver's seat. This CD started with Nusrat singing a cascading series of chant-like lyrics over a harmonium. The singing poked Clover awake, not in a good way, but in a nerve alerting way that made her slide forward in the passenger seat. But when the tablas joined, Clover was able to release a long breath as their rhythmic pop and thump settled any rattles that chambered around her head.

By the time they arrived at the race, Clover was a mass of meditative focus. Exiting the car, nothing but the one-two pattern of her breath could find her. Yes, there was a world of competitors walking around her—a world where mouths moved, objects collided, and nature swayed, but none of it registered a squeak over Clover's inhales.

Aware that Clover may have gone too deep into a pregame trance, Nanny A took her by the arm and walked her and her skis to the registration table. As with most cross-country events, there were barely any fans. Only family. And coaches. And coaches who were family. Nanny A wondered if, like her, they were coaches who were immediate family. She also wondered which of these coaches or family members were so passionate about the sport they'd shown up the night before, under the freeze of the moon, to set up ropes and flags and smooth the race path down to a Zamboni-inspired glass. But she was thankful someone made the effort to create this, even if they were a familial sucker like her. Smiling, Nanny A scanned the lay of the racecourse. She was looking forward to seeing Clover power through the straightaways, and, above all, she was happy one element was missing: William Jefferson Macklemore. And this, of course, was by design.

From the moment Nanny A heard of Bill, she knew she would not like him. Or trust him. Or want to engage with him. But she did know she would have to respect his unpredictable power. She'd heard the stories of what he did to Bobby, Snow Feather, his ex-wife Suzanne. She knew he was capable of vindictive stupidity and was powered by a shell of a male ego that was told too many times he was special. Or good-looking. *Jesus Christ, the pathetic fucking male I'm-told-I'm-good-looking-ego built of spit and straw*, she thought. And she knew he had the money and power in Fortooth to exact whatever he wanted. So, to protect Annabelle and her eventual granddaughter, she knew she would have to move to Fortooth to guarantee a fence, barbed and sturdy, stood between them.

Thankfully, it was known that cross-country skiing was the one winter sport Bill saw no value in. It was, as he put it once to a Fortooth reporter, "a sport for bored Swedish sadists to chase a fox they'll never fuck." But Nanny A knew what he actually meant was, that cross-country skiing had nothing to capitalize on. No money, no fan base, no sex appeal. So, at events like this, they had no Bill. What Nanny A did not know was, that even though the event did not have Bill in person, it had Bill in the form of a Sony DCR-VX1000 MiniDV camera operated by one of the organizers who happened to be on Glory Peak's payroll. Per his duties, this "organizer" was to film the event, keep Clover's race bib, and make copies of any race photos that featured her. Too worried about maintaining Clover's focus to register the stubby man filming from a wood bench, Nanny A brought Clover to the starting line and prepared her for the start.

First, she laid Clover's skis parallel on the track, just behind the line. Next, Nanny A planted her poles in front of them. Then, she released her bindings, allowing Clover to clip into her skis. Finally, she took the fleece off Clover's back and signaled for her to grab her poles and skate to the starting line. Which Clover did—almost running Nanny A over in the process.

"Hey!" Nanny A snapped, more out of reflex than anger. "You alive there?"

Confused, Clover turned around. "Yeah? What?"

"Nothing. You just . . ." Nanny A paused, staring at her granddaughter's pink face, lost somewhere outside the cosmos. Touching the back of her shoulder, she said, "Just get to the starting line. I'll meet you at the finish." And with that, Nanny A was off.

Two kilometers into the race, everyone realized it was not going to be much of an event. The competitors, though well-conditioned, were not used to the stinging morning wind and had no clue that to navigate it, they would have to purse their lips like a trumpeter and trade long, narrow breaths. For Clover, this was second nature, as she'd spent two seasons refining this technique. By kilometer six, she was half a kilometer ahead of the closest competitor. By kilometer eight, almost a full kilometer, and when she crossed the finish line, the second-place skier was almost seven minutes behind. Barely huffing, she unclipped her skis, placed them on her shoulders, and walked over to a waiting Nanny A, whose face was red and gleaming.

"Clove! Clove, you did it! You did it!" she exclaimed.

Sharing a small smile, Clover pulled her beanie off and released her curls. "That was a good run, Nanny."

"A good run? You little shit, you *decimated* them!"

Quickly, Clover's smile turned and her eyes widened. "Wait, do you think they're mad? I didn't upset them, did I?"

"No, baby—I mean maybe, but that's sports—sometimes you win, and sometimes you get your ass beat." Looking at Clover's eyes, it was apparent she did not anticipate this element of the race. The element of losers. "Listen, sweetie, this is good. It's okay to win, I promise you."

Clover released her brow, and happiness washed back over her face. "Okay, good. Because I really like this."

As Bill watched the video playback of his granddaughter crossing the finish line, a blood-warming sensation of pride trickled down his arms. Sure, the handheld footage was crap—the shooter was just a race organizer making a few extra bucks and obviously did not have an MFA in filmmaking—but it did capture something indisputable: Clover was a champion. And in her eyes, Bill could see the unquestionable steel-black stare that was pure Macklemore greatness. Sure, Bobby was air, but Clover revealed she was something harder, more resilient, more absolute—something titanium-like. And watching her plant, lunge, and glide, Bill realized he wanted to refine her. Not polish or smooth her edges but refine her as in extract her from a deep mine and turn her into an asset of great value. She would now be one of his projects.

And as he stood in his office and stared at the giant whiteboard that covered his south-facing wall, he saw the list of all his projects: The Lucky Mines Ski-In, Ski-Out Village. The Glory Peak Acro Fest. Finish Latest Chapters of Untitled WJM Autobiography. The board was littered with multicolored cursive and print scribblings, points written over points, and graphs half erased from sitting too long in the streaming sun. It was chaos, an ordered chaos, but on the bottom left corner of the board, there was something that confirmed this project would get special attention: a white, unmarked space.

Eager, Bill grabbed a red marker from his desk and walked toward the board. Then, in large uppercase letters, he wrote three words: Project Golden Thingy. To solidify their place on the board, he then spat in his hand and cleared the scribblings around it. Now the words appeared unobstructed, surrounded by enough space to do what was most important—grow into reality.

Many of the items on the board once had space like this, and as they grew greater and greater, details and dates filled in around them. This was how Bill measured growth, thoughts clustering around a breakthrough idea that spread like corkscrew vines from a beanstalk. Nearly every idea on the board was in some advanced stage of growth, and while on the surface they seemed a natural extension of Bill's blooming empire, they were all motivated by one thing—Bobby Mac.

Since Bobby Mac's disappearance, Bill had not slept through a single night. Not even a short one. His internal alarm was now programmed to go off three hours after sleep, avoiding any entrance he would make into the dream state. This was by subconscious design because Bill was not ready to acknowledge the moldy socks that sat like boulders in the hidden drawers of his soul. The drawers that stored the regret he felt over the failure of his marriage, for lying to his priests during confession, for accidentally driving over a dog in Milan and leaving it to bleed out on the cobblestone. And the drawer where he kept regret for letting Bobby go. It was with the sublimation of that drawer that Bill's manic expansion of Glory Peak sparked. From it came his idea to open the out-of-bounds areas in the hope that a skier would yard sale into a frozen Bobby Mac. Or that in deciding to turn the east side of the mountain into a half-pipe, a bulldozer would clear a buried path to his long-lost son. Or that in developing the Lucky Mines condominiums, a worker, while laying its foundation, would shovel deep enough to hit one of Bobby Mac's Timberland boots. But none of this happened. So, as he tossed in his sleep and came up with ideas that grew the tangle of thoughts on his whiteboard, Bill unconsciously continued to do one thing—explore every square centimeter of the Farangotta in search of his son.

What he did not expect to do in the process was reinvent the ski industry.

It happened on January 3, 1992. During a particularly terrible night of sleep, Bill somehow, kept finding his way to strobe like flashes of Pike's Pickled Pepper Peak. Pike's was a rugged chute that slithered down a fourteen-thousand-foot mountain, buttressed by the backside of Glory Peak and sharing a thin ridge with Miner's Gasp. Considered the unfortunate middle child of the Farangotta Big Three, Pike's Pickled Pepper Peak sat cranky and unloved by most locals and tourists alike. Bobby Mac, though, always had an affection for it—partly because of its moody, gothic-like spires of granite that suggested Edward Gory reinterpreting the works of Ansel Adams and mostly because few people ever ventured up, on, or around it—which meant it was pure.

Staring a hole into the polished grain of his ceiling, Bill wondered if Pike's Pickled Pepper Peak could possibly be used for backcountry skiing. He also wondered if maybe he could find a local free rider who was so stupid, extreme, and steezy, he would let Bill pay him $250 to ski down it and take photos of the descent. Bill would then plaster them throughout ski magazines, selling Glory Peak's unparalleled out-of-bounds skiing and Fortooth's unparalleled terrain as the best in lower 48. And maybe, most importantly, that skier would fall into a frozen Bobby Mac somewhere at Pike's base. Pulling on his bottom lip, Bill scanned his mental Rolodex of possible locals who had the skills—let alone reason—to do it. There were few to consider, with most either being too steeped in business or family responsibilities to take the risk. Reaching into the drawer of his nightstand, Bill pulled out a piece of chocolate he kept on standby. Believing it helped calm his thoughts, he bit into a chunk and chewed his way across every face he knew. It took him all of two bites before he settled on the perfect idiot to do it.

When Bill showed up on Gunther Wolfe's porch the following evening, his arrival was met with genuine surprise. Bill was not known to make house calls, and after Annabelle's disappearance, there was nothing connecting the two of them or any other reason to talk. Maybe at one point, Gunther dreamed of partnering with Bill to develop an empire, or condominiums, or maybe some tract houses with impressive attention to style and quality, but at this point in his life, Gunther's dream of building a real estate portfolio left with a southeast wind—the last remnant of his ambition, a small sweets shop he founded on Main Street.

The shop was named Das Fernweh, and it specialized in Bavarian chocolates. It also provided Gunther with a small but steady income that allowed him to indulge in what he did best: ski. But like most people who make it into their late thirties without a dream realized, a numbness crept over him, casting his days in melancholy. Medically speaking, it was textbook depression, inspired by the simple wear of enduring a mediocre life—but without the physical escape afforded by Annabelle to distract him from his own thoughts, Gunther just thought he was drifting closer and closer to death.

And then, Bill showed up. On his porch. And as Gunther watched the words steam from Bill's mouth in the early evening light, Bill presented Gunther with an unbelievable idea: he wanted him to ski down Pike's Pickled Pepper Peak. Bill's goal was to photograph its first descent and use the pictures to lure every ski jockey to the mountain, each one inspired to tear up every inch of its flinty crevices. Gunther understood the instinct and even respected the idea, but he was bothered that Bill's appearance came with no interest in real estate or franchise discussions of Das Fernweh. Digesting the offer, he realized if Bill was here, on his porch, near nightfall, he was somehow in a position of vulnerability, so Gunther masked his disappointment and invited Bill inside for some schnapps.

The ensuing negotiation was full of missed opportunities on both sides. Fuzzy from weeks of poor sleep, Bill was hesitant and passed up several chances to capitalize on revenue streams. Gunther, holding too tight to Bill's reputation as an unrelenting businessman, was tentative in his asks and insurances. Sitting silently across from each other at Gunther's kitchen table, it was apparent this was no stalemate of chess-playing titans, instead, just a couple of people who were unable to hide the fact that part of their essence had been chipped.

"So?" Bill asked, letting the word float, unhurried, in front of him like a cloud.

Gunther rested his chin in his palm and watched as the word fell to the table. He was fully aware his answer would be an eventual yes. But first, there had to be a bit of dance.

"It's dangerous," he said. "And I have not been training."

"You can have free access to Glory Peak," Bill countered. "Skis . . . anything you'll need to train."

"I have expenses. The import duties on the ingredients I have been shipping from Cologne are adding up," Gunther added.

"I'll assume all shipping costs for a year. We can set up a DHL account for you," Bill countered again.

"With something like this, health is always a concern," Gunther went on, absently stroking the hair on his chin. "Concussions, broken bones, residual knee traumas . . ." He waved his hand with each malady.

"I'll get you on the Glory Peak insurance plan. Best in the valley. Once again, for the year. You say yes, I'll have this all written up and executed by Monday."

Gunther rolled some imaginary felt between his fingertips and turned his gaze past Bill's shoulder to the bookshelf below his kitchen window. It was mostly filled with old newspapers and stacks of recipes he'd cut out of the magazines from the Fortooth Public Library—except for the bottom shelf. That was filled with two Bolex 16mm cameras and the leftover hats and scarves he had from Wolfehaus Real Estate. Now, the yellow of the fabric was muted, and for two years, he'd walked by the bookshelf without even noticing them. But there they were, staring back at him in octuplicate.

"Okay, Mr. Macklemore. I'll do it, but with one last consideration: I want my own team of people from Wolfehaus Media to film it."

Bill's brows bolted for his hairline. "Wolfehaus Media?" he barked. "What the hell is that?"

"My production company. If you are here, you must know about my time in Europe filming nature documentaries for ZDF," Gunther answered. "This way, if I die, I know I will be memorialized properly. No matter, you are welcome to have as many of the photos as you want."

Bill sat back in his chair and shook his head. He then ran his hand over his hair and pulled an imaginary strand off his index finger. "Hah, well, shit . . . I guess if you're dumb enough to risk death for some film, you can keep it."

Gunther flicked the imaginary felt from his fingers and released a laugh that never made it to the surface. *Why, yes*, he thought to himself. *I am that dumb.*

∿∿

The day of the descent was no different than most good wintery days in Fortooth. It was sunny but cold enough to keep the snow firm and had a variety of gusts swirling and searching their way up the mountains looking to battle it out for the alpha windchill position. Today, Gunther would feel their whistling skirmishes on top of Pike's Pickled Pepper Peak. And to get there, he would have to take a snowcat to Pike's base. The ensuing climb would be a bit of a challenge, but he made steeper and longer ones while summiting Nebelhorn. The key, as always, was to steady each step with a locked knee before taking the next small, patient step. It was a cautious approach but provided a German mountain man with steady German consistency. And simplicity.

Which was Gunther' strategy for filming. Simple classic coverage. There would be one helicopter, four cinematographers, three Bolex cameras, two Aaton XTR Prod cameras, ten thousand feet of Fuji 250D film stock, three PAs, and one sound recordist.

The problem was paying for it would prove to be very unsimple. Gunther had already twice remortgaged his house to open Das Fernweh and sold his collection of German tapestries to finance the launch of Wolfehaus Real Estate. He was, by all accounts, cash and credit poor—but he did have a deed to his house, a large list of production contacts, and semen. The budget for production, VHS manufacturing, and marketing was looking to be about $18,000. With the remaining equity he had in his house, he would be able to get $15,500. As a sperm donor, he would be able to make another $750. He would have to write checks for the remaining amount, and these checks would most likely bounce—but at the end of the run, he could be dead, and as far as he knew, debts did not follow you into the afterlife. If he was lucky enough to survive, he had no doubt VHS presales would cover the difference, pay back the bank loan, and buy back his sperm. Slushing up the mountain, he felt confident that there was money to be made in this operation and with each step, he repeated the soothing words of one mantra, *Just don't die.*

When Gunther reached the summit, his body temperature was near one hundred degrees. To relieve the possibility of overheating, he reached under the armpit of his Spyder shell and removed a swatch of duct tape that covered a hole in the jacket. Through it, he felt the frigid poke of cold air whoosh over him. It was invigorating. Skin warm, eyes dancing, he gazed at the wonderland around him. The sun was full, a light bulb floating in a sea of blue, and in the distance, a herd of alpacas stepped their way across Jade Ridge. Below him, collecting at the base of Pike's Pickled Pepper Peak was an audience of nearly everyone in town. Like the ice-cold wind speeding past him, their stares felt like a thousand jabs to his face. But despite their skepticism or the rising gales of winter, Gunther could not have imagined a grander image: he, on top of the most dangerous peak in the Farangotta, hair blowing in the wind, sun projecting his shadow long on the town below.

*Greatness,* he thought. *Annabelle, will you watch me?*

Scanning a path down the mountain, an outline of a ski route appeared. He would drop fifteen feet into Cagney's Boot, then make a hard right turn toward Pike's Pimple—a large rock outcropping that bulged over the mountain like an extended cliff. It was imperative he turned left before he hit the Pimple because if he didn't, he would launch to certain death in the trees three hundred feet below. To avoid that, he needed to find Cha-chee's Couloir, the shoot right under Pike's Pimple where he would have to carve near horizontal S-turns on a 45-degree pitch down Pike's Face, then charge into Pike's Alley, the final part of the chute which would launch him chest-deep into a sea of powder at the peak's base.

But that was just top half of the run. If he was still conscious, he would then have to thread through a dense collection of trees—at nearly fifty miles per hour, taking each turn so precisely that if he dug an edge too late or clipped a shrub that poked out unexpectedly, a collision of mortal magnitude would follow. But—and Gunther knew this was a near impossible but—but, if he made each turn with faultless arc and geometry, he would dump soft and steady into an open field of soft pack that flowed to the parking lot, his mission thankfully and miraculously complete.

Closing his eyes, Gunther pictured the cheers that awaited—and most important, pictured the grin of his colleague, William Jefferson Macklemore. He could already imagine Bill shaking his hand and saying, "Yes, my German friend, you are a man of skill and accomplishment." From then on, he would be by Bill's side as they built Glory Peak, Fortooth Bend, the Farangotta into world-regarded lore, enshrined in the hearts of skiers everywhere.

Anticipating the reward of the next twenty years of partnership, Gunther pulled his goggles from his side pocket, blew on the inside of the lenses, and furiously rubbed them. Then, as he started his internal countdown from ten, he pulled the goggles over his face, took one last look at the helicopter thudding steady in the sky above—every second of this moment already being immortalized on film—and dropped in.

He landed the fifteen-foot jump smoothly. His skis bounced soft off the fresh snow and his knees compressed, easily absorbing the shock that could have thrown his upper body out of alignment. When he stood back into his racing crouch, he was able to next dig his left inside edge into the snow and cleanly whip a 75-degree turn toward his next target—Pike's Pimple.

Sitting forty yards in the distance, it waited—a collection of fractured rocks sticking through a coating of white powder. Preparing to bank left, Gunther lowered into an angled crouch and grinned, a whistle of cold running through the hole in his jacket to the palm in his glove. This turn was going to be glorious, the perfect shift from his inside left edge to his right—until, twenty feet left of the Pimple, a man popped up with a Canon EOS Rebel in his hands. Like a sniper, he gunned twenty photos at the approaching Gunther. The problem was this man was in the line Gunther needed to ski to avoid launching off the Pimple, but before he could counter with a solution, Gunther heard the tear of his skis against rock and felt an unequivocal rush of air. Then, in a moment of ill-advised panic, Gunther leaned back and let his skis slip out from under him and before he could adjust, he was in a spiral down the mountainside. Sliding down the chute, he waved his arms for balance when his skis somehow found a perfectly angled sheet of ice that sent him flying into the air. For a moment, all he could see was vacillating images of untouched snow, seasoned with splashes of black rock, the occasional ponderosa pine, and empty sky blue. It was simultaneously all a blur and perfectly seen, until he shot through a four-foot-deep lake of powder waiting below.

From the parking lot, a collection of gasps passed through the spectators. Disbelief followed. A quiet disbelief that melted into the sad silence of mourning. They had come here to witness magic, and now they were left to digest the image of a man pinwheeling through the sky toward death.

All due to one poorly positioned cameraman.

So, when a small fission in the powder trailed its way toward the tree line, no one in the crowd imagined it could be Gunther—on his skis, body unharmed, fighting through the head-high suffocation of snow passing his red-hot skin. And no one in the crowd could have imagined, when his head did surface above the snow, like a shark's fin in a bad B movie, he would be determined to finish his run. But he was, and when he fully emerged from the powder, skis pointed toward the oncoming trees, everyone in the crowd stood, eyes in full-spread wonder, as Gunther proceeded to operate with such unconscious command that every decision that followed would be perfection.

First, he edged left past a tree. Then he darted between two forty-foot pines, then he charged a dip just below them, planted his poles and used them to launch off a waiting ridge twenty feet into the air. Glowing from the flight, Gunther then kicked his skis into a backscratcher and landed with a crunch and hockey stop so perfect he swore the NHL would be calling.

Out of breath at the base of Pike's Pickled Pepper Peak, Gunther leaned over, a bead of sweat falling from his cheek, and exhaled lung-emptying breaths. He was unaware of what just happened, but when he stood, and his blood pressure eased back to normal, he was finally able to scan the crowd in the parking lot. Their faces were all whiter than the powder he'd just powered through, and their eyes stupefied frisbees of black. Mouths half-opened, everyone standing silent minus nature, it was then that Gunther realized what just transpired.

Applause, which he hoped for, never came. Instead, something greater, deeper, and far more enduring than claps arrived. It was take-your-breath-away amazement.

Surveying the crowd, Gunther searched for one specific face to share this historic moment. But when he found it, there wasn't the expression of admiration he was expecting. Trying to place the look, Gunther hoped it was just disappointment, but it seemed like something worse. It seemed like, maybe, unpleasant surprise—like when you walk into a public restroom only to realize you chose the stall someone just vomited in.

Or maybe it was a look that Gunther never dreamed his future compatriot would have. A look that said William Jefferson Macklemore wished Gunther would have died.

# CHAPTER 8

## MARCH 1998

To describe Wolfehaus Media's fireball ascent to the top of the ski film world would be difficult. Not because it wasn't accurate but because there was nothing else to measure its success against. Sure, there was the occasional barnstorming ski film that rented out a theater, recited sardonic narration, and assembled slow-motion shots of Nordics bobbing through deep powder—but Wolfehaus Media was the first example of something new to the ski world. It was a media phenomenon. Kids traded bootleg copies of the VHS, then ripped the VHS, then put it on hard drives that were shared with skiers on all seven continents.

Before Gunther could set up his next printing of VHS tapes, he'd sold every single one, and before he could ship his next round of tapes, he was getting requests for new videos and suggestions on where to film next. As someone who had always expected success, Gunther was emotionally prepared for this journey. But as one who never achieved it, he was unaware of what it would take to continue and after the first month it became clear there was no way he could balance the growing orders with his trout fishing. So, he went to town in search of employees, but because everyone was in service to or employed by Bill or Glory Peak, no one was willing to risk their insurance on joining an upstart company with a foreigner. With employee options bleak, Gunther was prepared for this to be his latest commercial failure. That was, until one Monday morning when there was a knock at his front door.

Opening it, he saw Nanny A coughing into a balled hand. He wasn't expecting company, particularly his former lover's mother, dressed like a schoolteacher, with a scrunched face on his doorstep.

"Um, I, uh, can I help you?" Gunther asked, tucking his green plaid flannel into his corduroys.

"Yeah," she nodded. "You have any water?"

Before Gunther could answer, Nanny A was walking into his house and heading toward the kitchen.

Watching her grab a dirty glass on a drying rack next to the sink, he wondered if she'd just had a car accident or was simply rude.

"I have filtered water in the refrigerator," Gunther said. "It will taste less of rust."

"This is fine," Nanny A responded then turned on the faucet and filled the glass. Gunther watched her take a large gulp then place it in the sink. Waiting for her to say something, he put his hands in his pockets and rocked back and forth on his feet. She didn't speak; instead, she just scanned his kitchen, looked at the ceiling, then at her shoes. Finally, she looked at him and said, "I hear you need help?"

Gunther smiled. Word moved fast in town, even though it most likely wasn't on his behalf. Walking to the table, he sat and grabbed a pouch of tobacco from a hubcap doubling as a fruit bowl.

"Yes, that is correct," he started. "Wolfehaus Media is beginning to offer employment opportunities to the proper candidates. Are you here because you know someone who would be of interest?"

Nanny A smiled and walked to the kitchen table. Extending her hand to a chair across from Gunther, she asked, "May I?"

"Please," Gunther said, pulling a swab of tobacco from the pouch.

Nanny A pulled the chair out and sat. She next flipped her ponytail back, leaned forward, and rested her forearms on the table. Gunther was surprised by the intensity in her eyes and her proximity. Staring right at him, she said, "I would like to work for you."

Nodding, Gunther reached for a rolling paper in the pouch. Folding it into a V, he filled it with tobacco.

"I see," he said. "What is your experience?"

Nanny A shook her head and released a staccato breath. "Well, I have a PhD in cultural anthropology; created the Women's Studies Department at the University of Colorado Boulder; and founded the Anthropology section at their Museum of Natural History where I oversaw forty employees, a budget of one point two million dollars annually, and the women's studies scholarship program that, while I was there, gave away over six hundred thousand dollars in scholarship opportunities. You need to hear more?"

Gunther smiled and finished rolling his cigarette. Lighting it, he stood, walked to a filing cabinet that doubled as a kitchen counter, and pulled out twenty pages of checking account balances. Handing them to Nanny A, he walked to his sofa and took a large puff off the cigarette.

Scanning the printouts, she saw on page two there was a total of $18,000.76 in his account. Turning the page, she expected additional pieces of information detailing profit and loss or an itemized breakdown of overhead, salary, and benefits. But there was nothing—only a handwritten note from Gunther reminding himself to buy a BMW. Releasing a chuckle, Nanny A placed the checking statement on the table and said, "I cannot believe my daughter used to fuck you."

Gunther coughed out a burst of smoke so violent, he almost choked. "You knew?" he asked—partly from a place of shame but also partly, if not mostly, from a place of relief.

"She was my daughter, for Christ's sake," Nanny A said, shaking her head. Removing her L.L.Bean parka, she stood, folded it, and set it on the kitchen table. Beneath it was a wool sweater. It was intricate, done in the style of one of those Scottish sweaters with alternate patterns of triangles, lines, and circles. Draping wide over her shoulders and hips, it was obvious it was a man's sweater. This was how Nanny A dressed: linear, loose, her clothes smothering out all suggestions of femininity.

So, when she removed the sweater and set it on the kitchen table, Gunther was surprised to see the round bulge of her breasts spill out the top of her V-neck base layer. And he was also surprised to see a small sliver of skin peek out between the top of her pants and the bottom of her shirt. It was not warm in the house, so to take off two layers of clothing in the dead of winter suggested one thing to Gunther, something he was sure he was misreading. But watching her walk past him into his bedroom confirmed that everything Gunther just witnessed was indeed what he couldn't believe—a seduction. Unsure what to do next, Gunther took a beat, then extinguished his cigarette in the hubcap bowl. He next stood, ironed out his shirt with his hands, and walked toward his bedroom. Waiting for him in bed, her back to the door, was Nanny A's naked body under his covers.

Seeing her there, it triggered a blurry montage of all the women in his past. He saw Annabelle; he saw Barbara from Stuttgart; he saw his mother post birth, ready to breastfeed and bathe him. Uncertain of which woman to follow, Gunther slid under the covers and pressed his body into Nanny A's back. She was warm, and as she turned around to face him, he could hear his zipper slide open and feel her reaching for him. Falling deeper into her hold, Gunther imagined Annabelle appearing before him with every touch. Before long, he was lost in the memory of their first time—in his car, out by Punishment Lake.

It made sense their first time would happen there. In spring, when the grass dewed at sunrise and the snow gave way to the sprouting stems of the red columbines. That particular day, Gunther was scouting for a tract of land to relocate the alpacas. There were eighty-three of them—seventeen down from the hundred Annabelle had purchased from Gunther eleven months earlier. Her goal was to use the alpaca hair as fabric for a base-layer clothing company she and Bobby Mac started. Having learned of the poor wicking capability of cotton, she thought winter athletes needed base layers that were technically superior, environmentally friendly, and sturdy enough for use till their hearts exploded.

When Annabelle found Gunther, he was one year into his move to the Farangotta.

At the time, he was known as an importer of South American sweaters and was living out of a converted Airstream that doubled as an import shop. He had just spent three years filming the major peaks of Chile, Ecuador, and Peru for the German television broadcaster ZDF, and during his travels, he'd become an expert on the ins and outs of the alpaca sweaters he would sell by bulk in Fortooth. The winters were known to be cold here—not bone-snapping Montana cold, but cold enough to remind you that nature would beat you in a game of one on one, so it was no problem for Gunther to find steady, if niche, business in Fortooth.

Meeting her that first morning, a purple-and-blue scarf wrapped around her neck, he was touched by her sweet smile but not struck by the thunderbolt. Hair shiny, skin colored bronze by the sun, she was no doubt attractive, but what stood out to him most was the smell of her lavender hand cream. And her enthusiasm as she inquired about alpacas, the breathability of the fabric, how it handled water, and if it was cheap and easy to loom. Halfway through their first meeting, it became apparent Annabelle was not interested in purchasing alpaca sweaters but in purchasing alpacas themselves. Hoping to find the means to stay in Fortooth, Gunther realized if he helped Annabelle purchase a herd, his commission would be enough to buy some property and launch a proper business. Their talks spanned a year, and fourteen months after they'd met, he was arranging for the delivery of one hundred Huacaya alpacas at $118 per head. The plan, once they arrived, was to pen them on ten acres out by Punishment Lake. Teeming with a rolling buffet of the softest sugar-sweet grass in Farangotta, this would be their temporary home until the following spring, when they would be relocated to Bobby and Annabelle's barn and prepped for shearing.

In retrospect, Gunther realized that this planning had been their courtship. He'd sensed something was off with Annabelle's marriage, not just by the diminishing number of times she spoke of Bobby but by the frequency with which she would swing by his place to review plans they'd already reviewed. Excuses were found, items forgotten, thoughtful little gifts exchanged, all in the hope of getting an extra wink or accidental touch. Anything that allowed for the confirmation of connection.

By the time Gunther and Annabelle consummated the relationship, the force of expectation was so potent they could have started a car with the fuel tank on empty. The sex was fast and simple, Gunther barely in her when he came. But the after—that was long. Sitting in the backseat of his Volkswagen, they pressed their faces purple against each other and breathed in deep, plural gasps. For some reason, they would not let each other go, and with Gunther's flaccid cock still inside her, they couldn't tell where their pelvic bones started or stopped.

Nanny A had a similar feeling pressed up against Gunther. She could not let his body go. Unsure and not even caring if he came, she pulled Gunther as close to her as possible and dug her nose deep into his neck. It had the oat-scented musk of wet muesli, and the texture was complicated. His skin was soft, though not in a way that conveyed youth—it had the rubber of age, and the coarseness of too many days spent in the sun, but somehow his shaven face did not grate against her cheeks. Tracing her finger along his jaw, she searched for a scar, or a bite mark, or a scent—anything that could have lingered ten years later, like a faded tattoo on Gunther's skin. Anything that could have been a line to Annabelle.

*God, Annabelle, where are you?* Nanna A thought. *Do you know I miss you? And that stupid Coca-Cola shirt? I really don't care if you wear it. You can wear anything. Just come home. Please.* It was tough for her not to weep. Nanny A knew she was too hard on Annabelle, short, brusque even. *It was just . . . I thought you would be around. Long enough to not need me anymore.*

It was difficult for Clover to understand her grandmother's commitment to Wolfehaus. To her, it all felt weird and wasted. And what felt even more weird and wasted to Clover was why Nanny A wanted to spend so much time with Gunther.

*Gunther's an idiot*, Clover thought. An overeager lapdog who wagged his tail with such stupid vigor that no matter how much he tried to get a belly rub, she only wanted to drop-kick him down a flight of stairs.

"But how am I going to get to practice if you are working there every day?" Clover asked one morning when Nanny A informed her, she was going to be working at Wolfehaus full time.

"I'll still drop you off. And I'll see if we can get Gail to pick you up."

"Gail? Sheriff Dan's secretary? She smells like glue."

"Assistant," Nanny sternly responded. "And she likes you. And she can also bring you to school after."

"But why? You don't have to work, right?" Clover asked.

"No, but listen, Clover, and this may not make sense to you, but I want to be part of something. Gunther is on to something here. And he needs me to make sure it has a chance."

"But it's just freaking ski movies, Nanny."

"I know it seems like it. But they can be more. They can inspire dreams. They can be the anchor to a community that inspires incredible physical feats and celebrations of nature. And it's growing like Cabbage Patch Kids. We can create a revolution."

*You just don't get it, Nanny A*, Clover wanted to say. *I am more important than this stupid revolution.*

Not soon after this conversation, Clover stopped talking to Nanny A about Wolfehaus. Actually, she stopped talking to her about most things. Considering Nanny A was the one person on the planet whose company she could endure, it frustrated her that her only solution to this issue was to retreat. But it seemed better than fighting with her, and maybe if she hadn't started her friendship with Jimmy Harriman, she would have tried to reconnect with Nanny A. But Jimmy entered her life, and he quickly became the new *one person* whose company she could endure. If anything, it was easier to spend time with him, as he spoke less than Nanny A. And even less than Clover. But that didn't seem to matter as before long, she was spending all her school time, then all her after-school time with him. At first, their friendship seemed innocuous—just that comfortable routine of someone relying on somebody else to help navigate the pulls of life.

But then, people began to ask Clover if something else was happening— "you know, like, are you just friends, or something special" questions. Clover was initially oblivious to what these questions really meant. As she was oblivious to any narrative that implied their friendship consisted of anything other than comfort. Or safety. And as much as she had grown to love the world of Fortooth, the sun it provided, the trees it provided, and its firepit smells, one thing she did not love was the microscope it put her under. As granddaughter to Glory Peak's founder and the daughter of *the* Bobby Mac, she was second-generation royalty. Being so, it was impossible to not feel the pressure of eyes on her neck or hear the whispers of townies as she walked the streets. She did not ask for this appointment. And living in the shadow of her family, dead and alive, bothered her. Not bothered her like the dangling thread of a sweater does, but bothered her like a bone spur, its blunt pain coming with every step no matter what you did to try to avoid it.

Lucky for Clover, Jimmy, somehow, understood the discomfort she felt carrying the Macklemore name. Even luckier for her, Jimmy also understood the role he needed to play to take her discomfort away. As they walked to school, he would walk slightly ahead of or behind her, always knowing where to be so he could block the sight of Glory Peak from her periphery. And when they went to school, it was never through the tinted front doors like everyone in town but through the football field and then the gym, which provided the emptiest hallways to homeroom. If calibrated correctly, they would arrive two minutes before the first bell, and if ahead of schedule, they would kill the extra time balancing rocks by the school pond. Clover liked these moments, as Jimmy could place the rocks sometimes thirty high and build drunken stone skyscrapers that gave the finger to gravity and physics. Watching him dial his focus into every mineral, his eyes assessing the dents and rises in each stone, Clover would rub her nose and lose herself in an experience her grandmother would have described as "zen as shit."

With Jimmy by her side, Clover loved that her school days went by without much storm. She was always a B+ student, not because she couldn't be an A+ one but because she didn't want any extra attention from her teachers. Once in fourth grade, when she scored a hundred on a fractions test, her teacher suggested they meet after school for some advanced math tutoring. Pretty soon, Clover discovered it was just a ploy for the teacher to weasel her way into a meeting with her grandfather. Competitive at heart, she realized being a B or C student would be too much of a compromise but sliding by with a B+ was just enough to keep up a standard of better than good.

Besides, she had the academic success of Jimmy to sail on, one of the other things she prized about him. Like her, he had a strange, obsessive connection to ritual. And like her, he started his days in the basement of his home—but unlike her, it wasn't at a worktable with skis but at a coffee table sharpening pencils, filing away study cards, and checking the tips of his highlighters for ink. At first, Clover thought these habits were instilled in Jimmy by his father. He was an environmental engineer who carried the lessons of five years in the navy into their home. Not in a cruel way, as Clover noted, but in a way that celebrated the comfort and certainty of handling life with the peace and clarity that came with order and preparation. Through him, Jimmy found value in always being on time, always turning in his homework, and keeping meticulous notes in meticulous files in a meticulous room. What was unknown to both, and something that Clover soon recognized, was that their discipline started at a genetic level, enabling each one to embrace obsession like breathing. From the womb, they both were simply touched.

Before Clover befriended Jimmy, she remembered how he was bullied for this discipline. No one understood why, at the start of each class, he would line up two pencils, one red pen, one blue pen, and a green highlighter at the top of his desk, or why he would pull a tape recorder from his bag, label a tape in tiny and precise cursive, and proceed to record each class. One morning in fifth grade, Clover remembered passing Jimmy outside the music room. He was on the floor, sobbing in front of an assortment of broken cassette tapes. Unbeknownst to her, five minutes earlier, Jason Berger had ripped the tapes from his bag and stomped on them. Now, Jimmy was trying, and failing, to reel the exposed tape back into its broken cases. Almost crying herself, Clover watched him instead bunch the tape like tissues and weep into them.

These abuses Jimmy endured continued through eighth grade, up until the day Clover decided to sit with him at lunch to declare he was now off-limits. Being the granddaughter of William Jefferson Macklemore, she knew she had power, but being the granddaughter of Nanny A, she was taught never to abuse it. But sometimes, like on that day, she learned wielding it could have benefits. And they did because after that lunch, Jimmy knew he had found a protector. And as an unspoken thank-you—because they rarely spoke—he took it upon himself to make sure he was the same.

His guardianship came in several forms. Not just the blocking of her view of Glory Peak, but in other itchier ways—like sneaking onto Main Street and painting over Glory Peak signs. Or sometimes in ways that were even itchier, like when he would use his father's bowie knife to cut gashes into the tires of Bill Macklemore's Land Rover. Jimmy knew, like Nanny A, the danger of Bill's reach, and he also sensed Bill was somehow angling for a way into his granddaughter's life. Not able to stop him on a grander level, Jimmy figured, like a mosquito circling on a swampy day, he could annoy him with buzzes. Unaware that in these buzzings, Jimmy was laying the groundwork for an apocalypse.

# CHAPTER 9

## MARCH 1998—THE LE'ECHUWANNA

He Who Eats laughed when he opened the door. It was not every day Sheriff Dan Daley stopped by his house, so seeing him there, shifting back and forth on his doorstep, he knew this had to be some kind of *kemo-wabi* trouble. Eyeing Deputy Ron Booth leaning against a patrol car just over Sheriff Dan's shoulder, He Who Eats decided to ask the obvious: "What the fuck do you want?"

Sheriff Dan sent a glance to the ground. Almost whispering, he said, "We need to talk to you about the graffiti spray-painted on the Glory Peak billboard on Main Street."

"Why?" He Who Eats answered, scratching his armpit.

"Well, it's the third time someone vandalized a Glory Peak sign this week. And this image, well, it was large, and very inappropriate."

"Was it the image of a giant moose turd? Because that's what I would love to do on all those signs."

"It was a penis," Deputy Booth squeaked over Sheriff Dan's shoulder. Shifting his eyes at the deputy, He Who Eats noticed he was fighting a smirk.

"Well, besides the fact that I got a huge horse cock, what does this have to do with me?"

Sheriff Dan rubbed the side of his neck, his eyes still fixed on the doormat. "Well, there's been a lot of vandalism targeting Glory Peak, and umm, Mr. Macklemore, in particular. He, I mean, well . . . You have history—"

"History?" He Who Eats interrupted. "We don't got no history unless you want to talk about how I, historically, think he's a wolf scrotum."

He Who Eats watched Sheriff Dan lift his eyes from the ground and place them on him. They darted back and forth, then found their way back to the ground. "Listen, I'm not here to create any issues. I am just here to do my job," Sheriff Dan said.

"Bullshit," He Who Eats barked back. "You're here 'cause that fat *Wasicu* told your sorry ass to come down and harass me. You know what, tell him—actually, I'm gonna tell you this, too," He Who Eats said as he grabbed the door handle, about to slam the door. "Go choke on a mud-soaked donkey dick."

In Fortooth, it was commonly known the Le'Echuwanna hated Bill—but in reality, it wasn't hatred—it was something much deeper. The Le'Echuwanna saw Bill as a primal element of destruction. Like a disease that ravaged a body until it had taken from it the very thing it needed to survive, Bill was, in their eyes, a plundering fungus sucking the Farangotta dry.

For the first twenty years of Glory Peak's existence, they just sighed at Bill and the additions he was making to the valley. A ski mountain? Sure, why not? It was bound to happen if skiing was bound to happen. A hotel nestled against the mountain? Sure, why not? An expected carryover from a ski mountain. A condominium with ski-in, ski-out offerings, built on the side of the mountain? Well, that seemed a bit overkill, as no other outsiders needed to really buy winter homes in the Farangotta. But in 1996 when Bill decided to add Prospector's Goldmine, a multi-season hotel located just out of town, to the Glory Peak roster, the Le'Echuwanna saw this man with the flop of blond hair for what he was. The *Eh-Kar-lo*. Which translated to the great destroyer.

It was actually He Who Eats who recognized it first—a vision coming to him one night as he ate dinner by candlelight. Like most of the Le'Echuwanna, He Who Eats lived a modest life, one that did not reflect the financial resources he accrued. The tribe owned a variety of businesses, and unlike what was expected of Natives who were displaced by the white man, they did not descend into a vortex of alcohol, disrepair, or casinos. Instead, they learned from their mistake of selling land to Prescott Norville for much too cheap and put forth a strategy that would build strength via an accumulation of their own paper wealth. Which meant they started businesses. Their initial product was salt trout, which they sold in weekly allotments to the miners. This soon expanded into elk jerky, then to blankets and baskets, then to the inks and dyes they used to color the blankets, then finally settled into printing and paper production with the inks and dyes they made for the blankets.

Throughout the years, each of these businesses had the opportunity to expand into larger iterations, but the Le'Echuwanna knew if they allowed this growth, they would overtax the Farangotta's resources. So, they managed the growth of each business not by overharvesting but by instead focusing on building a system efficiency that increased margins and minimized cost.

They were able to do this because none of them took a salary and had an agreed-upon financial system where they divided 40 percent of their profits among each tribe member over the age of eighteen. With only fifty-six Le'Echuwanna left by the winter of 1998, that meant each Elder Elder was raking in $116,348 a year, a more-than-reasonable amount to live on and a dramatic increase over the allotments each Elder Elder received before He Who Eats took over.

Those allotments barely averaged $28,000, as the previous Elder Elder, *Se-Oh-Acha-Ho*, or as he was first known, He Who Paints the Sun and eventually became known as He Who Rubs the Staff, was fuzzy in his accounting. Alzheimer's, dementia, who knew what it was, had crept into his reign as chief and by the time he stepped down, the businesses were in near ruin as his focus shifted from efficient production practices to grinding against as many totem poles as possible.

Hoping his behavior could be curtailed to private moments, the tribe realized, like with a dog crooked from rabies, a tighter quarantine was needed.

So, to avoid the inglorious fate of chaining their leader to a kitchen table with an elk hide wrapped around his groin, they sent him to a nursing home in Delray Beach and elected a new chief. At first, He Who Eats was not sure he wanted the job. He enjoyed the idea of managing the tribe's businesses and knew he could quadruple its profit, but he also enjoyed managing a variety of meals and whiskey. And of course, there were the drugs. He loved the drugs. All of them. And unexpectedly, the Elder Elders did not care about that. They knew the practices by which they built the tribe were in jeopardy, so their concerns were focused more on keeping their community alive than on the legalities of weed. Furthermore, He Who Eats was blessed with the gushing force of the *Si-mah-neh*, the six-eyed trout that allowed him to see every world. At ceremonies, this force would appear so strong it would take his dancing to places not seen since James Brown discovered the fatback groove and somehow, despite his bear-size frame, his movements would be so graceful, so rhythmic, and so arhythmic, it was as if he conjured an orchestra of movement that transcended all the known knowns.

After a year of weekly persuasion, He Who Eats agreed to take the role of chief—and to only his surprise, he took to it with ease. He discovered that running the tribal meetings was simple, and as he began a greater interaction with his people, he developed a greater appreciation of their history. And the beauty of this was with this appreciation came a further mastering of the *Si-mah-neh*. Eventually, he could see births before they happened; pick a baby's gender just by smelling the wrist of the expectant mother; or at times, see his tribe's innermost thoughts, not through words but through their pupils as they contracted in light. For the most part, he was very capable of managing these visions, but on occasion, they burdened him with a future he did not want to see.

Receiving the vision of Bill as *Eh-Kar-lo* was one of those burdens. When it arrived, it was early January, after midnight, during a second dinner, this one a stew of elk and venison. He hadn't been out all day, as it was the time of year when the valley cold scraped faces like dull razors and was happy to be hunkered down in the warm hold of the home, he built himself. It held four bedrooms in a log cabin design, fixed together by oak and pine and slate. It had a kitchen that took up most of the bottom floor, not with counter space but with freezers, six in total, that held a collection of game meat and fish. And it had a living room that adjoined the kitchen with a large L-shaped sofa draped by a motley of elk hides, a stuffed reindeer hanging from the rafters, and three large televisions sitting on an east-facing wall.

During dinner, it was ritual for He Who Eats to sit in front of these televisions, scan what cable had to offer, and watch all three simultaneously. As it was already 1 a.m., the late-night pickings were slim, but his Dish was able to find *The Simpsons* on TV one, the surprising and charming escapades of *Sabrina the Teenage Witch* on TV two, and on TV three, *The X-Files*. Normally, when *The X-Files* was on, He Who Eats synced all three TVs to it, but having seen this episode before, he chose to balance it out with two splashes of half-hour comedy.

Looking back, it must have been the double splash of comedy that triggered the vision. That and the stinging fog of biting into a habanero hiding in the stew. Tongue numb, brows dripping sweat, the swell of eyelids blurring his vision, He Who Eats recalled watching Melissa Joan Hart on TV two talk about NSYNC and fake IDs when an animated Ed Begley Jr. leaped off TV one and landed on Sabrina. Angry, he choked her, the air squeaking from her lungs, and like a speared octopus, she flapped her arms and tried to purse her lips to conjure some magic. But the words never formed, and before long, she lay dead on the floor of the studio set. Confused by her limp body, Ed Begley Jr. proceeded to lift her right arm and pull her off the screen onto TV three, where Gillian Anderson stared into the eyes of a demonic doll. Then, seeing Ed Begley Jr. appear right behind Agent Scully, the doll shifted its gaze toward his eyes and dove for him. In a flash of white, the doll melted into Ed's body with Ed's skin flaking away to reveal Bill chewing on the carcass of an elk. Blood dripping from his mouth, Bill raised his arms to the sky, his hands now raging flames, and exploded into nothing, singeing He Who Eats' corneas red as all three televisions cut to snow.

Panicked, He Who Eats remembered jumping to his feet only to immediately keel over when his meal erupted from his stomach. Vomit on his feet, face, and hands, He Who Eats collapsed in a puddle of partially digested chili and grumbled through a coma sleep.

The following morning, He Who Eats called an immediate meeting of the Elder Elders. Meeting in their sacred mud hut, which had been patched together with decades of hardened Farangotta soil, the Elder Elders fell silent as they listened to He Who Eats' vision. Unfortunately, it did not take years of sacred teachings to understand its meaning: Bill would devour the valley until nothing but rot was left in the soil. The question then became, what would they do about it? Walking Toad had a very clear opinion, and with a stern, monotone voice, she shared it with the Elder Elders. "Mudhook has always been a scavenging dog. I think we should burn down Glory Peak."

"Hell yeah!" He Who Speaks chimed in.

Sacred Crow cackled next, her gray-black hair billowing like Einstein's in the hut. "Or we can grab a bow and hunt him by Punishment Lake. Eventually, it will happen. It is the quiet way."

"No!" interjected Pouting Trout. This caused everybody in the mud hut to go silent, as Pouting Trout seldom spoke. He was old and prone to disappearing midmeeting behind a snore, but when he did speak, his words were held gently, like bubbles on a finger, every tribe member trying their best to keep them from popping. Sitting in quiet, Pouting Trout took a long pull off his pipe and released the smoke into the center of the hut. Sunlight streamed through a hole on top and outlined the smoke as it coiled its way into S's and O's. Watching it, they hoped to find an answer in its squirming form, but it disappeared to nothing.

Looking at He Who Eats, Pouting Trout smiled. "You must perform the *He-atch-a-way*."

"Ah, come on, PT, I haven't even had my fucking Count Chocula yet—"

"Enough," snapped Pouting Trout. "It is the Elder Elder chief's way."

Releasing a low-rolling sigh, He Who Eats shifted onto his left leg, wobbled to his knees, and pushed himself up. Brushing the dust from his legs, he fluttered his hands and scanned the hut. They were all sitting cross-legged, their faces painted red and blue as sheepskins dressed their backs.

Clearing the crow in his throat, he brought his hands together in a booming clap and started mumbling a bass-heavy chant. *"Me-ah-wah-he, me-ah-wah . . ."* Pushing the chant through the chap of scarred lips, it soon lifted in volume through the room. The council, receiving the words, closed their eyes and began to thump on their inner thighs.

Following the drumbeat, He Who Eats let its rhythm enter the crown of his head and fall through his bones till it settled in the arches of his feet. Dancing followed next. High-step dancing with spins and claps and bows and salutations and sweat. Thick, beady sweat that flew off his body as he flicked his head from east to west. He was a blur now—a wet, heavy blur of hair and sheepskin. The chant, too, was a blur, a sentence that lost all meaning beyond the phonetic sounds of each pulsing syllable. Then, as the drumming turned thunderous and the chant a wailing cry, He Who Eats spun one last violent turn and collapsed to the floor.

Silence followed. The hut still, minus the dust, which swayed itself back and forth to the floor. Like a drunk waking from a hangover, He Who Eats teetered slowly to his feet and cleared damp hair from his face. Opening his mouth, he tried to speak, but only stutters and gasps followed. Finally, after he seesawed his towering frame to a firm stand, he revealed what he saw.

"We gotta buy ourselves some fucking land," he shared. And with that, pulled a large black hairball from his throat.

# CHAPTER 10

**FEBRUARY 9, 1988**

Bobby looked at Annabelle's fingers. Uncovered, a hint of blue, they must have been frozen fish-stick cold. The problem, and just one of many, was that there wasn't an oven set to 350 degrees to thaw them out. Watching Annabelle rub them, Bobby knew she was trying to trigger some blood flow, but after an hour submerged in a snow cave, he also knew the frigid design of winter was claiming its win.

For the most part, it was silent, but somehow, Bobby could still hear the scream of Annabelle's disdain. Knowing that any word, syllable, or letter he spoke could ignite the gasoline inside her, Bobby bit his lip and tried to stay quiet. But over time, as he watched her shiver in the cave's muted light, he finally said something.

"They tingling?"

"Not yet. Just cold." She huffed. "You'd think I'd be used to this by now, but fuck—the cold sucks."

Bobby could not argue. The cold did suck. But there was also a side of Bobby that thought the cold was incredible—the way it smacked your body to attention when you jumped in an icy lake, the way it numbed the burning pain of a shrub to the stomach when you misestimated a tree run, or the way it took the liquid heat of bourbon and smoothed it to a maple tinge on your first après drink. Yes, the cold could suck, but it could also be one of the most sublime gifts Mother Nature offered.

"I hear ya," Bobby answered, afraid to challenge her. "People always talk about your blood thinning when you go to warm places, but what about your blood thickening in cold ones?"

Annabelle coughed, then exhaled. "I know there's gotta be some plant or element somewhere that could warm up blood. Remind me when we get out to do some research. And then remind me to buy all of it."

"Done," Bobby answered. He then pulled a strand of hair from his head and tied it around his finger. Annabelle looked at him, perplexed, until she saw him finish a bow. He then added, "You know, just a reminder."

And it was—not for Bobby as much as it was for Annabelle. A reminder that although she'd grown to hate this man and despise the weak Polly-O String Cheese that made up his spine, he was, in certain rare circumstances, sweet. Stupid, maybe. Immature, a given. But still, underneath his selfish Peter Pan icing was a sweet filling of something lovely: chocolate cream.

Catching herself in a moment of nostalgia, she shuddered back to reality. "Aren't you cold at all?" she asked.

"Me, right now? Not at all," Bobby answered.

"Jesus, how is that even possible? It must be near ten degrees down here."

"Just about, but you know me, just doing the ol' Lawrence Taylor." Annabelle let out a sigh, or from the POV of Bobby's ears, a dismissive grunt. He shuffled in his seat. "You can dismiss it all you want, but I gotta tell you, my ass is rosy, my pits warm, and these fingers here?" He held them up and wiggled them. "I could play 'Free Bird' if I wanted. Just like Lawrence said, the cold is all mental, Belle. If you ignore it, it'll ignore you."

As much as she wanted to, Annabelle couldn't argue. Bobby not only looked warm but probably was warm.

Curious to get to the truth of it, she said, "Let me feel you." Bobby looked at her with one of those "Are you serious?" looks Anabelle had no patience for. "Jesus, Bobby, I don't want to sleep with you," she said. "Just get over here and warm me up for Christ's sake."

Disappointed, he crawled toward her and grabbed her hands. Watching him rub them, Annabelle wondered how long it would be till a flush of warmth found its way back to her fingertips. She hoped it wouldn't be too quick, because though her hands were cold, she was just happy to once again be touching Bobby Mac.

## JUNE 1981

Entering the Farangotta for the first time, Annabelle could never have imagined the winter cold that would wander every year, like a hibernating bear, and settle itself razor sharp in the valley. Because right now, all Annabelle could see was the sunblasted glory of a summer morning through the bug-covered windshield of her and Bobby Mac's Volkswagen Westfalia. It was June 28, 1981; they were twelve days married and riding not just the erotic bliss of a two-week-long honeymoon but also the sprouting expectation of what it would be like to make their first home. There were many options where to settle, but as tempting as the purple sunsets of Taos or the salt-scented sprays of New Haven were, it was a given they would settle in the mountainous bed of Fortooth Bend. Bobby's descriptions were too perfect, too Henry Thoreau, and as described to her over cuddles, the place where spirit and tree held hands so tight, a branch could be seen peeking a leafy finger out of nature's smiling mouth.

"Holy fuck, I mean Boulder is pretty, but wow," Annabelle shared as the van emerged from the dense pine forest that bordered the Farangotta. An open spread of sixty miles lay in front of her, and buttressing the east and west sides of what looked like the world's largest field were giant slate cliffs standing guard against anyone who tried to muddy the sky's blue. As the van chugged forward, staining the pure mountain air with the cough of diesel, Annabelle knew, regardless of whether she was still high from the two orgasms she had when they stopped to picnic or from the percussive giddiness of the Talking Heads album in the tape deck, that this trip to Farangotta, really, was once in a lifetime.

Seeing her reflection in the rearview mirror, she was surprised at the state of her appearance. Her hair fell long, a tangle of blonde and brown, and her face looked like a tripping Cheshire as it caught the sun through a rose-colored crystal glued to the dashboard.

"Hey," Bobby said, his smile now overtaking the rearview. "Not fucking bad, eh?"

"Not fucking bad? Are you joking me, Bobby? This is unbelievable!" she squealed.

Grinning, Annabelle watched Bobby release a howl that shot through the valley. Laughing, she then lunged for his face and gave him an open-mouthed kiss on half his lip and cheek. Bobby stretched his lips right to kiss her back, then reached for the volume knob to turn "Houses in motion" four notches down.

"See that, right beyond the Hangman?" he said and pointed at a shimmering distance just beyond the rock cliffs.

"That's what we call these cliffs around here. That, over there, is Punishment Lake, which is where I caught my first trout. She was a beaut—speckled, rainbow, and gold. Almost eighteen inches."

"Wow? Did you eat it?" she asked, hanging on each word as if they held the winning numbers of the lottery.

"Hell no. Only the Le'Echuwanna can eat fish from that lake. They settled this land, shit, I don't know . . . *way* before Columbus came. It's sacred to them. Most of this place is."

Annabelle nodded and returned her look to the lake. The sun bounced full into it, lighting a million small fires on its glassy surface.

"You know what else is special about that place, Belle?"

"What?" she asked, her tone more serious now.

"That's where Beverly Parilla gave me my first blow job."

"What? Oh my God, what a slut!" Annabelle laughed. Bobby grinned and adjusted the sun visor to the driver's side window. Annabelle then rolled down the window and pointed to the nearside of the approaching lake. "Bobby, pull over there. By the fallen tree."

"Why? We're almost there . . ."

"Because there's no way I'm letting you think about Beverly Parilla every time you pass this lake."

Bobby, once again, grinned. So did Annabelle because she was going to make sure Bobby had the best homecoming ever.

As much as the drive through the valley was greater than anything Annabelle could have imagined, the drive through town was exactly what Annabelle had imagined. She hoped to find the rustic combination of a Hollywood designed mining town with the down-home nostalgia of a Norman Rockwell Sunday. And she did. Main Street was one part wooden saloon, one part Romanesque style bank, three parts Edwardian bed-and-breakfast, and twelve parts Victorian department store. In all her dreams, she could not have painted, written, or dared to imagine a more perfect representation of Northwest prospecting anywhere.

Scanning the storefronts and restaurants, she mouthed names straight from a Wild West fairy tale. The Horned Pony Bar and Grill. Wesseleman's Sundries and Spirits. The Bull Yoke Saloon. Sweet Anna Mae's B&B. McClintock's Guns, Ammo, and Other Utilities.

Drunk on the sight of rusty signs swinging from porch fronts and fonts screaming to find a home on a Gene Autry album cover, Annabelle leaned back in the passenger seat and closed her eyes. It was almost too perfect. Too fantastic to dream.

Then, when she opened her eyes again, she saw it in the distance, rising at the end of Main Street, a mountain of near-perfect symmetry. It had paths cut down its face and shuttled hundreds of summer visitors up its incline courtesy of four-person chairlifts. It was regal, presiding over the valley with the authority bestowed on something that knew it was greater than anything else in its domain. Not just greater in size but greater in essence, its core purpose to remind all creatures that when the random accumulation of nature occurred as intended, anything on this playground was possible. Thunderstruck, Annabelle took it in.

"Is that—"

"Yep," interrupted Bobby Mac. "And fuck, it looks like it got bigger." Disgusted, he turned the Westfalia off Main Street and pulled in front of a Victorian storefront. A porch extended from it, with swings and picnic benches dressing its frame, and waiting in cursive over the front door was one last sign for Annabelle to read: Danu's.

The greeting was warm, the hug genuine, and the kiss on the cheek wet, but Annabelle still had trouble reading Bobby Mac's mother. Suzanne Joanne—formerly Macklemore but now once again Dempsey—sat across from the two of them in a leather club chair and sipped a glass of lemonade. Bobby knew the room well. Most would call it a living room, but as the entire apartment was mostly one large studio, one could argue they were just sitting in the kitchen or Bobby's bedroom.

Trying her best to appear respectful, Annabelle sat quiet, head still, eyes panning stealth-like across the room, hoping to gather any details she could. There were photographs. Everywhere. Some highlighting an older couple, from an older time, that Annabelle figured were Bobby's grandparents, but most of the photographs were of Bobby: Bobby, face chubby and smile broad in a little white sailor's uniform. Bobby, barely of walking age, laughing in a yellow snowsuit. Bobby, crying, his arm stuck down the ball return of a bowling alley. In total, close to fifty photographs of Bobby either decorated the walls or sat proud on tables and shelves. Annabelle wondered how she would feel if Suzanne was her mother, and she had to enter a room with these many photos of herself. The answer, without doubt, would be mortified. But looking at the comfort with which Bobby lounged on the sofa and attacked his lemonade, Annabelle understood he loved being here—in this shrine to himself.

"So have you heard from Dickface lately?" Bobby asked, taking a long gulp from his glass.

"Of course not," his mother responded. "If it wasn't for that giant wart he keeps feeding on the hill, I wouldn't even know he was alive."

Bobby smiled. He got warts and was always amazed how they seemed to sprout out of nowhere. Feet clean at slumber, and somehow when he woke, one would show its cauliflower face on his big toe.

"Yeah. It definitely seems bigger. Did he take over the Tit?"

"He sure as dirt did," Suzanne responded. "And the Nip. And rumor has it, he's making a bid for Fuckit Two."

"Wow." Bobby sighed. "I take it he already grabbed Fuckit One and Ballsack, then? He's gonna try and grab the whole damn valley."

Suzanne nodded and Annabelle listened, but for all she heard, they might as well have been talking in Swahili. In time, like any good transplant, she would learn the language of the terrain and realize they were naming three of the hills and peaks surrounding Mt. Forgotten. But for now, all she could do was listen and try to contextualize meaning.

Pulling a Virginia Slim from a side table, Suzanne turned toward Annabelle. "This probably sounds crazy to you, huh? The Tit, the Nip? We sound like a bunch of perverted old merchant marines."

Happy to enter the conversation, Annabelle cleared her throat and added, "Not at all. Was just trying to figure out what you were referring to. I knew it wasn't sexual."

"Hah!" Suzanne smirked. "It definitely is sexual. This valley was founded by men who'd save two months' salary for a spin in the saloon downstairs. Dogs—every one of them." Taking a drag of her Slim, Suzanne locked her eyes on Annabelle's. It wasn't an aggressive stare, but it did suggest a minor form of chicken. Not blinking, she held Annabelle's gaze, and as she did, Annabelle could feel her looking under every rug of her character.

Overwhelmed, Annabelle broke the look and grabbed for her lemonade. Her hands too wobbly to bring it to her mouth, she said, "So Bobby told me your parents came here in the twenties and set up this shop?"

Still looking at her, Suzanne pulled a stray piece of tobacco off her tongue and stubbed her cigarette out in a Luden's cough drop tin. "Sure did. Opened the first soda shop and general store in town. Used to be where McClintock's is."

"And now?" Annabelle asked, genuinely curious about what happened to Bobby's grandparents' business.

"Now? Well, didn't you see the sign? We're sitting right on top of it. It takes up near the entire block, largest retail store in the whole north side of the state."

"Okay, okay, Mom," Bobby interjected. "Let's not get spiky, here. She's not getting tested on any of this."

"I'm not getting *spiky*, B-Mac," Suzanne replied with a snort. "I'm just shocked you didn't point it out when you got here."

Bobby looked at Annabelle and rested his hand on her thigh. "Well, to be honest, I was just too caught up in my wife's gorgeous eyes."

Annabelle blushed. A moment later, she found her hand reaching for his, and when she found his palm, a breath of calm ran through her.

After an uncomfortable dinner filled with too much meatloaf and not nearly enough bourbon, Bobby thought it would be a great idea to head over to the Horned Pony for a nightcap. Annabelle was reluctant—the trip was long, and they had an early morning ahead of them, starting with meeting his father at the Glory Peak offices, but Bobby was warming to a nice buzz. So, as his mother tended in silence to a Virginia Slim and the dishes, he handed Annabelle her jean jacket and escorted her out the door.

Landing on the front porch, Annabelle interlocked her hand in Bobby's and followed him into the brisk night air. For the past two hours, all she'd wanted to do was laugh with Bobby about how insanely intense his mother was. Dying to share, she pulled him toward her and pressed the side of her head against his.

"Holy shit, Bobby, why didn't you warn me?" she said as he guided them toward Main Street.

Bobby chuckled and let the statement hang in the air. It wasn't that he was ignoring her; he was just absorbing this moment—the way she rested her temple against his as they walked, the natural smell of her skin as it mixed with the Fortooth wind and the remnants of his Aqua de Selva. It was a euphoric concoction that allowed him to float above town in his favorite state, air.

"Bobby? Bobby, you there?" Annabelle asked. Worried she'd overstepped a boundary; she imagined grabbing her previous question and stuffing it back in her mouth when Bobby pulled her toward him.

"What? Did I do something?" she asked. Smiling, his eyes sitting somewhere between sapphire and the ocean, he snugged her close and kissed her deep in the June night.

The rest of the evening was a blur. They entered the Horned Pony, and at the sight of Bobby, the whole room erupted in cheers, questions, and hugs. One by one, the entire bar came over to pirouette Anabelle on the dance floor or regale her with stories of Bobby in his youth. Before she could even pause for air, she was on her sixth shot of Cherry Heering and dancing by the pool table to "Pac-Man Fever."

Meanwhile, shifts of those same people came up to Bobby to swing high fives and land misestimated slaps on the back. Weaving through slurred conversations, he was happy to share stories of how he and Annabelle met, their hikes in Argentina, the rum in Brazil, their trip to Ecuador, minus the last day. Most of these stories were lies, and no one seemed to care, as Bobby was known to be capable of any physical feat known to man. If he could launch a daffy into a spread eagle off the far ridge of China Bowl, why couldn't he do a backflip off a bamboo bridge in Suriname or raft down the rapids of Iquitos in a canoe he dug himself? Here was the golden boy, finally back from exploring the mysteries of the world. Or not.

As the night waned and Bobby started his goodbyes, he noticed Annabelle's dancing turn to stumbles. Watching her try to overcome these wobbles and on shot eleven of Cherry Heering himself, Bobby lumbered over to her in a series of sidesteps that resembled a sailor fighting for balance on a storm-thrown boat. Finding her, he reached out for a hug, but as he did all Annabelle could do was collapse into his arms.

On the walk home, there were murmurs of love and liking his friends, all but that "bitch Rachel," and wanting dogs and the chickens that laid the blue eggs. When Bobby got her up the stairs and under the covers, she swore to him she would be the greatest wife ever. Kissing her forehead, Bobby assured her he knew, but before she fell asleep, she popped up and asked him one last question.

"Bobby," she said, grabbing his left shoulder, "I think your mom hates me. Do you think she hates me, Bobby?"

"No, not at all," he responded. "She's just like that. And she's probably pissed we eloped. But don't worry, it went good."

Watching Annabelle fall back onto the pillow, he saw a flush of relief fall over her face. "Thank God. I really want her to like me. And your dad. It would just kill me if he didn't."

But, before Bobby could respond, the roll of a snore escaped Annabelle's mouth. Now a little more sober, Bobby rolled onto his back and stared circles in the ceiling. As much as he could speak on behalf of his mother, he had no fucking clue what Dickface was going to think about Annabelle.

# CHAPTER 11

**JUNE 1981**

B
ill Macklemore knew damn good and well his ex-wife and adult son referred to him as Dickface—and frankly, he didn't care. He also knew damn good and well, from the moment he'd fixed eyes on her, that he did not like Annabelle. But if he had any chance of pulling Bobby back to Glory Peak, he knew he could not show this outright. In fact, he would have to act so enraptured by her beauty and grace that any nonpartial observer would have every reason to believe he adored everything about his new daughter-n-law. Even though what he really thought was, *This slag reeks of gin and needs a fucking haircut.*

So, Bill nodded as she spoke of the classes her mom taught in Boulder and smiled when she complimented him on his office and resort, but the whole time all he wanted to do was cock back his arm, reach across his desk, and punch Bobby in the face. It was obvious then and there, as one of Annabelle's unbrushed curls draped like a question mark on her forehead, that Bobby was on the verge of being a failure.

After this woefully disappointing introduction, Bill decided to tour them through the upgrades to the lodge and show them the area he was going to raze to install the Pacific Northwest's first gondola. Their walk was mostly quiet, and it was obvious Bill was dazzling Annabelle as she was eager to make a good impression. Hell, he could've said he planned to stake a Farangottan flag on his ass, and she would've replied with a vapid, "Wow, really?" she was so determined to be liked.

Bobby Mac, though? He was tougher run to groom. Bill knew what his son thought about the trees, the integrity of the mountain, and how he was partial to letting the valley sit untouched, nature sculpting the fate it thought best. There were moments when Bill tried to lock eyes with him, hoping to get a hint of approval, but mostly it was to see if Bobby was warming to being home. This, Bill knew, was the first step in bringing Bobby back to Glory Peak. There had been no talk yet of the death of Snow Feather or Bobby's sudden departure afterward. Bill was good with that and kept their talk focused on the mountain because he knew if the mountain called, it would be what tethered Bobby back to Fortooth. With the three of them standing at the future site of the gondola, Bill suggested they walk south along the crest toward the wider, shorter peak hiding behind Glory Peak. The one everyone referred to as the Tit.

Bobby had done his best not to think of the Tit since Snow Feather's death eighteen months earlier. And his best to forget its beauty, which sat raw and hidden at the top of a long rocky hike. Below it, he remembered a thick fabric of pines and shrubs crawling its way up the slope, but looking at it now, he saw a mountain cleared of foliage, with large empty areas that held a variety of ramps and oil barrels.

"What the fuck happened to the trees, Dad?" Bobby asked, the base of his right palm rubbing his forehead.

"I cleared them. See those ramps and barrels? When the snow falls on top, it's going to create jumps and falls and a bunch of different things the kids can do tricks on. Now that you are back, I was thinking you could run it. We could call it Bobby's Bandido Bowl. Chester's already mocking up some hats."

Bobby stared at the Tit. The once beautiful, bountiful, magnificent Tit. Inside him, as he cased the barrels, counted the ramps, and studied the fresh holes where trees once stood, a wave of anger rose.

Bill, oblivious to Bobby's mortification, smiled.

"Annabelle," Bill continued. "Did Bobby ever tell you how great a ski jumper he was? Not long jumping like one of those Scandinavian bughumpers, but trick jumping. I saw him once go off a jump, do a complete three-sixty with his skis pulled back and crossed like an *X*. It was a Picasso, I tell you. No one, I mean, no one had moves like Bobby Mac."

Bill, still oblivious to Bobby's visage, walked toward Annabelle and extended a bent arm. "You wanna take a closer look?" he asked.

When Annabelle grabbed Bill's forearm, Bobby broke. "Annabelle, don't."

Annabelle had never heard that tone before. Or seen that look. It was focused, penetrating, and fueled by pure and simple rage. Scared, Annabelle spun her head back and forth between the two.

"Y-you okay, Bobby?" she asked, sputtering. Bobby did not answer. He just walked toward her, grabbed her hand, and turned down the hill.

The walk back was silent. Bobby soon dropped Annabelle's hand, tucked his into the pockets of his Lee jean jacket, and stomped forward, never once looking over his shoulder to see if Annabelle was keeping up. It was nearly an hour by the time they got off the mountain and another twenty minutes by the time they got to his mother's front door—which he slammed open and shut, almost clipping Annabelle as she walked in behind him.

Bobby was already at the kitchen table, a beer open in his hand when Annabelle reached the top of the stairs. Concerned less about the eleven o'clock drink he was downing than his silence, Annabelle sat still across from him. Between them was an ashtray that held four half-smoked Virginia Slims and a plaid rubber placemat fraying at its edge.

Annabelle knew Bobby would speak when he was ready. So, she waited, and she practically suffocated, holding her breath while doing so.

Finally, after an eternity of puckered lips and false starts, Bobby spoke. "He fucking knows what that spot meant. He fucking knows, and he fucking tore it apart. Destroyed everything special about it."

Annabelle listened, unnerved by the edge in his voice.

"I-I cannot fucking believe him! I mean, I can, I *can* fucking believe him." Slamming the beer down, he looked at Annabelle. "Fuck, just promise me . . . Promise me we will never take anything from him. Not one fucking penny or ski pass or . . ."

Bobby's voice trailed to nothing. His eyes were red, about to shed tears.

"It's okay, babe, I promise," Annabelle answered. Then, she forced a smile and held back her tears.

The following morning, Bobby and Annabelle headed to the Prescott S. Norville Elementary School and High School. Tending to some weeds by the pond outside the cafeteria was Bobby's former principal, Toby Janks. Seeing Bobby, Principal Janks dropped the bushel of dyer's-weed in his hands.

"Ha! I heard you were back in town. I heard it, I heard it, I heard it! Get your butt over here." Christmas day happy, Bobby slid past the mound of pulled flowers to where the heavy up-and-down handshake of Principal Janks waited. For the first time, under a sober eye, Annabelle felt genuinely welcomed and Bobby, now all smiles, turned toward her.

"Belle, come meet Principal Janks. He's gonna get us jobs teaching the little shitheels here in town."

# CHAPTER 12

## DECEMBER 2000

Clover's seventeenth birthday came with low expectations. She was born on December 28, 1983—only three days after Christmas. This had taught her that most people would be recovering from the holiday or resting up for New Year's by the time her birthday came, so most were not eager to prepare for another celebration before the New Year. Fortooth was also a peculiar place this time of year, one that ran flush with the dirty, scavenging force Clover was conditioned from the womb to despise—the tourist. And in recent years, their numbers had multiplied. This influx was, of course, instigated by Bill, when, four years earlier, he invited the editor of *SKI* magazine to stay at his just-opened Valais Club. It was Bill's latest creation, a bespoke gingerbread hotel that rested halfway up Glory Peak's untamed south side. It was modeled after Switzerland's notorious backcountry mecca Verbier, as Bill had decided it was time the US embraced European-style resorting. With state-of-the-art saunas, an on-site chocolatier, five-star dining, and a singular wine list specializing in Oeil de Perdrix, the Valais Club was selected as *SKI* magazine's greatest ski-in, ski-out destination in North America four years running. Which meant the jet set had arrived.

Nanny A referred to these tourists as Gucci Pads—all après ski and no actual ski. It was an overly opinionated take by someone who did not herself know how to ski. But as someone who co-guided Wolfehaus Media to the top of the ski film world, she had over time appointed herself supreme judge of all things gnar and thrash. This was a far cry from her days as the supreme judge of all things culturally permissive and pro-woman. But her passion—that fervorous appetite to know more, say more, argue more, and believe more, that same passion that led to her dominance in academia—needed its outlet, so now extreme winter sports had its most vocal and unlikely overseer. And her gavel was ruthless. But it was this ruthlessness that brought the other type of traveler to Fortooth Bend searching for her approval—the sometimes long-haired, dreadlocked, or tattooed but always Patagonia-fleece-wearing snowflake.

The snowflake was, by all regards, the bread and butter of the ski world. It kept all ski-based economies in motion searching for that perfect alchemy of humidity, temperature, and air, which combined to create one of nature's greatest inventions: powder. When a snowflake found a location that excelled at delivering this—not just in volume but with a delicate, soufflé-like touch and confetti-like consistency—well, they stayed in that location. And took a job. And as Gunther Wolfe's exploits, captured so dizzyingly in the back country of Farangotta Valley, cycled throughout every snowflake's imagination, so began the arrival of the extreme snowboarder, skier, waiter, and bartender to Fortooth Bend. That meant this December 28 would not only be teeming with fur-lined Gucci Pads, but it would also be teeming with the weed-scented beards of the snowflake.

Clover had survived this confluence before, but with Wolfehaus's sales tripling, she anticipated a new form of chaos would overtake Main Street—and it did. So, as Nanny A knocked on her door at 6 a.m., the way she did every morning, Clover hoped, despite it being her birthday, things would be kept as normal as possible. Stepping into the kitchen, she saw her usual breakfast of Cream of Wheat, a fruit bowl, and ginger tea waiting on a set table. This was a promising start to as normal as possible. But then, an aspect of not so normal peeked its head from the fruit bowl.

A candle glowed and from the hallway, Nanny started. "Happy birthday to you. Happy birthday to you. Happy birthday, dear Cloverita, happy birthday to you."

Clover watched her enter the room. She was smiling, really grinning, her bright white incisors big enough to scare a rabbit. "Well, aren't you going to blow it out?" Nanny A asked, pointing at the candle. Clover wanted to say no. This was already too much attention, and she hadn't even left the house yet. Feeling Nanny A's smile grow as she pulled a chair up to the table, Clover reluctantly leaned over and released a slight breath of air. It fluttered the candle flame out.

"Wow, Clove, can you believe it? Seventeen! You're practically an adult. What a year, what a year!" Nanny beamed as she pulled the still-smoking candle from the fruit bowl and placed it back in its packet. "I can't wait to celebrate at the Yoke. Gunther is making a cake he swears will make chocolate taste new. And Libby said if tryouts finish by four, she'll be able to bring her crumble. You're gonna have so many desserts, it's gonna feel like Willy Wonka's."

Clover forced a smile and fished around the blueberries in her bowl. In the past year, after she noticed how sweets made her molars itch, she'd decided to give up all things sugar. She mentioned this twice to Nanny A, who clearly hadn't internalized the development. Spooning a strawberry onto her plate, Clover decided it wasn't worth bringing up again.

Still grinning, Nanny A grabbed a hat and pulled a large jacket over her shoulders, which hugged just tight enough to almost block out the Wolfehaus scarf draping around her neck. "Okay, pea. I'm off. Don't forget, the Yoke at six—and tell Jimmy he's welcome to bring his father if he likes."

Clover nodded and took a large sip of tea.

When she heard the front door close and Nanny A's Subaru spin away, Clover lifted the fruit bowl off the table and shattered it against the refrigerator door.

When Clover got to town later that day, she got the birthday gift she'd been hoping for—no one noticed her at all. The Gucci Pads paraded their way down Main Street in unseasoned shearling jackets and freshly bought UGGs while the snowflakes hot-boxed Toyota 4Runners, traded Widespread Panic CDs, and waited, high and hungry, for their Wolfehaus interview times.

Turning off Main Street, Clover looked into the morning sky and saw a crowd of clouds book across the blue. Snow was coming—not now, or this afternoon, but definitely that night. *Tomorrow*, she thought. *That's the day to celebrate. Fresh snow day.*

When she arrived at Jimmy's, it became clear he knew today wasn't worth celebrating either, but that it was at least worth acknowledging. Meeting her at the door, he greeted her not with a candle but with photographs of her cross-country skiing. Entranced, Clover slid onto his sofa and examined them.

"Your pole plant is too vertical," Jimmy shared. "You need to extend your lunge and plant at least eight inches farther. Then, when you shift your upper body into the pull, there'll be greater distance to leverage and that will help increase your speed."

Clover rested the photos on her lap and looked at Jimmy, who was now sitting across from her in his father's La-Z-Boy. "Wow, this means in a 10K, I can trim my time by—"

"Almost thirty seconds," he interrupted. Clover smiled because, like always, Jimmy knew how to do what she loved most—finish her thought.

As Clover and Jimmy walked along the muddy shoulder of Yeehaw Pass, they lifted their faces to the warming sun. A breeze ran over them, soothing the slight burn on their skin and reminding them that their decision to spend the day working on Clover's technique—instead of celebrating her birthday—was the right one.

Swinging by Clover's to grab two sets of skis, they slung them over their shoulders and started their march out to Paco's Rink.

Paco's wasn't really a skating rink, but it was a flat swatch of open terrain out by Punishment Lake. It was much closer than Prescott Loop, and unlike the tight single track of the Loop, it was as wide as it was long, providing a perfect canvas for Clover to practice turns, starts, and that endorphin-spinning action she loved most—sprints.

In that moment, it was her thighs that wanted that endorphin action the most. The walk to town, then to Jimmy's, then her house, and now to Paco's was giving them the feel of a warm-up. They were anxious, and with each step, itching more and more to get to skiing. But the more and more they itched, the more and more Clover realized they were itching in an unexpected way. The light blonde hairs on them lifted and tingled, somehow raised by a hidden static electricity even though a layer of long johns were plastered against them. This was no longer the normal adrenaline-pumped itching that appeared before practice. This was an itching so pointed it made her wonder if she was in a different body altogether.

Walking beside Jimmy, it took Clover almost the whole trip to realize the itching came in direct correspondence to his proximity. If he was close, the volume spiked. If he was far, the tingle leveled to a moderate swell—only manageable if she didn't focus on the sound of Jimmy's steady breathes.

When they arrived at Paco's Rink, Clover was so overwhelmed by this itch, she couldn't even look in Jimmy's direction. If she did, images would come. Images she never imagined before. Images she never in her life thought would be inspired by Jimmy. He was still whip skinny—no longer short, but still a rail—and his skin, nothing but a drape of fabric on a skeleton. His hair, once flat and bowl cut, now curled in messy tangles that poked out from the wool beanie he wore every day, and his eyes weren't the big blue of Jason Priestley's, but tiny little coals. Tiny little coals that, when caught by a soft sun, turned into the brown-green hazel of Fortooth's autumn. *Shit*, she thought, yanking her eyes off his. *I totally have a crush on Jimmy.*

This realization made the beginning of practice very awkward. Thankfully, Jimmy proceeded under the rules of standard operating procedure, which meant he made no suggestion of a flirtatious energy that could lead to a day spent humping each other's legs. Chastity was their tacit agreement, and as they stumbled through puberty, looking at each other like dolls from the eighties—all plastic and no gonad—it was unspoken, but agreed, that any thought of sexual expression was off-limits.

This was comforting to Jimmy. He was not adept at exploring his emotions, and had he known that Clover—while refining her lunge—was imagining what his penis looked like, he most likely would have gone home. Watching her dig her poles into the snow, a nearly right angle forming in the bend of her waist and buttocks, he did not see the lithe beauty of her body— only the platonic precision of her form.

Clover on the other hand was finding it impossible to shake the itching that came with Jimmy's gaze. So, she decided to practice her sprints south of Paco's Rink, which was sheltered by a grove of pines.

Hidden behind their bark, Clover once again felt safe, the trees' dense fill allowing her to relinquish thoughts of whether her body was adequate or even attractive. For the first time since she realized she had a crush on Jimmy— which was just about fifteen minutes ago—her blemishes and sags were once again just skin and appendages. Skin and appendages that transported her to that safe, solitary spot cross-country skiing provided. Lost in the sounds that came with the meditative repetition of her plants and lunges, she smiled as she heard a slight distinction in its patterning.

Her plants now landed with a deeper splash of slush. The scruff of her jacket as she pulled herself to the poles now extended a half beat. And the space between the slap of each ski now increased just long enough to make her wonder if she'd grown a foot. Following what Jimmy suggested earlier, she discovered that she was not just getting more efficient; she was also getting faster.

When Clover returned to Jimmy, it was in the bliss produced only by a perfect workout. Those endorphins she wanted ping-ponged through her, and for the first time, she found comfort in something she'd never found comfort in before—words.

"Jimmy, holy cow, it worked, it worked! I swear to you, I could, like, totally feel each lunge getting faster."

Smiling, Jimmy shifted the skis on his shoulder to make room for his poles.

"I mean, it was like seeing something in real time. Like I felt myself getting better. Do you think I could qualify for regionals this year? I mean, I think I could. I even think I could win. Wouldn't that be amazing?" Clover looked at Jimmy, whose head was nodding up and down.

"Jesus, Jimmy, what would I do without you? I mean, you really are the best."

Clover noticed Jimmy's eyes widen when she said that. Turning her stride into a small skip, she turned her head back and forth in bobblehead excitement. She could see Jimmy was excited, too, and in perfect sync, they turned their walk into a double time, almost running back to Jimmy's house.

By the time they entered Jimmy's bedroom and took their shells and fleece off, Clover knew they would be late for her birthday dinner.

What she did not know was how much she would enjoy her birthday dinner—not because Gunther's cake reinvented chocolate, or because Libby's crumble reinvented apple, but because Jimmy was sitting next to her, only a handhold away. Looking at Nanny A across the table, she wondered if she could see how happy she was. *Is this what my mom looked like the first time she introduced Nanny A to Bobby Mac?* she thought. *Did Mom's heart feel this big when she looked at my dad? So stupid big it was hard to breathe but also so weak she couldn't breathe fast enough.* Watching Nanny A, she couldn't help but want to hold her. She still had that big, toothy smile from the morning. And just when Clover didn't think it could get any bigger, she watched it double in size when the owner of the Bull Yoke waved away her credit card and told Nanny A dinner was on the house. *This is how it's supposed to be,* Clover thought. *This is how it's supposed to be, now.* Maybe tomorrow she'd ask Nanny A to go for a walk. Then she could tell her about how much she loved Jimmy. How she wanted to spend every waking moment watching him. How she wanted to swallow him up and chew him to nothing but protons she could swirl in her mouth. And how, after today, she was no longer a virgin.

# CHAPTER 13

**JANUARY 2001**

B
ill had no clue about his granddaughter's virginity. Whether she lost it, kept it locked in a safe fourteen feet under the garage, or even had a vagina at all. That information was irrelevant to anything important in his life. What he did know was her cross-country ski form was better, her times were faster, and if she kept training at this rate, she would be able to cut forty-five seconds off her 10K time.

Coming by this information was not easy. Currently, Bill had four videographers, one teacher, two officials at the Pacific Northwest Ski Association, two mechanics, and the owner of the Bull Yoke reporting on the happenings of Clover Dolores Macklemore.

Through them, Bill expected a video every two days that featured her practices, as well as a biweekly report from school describing the overall tenor of her mood. He'd also get a copy of her report card at the end of each semester, but her grades were of little interest to him. It was her practices, her daily attempts to refine her sport, that inspired Bill to keep being Bill. And that meant clearing more space on his board.

Project Golden Thingy now stood front and center. Underneath it was no longer an empty space bordered by half-erased thoughts. Instead, were bizarre, nonlinear thoughts, twisting, overlapping, veining their way across the white and all leading to one thing: Clover the Olympian.

*Hurt* sat next to *dig*, which sat above *grease* and below *scholarship*. If the words were ever connected in a way that deciphered Bill's tangled intentions, they would read, "Create a scholarship for the Pacific Northwest Ski Association, then build a Nordic Center to hold all of Farangotta's cross-country ski races." *Hurt* stood alone but represented the simple notion that if anyone challenged this agenda, well, Bill would hurt them. Sitting at his desk with footage of Clover playing on his big screen, he felt the overarching need to stand. Then, the overarching need to walk to his balcony. Standing on it, Bill surveyed the town below and the Glory Peak resort standing proud behind. It was in that moment, he resolved to bring the most boring sport ever created to Fortooth Bend.

〰️

The news of cross-country skiing coming to Fortooth Bend did not sit well with the Le'Echuwanna. They were in the process of securing a tract of land on the front side of Prescott Loop that would connect to the land they had purchased on the backside of Prescott Loop, and their closing was taking longer than expected. Per their accountant, it was because their cash situation was complicated. They had plenty of it, but because it was spread around several businesses, it was proving difficult to show what their exact revenues were to secure the multimillion-dollar loan for the purchase. But the bigger problem proved to be that they did not have access to the banks like Bill. So, when the first week of 2000 rolled in and *Fortooth Daily* announced Glory Peak Enterprises was opening a Nordic Center on land it just purchased by Prescott Loop, it was a shock to every Elder Elder in the tribe. According to the *Daily*, the center would have 1,200 acres of cross-country terrain, snowmobile courses, and sunset sleigh rides led by Clydesdales dressed as reindeer. Construction was going to commence in the summer, with a grand opening planned for the 2001–2002 season, and the inaugural Pilgrim's Challenge kicking off the first Farangotta cross-country ski season.

When He Who Eats heard this, it left him with a burning case of indigestion and a brewing batch of gas. It was a feeling shared by the rest of the council, who rocked back and forth in the Elder Elders' hut as Sacred Crow read the article aloud. Scanning the council, He Who Eats noticed a large depletion of their numbers, with several Elder Elders already spending their winters in the warm reaches of Orlando and others just dying off. Pouting Trout was still alive—just barely—and had lost such control of his countenance, all his votes were accented with a release of his bladder.

Overall, the meetings were barely tolerable now, the remaining Elder Elders whining their way through every topic and waiting to get to the point in the meeting when they could hear about their bank balances or ask for home computers. If not for the promise of the new blood about to join, He Who Eats would have set up a conference line from his house and led from his La-Z-Boy. But new Elders were coming, Budding elders. Sacred Crow's son, Fancy Glove, was in the process of preparing for his *Oh-sah-cha-me*, and it was hoped by the next Elder's meeting, he would be there in the mud hut along with two or maybe three more new Elders. Which was good for He Who Eats because not only would it allow for a perspective that better reflected the current state of Fortooth, Fancy Glove also had access to the dank weed, and with all the accounting He Who Eats was handling, he needed to get proper high, real soon.

"Shit buckets," He Who Eats chimed as Sacred Crow folded the newspaper. It was January and cold and dry in the Elders' hut, and for some reason, they were having trouble keeping the fire lit. "Well, I tell you, this sucks some mighty large mountain goat," He Who Eats continued.

"It sure does," Sacred Crow agreed, pulling on her braids. Her skin was flappier than He Who Eats remembered, and the ink of the eagle tattoo that peeked from under her shirt cuffs was now a weather-beaten pastel. Coughing, she said, "He's moving fast, the pecker breath. We got to find some way to slow him down."

"Slow him down?" He Who Eats answered, skeptical. "Nothing is going to *slow him down*. He's gone full-blown *Eh-cha*. The only way to combat him is to liquidate all our assets, then go after every acre through Parker's Pass. That's nearly thirty thousand acres we could shelter. That's enough for one hundred lifetimes of our people."

"Ohhhhhhh, ohhhhhhh, oh. I don't know, that sounds awfully speculative, Chief Eats," chimed in Squirreling Squirrel. Looking to his left, He Who Eats narrowed his eyes at Squirreling Squirrel. Squirreling Squirrel was closest in age to He Who Eats and the tribe's elected financial investment manager who, in He Who Eats' opinion, could be summed up by two things: passing on Microsoft stock in '83 and having the most shriveled set of bird nuts he ever saw on a hunt.

Taking in the tortoiseshell glasses at the tip of his nose and the Brooks Brothers flannel tucked into his thirty-inch waist, He Who Eats shot back, "Of course you do, ya' ant dick. Because if it was up to you, you'd hide your ass up on the *Ko-Ka-Po* and count your 3 percent interest rates in the mud."

Squirreling Squirrel shook his head and rubbed his wrinkled brow. "It saddens me, Chief Eats, that every time we discuss long-term financial planning, you resort to name-calling and cursing. It is the weakened foe who cannot find the right words to challenge the archer."

"Well, archer, I got a set of weak-ass words for you: bite my horse cock." Despondent, He Who Eats shifted his plea to the other council members. "I cannot believe you," he continued. "We have the info. We have the money. It's as apparent as the mole on Pouting Trout's nose. We gotta start moving lightning fast to get this land before the *Eh-Kar-lo* keeps feeding. We need to decide now."

Pouting Trout raised his hand to silence He Who Eats. His eyes nearly closed, a hangnail of separation between his lids, he reached into a small satchel made from a deer bladder he kept under his sheepskins. From it, he pulled four trout bones. "We will ask the *He-mah-no* for the answer."

Disgusted by this suggestion, He Who Eats snarled and hit the ground. "Come on P. T., this ain't roulette. We have to—"

"Enough!" Pouting Trout yelled. "This is the way!"

Unable to argue, He Who Eats bit his lip and grabbed his left forearm so tight, his nails broke skin.

He then watched Pouting Trout place the bones inside his palms, shake his hands, and hum, "*He-mah-no, he-mah-ne. He-mah-no-ne, he-mah-yay.*"

When he finished the chant, Pouting Trout dropped the bones on the ground. They assembled themselves into a distorted capital A shape, with one alone to the side. Seeing the lone bone, He Who Eats jumped to his feet and stormed out of the hut.

Outside, the sun shone brightly, and the village had a surprising liveliness. Most of the tribe was there to hear the council's verdict, and it being a Friday, they were also there to turn in the week's books and receipts for reimbursement. To the right of the main totem, in front of one of the four log cabins that functioned as a community center, post office, medical clinic, and cafeteria, He Who Eats saw Fancy Glove laughing with a bunch of teens. Storming toward him, he bellowed, "Hey, Fancy Glove, quit that clowning and get your ass over to my pickup."

Fancy Glove had never spoken to He Who Eats before, but he knew he had a temper that could split mountains. As they rambled along the dirt road that hugged the plateau of Hangman's Cliff Fancy Glove had no clue why he was in He Who Eats' front passenger seat. There were grunts and harrumphs and sighs and headshakes—but nothing explained why he was witnessing the full-blown drama that seemingly played out in He Who Eats' mind. Finally, after a crow-calling cackle, He Who Eats slammed the roof of the front cabin and turned toward Fancy Glove.

Face swollen, scrunched into a compressed mass of cheek and lip, He Who Eats' expression was unreadable, and Fancy Glove couldn't tell if he was gonna get screamed at for selling mushrooms to the ski bums or eaten. Just sixteen years old and making a late entry into puberty, he realized he had no hope if He Who Eats decided to pounce on him.

When He Who Eats asked, "You got any of that dank weed?" Fancy Glove let out a relieved breath. Fancy Glove did. He always did. And from his pocket, he pulled out two joints. Watching He Who Eats steer his truck right, he was surprised when he pulled off the road and parked at the south side of Punishment Lake.

"Gimme the big one," He Who Eats said. Hand shaking, Fancy Glove passed it over. Dangling it from his lips, He Who Eats pulled a lighter from his dashboard and sparked it. Next came a deep pull, so deep Fancy Glove expected him to finish the entire joint in one tug. Instead, He Who Eats pulled the keys from the ignition, opened the door, and dropped a "Come on." Watching him stomp ahead, Fancy Glove unclipped his seatbelt, sparked his joint, and followed.

The hike wasn't long or steep, but it was pretty, and Fancy Glove was surprised he had never been on it before. He enjoyed being outside, and he had what he and his friends thought was a respectable familiarity with the Farangotta. Enjoying the unobstructed view of the valley, he thought he'd share this place with them the next time they decided to take mescaline.

By the time he got to the top, He Who Eats was already hunkered down on one of the trunks of split pines that circled a firepit. Watching him relight the joint, Fancy Glove sat down on a pine trunk next to him, both puffing in silence as the whisper of a breeze rolled over them.

Almost done with his own joint, Fancy Glove watched He Who Eats assemble some wood in the pit and use the burning cherry of the joint to start a fire. Not sure what to do next, Fancy Glove decided to continue working on his joint and scan the surroundings. In the distance, down in the valley, he saw something move at a steady pace. It planted poles and lunged on a pair of skis, the only intrusion on an otherwise pristine snow-covered landscape.

"See that girl, way down by Beaver Ball Dam?" He Who Eats asked, his eyes also on the horizon. Fancy Glove squinted his stoned eyes in the direction of He Who Eats' pointing arm. "That girl is out here every day. Every single day. Getting her practice in. Never once has she done anything to screw this place up. And guess what? She's Bill's fucking granddaughter."

Fancy Glove perked up at that revelation. "What? Her?" he said.

"Yep," He Who Eats continued. "Probably around seventeen or something like that now. She lost her parents in the *Pay-ah-eh-ah-poe*. You were probably just three or four at the time. February '88. Jeez, what a wild freaking weekend. First time I realized I was small. Like a nothing. Just a spec in all this. God, to be swallowed up and drunk by Mother Earth, that's the dream." He Who Eats picked up a pine branch and poked the fire. Sparks leaped up and twisted into a funnel of smoke that lost its way to the blackening sky.

"Did you know them? Her parents?" Fancy Glove asked.

"Yeah, of course. Her dad was a legend. Could ski down any slab of mountain, long as it had a snowflake. Probably made more first runs than anyone in Farangotta."

"Did that piss you off—him ripping up our land like that?"

"Hell no." He Who Eats smiled. "He wouldn't do nothing like that. He was respectful. An archer type, you know, taking his time, making the most of each arrow. Man, watching him blaze a run was magic. It was like he floated on the snow—his skis moved so light, they barely left a mark. Your dad used to ski with him. Actually, *loved* to. Especially out on the backside of Pike's Pickled Pimple or whatever those snowflakes call it. They would hit just about any place that had snow and a slope."

"Wow. So, he must have been amazing, then?" Fancy Glove asked, knowing his father was considered by many to be the greatest snowboarder in Farangotta history.

"*Oh-sah-cha-me*, little buddy. The two of them, they were nothing but air." He Who Eats blew into the dusk wind and adjusted the wood base of the fire, losing himself to the ruby glow of its embers. Fancy Glove, lost in imagined videos of his father carving lines in two-foot powder, shifted his gaze to the silhouette of the young girl cross-country skiing. Her pace was steady, fast, each lunge and plant in perfect 2/4 rhythm. Taking a final drag, Fancy Glove nodded to himself.

*We both had air for dads. That* Pay-ah-eh-ah-poe *must've been some brutal shit if it took down air.*

# CHAPTER 14

**FEBRUARY 9, 1988**

In the history of the Farangotta Valley, no storm ever came close to the amount of snowfall that came that week. Huddled in their snow cave two hundred feet below the surface of Miner's Gasp, away from Channel 5, the *Fortooth Daily*, or local gossip, Bobby Mac and Annabelle had no idea they were victims to the largest snowstorm ever to hit the United States. Sure, they had picked up on suggestions of the scale—mostly in the form of the giant burps that rumbled through the snow layers settling around them—but Miner's Gasp was known for its unpredictable tectonic activity, having emerged from a still-shifting fault line over a million years ago. So, they assumed all rumblings were just the natural fallout of being closer than ever to the shifting plates, not the results of multiple avalanches falling and settling around them, building even more space between their ice cave and the search party above. Afraid to move and not sure if they did what to do or where to go, they ended up doing what no one in their situation ever wanted to do: wait.

They were spooning now, and Annabelle was doing her best to remember, despite Bobby holding her in his arms during a possibly life-ending situation, she no longer loved him. Feeling something stiff poke the lower part of her spine, Annabelle moved her backside away from Bobby to create some space.

"Sorry," Bobby mumbled. "Didn't mean to wake you."

"I was already awake—well, sorta," Annabelle confessed. "I didn't want to completely drift off, in case we hear the search party."

Rolling up, Bobby creaked into a seated position and rested his elbows on his knees. Annabelle, feeling a bone-chilling cold funnel into the space he'd occupied behind her back, now wished he'd go back to spooning her.

"Yeah, fair enough," Bobby said. "They probably tracked our footprints to the top of Wobble Trail. I'm just hoping we fell out in the Boneyard and aren't somewhere in the rock pitch. It'd be much easier to find us if we were closer to the base."

"Is there any way to tell?" Annabelle asked, shifting forward, her back now leaning up against the wall of the cave.

"Not really. I mean, we could dig and depending on the density of the snow, I could get a better sense of where we are—but that's gotta happen before it begins to freeze. Ice is ice, you know, and without an ice ax, it's just . . ." Bobby paused. "Well, actually I can tell by its color how dense it is."

"Really?' Annabelle asked.

"Yeah, the darker it is the thicker, the lighter the thinner."

Annabelle rubbed her eyes. Turning her look from Bobby, she began scanning the cave for areas where the snowpack seemed lightest. When they first landed, she remembered it all seemed bright white, but now it had turned various shades of gray black. Rolling on all fours, she thumped her palms against the walls and listened for a change in acoustics. But the thumps all sounded the same: muted and deadened by a wall of ice and snow.

"What I don't get," she whispered, "is why we can breathe. Based on the size of this cave, I figured we'd be out of oxygen by now."

Bobby leaned back and blew into his hands. "I was thinking the same thing. I figure we got an air source coming from someplace, like an invisible pipe leading—"

"To the top?" Annabelle finished. "That means it's not far to the surface!"

"Or" Bobby responded, "to a mineshaft, or rock cave, or some fracture in the mountain that has a bunch of stockpiled air."

Annabelle turned to him. She was disappointed in his response and even more disappointed in the tone he'd adopted—a tone of resignation.

"So, what? You're gonna do nothing?" she asked.

Sighing, Bobby crunched his abs and rolled to his knees. "I didn't say that, Belle. I just said that still having air doesn't mean we're close to the surface. But if you want, I'll try to find it."

As he moved into action, a sense of comfort ran over Annabelle. She personally did not have a solution to their predicament, but watching Bobby examine the walls let the tension in her rib cage release through her earlobes and for a moment, she felt something she hadn't felt since, well, since she could remember—relief.

No clue where to start, Bobby scanned the walls around him. On their surface they revealed nothing, but he knew there were certain fundamentals he could count on: the sun would always rise, snow would always melt, Suzanne Somers would give him a stiffy, and anything built would have some proof of construction.

Bobby decided to search for that proof. For something that showed him where the snow collapsed to form this cave and create an air bubble within a high-rise of powder. There had to be an architectural reason for it and running his fingers over the walls, he searched for that reason. He found old snow, new snow, snow with different consistencies, different textures, different colors. But still no proof.

Until his right index finger found a trace of narrative.

A scabby rift in the lower part of the wall. It scarred six inches above the floor and suggested the seam of something new settling on something old. It was a subtle differentiation, but the more Bobby rubbed his finger up and down it, the slight crack revealed a join where an avalanche melded with frozen snowpack.

Excited, Bobby turned to Annabelle and extended his hand. "Gimme your pen."

Fumbling in her pocket, Annabelle found her pen, then handed it to Bobby, who took it and started chiseling at the rift. At first, nothing happened. It was as if he was using a plastic straw to stab a rhinoceros. But then the snow above him began to splinter, and shortly after, snowpack started falling off the wall in book-size slabs. Watching them hit the ground, Annabelle said, "Bobby, Bobby, I think we should stop—"

"No, I'm almost there," he responded and sped up his chipping. The walls were now cracking and Bobby, hearing them splinter, glanced at the ceiling and said, "I think it's going to cave in on—"

He didn't even get to finish his sentence. Twisting its way through the ice wall, a deep fissure sprung, causing the cave to collapse and spray a haze of white so thick, it took thirty seconds to clear.

But when that haze did settle, it revealed an entrance to a partially finished mineshaft.

Fortooth Bend was, at one time, renowned for the profitable and dangerously drought-filled business of iron mining. It paid for the town, brought its first settlers, and left it near bankrupt as the quarries went dry and the mountains turned stingy. In Fortooth, four days would forever be etched into the minds of all Fortoothians: Pearl Harbor, John F. Kennedy's assassination, the opening day of Glory Peak, and the day Prospecting Services Limited closed the last of its iron mines.

Clearing the snow from his face, Bobby knew this was one of the rumored storage shafts Prospecting Services Limited built for mine maintenance. Back when the mine was active, the company figured it would be more efficient to store tools, fuel, medical and food supplies on the mountain instead of bringing them as needed from town. Over time, they drilled fifteen of these storage shafts, and when they left, they decided that instead of spending money to close them down, they would leave them burrowed in the mountains.

Taking in the storage shaft, Bobby anticipated if the elements were gentle and the protective infrastructure good, there would be enough resources to last them a month. And as usual, he was right. And wrong. Food was plentiful, but fuel was scarce. There were cots and blankets, but the blankets were nothing but the corroded remnants of World War II wool. Several boxes of fuses sat in a corner, but they were iced over four inches thick, so getting to them would take a jackhammer or a bomb.

Which they had—in the form of dynamite. A trunk of dynamite that had no match to light it. Shocked past wonder into awe, Bobby watched as Annabelle scurried into the rocky ribs of the mineshaft.

"Goddamn it, Bobby, if you haven't got a bushel of four-leaf clovers up your ass." She laughed, giddy with disbelief. If anything, this was at least a reminder of the ever-widening umbrella of luck that Bobby lived under.

And the incomparable entrepreneurial spirit of industry that powered Fortooth Bend. Six years earlier, in 1982 Bobby and Annabelle were gin-drunk on that very entrepreneurial spirit. It came from their morning hikes, their afternoon walks, and their making-dinner talks. At this point, they had settled into Fortooth life and enjoyed a homestead that kept the spirit of the valley alive. Money was not a concern; their salaries from teaching at Prescott S. Norville Elementary and High School were plenty, and Bobby's mother lent them the down payment for an old Victorian three-bedroom house on Angel's Bluff Lane, just south of Yeehaw Pass.

The purchase was the perfect starter marriage project as it allowed them to while their time away, refurbishing its floorboards, stained glass, and molding back to its 1883 state. They loved taking on the kitchen, which was an antiquated beast and marveled at their ability to replace the plumbing and install new gas stoves themselves. The work went fast and slow, but over time, every aspect of their Victorian was polished to its original gleam, and when the white porch swing was hung in place, they realized new projects needed to be found.

They were. Thirty Rhode Island Red chickens were found, bought, and cooped but eventually lost to the Fortooth coyotes. Herb and vegetable gardens were planted and provided bounties within the first year. Of course, there was talk of children, but never the specific talk of planning for a child, so Bobby made sure to pull out whenever he was five seconds away from ejaculating.

It was a warm time, a productive time, but also hinted at the flat edge of a plateau. So, something new was needed, something mad and dream-crazy to invest their dwindling passion.

On February 3, that thing arrived. Waking before his 6 a.m. alarm, Bobby stumbled into the bathroom with a full morning erection, eyes crusty, and still dazed from a night of bourbon and wine. Pulling down his long johns, he tried to angle his boner toward the toilet, but as he yawned and spun his head right, his thoughts fell to the wonderland outside the bathroom window. The sky was already a turquoise blue, and a light breeze danced over a fresh draping of powder. It was a rare powder. One so light and fine, the breeze lifted and twisted its flakes in dervishes along the white unspoil. Bobby dreamed of this snow and these mornings, and he knew, for the first time since he'd been back, that today was the day he was going to go skiing.

Skipping back to the bedroom, he saw Annabelle roll toward him. "Babe," she croaked. "Did you miss the toilet again? It sounded like you peed on the wall."

"Yeah, it's not good in there," Bobby answered. "But holy shit—look outside, babe!"

Reaching her arms back toward the headboard, Annabelle let out a yawn. Then, rubbing her shoulders, she spun to the edge of the bed. Through the window, a powder dust danced on their front yard as rays of amber swirled behind a large oak. *Yep, that's gorgeous*, she thought. Turning back to Bobby, she saw him shoulder-deep in the top shelf of their closet, pulling a sweater and ski jacket out.

"Are you going skiing?" she asked, still groggy.

"Yep!" Bobby answered with such a chirp, you'd think he'd just gotten permission to partake in his first sleepover.

"But you said you'd never ski or set foot on Glory Peak."

"I won't be," Bobby answered as he pulled a wool Kansas City Chiefs beanie from the closet. "I'm gonna go backcountry. There's an incredible drop in out by Goldfinger Alley. If I can get there by eight, I can hitch a ride on Tubby's snowcat, then climb up the rest."

"You're just going to climb to the top of a mountain and ski down? Isn't that dangerous?"

"Dangerous, babe? Are you kidding me? I did it all the time growing up. If you want to get the good pow, you gotta climb for it."

Before she could respond, Bobby planted a kiss on her forehead, was out the door and on his way to the garage to pull a pair of Dynastar skis, probably very rusty and definitely not tuned, out of storage.

Tubby was a notorious badger. A grumpy old badger who'd swipe anyone away with a morning "Fuck off!" if he felt it would give him something to laugh about later. But when he saw Bobby stomping toward him, skis and poles on his shoulders, he could not help but smile at the sight of Fortooth's greatest backcountry cowboy getting the saddle out. The town was waiting for this moment. Everyone wanted him to ski again. But everyone understood why he didn't—because his father was a piece-of-shit douchebag of a motherfucking fuckhead. And because of what happened to Snow Feather. But still, to see Bobby get back out there, blazing trails down a peak no one thought possible, meant maybe, just maybe, Bobby would stay in Fortooth forever.

Pulling alongside Bobby, Tubby shook his snowcat to a halt. Resting his skis and poles in the cargo bed, Bobby swung the passenger door open. Already glimmering from a light sweat, Bobby pulled himself into the cab. He noticed Tubby was smiling, so he answered with a smile and said two words: "Goldfinger Alley." Tubby, in turn, nodded, turned up the radio, and revved the snowcat forward.

As they arrived at the base of Goldfinger Alley, it would be impossible to deny the mounting adrenaline. Maybe it was the sound of Golden Earring's "Twilight Zone" booming from the speakers or the thump of Bobby slamming a bass drum on the dashboard, but energy was building with each creak of the snowcat's treads. When Tubby got to the base of Goldfinger, he was so juiced, he just about grabbed a pair of imaginary skis to join Bobby— but he didn't because he was sixty-three years old and had a sciatica so acute he couldn't bend his knee more than forty-five degrees. So instead, he turned down the radio and asked Bobby an obvious question: "You mind if I watch?"

Flashing his ten-thousand-watt grin, Bobby pulled a pair of mirrored Cébé sunglasses from his jacket and said, "Not at all, Tubbs. Not at all."

So, Tubby watched Bobby Mac from the cargo bed of his snowcat. At first, there was nothing special to see. A man with skis, switchbacking his way up a narrow pass between two rock cliffs, was a boring sight. But as Bobby shrunk to a small red dot at the top of the peak he'd soon plunge down, that adrenaline Tubby felt when they pulled to a stop flushed through him again.

Watching Bobby finally drop into the Alley, it took a moment for Tubby to notice he was even skiing. But when he landed, and a giant plume of white exploded around him, it became apparent a firework display was about to start.

The first turn was long—almost a full 90-degree twist that fanned a two-foot-high spray of snow at the cliff walls. The next one, another long turn that threw a nearly symmetrical spray of snow against a spot parallel to the first. From his truck, Tubby could see the outline of a giant S beginning to form in the otherwise untouched snowfall—one that suggested Superman but that Tubby actually knew translated to "Suck on this, Glory Hole." Watching the shape fill out, Tubby smiled because he knew as Bobby continued, he would draw a spiral so precise, it would look like needlework.

Sliding to a stop fifty yards from the snowcat, Bobby had no idea of the perfect path he'd stitched into the mountainside, but when he turned around and faced it for the first time, he knew he did good. Real good. So good, in fact, he did the run four more times. Each time adding another line of twine to the canvas. By the time he was done, the pass was nothing but a collection of helices so perfectly drawn, it was as if they were rendered by a draftsman. Smiling at their precision, Bobby knew it was time to return to the snowcat. Placing his skis in the back he stepped into the cab, nodded at a grinning Tubby, rested his face against the passenger window, and began to snore.

Stomping back into his house, Bobby knew today's run would be lost on Annabelle. Not because she didn't support him, but because she'd never skied before. He could, of course, try to explain it to her, but as literate as his metaphors would be, he knew they just wouldn't do the experience justice—especially the moment he'd spent airborne just before he landed in the Alley and had gotten a glimpse of what it might have felt like to be floating above the world like a god. Was he supposed to tell her that? That he was able to sit in the sky and defy all notion of gravity while simultaneously seeing everything for what it was and forgetting everything for what it was. She would have thought he was crazy. Or crazier than she already thought he was.

Greeting her in the kitchen, he opted instead for the simplest solution—brevity. "Hey, babe," he said as he saw her waiting at the table, still in her pajamas.

"Well, how was it?" she asked.

"Great," Bobby answered.

"Great, great? That's it? That's all you are going to give me?"

"Yeah, babe, it was great out there. An absolutely great day," Bobby added, moving to the refrigerator. Finding a Coors behind some cabbage, he walked to the sofa, a trail of slush melting off his clothes.

Scrunching her lips, Annabelle sat up in the chair and glared at him. "Jeez, Bobby, you're dripping all over the place. Come over here."

Downing his beer, Bobby stood and sludged over. His jacket was damp and as Annabelle pulled it off him, she saw that his underlayers were drenched.

"Holy shit, B, you're soaking!"

"I know." He smiled. "These long johns are great on warmth but shit for wetness."

"Well, we got to get you out of them ASAP," she responded.

Undressing him, she couldn't understand why Bobby didn't have a pair of long johns that kept him not just warm but dry—and also did something about the wicked end-of-day smell that infiltrated the rancid wool. It was then that an idea appeared. A big one. A giant one. And in that moment, on February 3, Annabelle stumbled—actually, collided headfirst—into her passion project. Her everything project. Her life-now-had-meaning project: Paca Joe, the world's first quick-drying, odor-fighting, environmentally sustainable, 100 percent alpaca-made base layers. If only she knew anything about alpaca fabric. Or base layers.

The good news was she had plenty of time to learn and, and with the academic skills she honed and then abandoned in graduate school, she had the ultimate foundation for exhuming the most relevant, irrelevant, obscure, and outrageous pieces of information on any topic that had an encyclopedia entry. Alpacas were in the first volume, but that volume wouldn't be the only tome she would devour to learn everything possible about the spitting camelids she believed held the key to her future. She knew Bobby barely read, so she knew that going on this adventure of researching, preparing, projecting, and Excel-sheeting a business model could risk alienating him on the day-to-day. As a result, most likely, this would not be something they shared only on their morning hikes. Or their drunk car rides home from the Bull Yoke. But she also knew the most foundational requirement of any entrepreneur was to take risks. And having no doubt that taking this risk would result in a multitude of dividends, she decided that regardless of what limited focus Bobby was capable of, he would have to join her on this ride.

# CHAPTER 15

**FEBRUARY 2001**

L ooking at the dailies from the latest Wolfehaus film shoot, Gunther sighed with boredom. Sure, the images were beautiful—seventy-two-frame-per-second sprays of powder off remote Alaskan mountains were *always* beautiful—but lately, no frame, filming location, or staggering report of increased sales could inspire in Gunther to do the one thing someone surrounded by success should do—smile.

Nanny A had created a machine. One so perfectly calibrated that *surprise* became a word without definition. This wouldn't have bothered Gunther if he, at least, still had the sex to look forward to. For years, the sex between him and Nanny A was a vortex of chewing and longing, and a physicality so raw it could have only been described as kink. Gunther was always amazed by Nanny A's initial willingness to go to these places. He expected, because of her age, her body would be fragile and lack the resilience of a woman in her twenties. But he was wrong—very wrong. The fire of her sadness fortified her in ways he never expected and sculpted her into one lean muscle ready to dig its way through any part of Gunther.

But then the company started doing well. And the fire she used to sweat through midmorning perversions blew toward the growing brushfire of Wolfehaus Media. No longer were there scouts ending with sex in rental cars or secret blow jobs in editing rooms. Now, there was just work and the occasional quickie that was mostly clothed and from behind. This troubled Gunther. And he knew if something did not soon change, he would be tempted, out of boredom, to destroy something of meaning. Which quite possibly could be Wolfehaus Media—or his cranium with a ball-peen hammer.

But then a solution came, and from the strangest of places: William Jefferson Macklemore, Gunther's detested, despised, but somehow still-admired foe. For years, Bill had rung in the New Year with the Huevos Rancheros Stampedo. A daylong celebration created by accident when the Danish water polo team fell asleep during a drunken New Year's Eve hike up Glory Peak. Lost and blurry eyed from finishing seven bottles of Cherry Heering, the team decided to stay overnight in one of the ski patrol huts. When they woke the next morning, it was to the rancid smell of vomit and diarrhea, as they all had soiled themselves during the night. Ashamed to emerge with their clothes covered in various forms of excrement, they opted instead to hike down the mountain nude, chanting the Danish national anthem and passing among them the remnants of their last bottle of Cherry Heering.

When they did arrive at the base, it was to the shocked laughter of the skiers in the lift lines. Buns rosy-red, their uncircumcised organs shriveled down to a half-eaten bratwurst, the tallest holding the empty bottle of Cherry Heering above his head like a Super Bowl trophy, most resort owners would have scoffed at the sight of the nude revelers cheering through their family friendly resort. But Bill understood the invigoration that came with mountain nudity—and how very few things felt better than the flap of your testicles on your thighs as you descended a thousand-foot vertical run on a fresh-powder day. So, instead of penalizing the Danes, he immortalized them when he ordered a bronze sculpture of their naked bodies to be installed outside the main lodge. And then, to ensure everyone knew the significance of the day, he created the Huevos Rancheros Stampedo—a fully nude bomber race that started at the top of Glory Peak and ended with a jump into a pool-size vat of Cherry Heering.

Once considered the coolest event in the ski world, the Huevos Rancheros Stampedo had now deteriorated into a spring cattle call for Gucci Pads eager for a story to share with their hedge-fund cronies about how they displayed their overly manicured junk while choking down shots from a ski boot. Now, no self-respecting snowflake would ever participate in such a thing. That said, the spirit of the event was something every snowflake couldn't help but want to be part of. And maybe, if something new was presented in a way that celebrated the event's original primal madness, there would be a reason for every genuine, next-generation snowflake to seek out Fortooth again.

Watching a shot of a snowboarder clip into his binding on his edit system, a half-asleep Gunther jolted to attention when a series of manic shouts came through his office window. Curious, he got up from his Avid and peered through the blinds. In the distance, he saw a collection of nude bodies splashing in a red pool—the overflow turning the snow around it a slushy merlot. If not for the reverberating echo of Nickleback's "How You Remind Me" screaming from speakers, it would have looked like the gruesome remnants of orcas feasting on seals.

*But they are having fun*, Gunther thought. *Those Gucci Pads and fraternity boys are having genuine fun. And Great Scott, they seem freeeeeeee.*

And that was all it took. A lightning bolt powered by Cherry Heering and scored by Nickleback to spark a way to make Fortooth a true snowflake's paradise again.

When Nanny A found Gunther the next day in his office, it was amid a myriad of scribblings. Looking him over, she could see he hadn't been home to shave, shower, or change his clothes.

"Gunther, what in God's name is all of this?" Nanny A asked as she closed and locked the door behind her.

Grabbing a wrinkled, coffee-stained paper off his desk, he handed it to her. Nanny A squinted as she tried to decipher his writing. "I can't make this out."

Sighing, Gunther stood up, reached across the desk, and turned the sheet of paper in Nanny A's hands upside down. With this new perspective, she could almost see what he wrote.

"It says 'Snow Ball,'" Gunther clarified. "It's the next thing we will do. An extreme skiing and snowboarding music festival. We throw it every year out by the Boneyard. We build an amphitheater, a terrain park, a half-pipe, invite every one of our skiers to it. Let them pick the bands, the music. It will be magnificent."

Looking at the paper, Nanny A saw none of what Gunther was describing. Just random words in cursive. Placing the paper on his desk, Nanny A looked at him. He was now searching through additional stacks of papers. "Okay, Gunther, but this does not follow our business model. We make ski films. I don't understand why you want to do this."

Finding a piece of paper, Gunther grabbed it and handed it to Nanny A. "So that we can do this," he said.

Looking at the paper, Nanny saw the sketch of a mountain, stick figures skiing down its slope, with the outline of something that looked like a wolf hovering above.

"What's this?" she said, her eyes now imagining a ski lift and slopeside restaurant on the sketch.

"That is Wolfe Mountain. Our future resort."

Nanny studied the sketch harder. The skiers now moved; the chairlift animated into operation; laughter and the swish of skis played in her mind. Looking up from the paper, Nanny A found Gunther's eyes. They were manic, his head vibrating; his teeth, almost chattering. *This is absolutely crazy*, Nanny A thought. But now, Nanny A could see it too.

"This is a big project," she shared. "It'll require our full attention. And we would need a way to connect all these dots. So, it feels . . . organic."

"I've figured that out." Gunther nodded at the paper Nanny A was still holding. "The winners of the Snow Ball will be featured in a series of films called Powder Puffs—which we will produce, of course. We will use these films to audition filmmakers for the company, and when we find somebody good enough, we'll hire him or her to replace me as chief creative officer so that I'm freed up to focus 100 percent on Wolfe Mountain."

*This is just insane*, Nanny A thought. *Beautifully insane*. Of course, they would have to find a way to secure a loan for land and production costs, and of course, they were going to have to hire an architect, a groundbreaking one who used clean, modern lines, and a chef who would create healthy and organic fusion-inspired dishes. There would be so much to do, and for the first time since she left her husband, Nanny A wondered if she could do this.

If she could take this step; this risk; commit the time and energy needed to keep this vision on track till it became real somewhere in the Farangotta. But before she could voice the concerns swirling through her mind, Gunther reached across the desk, took her hand inside his, and said, "Think of how much sleep Bill will lose over this. He's going to hate it."

And just like that, her fear was gone.

Clover did not understand it. She couldn't fathom why Nanny A would embark on another one of Gunther's dumb-as-dirt Wolfehaus adventures. This would mean longer hours at work, more time apart, and an increased and unwanted dose of Gunther.

Normally, Clover would have stared at Nanny A's feet as she shared this, but this was February 16, 2001, and she was no longer the Clover of December 27, 2000. So, instead of using her fork to slide around the crisp asparagus on her dinner plate, she placed it on the table and asked her grandmother a simple question: "Why?"

Surprised, Nanny A shifted in her seat. "Why? Because it's a good opportunity. And Fortooth could use another option for skiing—one that's not so dry and homogenized."

"Fine," Clover snapped back. "But I just don't get it. He's a moron."

"Who's a moron?" Nanny A responded, now fully aware of where this conversation was going.

"Gunther. Everyone in town thinks so. The guy's a joke."

"A joke? A joke! Let me tell you something—that guy created the biggest ski film empire in the world, and on top of that, he may be one of the greatest backcountry skiers in the world!"

"Yeah, but he's stupid, Nanny A," Clover said, this time with less spite. Looking across the table, she mumbled, "Please tell me you see that."

Nanny A sat down in her chair. Clover was confused by the sudden shift in her demeanor. No longer buzzing with enthusiasm, she now carried an air of seriousness, as if she was possibly getting ready to scream at her.

"Listen, Clover," Nanny A started in a calm voice. "We never had a chance to talk about these things. Me, working at Wolfehaus, and you, with all the time spent on your skiing. But one thing you should know, and I think this is one of the most fundamental lessons I can teach you and one that will benefit you for life to learn. And that's, all men are stupid." Clover reeled back in her chair. This was not only a jab at Gunther but her father, and most importantly, Jimmy.

"Not Jimmy," she whispered. "He's the smartest person I have ever met."

Nanny A, aware she'd nicked a nerve, pulled back from her impending diatribe. "He may be the exception. But besides him, each one of them—and pardon my French on this—are all dick and no balls."

Clover wanted to laugh, but there was still the pang of another wound festering under her fleece. The reason she responded sharply when Nanny A started this conversation.

"But what about my training?" she asked. "Next winter, they will be holding nationals at the Nordic Center, and I could qualify for the Olympic team if I place."

Sensing Clover's concern, Nanny A leaned forward and grabbed her hands. "I promise, Clove, I will always and—please look at me when I say this . . ." Shifting her face from the floor, Clover looked straight into Nanny A's eyes. They seemed strong, secure, no hint of quiver or dart to them. "I will always, always be here for your training. That is my priority."

For a split second, Clover tried to imagine Nanny A ditching Gunther and Wolfehaus obligations to attend one of her cross-country skiing competitions. Closing her eyes, hoping to broadcast this vision on the insides of her eyelids, she scrunched her face tight and tried to tune in an image of Nanny A cheering at a finish line. But no matter how hard she squeezed; no image would appear. Nanny A might have thought Clover's training was her priority, but time and time again she had shown Clover it wasn't. So, in that moment, she had to accept that Nanny A had just lied to her.

The only cushion to this blow was that Clover had Jimmy. And he'd already proven, time and time again, that not only was Clover's training his priority, but that Clover was as well. Jimmy valued her, which meant that whatever she prioritized, he prioritized, too.

This became evident over the coming weeks when, as predicted, Nanny A's support of her cross-country training petered, then dropped off altogether. And as expected, Jimmy's commitment to Clover and her training grew to the point that, come early March, Jimmy himself was on skis, rehearsing starts, practicing finishes, and drafting off her lead. Of course, at first, he couldn't keep up, but as his focus increased and his research became more obsessive, he evolved into the perfect sparring partner. It was his idea to run drills up steep terrain to increase shoulder memory and planting strength. It was his idea to ice-skate while pulling sleds to build up quadriceps power and speed control. It was his idea to focus on nose breathing and the regulation of heart rate for longer cardio consistency no matter the altitude.

Granted, this occasionally posed a problem because while he was day-lighting as her training partner, he was still moonlighting as her boyfriend. And sometimes, when he got too close while helping with her form or when his bangs fluttered over his eyes like the wings of a butterfly, making his face look like the cutest guinea pig ever—it became impossible for Clover to regulate her heart rate, no matter how slow and long she inhaled.

But despite those occasional flusters, her work was paying off. That winter, she won every race she entered and averaged a three-minute lead over whoever placed second. When spring showed up, it was official—she was a champion.

But like all young athletes who gained recognition for their success, her psyche took turns she did not expect. In some moments, she felt the flair of the peacock as she walked the school halls. In others, she wanted to slither out of sight like a garter snake. She was used to attention—the quiet murmurs and glances from gossipy locals who wanted to spread rumors about Bill Macklemore's weird, antisocial granddaughter. But with this newfound attention came something she wasn't prepared for—audacity. An audacity that came in the form of congratulations for things people hadn't witnessed or gifts from people she didn't know. But the place it came from that disturbed her most was the attention she got from the boys at school. They would hold a glance a beat too long, track her in the hall as she walked from one class to the next, or, most annoyingly, come to her via note, in the middle of class, when she was locked to the wood of her desk and couldn't avoid them.

The first and most regular of these notes came from Jesse Vanigan. Jesse was what most grandmothers would have referred to as a "real charmer." All but Nanny A, of course, who would have seen right through his borrowed hippie swagger to the wet puppy frailty his hemp necklace and flat brim hat tried to camouflage. Known for having a father who was "crazy rich," he was considered "super cute" by all the girls in school. But Clover had trouble seeing that. Because she was too preoccupied with how he made her feel—which was uncomfortable. Not just uncomfortable because of his aggressive attention but uncomfortable because something about it made her want more.

To a point, at least. And that point came when Jesse brought Jimmy into it. It was during an English class while Mrs. Porter was deconstructing *One Flew Over the Cuckoo's Nest* that Jesse made this foolish mistake. He was watching Clover out of the corner of a sleepy-dog eye, and though she tried to fight it, she could not help but inch the corners of her lips toward a smile. Watching back, she saw him fold a yellow swatch of paper. Next came the light tap of the paper against her shoulder. Looking to the floor, she saw a note at the leg of her desk. After slinking down to grab it, she unfolded it behind a textbook.

I WANT YOU, it read, in all caps. And I'll do you good. Deep good, it also read.

God, she hated him. *He's the worst!* she thought. But then, why did she feel a burst of itching under her right armpit when she read the note?

*Aaaargh, this is sooooo confusing*, she thought when another tap tickled her neck. Near panic, she scanned the floor around her. By her right leg was another scrap of paper. With her foot, she slid it closer and, once again, slinked down to pick it up. This time, it read: Come on, after school. Ditch that loser and meet me at Punishment Lake.

*Ditch that loser.*

Seeing those words, a bolt of anger ripped through her.

Before she could even think about how to respond and just as Mrs. Porter was saying something about a character named Chief, Clover was out of her seat, walking across the classroom, reeling her arm back, and slamming her fist into Jesse's left incisor.

Shocked, he fell backward in his chair, bleeding and unconscious on the floor. Clover herself was shocked at the swiftness of her punch—and it wasn't until minutes later that she realized half his tooth was lodged in the right knuckle of her index finger.

Clover's newfound public recognition may have come with its downsides, but it undeniably had its share of perks as well—which was made abundantly clear by Principal Janks, who, instead of bestowing the appropriate punishment of school suspension for knocking a classmate out, decided to allow her to finish her day in his office with full internet access.

Now, if she'd been able to use that internet, this wouldn't have been half bad. Unfortunately, though, Principal Janks had other ideas about how to spend that time, which included endless monologues that waxed nostalgic about how her long-dead parents were "the most ultimate couple ever."

Just when Clover thought she'd have to use her right hook on Principle Janks, the bell rang, and she was officially free. Leaving his office without a backward glance, she quickly found herself on the football field, where Jimmy was waiting.

"I don't want to talk about it," she said, rubbing her bandaged right hand. "Can we pretend it didn't happen?"

"Sure," Jimmy answered, then turned toward the ridgeline. Just as she was about to open her mouth to see if he wanted to hike to Punishment Lake, Jimmy added, "Actually, I was thinking we'd head out to Feather's Edge. We could get there by sunset."

Feather's Edge was a peculiar choice. It was not a particularly challenging hike or a particularly inspiring one, but it did give a clear, unobstructed view of the south side of the valley; the unspoiled side where the trees stood straight, tall, and green, all bark rockets pointing at the sky, never to take off.

When they got to the lookout, Clover was on edge. Since his suggestion where to hike, Jimmy hadn't added to the conversation. He just peeled away at the bark of a fallen branch he picked up along the way. *Is it possible he's going to propose? Or wait, is it possible he's going to break up?* Whatever was about to happen, she wondered if, somehow, she deserved it.

Sitting on a bench built for the summer tourists, they scanned the valley in silence. Winter was coming to an end, and the snow was resting in swatches over clay-brown mud. In a month, grass would return. In two months, the Fortooths would be slithering from their pits as the brown bears splashed through streams and chased trout. Breaking the branch in two, Jimmy took one of the pieces and pointed at a redwood, its crown peaking a full twenty feet above the others. At its top, on a fragile wood platform, stood a young Le'Echuwannan man shivering in the wind. He was naked, his long hair flapping like kelp in a swell. By all appearances, he should have been miserable, but he was chanting a sweet, delicate song that hovered over the valley like mist.

Clover watched as Jimmy closed his eyes and mouthed to the chant. *"Mi-esse, esse, ni-wanta tom yay. Mi-esse-esse ni-oh-wanta-tom-nay."* He then opened his eyes and looked at Clover. "I think that's Fancy Glove. You know, the kid who has the Purple Haze. Spencer said he stopped dealing. Had stuff to do in the council."

Clover looked back at Jimmy. He'd never spoken of the Le'Echuwanna before.

"Wait, how do you know this?" she asked.

"From Spencer. His dad does house visits for them. Most of the time, he just gives them an antacid, then sits around and listens to the gossip."

"Is there something happening? I mean, Jimmy, are you mad at me or something?" Clover asked. She was confused, not just about Spencer knowing so much about the Le'Echuwanna but also about who was sitting in front of her.

"It's called the *Oh-sah-cha-me*," Jimmy continued. "It's their rite of passage, I guess. Or that's what my dad says it is. If Fancy Glove makes it through the night without passing out, tomorrow he will be inducted into the council as an Elder. I know he's still young. My dad says they call the young ones Budding Elders; the old ones are Elder Elders." Jimmy turned his head from the pine and looked at Clover. "Did I tell you how my dad works with some of them to take care of the land?"

Jimmy's look was gentle, his pupils so dilated, deep, and black, Clover thought about climbing right into them. She loved him. Not for his crooked smile that was punctuated with one dimple. Not for the way he let cascading *fa-la-las* whistle through his nose when he slept. Not for any other reason than he was her best friend.

"Close your eyes," he said and reached for her hand. "Let's see if we can join him."

Clover was unsure of what this meant, but she closed her eyes, took deep breaths, and tried her best to join him. In those moments, she heard the rising sigh of the breeze, the rustling of the valley's branches, and finally, the soft repeating chant coming from Fancy Glove's lips. She had no idea what the words meant, but eventually, she disappeared into the ups and downs of their phonetic assemblage. It was soothing. So soothing that when Jimmy told her he enlisted in the navy and would be deploying for boot camp at school's end, she barely noticed the sting of his words.

# PART 3

West the wind, west the wind, as the lightning lights its way.
East the wind, east the wind, as the thunder has its say.

—As translated from the Le'Echuwanna
*Songs for Children between the Age of One and Air*

# CHAPTER 16

## MARCH 1982

There was no doubt Paca Joe was going to be big. In the world of 1982 ski apparel, the focus was on shells, waterproofing, goggles with glare reduction, and gloves. Skis themselves were always a priority, as were boots that gave great support and flex. Bindings, too, had technology thrown at them, but base layers—that core article of clothing that allowed all winter athletes to take on the elements—was a market ripe for expansion. And reinvention.

Up until that point, all reinventions came in two flavors: color or tech. Color just reflected the trends of current fashion. Tech, however, reflected a subtler trend, one that came with auditioning fabrics and thicknesses. In the early '80s, the most significant breakthrough in base-layer tech was polyester. Polyester mixed with rayon—nylon, polypropylene, spandex. And all these fabrics improved warmth and wicking, but the tax these synthetics brought on the environment was problematic, so a solution that reduced the carbon footprint was greatly needed.

Alpaca addressed this need. Deep diving into the world of natural fabrics, Annabelle quickly learned of the classic options of merino wool and cashmere. Cashmere obviously would be too expensive, and merino was a leading possibility till her mother reminded her of how the Indigenous communities of Peru used alpaca in high altitudes and cold climates. Always intrigued by how surprised an alpaca looked, she decided to test its heat retention herself and found it breathed better and dried faster than cotton, wool, or synthetics. And under further investigation, discovered it would be unique to ski fashion and could be branded as a boutique fabric, giving it an air of exclusivity that would appeal to both ski bum and ski brat. Surrounded by a town of wild winter athletes who would be her first customers, all she needed was a design aesthetic and a source.

Bobby remembered, clear as glass, the moment Annabelle presented him with the idea. It wasn't after sex, Annabelle knowing full well he would be too stoned from the numb of serotonin to have the conversation. It was instead during one of their morning hikes up the backside of Toucan's Tip—a physics-confounding peak of slate and limestone that culminated in a beak-like outcropping that hung over the valley. A top ten bucket list item for any serious rock climber, Toucan's Tip was one of the many spots in the Farangotta that made Bobby wonder if even God got drunk occasionally and had to live with the absurd decisions he made while under the influence. Having walked this trail a thousand times, and at least a hundred with Annabelle, Bobby knew every inch of this path, so when Annabelle stopped before the first major incline, he knew something was about to happen. Looking at her, he recognized a lip being bit and her head arching toward him as if she was trying to hear something.

"So?" she asked. "What do you think?"

Bobby looked back at her as though confused by the question. "Haven't I already made it clear?" He smiled. "I *love* it. It's a brilliant idea. I've been wearing the same Fruit of the Loom johns since I was twelve; I'd love something better."

Annabelle gushed with relief. She wasn't a crazy person, but all ideas born from electricity had the risk of seeming psychotic.

"So, what do you think about starting it with me? You have the technical expertise and could guinea pig it. I have some amazing ideas about styles and cuts. We've got some money stashed. It wouldn't take much more if we started small and focused on the locals and snowflakes."

"I could not agree more, babe. We get some snowflakes hooked on this, they'll spread it like wildfire. What else ya' think we'd need?" Bobby asked, reaching for her hand, a sign he wanted to start hiking again.

"Well, I'm thinking that with my mother's connection to the Centro de textiles Tradicionales, we can get all the fabric we need at next to cost. And then we can get a group here to design the patterns and cuts. Now that I'm thinking out loud, I wonder if we should just cut and sew here so if we have to, we can make adjustments."

"Nice. What are you thinking? Long sleeves, bottoms, socks—maybe a beanie or two?"

"I definitely want to start with long sleeves and bottoms. Find a way to give them a variety of colors and patterns. You know those bright orange and greens in those Quechua skirts? How cool would those be if we could get the base layers that color?"

Following behind her, it was easy for Bobby to get lost in her enthusiasm. Not only was he able to watch the curve of her buttocks flex and release in lean, steady steps, but he also heard mad passion in her voice. As Annabelle waved her hands Bobby listened, enraptured as she shared, in rambling sentences, how there was money to be made, an industry to change, and most important, an opportunity to water and feed their own root system—one without the manure-laced fertilizer that was William Jefferson Macklemore and Glory Peak. By the time they got back to their car, not only was Bobby in, he also saw the logo. It was the outline of an alpaca head facing forward, a snowy mountain morphing from its neck. *This is going to be monstrous,* he thought.

And expensive. Just a few months in, they discovered long-distance phone calls were legitimately underbudgeted. That opening a business account had surprise costs and monthly fees. That shipping came with an assortment of import taxes and the need for insurance. Looking at their savings, Annabelle soon realized there wasn't enough money to ship the first fabric order, let alone pay for the cutting, design, and packaging once they got the fabric.

And that was all before they had to decide what type of alpaca fiber to use. Based on her research, there were two types to choose from: Huacaya, a short and dense fiber that had a natural frizz and curl to it, or the rarer option, Suri, which had a more appealing luster that likened itself to silk. As much as Suri was Annabelle's preferred choice, it proved way out of their price range, so Huacaya became the consolation. And while closer in price point, it still was outside their budget.

As the numbers came in and the dream of building a clothing empire started to become a distant reality, Annabelle's temperament soon took on one of a deer who accidentally stumbled into a fenced-in ranch. At first, there seemed to be freedom to run and forage, but soon it was apparent that even though it had some access to necessities, the barbwire denied its ability to move forward. Bobby, bothered by the sanding down of his wife's enthusiasm, decided he had to help her find a way.

His solution, at first, brought a headshaking no. It was, of course, presented on a morning hike and came with, so Bobby thought, the ability to operate with resource and speed. But Annabelle had strong reservations. Looking at her as they paused on Coyote Toe Trail, Bobby asked the obvious.

"Why the fuck not, Belle?" The words weren't sharp, but Annabelle was surprised by the lack of compassion in them. She was also surprised by how fast he followed the question with a volley of explanation: "We'd have the cash tomorrow, could treat it as a low-interest loan, carve out decision-making control and all that stuff you talk about. And-and-and," he stuttered, "you wouldn't have to stress, and we could just get the game started!"

Annabelle did not know how to take Bobby's statements. Now that the shine of their sex had cooled, she had to come to terms with his annoying dependence on sports analogies and his favorite and most overused phrase, "all that stuff."

Standing there, steam releasing from her enlarged nostrils, she responded, "Because your mom is a cold bitch and won't even talk to me!"

Around them, the mountainside woke. Four-legged creatures darted for cracks, and birds scattered, all but a red-tailed hawk, which sat on a nearby tree, pruning his feathers. Bobby was dumbstruck by her yell. He then answered the only way he knew—with a laugh.

"Ah, come on, Belle. Her being a bitch just shows how much she likes you. It's a sign of love."

Unmoved by his answer, Annabelle continued, "It isn't a sign of love, B. She just stares at me and examines every move as she smokes those gross fucking Slims. I feel like I'm a rat in some experiment I didn't agree to be part of."

Now, Bobby laughed even harder. "You are, Belle. We all are. It's like she has us all behind some glass cage that only she gets to look through. But (a) she hates my dad, so helping us get this going without him will send her sky high. And (b) she can stock the line in her shop, so that's a guaranteed order. From where I'm sitting, that's a pretty comfortable first-quarter lead."

She knew he was right. It was obvious to anyone with a synapse. But she also knew the decision could be wrong. That somehow, somewhere down the line, she could be asked to slide over and let someone else take the wheel.

To ensure that never came to pass, Annabelle prepared for her meeting with Suzanne as if she was meeting with the CEO of Wells Fargo. There was a prospectus, projections, bound packets, design elements, biographies of her partners in Peru, clothing patterns, and the beginnings of a marketing campaign. Sitting in front of Suzanne, hair pulled back, a denim button-down ironed and tucked into mud-colored corduroys, Annabelle looked as if she was interviewing for a teaching position at a Northeast liberal arts college. Or as a ceramics instructor. Either way, as Suzanne flipped through the proposal and pulled long drags from a Virginia Slim, Annabelle had the slight worry she was going to be punched in the face. Pausing at a page, Suzanne dropped a dangling ash into her coffee mug, then lifted the page closer.

"What's this?" she asked, eyes scanning an image of an alpaca looking at her with the base of a mountain morphing from its neck.

"That's our logo. Bobby designed it. It leans into the regal nature of the alpaca and celebrates its symbiotic relationship with the mountains."

"I like its eyes. Good work, Bobby."

Annabelle smiled at the compliment. The eyes were damn good— and hard to render without diminishing the alpaca's spirit. That spirit of a prepubescent Snuffleupagus mixed with the arrogance of being able to manage the craggiest mountain terrain Mother Earth could jumble.

Done scanning the documents, Suzanne placed the papers back on the table, then stubbed out her cigarette. "Well, I got bison and elk defrosting . . . Which one do you want for dinner?" It was the most anticlimactic yes Annabelle ever got.

Later that evening, as they left Suzanne's, Bobby saw a lightness in Annabelle's walk that he'd never seen before. She was on her toes, taking large, arcing steps like an astronaut crossing moon rock. Relieved, Bobby began to anticipate the possibility of a romantic pit stop on the way home. But there was no stop—just Annabelle running through a calendar of to-dos and the tapping out of ideas on the steering wheel. She was still talking as she pulled into the driveway and still talking as they walked into the house. Bobby hoped with each step the tone would shift when they entered the bedroom. But it never did. Annabelle, instead, beelined for an alcove off the kitchen, turned on a light, then the computer. As it hummed to life, she settled into a small wooden chair and rubbed her hands.

"Bobby, where you going?" she chirped.

Bobby, still on his way to the bedroom, stopped halfway up the stairs. "I thought we were getting into bed," he said, truly thinking they were.

"What? Babe, we got a ton to do if we want to get the fabric shipments in by next month. Put on some coffee."

Dropping his head, Bobby turned around and headed back down the stairs. This was not the way he wanted to celebrate this victory. And if Annabelle was aware enough to hear how slow his steps moved, she would have recognized his disappointment. But she did not hear them. Or his sighs. All she heard was coffee.

# CHAPTER 17

**FEBRUARY 10, 1988**

Staring at Bobby in the storage mine, Annabelle had no clue what he was thinking. They must have been here almost twenty-four hours, but he was acting as if they were on day one of vacation. His body language was comfortable, his energy casual, as if waiting on a mai tai, and as she watched him examine a can of twenty-year-old baked beans, he seemed almost peaceful as he sat cross-legged on the freezer-burned surface of a military cot. To his left was the inconsistent sputter of a kerosene lamp looking for fuel, and if Annabelle silenced her thoughts enough to listen, she would be able to hear him murmur the ingredients on the label. He seemed engaged, but possibly only due to hunger. Watching him, Annabelle wondered if Bobby even liked life. Granted, at times, she knew its responsibilities deadened his sail, but she thought he liked it. At least enough to want to keep living.

"Well, I think we just roll the dice on this," Bobby finally said. "I mean, we either die from hypothermia, or whatever fungus we got in here. So, considering the options, it might just be Hail Mary time." Bobby chuckled. He then grabbed a rusty screwdriver from a wooden trunk and hammered it into the top of the can. Peeling back the top, he marveled at the syrupy sweetness somehow still protected in the aluminum.

"No mold," he confirmed, "and smells like it's still got that ol' Heinz flavor."

Bobby hopped over to Annabelle and handed her the can. She accepted it and the makeshift spoon he fashioned from the lid, then dug in as Bobby went back to inspecting the remaining rations.

A minute later Annabelle scraped the can, placed it by the foot of her cot, and coughed. Knowing full well neither of them wanted to broach the topic, she decided it was time to address reality.

"So, what do you think they're doing up top?" she asked.

Putting down a tin of potted meat, Bobby looked her way. "Probably still searching. But I'm not sure what tracks they'll have to follow up on. Seemed like a storm was heading our way. So, that means visibility issues 'cause that new snow would cover up our footprints. They know where the car is, though. And your mom knows we like this hike, so they should be able to put it together."

"God, she's probably on a tear right now. Probably cursing Sheriff Daley up and down Main Street to do something."

"Jeez, that poor guy," Bobby added. "He must be wishing every night he never helped her with that tire."

"Right?" Annabelle laughed. "No good deed . . ." She reached for the empty can of beans, forgetting she'd already polished it clean. Placing it back at her feet, she decided to broach another topic they'd been avoiding. "How do you think Clover is doing?"

Annabelle released the words gently, hoping they would land soft on Bobby's lap, so soft he would barely feel them. But by the look of his eyes, Annabelle saw they landed like a spear to the throat.

"I don't know," he said, his voice flat and faint. "Probably taking it in. Probably still trying to figure out what's going on. I don't think she's crying, but I also don't know with her. It's difficult to figure out what she's thinking sometimes, but she's just four, so..."

It was easy to pin the blame on Clover's age, but Annabelle had been the same way and never grew out of it. *That is 100 percent my genetic contribution to the conversation*, Annabelle thought, but couldn't bring herself to say out loud. Following form, she looked up at Bobby, her face revealing none of the guilt she felt below.

# CHAPTER 18

The weeks leading up to Jimmy's departure were filled with the gooey blur of summer. As sunlight edged deeper into the hours usually held for night and freedom replaced the predictability of school days, Clover tried her best to find some grounding. But with her training now reduced to her least favorite pastime on the planet—running—it was difficult for her to find comfort without the winter ritual of stepping into bindings.

Jimmy was also less available now, spending his free time preparing for his next phase of life. This consisted of mornings spent in silence while walking the forests and evenings spent in observation while hiking the mountains. He was "conditioning himself," he explained to Clover, to become "situationally aware"—a skill he heard was needed to excel in the navy.

*The navy, the stupid navy*, Clover thought. She understood why he enlisted. His father did, and his grandfather did, and his uncle, who was now a rear admiral overseeing the US Indo-Pacific Command. They all used it to pay for college, which is what Jimmy was going to do once his tour was over. The plan was that Clover would wait two years, qualify for the Olympics while Jimmy avoided unnecessary gestures of extreme bravery, and then when he returned, they would move someplace in Colorado where he could get the best electrical engineering degree, and she could work toward her second gold medal.

Clover, of course, wanted to support this plan, but two years without him would be a gut-burning pain. Like how she imagined hot acid felt as it poured down your throat, dissolved your innards, and burned your entire being into a pile of ash. It was all too much, the thought of Jimmy leaving. So, to stave it off, she resolved every night to swallow up all their bed allowed. Head resting on his chest, her fingers memorized every pore of his skin, and her nose breathed in every particle that made up his pinecone musk. They were forged during this time, a braid of one—except for the night before his departure, where instead of nudity, kissing, or tickles, she got Jimmy lying in bed, lost in his ceiling. Watching him but afraid to say anything that could disrupt these last few hours, Clover wondered why, even though she was nestled in his armpit, she felt lonelier than ever.

The next morning when Jimmy left for Naval Station Great Lakes, there were no tears, sex, or fighting, just a deep look into his eyes. And a hug. One Clover held so tight, he could have evaporated in her arms. Pulling back, she took in a breath and held it in her throat, using it to block the tsunami of emotion she felt rising from her heart and threatened to split her in two. Clover could tell Jimmy was fighting something, too, as his eyes began to outline with tears. Staring into his large round pupils, she saw something deep and warm enough to let her know that he and this were forever real.

Later that night, during dinner, Clover searched for a reason to eat, but the sadness she felt from Jimmy's departure numbed her. Nanny A, on the other hand, couldn't stop eating. Nor could she shut up. Watching Nanny A blather through mouthfuls of seco de carne and ramble about Wolfehaus's latest run of Power Puff movies made Clover want to rip off her ears and scream.

"Clove, not only has it doubled the sales of our last DVD series, but because of the option to try out for next year's Snow Ball if you register now, our mailing list has multiplied by maybe tenfold. It's like I told Gunther—if we're gonna rope 'em in with the promise of a free year of skiing or boarding, they gotta give us something in return. My next thought is we set up some kind of subscription service where they pay monthly and get a new DVD. Like a wine club. This way, we are pushing the old and new catalogue."

Clover listened and ran her spoon through her stew. If she twirled it just right, she could see one of Jimmy's curls in its wake. Many times, she thought of sharing her feelings regarding Jimmy's departure, but sensing they would be lost in the vortex of Nanny A's monologue, she opted to carry them alone. Excusing herself from the table, Clover emptied her leftovers into a Tupperware and headed for the front door.

"Wait, Clove—I didn't even get to the good part about what this means for us, moneywise," Nanny A pleaded, hoping this would bring her granddaughter back to the kitchen table, but Clover could barely bring herself to turn around.

"That's okay, Nanny, we can talk about it tomorrow," Clover offered, knowing full well that moving forward, she would avoid as many dinners with Nanny A as possible.

"Great," Nanny A responded. "I'll leave dessert in the fridge—and don't worry about cleaning up. I'll just . . ."

Clover didn't hear the rest of the sentence as she shut the front door.

Around her was the cloudless eve of the Farangotta. And though it was five after nine, the sun still hung like a dying light bulb and would probably hold on till about nine thirty or so, when the moon would take over the broadcast. If she walked fast enough, Clover could get into town before nightfall. And if she walked through the forest, she could also enjoy the changing of its orchestra as the diurnal animals retreated to their dens and handed their keys to the bats and owls that worked the night shift. Turning toward MacGregor's Ole Copper-Spoked Pass, there was still plenty of sunlight out, inspiring Clover to wonder if she would see the alpacas up on Jade Ridge.

They were rumored to summer there, along the moss-covered terrain that stood in thin spires west of Miner's Gasp. Many times, during his training, Jimmy studied their silhouettes as they paused to take in the unbroken view of the valley and feast on its tangy lichen. This was grade A grazing, and the perfect place for the herd to rest before they disappeared to the other side of the ridge to slumber. According to Jimmy, there were 139 now, almost a full third more than when Clover's mother first shipped them to Fortooth. With breeding like that, it would only be a short amount of time before they were as native to the valley as the Fortooth itself. Like the bighorn sheep who one hundred years earlier checkered themselves up and down the slopes and ridges. They were the original wardens of the land, the ones who tended to its grass and battled in thunderous, headbutting jousts for the alpha seat on the mountains. Over time, from disease and hunting of the white man, they disappeared, rumored by the Le'Echuwanna to have climbed a limestone crest to the Second World, where guns and virus could not find them.

But that was a century ago, and the only remnants of their domination were the horns the Le'Echuwanna blew and used for ceremonial dress. Winding through the pass, Clover kept her eyes on the ridge, hoping to see tufts of white along the rocks. *Maybe*, she thought, *the alpacas, one day, could create an army—like the sheep before and make sure everything in the Farangotta stays in balance.* But scanning the ridges, Clover saw none, and twenty minutes later, as she got into town, she would just have to hold on to the stories Jimmy shared.

Town that evening had that peculiar still energy of a summer destination shuttering its doors. The few bed-and-breakfasts on Main Street were open but empty, and the Glory Peak resort and condominiums were closing, section by section, to rest and rejuvenate before the winter season returned. Outside of winter, this was Clover's favorite part of the year, when the empty streets allowed her the opportunity to explore undetected.

These explorations started as a child. Silent, she would skulk through alleys and watch through windows as her neighbors did their business. Clover never did this to satisfy some perversion or because she was driven by an investigative curiosity to uncover the dark secrets of her town. She did this because she hoped that through these windows, she would catch a glimpse of what a family looked like. A nuclear family, a Norman Rockwell family, a single-parent family. Any family with a parent, a child, and a loving ritual. For the most part, Clover just saw families in front of the television or snapping grumpily as they shared a meal in an underlit kitchen. But once, she saw a father helping his son piece together a model tank while Steve

Miller Band's "Fly Like an Eagle" sang from a stereo. And another time, she spied a mother rocking a young child in her arms. She couldn't remember what lullaby she was singing, but she never forgot how the mother's parched lips stuck together as she whistled the words. It was the promise of these discoveries that pulled her into this stealthy alter-life, and it was this promise that inevitably led to her grandfather.

Bill being Bill, he was always easy to find. All she had to do was spot his fire-engine-red 1976 four-door Land Rover with the Glory Peak emblem painted on its front doors. Usually, it was parked outside the Glory Peak offices, but sometimes, depending on the time of night, she would find it in the roundabout of Bill's driveway. He didn't spend much time in the local haunts, and from what she could tell, he was either working, eating, or drinking brown liquors. Often, he was up late, and if she spied him at home, it was usually alone, in his study, with a variety of binders, though a few times, she saw articles of lingerie draped over the leather arm of his office sofa, and during those times, a beige Lexus SUV in the driveway. On those nights it was always a risk to investigate as eventually he made it to his study to work, sometimes showing up almost naked, his hardening belly draped over tighty-whities like a mushroom cap.

Hating the sight of his near-naked body, she preferred to see him at the office, but sometimes the need to know rang too loud and brought Clover to a yard and pine tree she could sit under to watch her grandfather just be.

This night, she was happy to see his Land Rover in town. So, she took her familiar seat on the second-floor fire escape of the movie theater across the alley from Bill's office. Through the window, she could see him in a navy-blue Glory Peak polo and brown cargo shorts that fell loose at his knees. He stood in front of a large whiteboard covered in doodles and nursed brown liquor from a crystal tumbler. Watching him shuffle back and forth to the board, he occasionally circled words, underlined others, and connected some with a medley of directional arrows.

At first glance, there seemed to be a frantic sort of mania to the way he scribbled ideas on the board, but as Clover got lost in the theatricality of his gestures, they took on the impassioned aura of a conductor driving his orchestra to the most baroque reaches of their instruments. Finally, when the pacing and the scribblings ascended to the final movement, Bill drove home an emphatic crescendo and circled one word with a barrage of exclamation points. Hypnotized, she watched him take two steps back to admire his work. She then watched him turn toward the bottle on his desk and reach for a refill.

It was only then he saw his granddaughter's dirty blonde waves. Stunned, he placed his glass back on his desk, and like a hunter who stumbled on a deer, bent over, eating acorns, he stood frozen, and tried his best to not scare it into the forest.

Clover had the same instinct. And for thirty-four seconds, they both held their breath. Complete silence. Until Bill's office door opened, and someone entered with a banker bag. Then, Clover was down the fire escape, sprinting through Main Street, and heading back into the forest surrounding MacGregor's Ole Copper-Spoked Pass.

The following morning, when Clover was returning from a run around Punishment Lake and saw Bill's red Land Rover waiting outside the visitor's center, she was not surprised, just disappointed. Disappointed it took him until 10 a.m. to find her.

Hair brushed out, face shaven, he leaned over the hood and reviewed a scroll of architectural drawings. Still huffing from her workout, Clover glanced him up and down. Then, without saying anything, opened his passenger door and got in, ignoring the construction plans for the Nordic Center on the dashboard.

Driving down Yeehaw Pass, a filter of surreal discovery overtook her. Clover had been down this road a million times and knew every rock, tree, and hill that lined it, and for years, they all sat pretty and then, over time, became nothing special. But today, each shrub, blade of grass, and flower glowed fantastic. Normally, it was the sun or wind that amplified these elements, but Clover knew it was the simple presence of her grandfather, next to her in a car, that made her think she had entered a fantasphere.

This first morning, all they did was drive in silence. The second, third, fourth, and fifth mornings were just more of the same. Clover was hesitant to start a conversation and as much as she enjoyed spending time with this person whose shadow seemed to follow and fall heavy on her family, she knew

Nanny A hated him and her mother too. She wasn't sure about her father, but Clover knew he had never introduced her to Bill. Until now, she carried his name like a book bag she was never allowed to open. His genetic lineage weighing on her shoulders, traveling wherever she went, but somehow, never able to be taken off her back to examine what was inside. Bill was a stranger and her grandfather, a legend and, per Nanny A, the devil. Wondering about him for the last seventeen years, all she wanted to know was whether they would get along. On terms they defined themselves. That told her, *Yes, we are connected; yes, we are family; and yes, Clover, I care about you.*

Finally, on the sixth day of their time together, roughly twenty minutes into the drive, Bill mustered up the pluck to speak. Adjusting the rearview mirror, he said, matter-of-factly, "I hear you're a good cross-country skier." Eying him in the rearview, she revealed the tiniest arch of a smile, then turned her gaze to the neon green of a passing pine.

# CHAPTER 19

## SEPTEMBER 2001

I f Nanny A knew Clover was spending her mornings with Bill, she would have shat a limestone tepee—but she didn't. This was not necessarily because the idea of Clover spending time with Bill would be unheard of but because it never occurred to her that Clover would lie to her.

Nanny A believed Clover when she said she was extending her training to three hours, and she believed Clover when she said she befriended a vacationer who was training for the New York City Marathon. Sometimes, Clover told her she would miss dinner to hang in town with this vacationer, and other times, she told her she and the vacationer were going to spend Sundays exploring Mt. Frederick. And because she would always come home safe and smiling, Nanny A had no problem buying into the existence of this no-named vacationer.

After all, Wolfehaus needed her guiding hand—actually now, because of its size, Wolfehaus needed *both* her guiding hands, and if that meant letting up on Clover's leash, it was a growing pain she accepted.

Gunther respected Nanny A for allowing Clover this independence, as he believed that through independence, one found fortitude. Internally dismissing Gunther's philosophy as horseshit, Nanny A feigned agreement, knowing she had to keep Gunther's trust. That was, if she was going to take the lead in procuring the most important ingredient for Wolfe Mountain: land.

And she knew just the type of land she needed. Unlike Bill, she did not need a large heaven-pointing peak that rose stiff and hard with the sole purpose of inspiring awe. She needed something welcoming. Something that could wave hi and smile as it gave the snowflake the comforting hug of a snow-lined womb. This would be a challenge to find in Farangotta Valley. The valley was known for magic, but it was also known for chaos, a chaos that found form in hills, peaks, spires, lakes, and rivers. Cliffs emerged in parallel over an empty valley. Spires of rocks jutted like baobab trees as lakes formed from snow in a rocky bowl that, over time, collected in varied depths at the base of thirsty mountains. Tectonics, those underlying plates doing their dance just below the earth's crust, were up to nothing but trouble in the Farangotta. They were the punks of the geothermic music scene, looking for that spat of reason to get iron punching and limestone moshing. Ten million years ago, as the planet was finding its shape, these plates fought, brutal colliding fights that sent fragments of earth around like shards of glass in a head-on collision. It got dirty. And violent. But when the activity settled, a Seussian wonderland was left in the Farangotta.

Since moving to Fortooth, this was the one thing that never settled right with Nanny A. Farangotta Valley was not a place sculpted by Mother Earth. It was a place forged by Father World. Though the springs were lined with the florid ripeness of sprouting flowers, this was not a feminine land, and she wanted a feminine land. But everywhere she looked, she just saw phallic verticals and round boulders of gneiss, the geological equivalent of a parade of cocks and balls.

*Where is the fucking vagina?* she thought. The yonic cupping of a slightly sloping hill that ebbed and flowed in a D-cup of a mountain ridge, one that spread wide and warm for two to three miles.

In her first week of scouting, she found nothing. Her second week, even less. In her third week, she opted to stop using the car and investigate by foot. This choice pointed her in the right direction. It increased the scale of the environment and returned it to one of proper human dimensions.

She could now feel a discovery around a bend and better digest the sensual experience of trekking through a pass to a clearing. And then, one Sunday, during her sixth week of scouting, she stumbled onto her sleeping lady.

It waited several miles, beyond several peaks, behind the backside of Punishment Lake. To find it, she not only had to traverse hills but also push through a forest of pines so thick it obscured everything on the other side. Most people would have given in to this shield of forest, figuring it either went on forever or dead-ended at the base of a cliff. But Nanny A, for some reason, was pulled to what waited behind this pine curtain. And as their stacking thinned, and revealed a blossom of grass, she knew Wolfehaus had found the Farangotta's vagina.

Gunther agreed. When he finally made it through the dense pine, all he could say was, "*Meine gutness, meine gutness, meine gutness!*" Amazed, he ran his right hand through his hair and left it there until he realized that what lay in front of him looked like the spread legs of a sleeping woman.

Before him ran two ridges that ascended to a ledge. The ledge, wide and flat, rolled out for nearly two hundred soccer fields, then rose to a steep peak curved like a crescent moon. As he stared at what looked like an enormous amphitheater, a massive mirage of transparent overlays appeared where the main bowl and terrain park would sit.

The only problem, Nanny A later discovered, was the Le'Echuwanna had found it first. First in ritual, then in deed. This was the first lot of land they purchased when they decided to block Bill. Upon hearing this, Gunther resigned to search for another location, but Nanny A, realizing this information could help her accomplish something richer, decided to try to gain an ally in the creation of Wolfe Mountain.

She had never been to He Who Eats' home before. But every time she drove Yeehaw Pass, it came into view next to a large slate boulder on the flat of Copper Bone Ridge—a squat, two-story log cabin standing proud at the top of Sleeping Camel Lane. Before her scouting, she never had a reason to visit He Who Eats. But that was before she found the sleeping lady. Now things were different. Now she had a reason to chug her Subaru into his driveway, exit her car, walk to his front door, and press his doorbell where a loud lion's roar answered in a run of octaves.

When He Who Eats opened the door and stood before her in a flannel robe covered in palm trees, Nanny A realized this may have been a bad idea.

"You lost?" he asked pulling a bag of Skittles from the robe's pocket.

"Uh, no. This is actually where I want to be," Nanny A responded, arching her neck in an unconscious effort to seem as tall as possible.

"Where you actually want to be, huh? Well, I guess, then, why don't ya be inside? The 'squitos gonna bite my ass up if I don't get on some pants." With that, He Who Eats turned and walked into his living room.

Nanny A followed and on entering was struck by two things: the gamey smell of a stew cooking and the three enormous TVs all playing the same episode of *Futurama*. Scanning the room, she was impressed by the wide array of animal pelts and the headdresses embroidered with rust-colored beads and turquoise pebbles that hung from his walls. They reminded her of her previous life, teaching about the Achuar, and the Balinese fertility masks she collected on research trips.

Meanwhile, He Who Eats grabbed a pair of adidas track pants from his La-Z-Boy, pulled them on, shuffled over to the kitchen, and ladled out two bowls of stew.

Understanding the gesture, Nanny A grabbed a bowl and sat. A spoonful in, she was impressed.

"Is that elk? Holy shit, how'd you make it so tender?" she asked between bites.

"'Cause I'm a good fucking cook," he replied. "You think I got this swimsuit body piling shit into my mouth?"

He Who Eats then slid a small bottle of hot sauce toward her. Nanny A grabbed it and doused her stew.

"Whoa, whoa, settle down there, *gori-sabe*. That's some good old-fashioned fire juice. It'll burn a hole right out your sphincter if you don't watch it."

Nanny took a large bite and swallowed without a hint of discomfort. "Spice doesn't bother me. Actually, I love it. Sometimes I'll chew on a jalapeño just to wake up in the morning—it's better than coffee."

He Who Eats laughed and drank the remaining stew in his bowl in one large gulp.

"So, I guess you are as crazy as everyone says?" he said, grabbing a weathered leather pouch from a kitchen drawer. Shuffling back to his chair, he pulled a white pipe, carved from the antlers of an elk bull, from the pouch, then shook the contents on the table. "*Jimmy-waka-wa*," he shared as he lifted a large bud of marijuana from the table. "Some freshy-fresh Purple Haze."

It had been almost seventeen years since Nanny A smoked weed, and halfway through the first bowl, all she could think was, *Why haven't I been doing this every day?* Laughter, hunger, the desire to dance—that overall feeling of lightness. This would have gotten her through sleepless nights. This would have inspired her to eat breakfast again. This would have softened the slow, steady bleed of her heart that started the day the police called off their search party and declared her daughter dead.

Instead, all she'd had in the name of medicine was Gunther and Wolfehaus. Sitting on the sofa with a bowl of peanut M&Ms in her hands, she watched the three televisions play *Candid Camera*. She had never heard of the Pax Network before, but He Who Eats assured her they had some "quality programming," and she was happy to follow his lead. It was hard not to. He had no sense of accommodation when he spoke, and everything he did, whether it was pass her another bowl of weed or decide what to watch, came with a refreshing air of alpha authority. It was a relief not to have to make decisions and a greater relief to be around a man she did not have to mother.

When they finished the *Candid Camera* marathon two hours later, He Who Eats rose and suggested they go for a sunset walk. Grabbing his Kansas City Chiefs beanie, he handed her a pair of gloves large enough for a polar bear and led her outside.

Nanny A was not prepared to be outdoors. Though the sun was taking its final steps of the day, it still shone a potent sherbet orange and its warmth brought her a wide smile. Not knowing where to go, she was happy to let He Who Eats lead and followed him north as he fought huffs up a hill to the left of his house.

Walking almost in stride with him, Nanny A searched for words to start a conversation. Figuring the weather was too obvious to use, she glanced at his hat and said, "You know my son-in-law was a Chiefs fan."

"Yeah," answered He Who Eats. "Was it because he was an ignorant white bigot? Fucking Chiefs. *Redskins*. Let me ask you a question: Why do you think the NFL is still pushing that cowboys versus Indians shit? You guys don't feel like you got enough fucking wins under your belt?"

"I don't know, I don't really follow football," she answered.

"Of course, you don't. You're some type of professor, aren't you? So, riddle me this, Professor—why name two teams the Cowboys and Redskins if ain't for some hick white man still living out some boyhood dream of seeing some Little Bighorn shit? It's fucked up. You don't see us setting up a team of horse riders to chase down a team of wagon-riding *pi-ohs*, calling us Buffalo Hunters and you guys the White Douchebags."

Nanny A laughed. "True. But our country was built on the hubris and idiocy of the patriarchy. None of this would be here if it wasn't for the white man's intent on showing his penis to the world."

"Hah! That's some funny shit to hear from the woman who wants to take over the *Pe-ah-eh-oh*."

"The *Pe-ah-eh-oh*?" Nanny A asked, head tilted.

"Yeah, the *Pe-ah-eh-oh*—that range behind Punishment Lake that looks like a big-titted lady lying spread eagle on the ground. It means birthing mother."

"Hah! What a perfect name. What do you think about stopping up there at the ledge?" Nanny A pointed to a spot fifty yards uphill. On it waited two beach chairs and an Igloo cooler.

He Who Eats gazed at it, then back toward her. "Where the fuck do you think I was fucking taking you?"

# CHAPTER 20

## SEPTEMBER 2001, CONTINUED

D rinking his beer as the sun bled out, He Who Eats did not hear a single word Nanny A said as they sat atop Copper Bone Ridge. He did notice the passion in her eyes as she paced, pantomimed gestures of skiing, and emphatically slammed fists into her palms.

When she finished, He Who Eats just breathed deeply and turned his gaze to Jade Ridge. On it, he saw the silhouette of forty alpacas munching the sweet and tangy moss carpeting the limestone ridge. If Nanny A took a moment to observe the surroundings, she would have been blessed with this sight—the once alien, now fully organic sight of her daughter's alpaca herd living out their bliss in the Farangotta Valley. But instead, she was pitching He Who Eats on chairlifts and strudel.

Eager for an answer, Nanny A pulled a chair up next to him, her back facing the wonder of the forming night.

"So, what do you think?"

Taking a swig of beer, He Who Eats looked her straight in the eyes and said, "I think you got the biggest dick out of any *gori-sabe* I've ever met."

And that was the end of the meeting. Ten seconds later, with the sun near gone, He Who Eats rose from his seat, walked Nanny A to her car, and tucked her into the driver's seat. As the engine revved, he handed her a bud wrapped in aluminum foil and watched her disappear down the dirt road back to Yeehaw Pass.

*Poor fucking woman*, he thought. *She caught it. The mah-ne-mo. The swollen hunger.*

Turning toward his house, he could only imagine how sad her daughter, Annabelle, would have been if she'd heard Nanny A talk this way.

Thinking back, He Who Eats always liked Annabelle. Maybe it was the wild curls of her hair or the way she looked at the sky. Actually, it was neither of those things, he realized; it was his sense that she always aimed to be kind.

Which, after spending four hours with her mother, was something he learned was part of their genetic makeup. He saw kindness in Nanny A, but he also saw how the heartbreak of a mother who'd lost her daughter had turned that kindness into a need to feel something. Anything. No matter how toxic the feeling.

"Shit," he said to himself. "The *mah-ne-mo* is a dick."

But regardless of his compassion, he knew there were bigger things to contend with now. Nanny A had shown her cards and revealed that the Farangotta was no longer exposed to the ravings of one egomaniacal plunderer. There were now two. And the council needed to know.

But not until after He Who Eats had eaten more stew. And slept.

It was always a rare treat to see He Who Eats before eleven in the village. He was known as a *hoot-hoot*, a night owl, and showing up at 9 a.m. on a Tuesday meant one of two things: he was either still up from the night before, or something urgent, like death, was imminent. Stomping into the rec center library, He Who Eats saw a collection of teens working their way through a computer programming class. Teaching them was Squirreling Squirrel, who put down his marker when he saw He Who Eats.

"Well, hello, He Who Eats," he said. "How nice to see you this morning. Do you want to sit in and review DOS with us?"

"Hell no," He Who Eats barked. "I wanna get the council together ASAP."

"Well, we're not done with class," Squirreling Squirrel answered.

"Well wrap it up, nutbag. I'm gonna get Fancy Glove to spread the word while I prep the hut."

Shuffling through the mud hut, He Who Eats groaned at the amount of work needed to prepare for the Elder Elders' meeting. Normally, he showed up and it was already set up—one of the perks of being chief—but in assembling the pelts, prepping the fire, and filling the tobacco pouches, he realized this was just unnecessary dressing for what was, in fact, an emergency meeting.

Annoyed, he dropped the wood on the hut floor and walked back to the rec center. Deciding the small library was fine to hold court, He Who Eats lifted the kids from their seats and pulled their chairs into a circle formation.

Through the rec center windows, he could see the Elder Elders arrive. First was Pouting Trout, with Scared Crow helping him from her Volvo station wagon. He was frailer than at the last meeting, his skin so thin and translucent he looked like a skeleton dressed in plastic wrap. Behind them was Lady Dog. It had been a year since she'd last shown up for an Elder Elders' meeting, and outside of the *Oh-sah-cha-me* ceremonies, she mostly spent her time managing the paper mill and detangling her waist-length wild grays, which spread from her scalp like a litter of snakes. In the distance, driving as crookedly as one could while following a straight road, he could see Sleeping Mouse, the tribal lawyer who also managed their real estate portfolio. Unlike Squirreling Squirrel, he understood the value of action, and while his decisions were tempered with caution, his attendance showed promise.

Before they began their walk toward the mud hut, He Who Eats exited the rec center.

"Hey, yo!" he screamed. "We're not meeting up there! I set up a prayer circle in the library."

Groans and murmurs followed as everybody turned toward the rec center and walked into the library. When Squirreling Squirrel and Fancy

Glove finally arrived, Pouting Trout shared what was running through everyone's mind.

"He Who Eats," he started, "this is not a proper ceremony. What is your intention here?"

Annoyed by the time wasted even asking that question, He Who Eats shot back, "With all due respect, my wise Elder Elder, I don't fucking give an eagle's ass if this is a proper ceremony. We got some major problems we have to move on."

"He Who Eats, how dare you!" Lady Dog hissed. "That is not the tone of ceremony!"

"Lady Dog," He Who Eats punched back, "with all due respect, you haven't been to a meeting in nearly a year, so you can take your self-righteous talk of ceremony and smoke it out your canoe. Like I said: We. Have. A problem."

"Okay, okay, everyone," Sleeping Mouse interjected. "Chief He Who Eats has obviously woken early with much reason to call this. As our leader, it is his prerogative to make this meeting what he feels is best. One suggestion I do have is this: Chief Eats, for the tribal minutes, let's list this not as an Elder Elders' meeting but instead a tribal council meeting. That way, we can allow for a more casual exchange that is less about tradition and more about business."

"Sounds perfectly fucking fine to me, Sleeping Mouse. Fancy Glove, make a note in the minutes that this is a tribal council meeting."

Fancy Glove nodded and pulled a worn composition notebook from his JanSport bag. Undoing a rubber band that held it together, he entered the date: September 8, 2001.

The council was now formally in session.

Immediately, He Who Eats snarled into story. He shared of Nanny A's visit, the information that Wolfehaus was planning to build a ski resort to rival Glory Peak, and that they were looking to buy the *Pe-ah-eh-oh* from them. Everyone hissed and sighed as they listened and slapped their thighs when He Who Eats ended with, "And then I sent her stoned ass back to that Kraut's house!"

Settling in his chair, He Who Eats watched his words hover like smoke.

The Elder Elders had trouble receiving this information. There were just too many things to disbelieve. Wasn't Nanny A a highly regarded academic who started her career championing Indigenous people and feminine power? Wasn't this the mother of Annabelle Macklemore, the empathetic young woman whom they allowed to place an alpaca herd on their land? Wasn't Gunther just a failed Olympic skier squeezing out some dollars to make ski films and sell water bottles? Did this mean that Bill was no longer the only land-chewing *Eh-Kar-lo* in the valley?

"Aye, she has the *mah-ne-mo*," Sacred Crow shared. "That dirty hunger. It was only a matter of time. No one can stay pure when they lose their daughter like that."

"It is the *pi-oh* way," added Pouting Trout. "Since they came here from the Eastern Lands. First, they took the stones; now they want their holders."

Sleeping Mouse was much less impressed by the information. Rubbing his chin, his business side took precedence. "Are you sure she asked for our land?"

"Sure as fucking lint, I am. And I'm sure as lint she wants to build another resort there. She spent near thirty minutes talking about it like a cracked-out conjurer."

Sleeping Mouse continued rubbing his chin. He quickly pulled a BlackBerry from his jacket and ran some calculations. Moments later, he leaned back and heaved a sigh of relief.

"There is no way in hell they could afford a down payment of that size or get a loan to build something that competes. We are talking at least four million in cash."

"Yeah, but not for the land," He Who Eats countered. "If they do go that far out, she could get two thousand acres for probably a million dollars, if that. It's no man's land, *kemo*."

"Sure," Sleeping Mouse answered, "but they'll then have to spend another two to three million, to hire architects, get legal and the permit process going. There's no way they have the cash for that."

Putting down his pencil, Fancy Glove raised his hand and shared what he knew the Elder Elders did not know. "Excuse me, Elder Elders and Lady Elder Elders, I know I am just a Budding Elder, but I'm hoping to give some perspective here. Wolfehaus is probably the biggest up-and-coming ski brand in the US. Their videos are everywhere, they also started selling clothes and snowboards last year, and they just launched the fastest-growing outdoors magazine around. It's pretty sick, actually."

"How do you know this?" snapped Lady Dog. "That sounds absurd. Don't you agree, Squirreling Squirrel? Just absurd."

Squirreling Squirrel scanned the room, looking for an answer.

"Well," responded Fancy Glove. "Everyone I know either watches their videos or sports one of their stickers or shirts. It's the cool shit."

"Language, language," Lady Dog snarled. "You have not earned that right yet."

"Well, *I* fucking have, ya wet weasel," interrupted He Who Eats. "So now, not only do we have a vision, a woman with the thirsty hunger, but we also got a new *Eh-Kar-lo* with a shit ton of money to gobble up the valley."

Even Pouting Trout could not counter. But he tried to. "Let us ask the bones," he suggested, grabbing the pouch tied to his waist.

"Come on, Pouting T, we already said this is not an Elders' meeting. It's a fucking tribal council," He Who Eats huffed.

"Please—let's just *please* ask the bones," whispered Squirreling Squirrel. Watching him squint his eyes, it was the first time He Who Eats had a tinge of compassion for the man. He Who Eats next rubbed his head, about to be as surprised as everybody else over what he was about to agree to. "Fine," he relented, "but this doesn't mean what comes up is law."

Nodding, Pouting Trout reached into his pouch, grabbed four bones, and shook them in his hands. Blowing on them, he dropped them to the floor. A rhombus took form.

"Yes, fucking yes! We are going to war, we are going to war!" He Who Eats screamed and slapped his knee.

"Um, excuse me, Chief He Who Eats," Fancy Glove interrupted. "I do not mean to correct you, but based on our language lessons with Squirreling Squirrel, it actually translates to sharpen the sticks."

"So, what are you fucking saying?"

"He's saying," clarified Sleeping Mouse, "that we gotta get our ducks in a row. But it's not time yet to release the wolves."

He Who Eats stood outside of the rec center, waiting for everyone to leave—everyone except Fancy Glove. He knew he'd be the last one out, as the young ones always jumped on the internet and played with whatever computer things they could. For nearly twenty minutes, he paced around his pickup and munched through a bag of Twizzlers. Then, when the sugar spiked to an unbearable level, he stormed into the rec center, where he found Fancy Glove at an iMac. Startled by He Who Eats' approaching footsteps, Fancy Glove logged out of his AOL account, grabbed his JanSport bag, and looked up just in time to see He Who Eats plant his large body right in front of him.

"Chief," Fancy Glove said innocent. "I didn't mean to challenge you. I was just . . ."

"Follow me," He Who Eats barked, balling up the Twizzlers wrapper and throwing it at the nearest trash can. It hit the rim and bounced under a desk somewhere. "Don't ask any questions. Just come with me."

While He Who Eats drove them toward Punishment Lake, Fancy Glove packed a fresh bowl of Northern Lights. Surprisingly, He Who Eats declined when Fancy Glove passed him the pipe. Watching a falcon soar in the distance, a Fortooth dangling like rope from its beak, He Who Eats turned the radio silent and looked at Fancy Glove.

"So . . ." he said. His voice was a mellow baritone that had none of its normal thunder. "So how many of your friends do you think want to do the ceremony?"

Exhaling a deep cloud of smoke, Fancy Glove croaked out a quick "I don't know" before he entered a coughing fit.

"Come on, dude. You're the guy, right? The kid who's gonna take this over one day? So, how many?"

Officially high, Fancy Glove had no clue how to respond. *Take this over? What the fuck does he mean?* Hell, he just wanted the Elder Elder's salary—and to use the paper company to create a better rolling paper than Zig-Zag. Becoming chief wasn't something he'd given one gram of thought to, not even when he was weed-tripping high.

Fancy Glove shook his head. "Whoa, Eats, I mean, Chief, I don't know about all that—I'm just digging on learning about what we got here, that's it."

"Yeah, yeah . . . of course, you are. That, and figuring out how to use the paper company for something sketchy you got planned. But you're fucked. I seen it in your eyes. You got the warrior thing going."

Laughing, Fancy Glove took another hit off the pipe. "That's crazy, man. I can't even use a bow. I'd need, like, a grenade launcher to hit an elk."

"Eh, who cares about aim?" He Who Eats chuckled, waving a hand. "But I am telling you now, if you're going to be chief, you're gonna need some warriors."

"For what, dude? I ain't going on a raid."

"So wrong," He Who Eats countered. "We're gonna plug in the speakers and throw ourselves a fucking war party."

# CHAPTER 21

**NOVEMBER 1982**

A t the end of the day, the success of Paca Joe relied on sourcing. Ordering the fabric straight from Peru was proving to be cost prohibitive—and that was even if they blended it with wool, left it undyed, and opted for the lowest-quality alpaca yarn available. Taxes and shipping were just too much, making it impossible for Annabelle to bring sustainable Peruvian alpaca products to the Farangotta.

But Suzanne Dempsey had an idea. In fact, Suzanne had many ideas. And to Annabelle's surprise, all of them were pretty good—a natural outcropping of her time managing Danu's books and the leftover research she had from when she planned to move to London and get into fashion. She knew the process of pattern design, making samples, how to turn the samples into production, and what it would take to sell and distribute the product. And as an added bonus, because of the consistent buying Danu's did over fifty years, Suzanne was friends with all the sales reps in the outdoor clothing space. So, she knew what to charge, what the margins should be, and what expenses would be eaten up by the dinners needed to charm the whiskey-holics who bought the latest CB Sports jackets.

Inhaling a thoughtful drag from her just-lit Slim, Suzanne studied the latest first-run projections. The budget was too tight, and with just one bad batch of fabric or delay in delivery, she knew Paca Joe would fall into bankruptcy. Emptying a Sweet'N Low into her decaf coffee, Suzanne placed the projections on the table and looked at Annabelle.

"The fabric costs are too high," she said, stating a fact they all long avoided.

"I know." Annabelle sighed. "And I cut them down as much as humanly possible. It just costs so much to get it here."

Suzanne nodded and emptied a tablespoon of Coffee-Mate into her cup. After a few seconds of clanking her spoon around, she had an idea. "If only there was a way to source alpaca *here*."

"What do you mean?" Annabelle asked.

"I mean, if only there were alpacas here. Somewhere in the valley. A herd of them we could reuse every season and then not have to deal with the fluctuating cost of shipping. It's like if you were making beer and grew your own hops—you could control your production costs much more effectively."

It took a beat for Annabelle to understand where she was heading. She never thought about the possibility of owning an alpaca. Maybe a pygmy goat, but never a Peruvian camelid. Or a herd of one hundred Peruvian camelids.

"But how would one do that?" Annabelle asked. "I mean, how does one buy an alpaca? It's not like there are any farms or whatever around here."

"Can you ask your mother? Wouldn't she know of some vendors through her travels?"

"Possibly, but . . ." Annabelle shook her head, thinking of Nanny A's stringent ethical beliefs on white colonialization. "She would never condone taking a resource and income stream from an Indigenous culture."

"Gotcha," Suzanne responded. She then took another long drag from her Slim and an even longer sip of her decaf. "Sheriff Daley was telling me the other day about this German fellow who's squatting out by Miner's Gasp. He's converted his campsite into some sort of trading post that specializes in South American bags and clothes. Maybe he has a line on something?"

"Wouldn't hurt to ask," Annabelle said, shrugging. "Should we stop by?"

"Let me see if I can move my four o'clock doctor's appointment," Suzanne said.

"It's okay," Annabelle said, getting up from her seat. "I can head over myself. I'll call if I hear anything promising. Can you stay by your phone, just in case?"

Suzanne nodded dutifully, then glanced at the phone she had hitched to the wall.

Driving the winding pass toward Miner's Gasp, Annabelle took in the orange and yellow dotting the valley. She knew fall would soon crawl to a stop and white would next take over as the predominant color. These transition moments always unnerved her, preferring the destination of winter and summer to the in-between seasons that buttressed them. But somewhere on her drive, she wondered, *What if summer and winter were the transition seasons to spring and fall? Could the destination be in the withering of life and then in its rebirthing?* Her womb seemed to think so and pulsed as she steered her Subaru toward an Airstream in the distance.

For a temporary trading post, there seemed to be a lot of permanence in place. Cinder blocks steadied the Airstream's wheels, and around it, several tables waited with bags and jewelry. Next to them were clothing racks and across from that, a furniture section assembled to look like a living room. This was a showroom, one that only needed walls and a ceiling to call itself a shop.

As Annabelle parked her car next to a picnic table, Gunther Wolfe, the owner of this incredibly niche trading post was already walking toward her. He was far taller and far blonder than Annabelle imagined and peeled an orange in practiced pulls.

"Well, hallo, and *guten tag* to you!" he bellowed, his teeth as large and square as Rummikub tiles. "You have made it to the Andes Bizarrrré."

Annabelle offered a handshake, resisting the temptation to correct his pronunciation of *bizarre*.

"Thank you," she responded. "This is quite a setup you have here."

"You think? I have been trying my best to make it feel as welcoming as possible. In Peru, it is all about hosting. The invitation in and the sharing of community."

"You've been to Peru?"

"Ah, ya, of course! Peru, Ecuador, Chile, Argentina . . . Wherever there is fresh snow. And Pisco, of course."

"Ah, yeah, I miss the Pisco," she shared, a warm smile of nostalgia on her lips.

Gunther clapped his hands. "So, you have been to Peru, then? Amazing!"

Annabelle nodded and proceeded to share a brief history of her travels in the jungle. Gunther then countered with stories of his travels and how they evolved into the import and sales of these products, as he needed a way to support his powder addiction. Impressed, she asked where he sourced his sweaters.

Eager to share, he spoke of a weaver he worked with in Huancayo who could loom to the specifications of the larger Western figure. Gunther seemed to know a decent amount about alpaca yarn, and as he spoke in confused but formal English, Annabelle wondered if he was dumb or just one of those people whose happiness made them seem out of touch with the real world.

When Annabelle gathered enough information to report back to Suzanne, she decided, in the name of generosity, to go with happy, tarnished by a slight tint of stupidity.

Bobby was skeptical at first. He had no idea where to buy an alpaca, how to buy an alpaca, or where to put an alpaca, but when he saw the look in Annabelle's eyes, he accepted he would soon be a father to one hundred alpacas. Furthermore, his mom supported the idea, he learned when the three of them sat down that evening for a makeshift meeting at the Bull Yoke. Listening to the rationale, it was difficult for Bobby to argue, but he still had one question . . .

"How the hell are we supposed to take care of an alpaca?" It had only been three hours since Annabelle met with Gunther and Bobby barely had time to chew on this major change of plans, let alone the piece of venison in his mouth.

"Bobby, dear," his mother responded, "they are not delicate creatures. They're grazers. And if there's no grass, they'll eat hay. Just imagine furry cows."

"And shearing them? You know people who can shear them?"

"It's just like shearing a lamb. We know where to get clippers, and I know people in Portland who are willing to come down and manage that process," Suzanne answered.

Bobby jabbed a fork at the gristle on his plate. There was just one last question. "Well, we have no room at our place, so where we gonna keep them?"

Lighting a Slim, Suzanne smiled and said, "I was thinking I could buy the land behind the football field and lease it back to you guys. It's a large pasture and has plenty of room for roaming."

Just then, Walter Johanneson, the owner of the Bull Yoke, emerged with a chocolate lava cake sprinkled with powdered sugar and set the dish in front of Bobby. Swallowing the venison in his mouth, Bobby reached for a spoon, dug into the lava cake, and took a bite. A large chocolate-covered smiled followed.

"You look mighty happy over there," Suzanne observed.

Bobby swallowed the chocolate. It was rich, a slight aftertaste of cinnamon and coffee. It did make him happy, but the dessert still couldn't answer what Bobby was thinking, *Do I even have a say in any of this?*

Walter Johanneson had owned and worked at the Bull Yoke for most of his adult life. At twenty-eight, he opened it with the money he made while working for Prospecting Services Limited as a dynamiter. Not wanting to leave Fortooth when the mines shut down, Walter moved into a career he never expected—restaurateur.

There was need, of course, for a good steakhouse in town, and with his hunting expertise, he could source all the game they would serve from the valley. However, he had a lot to learn about the ups and downs of running a restaurant, and when the snow didn't come in the winters of '79 and '80, he would have lost the Bull Yoke to bankruptcy if not for a loan from William Jefferson Macklemore. A loan that came with a flexible payment plan and low enough interest rate that Walter knew, immediately, there had to be a catch.

And he was right. There was, albeit a minor one: Walter would receive the loan that would keep the Bull Yoke alive in exchange for gossip. Any circulating news or business-related gossip Walter came upon at the Bull Yoke, whether by local or tourist, would be reported back to Bill.

And the development of Paca Joe was precisely the sort of news that required reporting.

However, when Walter shared the news that Paca Joe was about to import a herd of alpacas to support a new sports-related clothing line founded by his ex-wife, son, and daughter-in-law, Bill feigned indifference. He also feigned indifference when Walter shared that Bobby Mac seemed to be in good physical condition and had an appetite that suggested he was skiing.

Thanking him with a double-fisted handshake, Bill watched Walter leave his office. He then walked to his giant whiteboard, selected a red pen, and wrote in uppercase, NO GERMS.

Two weeks later, the Fortooth city council passed legislation outlawing the international import of animals in Farangotta County. The aim was to protect the local livestock from foot-and-mouth disease. Somehow, this news never found its way to the *Fortooth Daily* or to the citizens of Fortooth. Which was why Annabelle continued meeting with Gunther to discuss alpaca lineage, shipping costs, quarantine issues, and barn building. Gunther had found a farm in Huancayo willing to sell a tenth of its herd and then positioned himself as the agent of sale. His commission on the deal would allow him to purchase the land he squatted on, build a house, and launch a real estate company. It also allowed for more time with Annabelle. He was very much enjoying her visits and the yerba maté they shared, and as a skier, he hoped once they got their footing, he would be the first athlete sponsored by Paca Joe.

It took a little under a year of planning, but finally Paca Joe was about to launch. Real soon. And with the delivery of the herd three weeks out, Bobby,

Annabelle, and Gunther decided to install a perimeter fence around the land Suzanne purchased behind the high school. For three days they dug and sweat, each one running a future in their head they wanted to share but for some reason could only keep to themselves. As Bobby hammered the last fence post in place, Gunther approached him and Annabelle with a ceramic jug. Smiling that innocent-or-maybe-stupid full-toothed grin, Gunther popped the jug and handed it to Bobby.

"In spite of the time we have not yet shared, Mr. Macklemore, let's share a nip."

"Pisco?" Annabelle asked.

"No, *chicha morada*. A special brew. I buried it underground for thirty days."

Bobby, broadcasting a Cheshire cat–grin, grabbed the jug and took a nip so big it led to a nap on the field. Annabelle followed with a sip too. Her sip pushed her home, to her bed, where sleep and a dream lined with alpaca hair felt so real it almost tickled her awake.

At 8 a.m. the next day, Annabelle, Bobby, and Gunther met to add the final backer rails to the fence. Waiting, to their complete surprise, was a summons stapled to the fence gate obstructing further construction and declaring the property condemned. Reading the notice taped to the entry gate, Bobby kept focusing on one word: animal.

"Shit, Bobby, what the hell is going on?" asked Annabelle. She was more calm than alarmed, only because she noticed a swelling anger in his breaths.

"Let's head to Suzanne's—I mean, Mom's—I mean, let's just get into town." Walking toward the pickup, Bobby noticed Gunther wasn't following. Turning around, he asked, "Aren't you coming?"

Gunther rested the shovel on the ground. "No. I think it is best you have your initial investigation."

Disgusted, Bobby opened his car door and gunned the engine.

Suzanne, of course, knew what happened the second Bobby shared the story. Grabbing a Slim and a lighter, for the first time, Annabelle saw Suzanne Dempsey have trouble lighting a cigarette. Her hands were shaking, and instead of fighting with the lighter, she broke the cigarette in two and kicked the kitchen wall.

When they entered the police department twenty minutes later, their chambers were loaded with a hollow-point round of "We want answers."

Sheriff Dan Daley expected this and emerging from his office, he knew it would take more than some soothing words to calm Suzanne down. Walking up to her, he hoped a smile would cool her boil.

"Dan," she began, pointing her car key at him, "do you want to tell me what the hell is going on here?"

"Sure thing, Suzanne," he responded. "How about we bring this conversation to my office?"

"Hell no! I want some answers now!" Suzanne barked.

Dan, still smiling, spotted a stack of papers on a nearby desk. He lifted them and placed them on the reception desk in front of her. Incensed, Suzanne batted them to the floor. Sheriff Daley then spotted a paper cup filled with water and placed it on the receptionist's desk. Suzanne swatted it into the wall, the water exploding over the waiting area.

Clearing the drops from his face, Sheriff Daley then asked, "Are you *now* ready to talk in my office?"

Sitting in Sheriff Daley's office, all Suzanne could do was harrumph. Harrumph and mumble, "That fucker."

Sheriff Daley understood her frustration and tried his best to explain this was all beyond his control, but she could not hear him. None of them could—especially Annabelle.

Trying her best to digest the facts, she asked, "So let me get this straight—a council meeting was called to order, which led to legislature restricting all invasive species and livestock in the Farangotta Valley?"

"Yes, ma'am," Sheriff Daley politely responded.

"I guess I am just confused. How does this just . . . happen? I thought people had to vote on something like this before it gets passed."

"Sometimes, yes. But this was an emergency meeting called when it was discovered you were planning on bringing in foreign livestock. There was concern over the possible spread of foot-and-mouth disease and other undetected viruses. The property is also close to the school, so there were additional concerns about safety," Sheriff Daley answered.

"That fucker, that fucker!" snapped Suzanne. "I'm going to cut off his foot and shove it in his fucking mouth!"

Suzanne's scream rattled everyone's ear. Scrunching her eyes, Annabelle grabbed her temples and asked, "So okay . . . I mean, that seems incredibly reactionary, and also, that's like, the whole point of quarantine. But I just don't understand. Who has the authority to call that meeting?"

Sheriff Daley scanned the room as it waited for an answer. In truth, everyone knew whose name he was going to share.

"Listen, guys, it's not like I wanted my deputy to post that sign. It's legal procedure, and I say this sincerely—it is my job to protect the law."

"Yeah, yeah, we know, Dan. Just following orders. If your mom was alive, she'd be having a seizure right now out of shame," Suzanne hissed.

Embarrassed by his mom's jab, Bobby jumped into the conversation. "Listen, Sheriff, I know this is a shitty position to be in, and I know you are truly not trying to harm us, but what are our options here? Like, do we have any? This is game time. The herd is coming in a week, and a month after that, they're supposed to be out of quarantine, waiting for us to pick them up."

"Well, you could appeal to the council to repeal the statute, I guess . . . but you'd have to get a meeting called, then convince two-thirds of the council to change their vote."

"That fucker!" screamed Suzanne. She then followed with a kick to the steel front of Sheriff Daley's desk. His cup of pens flew back, and his lamp wobbled to the floor.

"Let me ask you another question," Suzanne added with a snarl. "If you get a call on the radio in about twenty minutes asking to investigate a commotion out by Glory Peak, you think you could hold off on responding for a beat?"

"If it keeps you from burning down my office, without a doubt," Sheriff Daley said, reaching for a felt-tip marker on the floor.

Annabelle was petrified by the Suzanne she saw in the driver's seat. Her nose snorted staccato, and her hands gripped the steering wheel with enough power to bend it into a right angle. A nervous glance at the speedometer confirmed Annabelle's suspicions—they were going at least forty miles over the speed limit.

Bobby, sitting beside her, shared Suzanne's anger. Face swollen red, he squeezed the passenger side of the dashboard and dug his nails deep into its pleather.

"Goddamn it, Bobby, goddamn it! That piece of shit! I'm not going to let him ruin this for us! I promise you—I promise you *both*—over my parents' dead bodies, this interloping piece of shit is not going to kill this!"

Watching the town blur past, Annabelle realized this fury went deeper than any alpaca herd. It went to the night of Suzanne's wedding, the dream Suzanne had given up, and the reality that the Prince Charming she fantasized of at age six was nothing more than a Disneyfied lie.

Suzanne began to quiver as tears edged from her eyes. Through muted sniffles, the faint sound of her pleas filled the car. They were hard to decipher, but Annabelle finally made out the words: "God, help me, please don't let this son of a bitch ruin this for me again."

When they pulled in front of the Glory Peak offices, Suzanne seemed to have regained her composure. Wiping her puffy eyes, she looked at Bobby and Annabelle and said, "You two get out of the car. I'm just going to get something real quick."

Bobby eyed Annabelle, then looked at his mother and said, "Get *what*, Mom?"

She didn't answer. She just exited the car and walked to the trunk—where she pulled out a rifle case. Unpacking a double-barrel shotgun from it, she loaded two shotgun shells into its chambers.

Again, Annabelle and Bobby eyed each other, but this time much more severely. Before they could ask any questions, Suzanne pointed across the street and said, "Wait there."

Then, she walked over to Bill's green Land Rover sitting outside the Glory Peak offices, aimed the shotgun at the hood, and squeezed off a shot.

The hood exploded off the chassis and tumbled through the air. Naked to the world, the engine now revealed a softball-size hole and hissed from a ruptured waterline. Walking to the driver's side door, Suzanne next smashed the butt end of the gun through the driver's side window. Hearing the onslaught, people began to stumble onto the streets. Confused by the sight of Suzanne cocking the hammer of the second barrel, the crowd chattered as she aimed the gun at the dashboard and blew two-thirds of it to dust.

Bill, alarmed by the sounds of people screaming, ran to the railing of his office balcony to see what was happening. He arrived just in time to see his ex-wife load two more shells into her shotgun.

"Suzanne, what the hell are you doing?" he screamed.

Clicking the chambers of the shotgun shut, Suzanne walked to the back of the truck, raised her gun, and unloaded on the rear door. The spare tire hanging from it burst to nothing, the door now dangling from a warped hinge.

Suzanne then turned toward the balcony and screamed, "I am not letting you ruin this, you sack of shit! There is no way you are stealing this from me or Bobby!"

"Stealing what?" Bill pleaded. "I have no idea what you are talking about!"

Now walking toward the passenger side of the truck, Suzanne pointed her last shell at the spotlights on the roof.

"This is my fucking town, you scavenger! I want you the fuck out of it!" she yelled and pulled the trigger, firing into the lights. A flurry of sparks and glass shot onto the street and sidewalk. By now, everyone in the shops had filtered outside—tourists and residents both lost in the spectacle. Shockingly, no one attempted to intervene. Including Bobby, who watched proud as his mother swung the shotgun like an ax at Bill's windshield.

It was a sight, one so mesmerizing and unbridled, it held everyone's attention. And perhaps that was why nobody noticed when a spark from the blown-up headlight hit a puddle of gasoline and ignited into a full-fledged flame.

Practically frothing, Suzanne stood herself on the front bumper and hammered the exposed engine with the stock of the shotgun—unaware that, behind her, the flame began to trail towards her.

Bill, however, saw it from his balcony. Concerned, he pleaded for Suzanne to stop, but she couldn't hear him through her own shouting.

"You piece of shit!" she yelled. "I won't let you get away with your sick shit again! I know what you did. I know what you—"

And that was it.

As Suzanne's last swing dislodged the fuel line and emptied unleaded on the flame, she did not hear Bill's final scream of "Suzanne, please, I'll stop!" Or the sound of the fireball that exploded around her.

# CHAPTER 22

**FEBRUARY 10, 1988**

Annabelle didn't want to risk falling asleep, but it had been a long day. She'd gotten up early, met her husband to sign divorce papers, fell through a hundred-foot crevasse, and crawled into a temporary mineshaft.

Any of those events would've justified a deep sleep, but combined, they added up to something that suggested it all was too terrible to be real. Maybe it was a dream. And if it was, she wondered, if she did allow herself to sleep, would that mean she'd wake back up? Or would she just experience a dream within a dream and curate a whole different reality? One with Clover, her mother, and Paca Joe in every sports store in the United States.

Or one with a happy Bobby Mac; a happy Bobby Mac who never cheated on her, so she never cheated on him right back, and so they would have stayed together the way they always planned.

Opening her eyes, she rolled to her side and saw Bobby across the shaft. He was lying on his back, his right arm folded under his head as he stared at the ceiling. His clothes were tight, way too tight, and scrunched at the sides, revealing a four-by-six-inch scar below his left ribs.

She knew there were more scars, ones she couldn't see—like the one on his left shoulder and one that zigzagged from his nipple to his hip. A good portion of his upper body was covered in scars from when he caught fire the morning he tried to extinguish his mother as she burned to death on Main Street.

"Do they hurt?" she asked, her voice tentative, even childlike.

Surprised by her question, Bobby pulled his jacket down to cover his scars, forgetting for a moment that she'd seen them all before.

"No, not really," he said. "They, um . . . pull sometimes when I stretch too hard, and then there's sorta a dull pain. But nothing really besides that."

Looking at him in the flicker of the gas lamp, Annabelle remembered the day of Suzanne's funeral. Bobby, still recovering from his burns, could barely move. He had been silent the whole morning and navigated the day with the aid of a walker. Unable to raise his arms, Annabelle shook all the hands and received all the hugs on his behalf.

Everything that day was a gauzy blur, and it took what felt like a decade to return home. Getting into bed that night, she remembered how Bobby was curled in a C on his left side and how she curled up gentle just behind him. Then how hearing the light welp of his breathing, she pressed her lips against his. There was still a hint of Vaseline on his bandages, so she undressed him gently and placed her breasts soft against his chest.

It was the quietest love they'd ever made. She remembered drinking his tears as they fell and how, at climax, both their bodies quivered, and their hearts pulsed back and forth on the same beat.

Releasing a yawn on her cot in the mineshaft, Annabelle's entwined lashes blurred the memory. The memory then disappeared, replaced on the insides of her closing eyelids by a face, Clover's. Not four-year-old Clover, but the face of an older Clover, an eighteen-year-old Clover staring straight through her.

Now about to pass out, Annabelle just wanted to know one more thing. "Why, Bobby?" she whispered. "Why wasn't it enough to fight for for?"

## NOVEMBER 2001

Clover's appetite for early mornings grew with her senior year of school. It did not take long for her to understand there were limited hours in a day, and if she wanted to increase her training, she needed to get out there with enough time to maximize her conditioning—especially if she was spending her afternoons with Bill. Which, by now, was habit. She would meet him in the field that abutted the high school football stadium, where he waited in his red Land Rover. Clover had never seen his previous Land Rover, the one painted heritage green. And as long as he greeted her with hot chocolate or a roast beef sandwich with mustard and gherkins it didn't matter what color the car was. Especially if he had the legendary Glory Peak oatmeal cookies with him.

The rides themselves would vary in length, but the conversation would always focus on two things: her skiing and the inaugural race of the Glory Peak Nordic Center. Per the convos, Bill planned on having press at the event, and his publicity team was preparing full spreads in all the ski and travel magazines. He also informed her that he invited coaches from the US national team, figuring one day, they would use the Nordic Center as a training center for the Olympic cross-country ski team.

This information gnawed at Clover. She couldn't help but worry that he was pulling strings, moving pieces into place, somehow working to secure her victory as a cross-country Olympian before she'd even gotten the chance to compete for the gold. Clover had no problem with the idea of becoming an Olympian; it was what she worked for and what she really wanted, after all. But she did have a problem with it being given to her.

One day, as they walked the grounds of the soon-to-be-opened Nordic Center, she began a conversation long overdue. "Why did you never try to see me?" she asked in a tone without judgment—just a matter-of-fact query from an unemotional interrogator.

Bill laughed. Then laughed louder. He knew that someday this conversation was bound to happen, and here it was.

"Well, I tried," he said after his laughter died down, "but your mother made it clear that I was not welcome anywhere near you . . . and your father, well . . . we weren't on speaking terms when you were born."

"But weren't you curious? I *am* your only grandchild."

"Of course, I was. I'd inquire with whoever I could and read all the stories about you in the paper."

This, of course, was a drastic understatement. He had a full library of videos, pictures, and reports that stitched together a detailed biography of his granddaughter.

"But why didn't you try harder? You let them win." And for the first time in the exchange, Clover's voice betrayed an emotion. Anger.

"I didn't let them win," he responded. "And besides, it wasn't about that . . . You've got to realize, there were a lot of nuances to our family dynamic back then. As much of a cop-out as it sounds, things were complicated. In the end, it was about letting them feel like they won."

At this point, they stood by what would become the finish line. Flanked by bleachers and a large concession stand, Bill lifted a fallen café chair and arranged two seats at a table.

"So, let me ask you something," he added, brushing some November leaves off a tabletop. "Why do you like it?"

Clover had never been asked this question before. Nanny A, Gunther, and even Jimmy had never asked why she chose cross-country skiing. Looking out at a field that would soon hold several Nordic ski tracks, Clover thought and sat on an unfinished wood bench.

"It's mine, I guess," realizing as she said it out loud that her reason for loving cross-country was just that simple. "Because when I do it," she continued, "it has nothing to do with any of you."

It was not the answer Bill expected but far be it from him to question the motivations of a champion.

As the days led up to the inaugural 2001 Glory Peak Pilgrim's Rhapsody, Clover's focus was unprecedented. She woke at 5 a.m., waxed her skis until 5:30, and was out at Prescott's Loop by 6 a.m. Her goal was to start practice before the sun rose and to be a quarter through it when it hung full above the horizon. This way, she could watch the animals stir awake and watch He Who Eats lead the younger members on a hunt. Most mornings, they would skulk through the forest and hide under the snow, camouflaged by coyote pelts and pine shrubs. And some of the time, they would shoot arrows at trees, with He Who Eats instructing them how to maximize power and accuracy. Most struggled with the accuracy part—except for one skinny guy with a flop of long black hair.

Clover knew him as Fancy Glove, the kid who sold the super kind bud and whom she and Jimmy had watched sit naked in a tree and chant.

To her surprise, even as He Who Eats trained them, he still found time to leave Clover a thermos. But it was no longer filled with hot chocolate. Now it was a concoction of epazote, rose hips, cinnamon, rosemary, and star anise. The young tribesmen also carried it in their canteens, and if Clover had a chance to ask He Who Eats what it was, he would have told her what he told them: warrior juice.

Three weeks from race day, Clover informed her grandfather they needed to hold off on their meetups so she could focus on training. She would have said the same thing to Nanny A, but Nanny A was so entrenched in meetings with banks and architects that Clover seldom saw her. Which was okay because Clover was zoning. Her only distraction being the looks thrown at her in school by Jesse Vanigan. With Jimmy now gone, Jesse had resumed his slow-motion gazes, despite Clover's very public right hook. These looks of his unsettled her more than before because without Jimmy to take the edge off, her energy was skittish. And primal.

On the morning of the race, Clover did something she'd never done prior: masturbate. Once in bed, as the nerves shocked her awake, and then once in the shower, as they found her again under the warm water.

When she got to the kitchen for breakfast, Nanny A was there, and so was a bowl of piping hot Cream of Wheat. Grabbing a spoon, Clover wobbled toward the bowl, the shake in her grip too obvious to hide.

Nanny A shifted her gaze from her cost reports. "Is everything okay?" she asked. Clover didn't respond and placed the spoon back on the table.

"Baby," Nanny A continued. "You are going to do great. You got this." Forcing a smile, Clover rose from the table and went to the basement for her skis.

When they arrived at the brand-new Glory Peak Nordic Center, it was to the largest cross-country skiing crowd ever assembled in the Farangotta. State-of-the-art concession stands whipped up mocha-frosted lattes, as local news crews charged their camera batteries, and spectators laid out crisp twenties for Nordic Center beanies and hand warmers. Thanks to Bill, the future of cross-country skiing in the Pacific Northwest now had a face, and it fed on café-grilled egg croissandwiches.

Not surprisingly, the scene overwhelmed Clover. The quiet she'd hoped to find while preparing on the track was instead supplanted by a rodeo of cackles, microphone announcements, and hollers. And the participants—well, they seemed like they were from a different sport altogether. Their clothing was skintight, their helmets were aerodynamic, and they stretched and warmed their limbs with a professional intensity Clover had never seen before.

Scanning the crowd, she hoped to see Bill—his face hidden behind his mirrored Cébé sunglasses and the rest of him hidden behind a crowd of spectators—but he was nowhere to be found. Instead, she knew, he was sitting back at his office letting Nanny A feel like she won.

Dragging her eyes off the crowd, Clover stepped up to the starting line and scanned the field of participants. Their poles were planted, their skis sliding back and forth—and one, with an electric-blue skintight one-piece, stretched her arms to the sky, as though in prayer. She was tall, her shoulders broad, and her latissimus dorsi fanned out like that of a young Bruce Lee.

But it was her thighs, which bulged wide past her hips, that gave Clover the most worry. They were monsters—swollen monsters of anaconda cable that revealed the hours and years she must have spent in training. Looking down at her long, lean legs, Clover wondered, for the first time ever, if maybe she'd lose this race.

Rubbing her hands to bring some warmth back, Nanny A pulled Clover's race bib from her pocket and tried to hand it to her. Clover, however, had her focus locked on the flexing ankle muscles of Big Thighs in Electric Blue, completely unaware that Nanny A was standing beside her.

"You sure you want to do this?" Nanny A asked.

Snapped out of her daze, Clover blinked back at her grandmother for a few seconds before looking down the racetrack. It was an all-white imprint on an otherwise untouched expanse of snow that carved its way toward the trees where it then disappeared in the pines.

"Hey, Clover, you sure you want to do this?" Nanny A asked again.

Clover cleared her throat, but even then, her voice wouldn't come. Instead, she offered Nanny A a silent nod that she wasn't altogether sure she meant. There was more to their exchange after that—probably Nanny A asking if she was all right or reassuring her that this wasn't a big deal and that she had this race in the bag—but it all passed in a groan of sound.

Before she knew it, Nanny A was gone—Clover didn't even know where—leaving her dazed somewhere in the middle of the starting line. No longer was there a rodeo of noise, just silence. A silence so long, Clover swore the other racers overheard the beating of her heart.

When the starting gun went off, it took her a moment to realize the race had even begun. Transfixed by the stampede of competitors lunging for the front of the pack, Clover stood frozen. But then, the shrill sound of Nanny A screaming, "Go, Clove, go!" snapped her back to reality, and she dug her poles into the snow and pushed after the pack.

It took five minutes for her to catch the next competitor. Passing her on a small hill, Clover took a deep breath and finally eased into the rhythm of her motion. *Breathe in, double-plant poles, pull forward through the shoulders, spread the skis in a V-shape, then push off the back leg.* With each move she could practically hear Jimmy beside her, coaching her the way he used to.

*This is just another practice*, she told herself. *A practice with other people.* All she needed to do was breathe, plant, breathe, plant, again.

Settling into the comfort of this pattern, Clover glided past thirty of the competitors in the meat of the pack, sometimes two at a time. There were three still ahead though. The third-place skier was going to be easy to pass, seeing as she pretty much handed her position to Clover when she keeled over on a downhill stretch. The second-place leader was going to be more of a challenge, as her form was rock solid, but her breathing was not, and instead of taking calm breaths through her nose, huffed big and fast through her mouth. Soon her fingers would tingle, and when they did, her efficiency would wane, and then, of course, Clover would pass her.

And she did exactly that as she exited the long, left turn that led to the finish line, leaving the second-place racer nothing but a dot receding over her left shoulder. Planting and pulling, Clover now had to focus on one last racer—Big Thighs in Electric Blue.

If it wasn't for the technique she'd spent the last eighteen months honing, there would be no hope of a ticker-tape finish. But there were hours spent on the singular purpose that in a straightaway, there was no greater, faster, or more efficient cross-country skier on the planet than Clover Dolores Macklemore. Closing her eyes, Clover gave herself over to faith. Faith in her pole plant; faith in her edge; faith in her abdomen, abductors, gluteus, and rhomboid. Faith in Jimmy, who was somewhere in the Persian Gulf, thinking of her, and faith in her parents, whose frozen skeletons sat on the top of Miner's Gasp, watching, cheering, and clapping their skeleton hands as Clover dug deeper and deeper with every skate and plant. And while Big Thighs in Electric Blue did not waver, Clover released a final burst of muscle that kicked her into overdrive and carried her over the finish line by a curl.

The crowd erupted. A photo finish; a come-from-behind victory; a rookie-taking-down-the-favorite, underdog sort of win—the race couldn't have been better sculpted to highlight the possible drama of what William Jefferson Macklemore thought was the world's most boring sport. Cross-country skiing had officially arrived in Farangotta.

Fighting through a crowd of spectators and reporters, Nanny A grabbed Clover with so much force, she almost pulled her out of her bindings. Still high from the finish, Clover tried to relax her body's desire to keep skiing and wondered where Big Thighs in Electric Blue went. She wanted to give her a handshake—a hug, even—something to let her know she was sorry she had won.

It took a minute of scanning the crowd for Clover to find Big Thighs in Electric Blue. She was standing in the distance, behind a tree, at the far end of the parking lot. Watching her there, a stir of sadness woke in Clover. *Didn't she have family or friends there rooting for her? Someone to console or congratulate her after coming in second?*

Walking toward her, Clover watched as Electric Blue bent over and began digging around in her bag. Maybe she was looking for a protein bar or some medical tape to wrap her hands, but instead she revealed something Clover would never forget.

A stack of cash. Electric Blue was stuffing a huge stack of cash into her bag as a moment later, one of the event's organizers emerged from behind a copse of saplings to her left and offered Electric Blue a handshake.

Just like that, Clover took off for Electric Blue. But when the organizer laughed to himself and pulled a cellphone from his pocket, Clover turned and decided to follow him instead. Hiding between SUVs in the parking lot, she kept a safe distance, but then, when he reached his Ford Bronco, Clover saw the one thing in the world she hoped not to see—the Glory Peak logo on the driver's side door.

The awards ceremony was a haze. Clover did not want to stand on the podium. Did not want to pose with a trophy. Did not want to spend another moment at the Glory Peak Nordic Center. And when the crowd—and Nanny A—cheered for her, she felt her face go red with shame. Big Thighs in Electric Blue, despite scoring second place, was nowhere to be found, and selfishly, Clover was happy about that. To face her would've been too humiliating.

On the drive back, all Clover could do was focus on the acidic storm rumbling in her stomach. She wanted to puke—all over the car, all over the valley, all over her grandfather. Nanny A was oblivious, of course, and rambled on and on about celebrating and Wolfehaus featuring her in a series of cross-country videos and how this was the perfect start to Clover's professional career. When she suggested filming her on an ice trek in Greenland, that was the final straw.

Clover vomited a cluster of Cream of Wheat on the windshield.

Screeching to a stop, Nanny A asked the obvious: "Oh my God, Clover, are you okay?"

"Yes!" Clover screamed back—even though the pitch of her scream contradicted her statement. "I just want to get home!" At least she meant that part.

Putting the car back in drive, Nanny A revved toward the house. As she parked in the round of the driveway, Clover shot out the door and ran to her bedroom. Jumping onto her bed, she released a flurry of sledgehammer punches at her pillows. Rolling onto her back, she then released a flurry of kicks at the ceiling. Snapping to a seat, she turned towards her windows and saw Glory Peak, sitting like a turd in the distance.

She had to go to town. Now.

Passing a concerned Nanny A coming up the stairs, Clover ran out the front door and headed toward MacGregor's Ole Copper-Spoked Pass. Chugging down the trail, she got to town in record time, oblivious to the herd of alpacas observing her from the lip of Jade Ridge.

She began pacing outside of Glory Peak's offices as soon as she arrived. She had never stepped foot inside them before. Unsure of what to do, she placed her palm against her forehead and rubbed it furious. Then, wiping any evidence of tears from her eyes, she opened the front door and stepped in.

It was evident right away that she was unexpected. Everyone in town knew who she was, and everyone in the office knew who she was to infinity. Sizing up their reactions, Clover walked over to the receptionist.

"I am here to see my grandfather," she said.

The receptionist, holding a watering can above a wilted petunia, stared back at her, eyes wide open.

Clover stepped closer. "Is he here?" she asked, enunciating each word. Still unsure how to respond, the receptionist continued hydrating the petunia, water now overflowing on the floor.

Shaking her head, Clover stormed past her, up the stairs to Bill's office.

On entering, it did not hold much of a surprise. She had seen it hundreds of times from the fire escape, so she knew its landscape. But the smell was something she did not expect. Musty, moldy, it hovered someplace between fresh moss and dirt after a rain. Scanning the shelves, she saw photos of her grandfather and Glory Peak throughout the years. They did not interest her; she inventoried them before. But something did—the giant whiteboard on his west wall.

Walking toward it, she saw half-smeared words, the ghost of sentences under recent ones next to partially written ideas. For the most part, she recognized it was gibberish, but there was one section, on the mid-to-left side, that grabbed her attention. On it, in large capital letters, was Project Golden Thingy. Around it, written in red and blue, were the words dig, grease, hurt, and scholarship. And most freshly written and underlined, wampum.

Most people would not have understood the meaning of this collection of nouns, but Clover was a Macklemore, and whether or not she wanted to accept it, she spoke Bill. So, it didn't take her long to decipher his riddle, and when she did, her worst fears were confirmed: Bill had been orchestrating the success of her cross-country skiing career.

Her heart now pumping as fast as if she was racing, Clover searched the office and found a letter opener in a side drawer. Pulling her first-place medal from her pocket, she walked over to the board, placed it over Project Golden Thingy, and slammed the letter opener through its ribbon.

Seconds later, she was back on Main Street and, shortly after, turning left onto Penguin Tip Lane. Within fifteen minutes, she was at the door of a large wood-and-stone mansion ringing an echoey doorbell. It took a moment for the organ reverb to settle, and when it did, the door creaked open to reveal Jesse Vanigan. He had a half-smoked joint in his mouth and, unsurprised, cleared the doorway for Clover to enter.

Biting her lip, she stepped in and took in the cavernous living room. Weird, massive canvases of geometric grays filled the walls, and rectangular brass sculptures sat on shelves and floors. Everyone in town knew Jesse was rich, but this somehow seemed movie-rich, where butlers pulled wine from cellars and disinterested parents talked of St. Barts trips and whether they needed a larger yacht for the crew.

Strutting toward the kitchen, Jesse slinked onto a stool at a large wooden island. Not sure what to do, she followed and stood next to him. Staring her up and down, he took a hit off his joint and offered it to her. She waved it away and instead took a deep breath and arched her toes. No longer capable of avoiding his eyes, she lunged forward and smashed her lips against his. After a long and sloppy kiss, Clover pulled back and stared at his face. A trail of smoke crept from his right nostril. Watching it twirl up his cheek, Clover pressed her nose against the side of his face and inhaled the fume, fully knowing she would never cross-country ski again.

# CHAPTER 23

**MARCH 1983**

The weeks following Suzanne's death were filled with silence. A brutal silence. For Bobby. For Annabelle. For their house. And two months after the love they made the night of Suzanne's funeral, Annabelle confirmed what she had already known—she was pregnant. At first, she did not want to tell Bobby, he was still too lost in sadness. She wanted this to be happy news, but that wouldn't happen until he finished grieving. And so, she'd waited.

But when Bobby stopped coming home for dinner and instead spent his nights wandering the backcountry, she knew she had to share the news. So, at the end of her second month, over a dinner of pilaf and Kraft macaroni, Annabelle told Bobby he was going to be a father. At first, there was no response. Then Bobby grabbed his mug of Molson and downed it in one gulp. Ecstatic, he threw it against the wall, ran to Annabelle, lifted her in the air, and twirled her like a figure skater.

"I'm gonna be a daddy! Are you shitting me, Belle? I'm gonna be a daddy!" Bobby beamed in ways Annabelle had worried he never would again. Placing her back on the floor, he sprinted to the storage room and came back with a brown paper bag.

Relieved, Annabelle asked, "What's in the bag?"

"You'll see," he said. Then smiled, grabbed her hand, and walked her to the car.

When they got to the top of Feather's Edge, the moon hung like a diamond drop pendant in the sky. Sitting Annabelle on one of the stone benches, Bobby unrolled the top of the paper bag and took out an assortment of fireworks. Handing her a Roman candle, he made sure the fuse was dry and visible.

"Okay," he said, "the key is to dig as deep as possible in your heart and wish for what you want. Boy or girl. And then we light it, okay?"

Annabelle closed her eyes and took a giant gulp of the Farangotta night. Then, like a ghost appearing before her, the vision of a girl named Clover came into focus. Opening her eyes, she looked at Bobby. He was pulling a bottle of Fireball from the bag and a box of long matches they used to light their fireplace.

"Hot damn, we are gonna get crazy tonight. You ready, Belle?"

Annabelle looked him over as he lit two matches on the bottom of the box, then took a giant swig of the whiskey.

"Okay, I'm ready," she said. The problem, she realized, as Bobby spat the whiskey in his mouth on the match flame, igniting a flash of fire in the night, was that Bobby was not.

⋎ℛ

For the next two months, instead of sharing in the excitement of Clover's upcoming arrival, Bobby focused on winter. Snow came fast and dry and long that season, one of those rare Farangotta years that had snowfall through June, and Bobby insisted on getting first tracks every morning and last rounds ever night at the Horned Pony. The drinking never bothered Annabelle in the past, and it really didn't now. The problem was that Bobby chose to spend his time at a bar, with people she didn't know, over her and their soon to be born daughter.

There were other concerns, too. Like the herd of alpacas that needed to find a home and what to do with Danu's and the employees. With Bobby gone most days, Annabelle would travel out to Gunther's to share yerba maté and relay her heartbroken concerns for the herd.

"Just imagine," she would say. "Just imagine you wake up one morning and you are shuttled onto a truck, which you probably had never seen before, and then onto a plane, which you probably never even knew existed, and sent to a place as far off from yours as possible. And instead of grazing on a field, you're locked in a warehouse, listening to a language you can't understand. I mean, how would you know where you were? Like, as in, whatever world you understood—and I guess, for them, that's alpaca world—how would you know where you were in alpaca world?"

Gunther would always nod and answer with the same "Good question," then return to building the porch he was adding onto his house.

Thankful for his ear, these conversations with Gunther were almost enough to weather the days. But when, one morning, she found Bobby passed out in the laundry room, covered in puke and urine, she knew she needed to call in reinforcements.

## JUNE 1983

Nanny A never expected to move farther west than Colorado. Boulder was perfect for her—and as her women's studies courses gained national recognition, and her four bedroom Victorian overflowed with the Balinese, East African, and Ecuadorian artifacts she collected from her research adventures, Nanny A began to think she had done the thing few people in life got to claim—won.

But, as the pendulum swings its bulbous base both ways, when it was discovered Nanny A was sleeping with a senior named Jack Dempsey Florence-Schwartzberg, life turned south—fast. As was stated in the university bylaws, it was forbidden for a professor to have any sexual relations with a student, and if discovered, it would result in immediate termination. However, due to Nanny A's visibility as department head and her regard within feminist academia, the university chose to suspend her for the year rather than fire her outright. So, when Annabelle called and asked her to come to Fortooth to help with the pregnancy—and secretly, to help her with her drunk, absent husband—the timing could not have been more Seiko.

It took her no more than two days to find a renter for her place, and while it was, at first, tough to step away from her department, she realized her attachment was more ceremonial than genuine. Within a week she was packed, and the night before she left, she celebrated her "vacation" with merlot, rainbow trout, and Jack Dempsey Florence-Schwartzberg's enthusiastic attention at the Stanley Hotel. Slipping out to the dewy haze of a Monday morning as Jack snored in the hotel room, two thoughts jostled around in Nanny A's head: *Thank god, I don't have to give another fucking lecture*, and *I hope Jack's next girlfriend teaches that poor kid how to give oral.*

The drive itself was unmemorable. There was Cat Stevens's *Greatest Hits* on replay, a BBC audio recording of *The Hobbit*, and terrain that seemed nice, but if asked, she would offer the same response she gave when asked about the writings of Stephen Jay Gould: "Fine."

After twenty-three hours and a steady serving of coca tea, Nanny A finally pulled into the valley. Looking at the massive granite cliffs that flanked both sides, her first thought was that of a coffin waiting to close. Her second was a fleeting thought of Jack Dempsey Florence-Schwartzberg accompanied by a sigh and a slight itch to her inner thigh. She realized she would need a new lover soon. One who allowed for steady relief from what she knew was going to be the hokey boredom of a town stuck in the snow-covered Americana of a once better time. And one more appropriate for a fifty-one-year-old.

Turning left onto Yeehaw Pass, she was already beginning to loathe the idea of feigning interest when the locals talked about what the town was like when the mine was open. Lost in a swirl of snarky retorts, she barreled ahead, oblivious to the oncoming pile of shards in the middle of the road. As she plowed through it, a sharp rock stabbed her tire and sent her toward the shoulder, forcing her to slam on her brakes and send the boxy ass of her Volvo in a fishtail.

Livid, she placed the car in park, pushed open her car door, and examined her front right tire. Spotting a large hole, she let out a primal "Fuuuuuuuuck!"

when, down the road came the rickety Ford Bronco of Sheriff Dan Daley. Easing to a stop, he exited his car and walked over.

"So, what do we got here?" he asked in a voice with less drawl than she expected.

"I ran over a freakin' rock pile. Goddamn tire is shot," she responded, trying not to judge his mustache or the mirrored aviators he wore.

"Well, that happens on occasion out here. Nothing a tow and Jim in town can't fix." Nanny A looked at him. Her face reflected in his glasses, and she wanted to take the toothpick out of his mouth and throw it into a fire, but the side wrinkles that peeked out from behind his frames suggested both a smile and a genuine welcome to Fortooth Bend.

Overall, Sheriff Dan Daley wasn't half bad—at least that was Nanny A's initial impression of him based on their banter during the drive to Annabelle's. By the time he pulled his Bronco into her daughter's driveway, Sheriff Dan offered her his card and said, "If you're ever interested in getting the best nature tour in Fortooth, give this guy a ring."

Nanny A glanced at the plain white card with bold black letters. "This guy? You mean Sheriff Dan Daley?" she added with a laugh, pointing at his name on the card. The sheriff went red, realizing his joke hadn't landed the way he'd hoped.

"I was trying to be clever, but I guess—"

"I'm not expecting to be here long," Nanny A interjected, swinging open the truck door and stepping out onto the gravel driveway. Ducking slightly so she could see the sheriff's red face through the passenger window, she added, "But if I've got time, I'll be sure to give *this guy* a ring."

The sheriff grinned, a whole new hue of red covering his face. Nanny A grinned, too, and began walking toward Annabelle's house, deliberately not turning around to wave goodbye.

Despite the ragged herd of alpacas wandering outside, the exterior of Annabelle and Bobby Mac's house was nice. Much nicer than Nanny A imagined. But stepping through the door told another story. There were dishes piled head-high in the sink, unfolded laundry thrown on every inch of the sofa, and the outline of a puddle on the floor that looked like spilled beer but smelled like urine. Then there was her daughter standing in the kitchen, way too skinny for a woman three months pregnant.

Nanny A opened her mouth to say something, but she wasn't sure how to phrase it. In the seconds that she scrambled for words; her eyes locked with her daughter's.

"Honey, this is . . . Listen, we'll sort all of this out, okay?"

Annabelle nodded—her eyes wide, stoned, lost somewhere in the living room walls. Nanny A couldn't even tell if she was alive. But then her facial expression woke and in two strides, Annabelle made her way to her mother, just in time to weep in her arms.

After her cry, Annabelle wiped her face, sat at the kitchen table, and watched her mom load the dishwasher. No clue where to start, she just blurted out, "It's not that I don't sympathize—his mother was great—and I mean, she was amazing, even if, at first, I didn't think so. And she was so incredible with Paca Joe."

Nanny A wasn't sure what to say to her daughter. In moments like these, she knew it was often best not to say anything. Her purpose here was to patch a hole in the vacuum seal of her daughter's sanity, not to dose out opinions about the life she built in this relic of a town founded on the misguided self-importance of white manifest destiny.

"I mean, like I said, I get it—I get that losing Suzanne was horrible," Annabelle continued, shaking her head. "I was there, for God's sake! I watched her shoot up Bill's car, watched the gasoline and . . ." Annabelle paused, her eyes filling with tears all over again.

"But, Mom, it's been months now, and we've got a girl coming. And I need him here. I need him helping." Annabelle sniffled, using her forearm to wipe her nose. "I mean, I nearly piss myself every time I feed the alpacas from all the bending over."

Pausing from the dishes, Nanny A turned to her daughter. "Wait, you're telling me he's not even helping you feed the alpacas?"

"No," she responded. "All he does is ski and prep his gear. He doesn't even speak to me during dinner anymore, and half the time, he's in town until two in the morning, and then . . . I don't even know."

Nanny A held still. Then, slowly, she wiped the suds off her hands, turned to face her daughter head-on, and asked, "You don't think he's having an affair?"

Annabelle blinked a few times, her eyes returning to that stoned, lost-in-the-walls look Nanny A saw when she arrived. Shaking her head, Annabelle said, "No, no . . . he's not having an affair . . . I just don't think he's ready for this."

Nanny A confirmed her daughter's theory when Bobby returned home. He smelled like chili, cheap bourbon, and avoided every one of her attempts at eye contact. Before she could even inquire about how he was feeling about becoming a father, or the launch of Paca Joe, or anything at all really, Bobby was already excusing himself from the conversation and driving back to town.

Over the next month, Nanny A watched in disbelief as Bobby continued this disturbing behavior. Knowing she would soon be back in Boulder, she chose not to address the problem. Instead, she focused on what life would be like if she brought Annabelle back to Colorado with her. Yes, it would interrupt her visits with Jack Dempsey Florence Schwartzberg, and did she really want to be playing wet nurse at fifty-one to her depressed, unemployed, single daughter?

This option, however, became irrelevant when she checked back in with Dean Plitzker, who ran the College of Arts and Sciences. In a rambling, stuttering, poorly phrased phone call, Dean Plitzker informed Nanny A she was being removed as department chair and would not be allowed to return for the fall semester. He additionally informed her that the university, out of respect for her groundbreaking accomplishments, was prepared to keep her tenure status if she would sign a confidentiality agreement regarding her dismissal. Accepting her time there had run its course, Nanny A agreed, and minutes after the call, informed Annabelle she was moving to Fortooth to help with Clover and Paca Joe. Ecstatic, Annabelle began talk of turning the garage into an apartment. But Nanny A quickly shot that down. If Sheriff Dan Daley was to become her lover, she needed all the privacy she could get.

The plan moving forward was simple. She was going to drive back to Boulder, put her items in storage, place her house on the market, and return before Annabelle went into labor. She still had five months before her due date, and that would give her plenty of time to wrap up twenty years of her life and make it back for last-minute adjustments to the nursery. Seeing Bobby splayed out on the living room sofa the morning of her departure, she decided it was time to talk. It took her a few minutes and a rough amount of shaking, but she was finally able to wake him, the crusty remnants of ketchup and barbecue sauce still on his chin. "Abigail," he mumbled. "What's going on? Is Annabelle okay?" Kneeling in front of him, Nanny A grabbed his hands and looked him right in the face.

"I'm heading back to Boulder. And I am sure Annabelle told you I'm going to move here for a bit to make sure you guys have an extra set of hands with the baby and to help get all the Paca Joe stuff back on track."

It took a beat for Bobby to register her words. "Oh yeah . . . Annabelle told me. You're getting a place, right? Or should we start work on the garage?"

"No, I'm gonna find my own spot. But listen, and I need to make sure you hear me on this, Bobby," she said, waiting a few breaths to make sure his eyes meet hers. "I need to know you're going to take care of Annabelle while I'm gone. It's just ten days, Bobby, so ante your shit up and make sure nothing happens to my daughter."

Bobby wasn't sure how to respond. Taking his hands from Nanny A, he began to rub his eyes. "I, uh, yeah, sure, uhhhhhh . . ."

Nanny A reached for his face and grabbed his chin with her right hand. Bobby's eyes spread wide. "Wrong answer," she said, her voice direct, almost even flat. "Promise me, Bobby. Promise me you will stop being such a spoiled little man-child and make sure Annabelle and your unborn child will be okay."

Barely able to move his lips, Bobby released a faint "Okay."

For the next five months, Bobby was a man of his word. But as the snow fell in December, his promise became harder to keep. Specifically, December 27, when he woke early, made Annabelle a fried egg breakfast, and dropped her off in town for doctor's appointments and bank meetings. Returning to the house, he then settled into the fix-it work he needed to do on the alpaca pen they had built along the front side of their house. By noon, he was able to get the hinges on the door replaced, and by three, the rotted two-by-fours in the hayloft were swapped out with new wood. At this point, he was sweating and hot, despite the cool winter air, and wanted a drink. What showed up, instead, was Tubby's son, Baby Tubbs, and Baby Tubbs's best friend, Lou Paul Ginger. They weren't invited, but they did have two brand-new Yamaha Phazer snowmobiles just picked up from Harold's Sports World off highway 690 and were excited to test them out at the base of Goldfinger. At first Bobby was hesitant to abandon his work but eventually succumbed when the promise of Southern Comfort and Thai stick was presented. Looking at the belly peeking out over Lou Paul's belt buckle, Bobby asked, "You promise me we'll be back by six?"

"Hells yes," Lou Paul responded, flashing a chipped incisor.

"Actually, five forty-five would be better," Bobby added, then corralled the nearby alpacas into their pen. Grabbing Baby Tubbs's bottle of Southern Comfort, he settled into the back of Lou Paul's Ford Bronco and watched the snowmobiles rattle on the trailer as they headed down Yeehaw Pass.

When Annabelle returned from town and realized Bobby was nowhere to be found, she was livid. Not only did Bobby forget to pick her up at six like he'd promised, he also didn't finish installing the latch on the alpaca pen, and she found half the herd roaming around the front yard. And then when she did get into the house, she saw the freezer door swung wide open, ruining the pint of Haagen-Dazs coffee ice cream she spent all daydreaming about.

Slamming the freezer door, Annabelle shouted, "You motherfucking, cocksucking, fuckface!"

Her anger shot through the house like a fireball. Unable to wrangle it, Annabelle punched a kitchen cabinet, then kicked the wooden cutting block. Tears followed, and after, a wailing slump on the floor. Finally, when the anger trickled to nothing, and her breathing returned to normal, Annabelle sat against the refrigerator door. Grabbing the handle to pull herself up, a sharp bolt of electricity shot from her lower spine to the bullseye of her belly button. The baby inside her was moving. Kicking. Punching with open, pointy fingers. It wanted out. Now. Sweating, she walked to the couch and tried to sit as a stronger wave of pain rose from her spine to her abdomen.

"Holy... wow!" she screamed. Her face now dripping sweat, she waddled to the phone in the kitchen. Gasping as another contraction hit, Annabelle grabbed the receiver, then tapped 911 into the keypad.

When a voice finally answered, she sputtered, "Help. I need help! I think I'm in labor." Fighting the rush of heat running through her body, Annabelle looked at the front door. "Bobby," she wheezed. "Where the hell are you?"

The answer was on a snowmobile circling the base of Goldfinger. Purring, the Yamaha hugged the ups and downs of the mountain base and slid into left and right turns with a smoothness that made it feel more motorbike than snowmobile.

Grinning that ten-thousand-watt grin, Bobby speed through each turn as 150 gallons of liquified courage warmed his veins. But when he slowed and looked up at the fingernail clipping of a moon, a reminder of life off the snowmobile appeared. It had stars for eyes and the shy smile of a sleeping Annabelle.

Seeing her, Bobby squeezed the snowmobile's brakes and skidded to a stop. Then, turning the snowmobile around, he felt a large gasp of air fill his heart. He needed to be back home. Immediately.

Panic flooding through him, Bobby gassed the engine and aimed the snowmobile at the large shoulder where Lou Paul's Bronco was parked. What he did not count on was Lou Paul and Baby Tubbs careening, like a drunk duck, toward him on the other snowmobile. Yipping and hooting, they launched off a fallen tree trunk and came straight for the heart of Bobby's snowmobile. As he darted right to avoid them, Bobby's snowmobile now aimed straight at the Bronco.

The collision that happened next was too fast to comprehend. A roar of metal was released through the valley and Bobby was somehow launched onto the hood of the Bronco, then into a snowbank. When Bobby woke two hours later in the intensive care unit of Farangotta County General Hospital, he learned that he shattered his left kneecap and fractured his right clavicle. He also learned that his daughter, Clover Dolores Macklemore, had entered the world. She was sleeping in the maternity ward while her mother, who was found unconscious among a herd of nervous alpacas, was being treated for hypothermia.

# CHAPTER 24

## FEBRUARY 2002

For months, Bill Macklemore waited in the parking lot of the Glory Peak Nordic Center for his granddaughter to show up. Like clockwork, he would arrive at 3:27, wait thirty-three minutes, and drive back to his office when Clover inevitably didn't arrive. He'd then meet with his staff and discuss expansion plans into the Boneyard.

The rumors he'd heard about Wolfehaus building a competitive resort proved to be true, and to stymie their growth, he started buying up swatches of land around the valley. In addition to being the largest employer in the Farangotta Valley, Glory Peak Enterprises was now the largest landowner. An impressive return on the five-thousand-dollar loan Bill needed cosigned by Suzanne for his initial lease payment on Glory Peak.

Scanning his office of employees, all he could think to himself was, *God, I wish Bobby was here to see this.* But his son wasn't, and in many ways, never was. Looking at all the eager faces ready to cut themselves for his approval, Bill wished one of them had the spine to challenge him. Tell him his font choice sucked, or the name of the beet salad was stupid, or that he should wake his old ass up and start doing something that didn't have the stale smell of typewriter ribbon.

After the head of business development finished his report on bumper sticker sales, Bill excused the employees from his office. Alone, his body started to itch, and his skin began to turn red. He was having a hot flash of some sort, one that came with an oncoming wave of needlelike pricks. His throat beginning to close, Bill pulled off his fleece and turtleneck. Still gasping, he opened his balcony doors and stepped shirtless into the cold winter air.

His nipples stung, but relief soon took over. Relaxed, half nude on the balcony, Bill drifted to memories of skiing down the Italian Alps and the feeling of his testicles touching snow as he made love to Chiara on a winter hike. *He could have loved her*, he thought. Or maybe, he could have liked her. But he left her, even though she'd wailed and cried and begged him to stay. He had truly loved that passion of hers—the passion she had for *him*. Even now, as he closed his eyes, he could smell the waxy scent of her red lipstick.

But then, he snapped back to reality and opened his eyes just in time to see a curly-haired dot scurry along the far edge of Main Street. He knew who it was, and he knew where it was going.

Returning to his office, he stood in front of his whiteboard. It was as blank as the day he'd bought it, and while most of the residual writing was removed, if he pressed his face against the left side, he could see the faint writing of Project Golden Thingy.

"What a fucking disappointment," he muttered. "Trading everything for some pot smoking, trustafarian loser whose parents couldn't give a fuck about him. No amount of screwing was worth it."

Bill, of course, was right, and Clover would be the first to admit it. Although she and Jesse had a ton of sex—all over his house, all over town, and in a variety of positions—her grandfather was undeniably right, it wasn't worth throwing everything away for. But that wasn't why she'd found herself at Jesse's house three months ago; she did that because it was an easy thing for her to do.

She had time now. And with Jimmy gone and her grandmother pretty much gone, the options for how to spend her time were pretty limited. So, sex seemed like an easy decision. And when it was mixed with weed and vodka, an option filled with a plethora of sensations.

Despite Clover wanting it, somehow, Jesse had a direct feed to Clover's sensations. Somehow, he knew how to light a fuse at her clitoris and send a flame down her legs and up her fingertips. Unlike with Jimmy, these moments did not touch her in the back of her rib cage, where her bones met her spine, but they did scream and dance on her surface. And even though she wanted these moments to exist beyond the realm of sloppy passion, she knew they only served one purpose: to dull the sharp-edged reality of feeling abandoned, uninspired, and unloved.

The reports Bill received on his granddaughter supported this. He did not have a degree in psychology, but it was obvious that Clover was lost. It was also apparent Clover wanted nothing to do with him. Beyond her avoidance of the Glory Peak Nordic Center and the Glory Peak offices, he could no longer doubt this fact when, one Tuesday, he pulled up to a stop sign at the edge of town and saw Clover walking to Jesse's house. Deciding to follow her from a distance, he eventually spun up the courage to roll down his window and call to her. But when Clover heard his voice and spotted his car, she grabbed a rock and launched it at him. Five more rocks quickly followed. Taking the hint, Bill drove back toward town.

But still, with all that, Bill was her grandfather. And he had a patriarchal duty to make sure no line of DNA burned to ash on his watch. Or in his town. Examining his options, he realized he would have to do the one thing he dreaded more than eating cauliflower.

He would have to speak with Nanny A.

Bill had never been inside the Wolfehaus headquarters and while he drove by the large yellow warehouse many times, he never actually got out to inspect it. The parking lot he noticed, which used to sit empty, now held converted Westphalia vans and rusted Toyota 4Runners, and the land beside it, also once empty, now housed several skate ramps and half-pipes. *There's some grit*

*here*, he thought as he exited his Rover and trucked toward the front door. *Shame it's wasted on a bunch of degenerates.*

Inside the building was exactly what he expected: a large open area divided into a Tetris-like mass of cubicles. One wall was used for rock climbing, another had a basketball hoop, and another had a collection of pinball machines beeping along it. "Fucking reefer heads," he mumbled. Walking up to a young receptionist with large dreadlocks in her hair, Bill could only laugh.

"Hey there," he started. "I'm here to talk to Abigail Charters."

"Who?" the receptionist drawled back, genuinely confused.

"The old lady who runs the joint. You know, the one who's always in that purple fleece."

"Oh, you mean Nanny A." The receptionist nodded back as she twisted her dreads tighter.

"I don't, like, mean to be rude, you know, but . . . is she expecting you?"

"Listen here, you nutcake, just point me to her office."

Fighting back a laugh, the receptionist pointed to a far corner office and giggled. "Okay, dude, chill."

If Nanny A had $20 million to bet on whether William Jefferson Macklemore would have ever come to her offices, she would have easily taken that bet. And on this 32-degree day, she would have lost that bet. Seeing him at her door was extraordinary—but the sort of extraordinary that was dipped in a paint of hate and disgust. Unable to respond to his hello, she watched as he entered her office and sat across from her in a chair cobbled together from old skis. Next, she watched his lips move, so she knew he was speaking, but it still took thirty seconds before she could hear anything come out of his mouth.

Shaking her head as she looked at him in her chair, all she could say was, "Come again?"

"I said, you've got a real great space here. It's got a lot of grit."

Perplexed by what Bill meant, Nanny A leaned back in her chair and studied the folds around his eyes. "Okay, thanks, I guess," she responded. Then, firming back up in her chair, she looked him in the eyes and asked, "What the hell are you doing here, Bill?"

Bill smiled and shook his head. As much as he wanted to, he could not hate Abigail Charters. She had a tungsten set of balls, and Bill was always fond of someone with big balls.

"Okay, then, Abigail. We'll avoid the small talk. I'm concerned about Clover. I've been hearing some chatter about her spending all her time with that Vanigan kid, and from what I gather, he's quite a shitheel."

Chuckling, Nanny A leaned forward, took a pen off her desk, and placed it in the ceramic mug she used as a pencil holder.

"*That's* why you're here? Because you are concerned about Clover's reputation?"

"She's still my granddaughter. And she's still young. I don't want her stepping off a cliff she can't climb back up."

Smiling, Nanny A grabbed the mug and fiddled with the pens. "Well, well . . . isn't that awfully paternal of you. Coming in here with your masculine swagger and throwing concern and compassion our way. Lemme guess—you're next gonna come up with some suggestions on what we can do to bring her back to a state of proper feminine decorum?"

"Well, I'm not exactly sure what all that means, but I do think it might benefit her if she got back to her cross-country skiing. From what I also hear, she's real talented there."

"Ah, so that's it!" Nanny A snorted, sitting back in her chair. "Bill wants to finally get his little Olympian. You're sure your ego can handle it not being for downhill?"

"Listen, Abigail," Bill said, fixing her with a glare. "I'm not here to spar with you. Especially regarding my intentions about protecting my granddaughter. I just think, well . . . I just think if there is something we can do, we should do it."

"Just like when you could have done something for Belle and Bobby?" she fired back.

Watching Bill slouch in his chair, she knew her shot had landed. Then, watching him slide a shaking hand through his thinning hair and cough into a fist, she knew her shot had landed deep.

"You know I have to live with it, too," he said quietly, almost as if in thought.

"Good!" she cried. "You fucking killed them! You and your pathetic excuse for a male ego sent them straight to the morgue!"

Swaying his head back and forth defiantly, Bill stood up and looked at Nanny A. "So, you want to keep up this whole thing?"

"Damn straight I do!" she responded.

Neither moving, they each waited for a blink or a twitch to break the stalemate. But when none came, Bill took the lead. "Well, okay," he said then turned and walked to his car.

The following hours and days were filled with a flurry of phone calls and a flurry of research regarding zoning rights, commercial building restrictions, and deed information. Both Bill and Nanny A were in attack mode, each trying to grab as much land as possible or block the other from buying as much land as possible. On Nanny A's side, she had cash in the bank and the ability to buy parcels without too much exposure. On Bill's side, he had access to the banks, long-standing relationships with the politicos, and knew how to navigate the ins and outs of Fortooth real estate. So, while Wolfehaus was able to amass a decent swatch of real estate with small incremental purchases, Bill was able, over time, to make larger land grabs. Unfortunately caught in the middle of this game of Monopoly they never agreed to play, were the Le'Echuwanna.

Fortunately, they had the land allotted to them by the US government, and fortunately, they had the land they purchased in anticipation of needing a way to preserve their life. But when word of the real estate war between Bill and Nanny A reached He Who Eats, his worst fears became a reality: they were going to be bought out of the valley. And as he shared this information at the weekly Elder Elders' meeting, so came the same avoidant responses.

Pouting Trout rolled bones, and Lady Dog spat venom at all the white people in Fortooth. But as much as he pushed for it and presented all the reasons, He Who Eats could not get a consensus on launching a war party.

All he could get were opinions on what type of IRAs they should set up, whether Apple was a better investment than IBM, or if AOL had a better hold of the internet than Yahoo. Exhausted by the swirling pool of denial, He Who Eats jumped from his sitting position and reared like a stuck bear.

"Jesus Christ, people! What the hell are you doing? We can't avoid this like a bad fucking marriage. This is our land! We must defend it!" Scanning the hut, He Who Eats hoped someone felt his outrage. But there was nothing—just hanging heads and wandering eyes.

Squirreling Squirrel pulled his glasses off his face. Rubbing them, he said "The other day, I spoke with Jumping Tooth in Orlando. He said the Seminoles had land near the Everglades they would be willing to sell. We could get thousands of acres there for half the price of what we would spend here. He also said there's an abandoned pipe manufacturing plant we could turn into a paper mill and printing press. He said great progress has been made in using mangrove trees for paper pulp."

Murmurs of "interesting" and "ahh, good" followed. He Who Eats, disgusted this idea was even being entertained, reached to the sky like a backwoods preacher and fell to his knees.

"By the power of Lady Nature and Father Wind, are you serious? Seminole land, mangrove trees? Am I in the *Na-oh-wah* twilight zone?" He looked around at everyone and glared. "I am fucking done! I am calling a *La-mah-oh*. Right now!"

A hush blew through the mud hut. *La-mah-ohs* were wartime actions allowed only through absolute executive power. They were very much against the democratic grain of the tribal council, but when decisive actions were needed, they were the fastest way to achieve action. The one hitch, however, was that they needed a second to ratify the action. Looking at the Elder Elders, He Who Eats discovered none of them were prepared to ratify it.

Then, just as He Who Eats was about to rear back and kick one of the wooden poles that supported the mud hut, a skinny hand rose among the seated. It belonged to Fancy Glove.

Locking eyes with He Who Eats, he said, "I embrace the duty, I embrace the law. I breathe the spirits, I sit in awe . . ."

Sighing, Lady Dog reached for a drum and began to chant. The beat was steady and solitary as the council started to sing "The Song of the Arrow Way."

# CHAPTER 25

**MAY 2002**

"Huevos rancheros, ya little motherfucka! You have a major set of huevos rancheros!"

He Who Eats was elated as he drove his pickup truck toward his house. Fancy Glove, who was normally one to relish these drives, just stared out the window and looked at the shadow of something he could not make out hovering over the side-view mirror.

"Jesus, did you shift the hut! I mean *Pay-ah-eh-ah-poe* shifted it. Did you see Squirreling Squirrel's face? He shat a Dutch biscuit right on the spot. I could smell it, I tell you!" He Who Eats slammed the steering wheel. Fancy Glove, watching, tried to smile, but the shadow he saw hovering over the side-view mirror kept blocking his light.

"What's wrong, *baby-sabe*? You scared or something? I don't want no second-guessing coming this way. We gotta be war-ready if we are going to make this count."

Fancy Glove didn't disagree, and he wasn't second-guessing. He was sure as stone this was the right decision. But as he turned toward He Who Eats, he saw the shadow that was hovering outside slide inside the truck and fall long over the driver's side interior.

"I think I have the *Si-mah-neh*," Fancy Glove shared. Immediately, He Who Eats stomped on the brakes, the car sliding with such force, Fancy Glove almost shot through the windshield.

Taking a moment to let the gravel settle around them, He Who Eats gently asked, "Are you serious?"

"Yeah . . . last night, when I was in the tub, I had a vision. At least, I *think* it was a vision," Fancy Glove shared. "Fuck, I don't know—I was super high. Like, tripping high."

As one who possessed the power of the six-eyed trout and thus understood how overwhelming the vision highway was, He Who Eats leaned forward, his face coming into a white shard of sunlight.

"That don't mean nothing. I've been high plenty of times, but that never started or stopped the *Si-mah-neh*. Usually, it just helps break down the dam the first time." He paused for a moment, the world going quiet around them, as though it wanted to eavesdrop. Then, he asked, "What did you see?"

"Hornets," Fancy Glove said. "A cloud of hornets swarming the valley. They were so thick, they covered everything—almost like a snowfall, but black. There was no color, just this breathing mass of insects chewing on stuff until there was nothing left to chew but each other."

"Then what happened?" He Who Eats whispered.

"Then, they flew off, carrying away Laughing Bear, Tickle Toes, the whole tribe. I ran after them, but just as I was about to grab Pouting Trout's leg, I fell off a cliff. And fell, like, forever, until I woke back up."

Taking in lung-filling breaths, He Who Eats rubbed his hand on the dashboard. "What if I told you I had the same vision? But instead of missing Pouting Trout, I caught his leg, and when I did, he turned to ash in my hands."

Looking at He Who Eats, Fancy Glove realized he was no longer watching from the sidelines. He was now a star player in the game. And as a star player, he was expected to take the ball and run.

"Listen, He Who Eats," he said, "as we get ready to deal with this shit— the war for our land and the fight against the *Eh-Kar-lo*—can you do me one favor?"

"Of course, *baby-sabe*. Whaddya need?"

"Can you just call me Grant, like everyone else?"

He Who Eats laughed, then with a smile he put his pickup back in gear and started the drive back to his house.

For the next two weeks, He Who Eats' home was the de facto command center for the war party. There were morning drills on the hillside—as it was decided predawn was the best time to attack—while camouflage and bow practice were held in the late afternoon to help everybody get used to shooting and hiding in suboptimal daylight.

During the training, Grant moved into his leadership position with ease. This didn't seem to surprise He Who Eats as much as it surprised Grant. To wake up one day and be leveled above your friends, this idea scared Grant. He'd known these people since birth. They'd seen him fall, fart, make jokes that didn't land, and roll broken and barely smokable joints that would have gotten him kicked out of Jamaica. But when their chief, He Who Eats, told them he was going to be their leader, they nodded and followed.

That was the way of the Le'Echuwanna—unconditional trust. And trusting He Who Eats' decree was as simple for them to do as eating when they were hungry. It was in their nature. And proof of Grant's behavior only made their adherence all the easier.

All six in the war party acknowledged how quickly he excelled in their training drills. In particular, his ability to camouflage himself amid the myriads of ecosystems that appeared and disappeared without warning in the Farangotta. One minute it was high-altitude shrubbery, dense and pale green, the next, aqua mountain lakes, sparkling and serene. It didn't make a difference; his preternatural stealth was so strong that it nearly rendered him invisible no matter the location or time of day. This—along with the Northern Lights–Purple Haze hybrid he shared after dinner while they sat by the fire and sang—made him a leader they were happy to respect and follow.

As he watched them train under the half-light of morn, He Who Eats would have smoky visions of Le'Echuwannan life before electricity, when the simple needs of feeding, breeding, and leading were the only matters of concern. This was as it should be, and if Matt Groening had the ability to broadcast *The Simpsons* in the 1600s, He Who Eats would have taken a DeLorean back there in a second. But there was no DeLorean. And cable only existed courtesy of Time Warner, so these moments in their Mountain Hardware jackets, passing small Graffix bongs in his living room, became the moments worth living and dying for.

The night before their first raid, a somber breeze washed through the house. There were no bong hits, no bourbon chasers, no buffalo wing runs. There was just quiet—and an appreciation for the wind, and the trees, and the moon. Doling out bison chili, He Who Eats reviewed the plan. They would drive six hundred yards from the Wolfe Mountain construction site. Then, waiting in the pickup, He Who Eats would signal Grant to sneak though the construction fence and place ten containers of nitroglycerin in small wooden pipes along the back of the site. At that moment, the other six warriors would get into position, shoot lit arrows at the containers, and ignite a massive explosion that would trigger a rock avalanche onto the construction site—burying it until summer.

Examining the room, He Who Eats watched the warriors attend to their details. Some were cleaning feathers at the end of arrows; others were figuring out the designs of their war paint. That night, no one slept and when He Who Eats' alarm went off at four o'clock that morning, everyone was already dressed and waiting.

Outside, the remaining dark seemed to know something was ahead. The moon waned, barely visible behind splatters of clouds, and a fog ambled its way through the valley floor. Taking in the surroundings, He Who Eats knew what these signs meant. The morning would arrive in gray scale, and the wolves and jackrabbits would confidently run the valley floor, aware their pelts would blend into the white of the fog. Which meant this morning was going to have movement because hunting would happen, and the food chain would wake hungry into action.

It took all of two minutes for Grant to load the warriors into He Who Eats' pickup. All silent on departure, He Who Eats eased his truck down his driveway and pointed its wheels at the road leading to the Wolfe Mountain construction site. Seeing the construction site in the distance, He Who Eats began to have a bizarre feeling of admiration for all the work Nanny A had done. Not only had she found the money to start construction, but Nanny A had also found a warm, inviting piece of land—one that looked like a semicircle of arms waiting to squeeze off a bear hug as much as being the perfect place for a ski mountain. And He Who Eats had to admit that what Nanny A, and that ball sack Gunther, had built off one video was amazing. To create an alternative to the unchallenged reign of William Jefferson Macklemore was a wonderful idea, but still, when he'd sat with her during that sunset months ago—Nanny A's arms pinwheeling enthusiasm and unending trails of ideas and explanations—he knew that however potent the fuel was that powered Wolfehaus, it was also too potent for her to control. And if that was something she could not control, that meant the Farangotta's balance was at risk.

Creeping to a stop at the perimeter of the construction site, He Who Eats chuckled at the sight of a warning sign that read, All trespassers will be shot, quartered, pickled, and fed to the wild alpacas.

"Fucking Nanny A," he muttered. "She's got brassy ones." Then, sliding the gearshift into park, he motioned for the warriors to exit. One by one, they hopped out of the cargo bed and disappeared under white parkas into the thickening fog. Sighing, He Who Eats turned to Grant in the passenger seat. Feeling a surprising sense of paternity, he pulled him in for a warm, tobacco-scented hug and whispered, "*Heh-ah-cha-mo.*" Air, it meant, be air.

Patting him on the shoulder, Grant exited the car as though on mute and dissolved into the cloudy vapor of dawn.

Almost immediately after, as He Who Eats predicted, the animals came out to play. First, he saw a rabbit sprint into a field. Then, beyond the field, slinking toward the edge of the tree line, a wolf on its belly. An eagle appeared next, gliding in the dark gray sky, and when it saw the rabbit huddled in the snow, it turned its beak left and dove for it, inspiring the wolf to attack. The rabbit, somehow, avoided them both and sprinted back into the woods just as a fox walked onto the field, a field mouse hanging from his mouth. Tracking the fox, He Who Eats wondered why the field mouse's tail did not flap and why there was a perfect consistency to the shape of its body. And that's when he realized—it wasn't a mouse in his mouth, but one of the wooden pipes he filled with nitroglycerin.

"Fuuuuuuuck," He Who Eats mouthed as he filed through his mind for the appropriate response. He was confident he did a good job packing the nitroglycerin in the pipes, but he also knew that nitroglycerin was a contact explosive, and its already delicate disposition would become more unstable over time. With the wrong jolt or movement made by somebody who did not know its dangers, devastation would be the outcome. Knowing there was only one thing to do, He Who Eats pulled a quiver and bow from his hunting rack, unlocked the car doors, and exited.

Crouching in front of his truck, he raised the bow and took aim at the fox. Clear in his sights, he was just about to release the arrow when the wolf lunged from a hidden spot, sending the fox back into the forest—wooden pipe still in its mouth. Not wanting to leave the car but knowing if the bomb was discovered, it could lead back to the tribe, He Who Eats brought the bow to his side and ran after the fox.

It was not difficult to track. A light rain had fallen around midnight, so his paw prints appeared like clovers on the ground. Slowing his run to a walk, He Who Eats bent the top of his body parallel to the ground and slid up to a fallen cedar. Through its decayed holes, he could see the fox at the base of a grove of aspens, the small wooden pipe still hanging from its mouth. Raising the bow for a shot, He Who Eats watched as the fox slinked behind broken tree trunk. With no apparent shot, he circled the trees for a better angle—finally finding a clear vantage to the fox's chest.

Aiming the bow, he tuned in to two sounds: the crackle of the wood as the fox chomped and the whomp of the bow as he pulled the arrow to his ear. About to release it, he then heard a third sound, the earth-shattering sound of nine bombs going off and the body-shaking waterfall of a rock avalanche in motion.

Petrified by the sounds of the explosion, the fox sprinted deeper into the woods. Late to its exit, He Who Eats released the bow string and watched the arrow land in the fox's hindquarter, tumbling it into an aspen and the nitroglycerin pipe towards a rock jutting through the ground.

The war party, having successfully destroyed any potential of Wolfe Mountain, ran back to their chief's pickup truck. However, when they arrived and discovered he wasn't there, everybody began to panic—and none more than Grant, who knew something must have gone wrong. A split second later, when they heard an additional, unplanned explosion boom nearby, his worst fears were confirmed.

"He Who Eats," Grant whispered. Not having to say more, he sprinted toward the explosion, the war party right behind him.

Not fifty yards into the forest, they saw a large mass crawling on the ground. Covered in a layer of dirt and scorched grass, it scrambled in jerky, desperate lunges. Finally reaching it, Grant extended his arms, and He Who Eats fell into them. Spit and blood shooting from his mouth, He Who Eats tried to form words through his hyperventilating body.

"M-my foot!" he sputtered. "You have to go back and get my foot!"

Watching He Who Eats' eyes flutter and close, Grant swallowed every ounce of air he could and tried to pull He Who Eats onto his shoulder. But he could barely roll him off the ground. Looking at the other warriors, he yelled, "Grab him, grab him!" They all kneeled and reached for an appendage. It took all six of them to drag him to the car and strap him into the cargo bed.

# CHAPTER 26

## JANUARY 1984

A full week passed before Bobby was released from the hospital after his misadventure with the snowmobile. By that time, Nanny A had returned to the house, set up the nursery, and moved into a brick colonial, two short country roads from Annabelle, Bobby Mac, and the seven-day old Clover.

Without a doubt, Nanny A was pissed at Bobby. He had failed to keep his promise—which meant she would never trust him again. But she also knew Annabelle was still moon-blissed from just giving birth, so she had to do whatever she could to give them a grasping chance at moving forward. Which meant she supported Bobby as he navigated a cast that went from his left leg to his right chest. Fed him when he kept dropping his fork. Drove him to doctor's appointments and rented him movies from Video Hut. She did not, however, talk to him. Or look at him. At first, the discomfort was scorching for Bobby, every moment of silence a needle stab to his heart. But over time, it was welcomed—a public sort of privacy that allowed someone buried in shame to slink through the day.

But there was still so much to manage. And Annabelle realized that even with Nanny A's help, taking care of a fresh baby and a herd of alpacas was bordering on the psychotic. Thankfully, Paca Joe was alive due to the iron scaffolding of Suzanne's infrastructure. The shearers she found in Portland came down just as planned, and they harvested 712 pounds of alpaca hair, which they passed off to weavers just south of Mount Shasta. When done, they had ninety-six yards of usable fabric ready to dye and stitch into their first line.

This was the part of the process that scared Annabelle. As it fell on her to oversee production right there in Fortooth, out of a small auto body shop she'd converted into their factory and distribution center. She would only have six months to settle into motherhood before production began, and without Suzanne, it felt akin to devising a plan to rob Fort Knox.

Taking care of the alpacas was also a challenge she'd underestimated. Every week they ate through their weight in hay and possessed an intelligence she didn't predict. They could open the latch to the pen and open the front door to the house. Though they moved slowly, they always moved, and many times, Annabelle would come home to discover they wandered off the property. This, in particular, wore on the town, as they were often found grazing along Yeehaw Pass or leaving large collections of bean-size turds in front of the high school. Still healing, Bobby was useless in re-penning them, so Annabelle turned to Gunther to truck them back home. Always gentle when she approached him, he was happy to lend an ear when she vented about Paca Joe, and eventually, her marriage.

By February, Bobby was able to walk again, courtesy of a ski pole he converted into a cane. His shoulder was still in a sling, but he could at least push a stroller or rub Clover's back and rock her to sleep. It was in these moments Annabelle remembered why she fell for him. And even Nanny A almost understood when she once witnessed Bobby lying next to Clover in her crib, massaging her scalp and singing "Blackbird." Though most times she wanted to kick him, she recognized on occasion his ability to channel love.

Meanwhile, Annabelle still had to find a solution to their alpaca problem, but when she tried to discuss the matter with Bobby, he barely engaged. In fact, the most she got out of him during these brainstorming sessions was an unenthusiastic "I told ya so."

Despite his indifference it was abundantly clear something had to be done. Especially after one night, when Nanny A came by to drop off a quinoa salad and saw a male alpaca rubbing a pink erection against the porch swing. When she attempted to bring him to the pen, the alpaca reared and kicked her with his hinds. He then spun and charged her, chasing her back into her car, where he proceeded to spit on her windshield and butt his head against the side mirror. Twenty minutes later, when Annabelle returned from town, she had to chase the heated alpaca into the pen with a hose. And just when she thought things couldn't get any worse, Deputy Ron Booth showed up with news that a new ordinance was passed prohibiting the open grazing of alpacas, and how if they were caught on public land, they would be remanded to animal control. Petrified by the thought of losing them, Annabelle begged Bobby to reinforce the pen, raise the fences, and build a padlock system that would guarantee they wouldn't escape.

"You know they're still gonna get out," he said, scratching the inside of his right ankle with his ski-pole cane.

"Not if you make the fence six feet high and stake it with four-by-fours, that will keep them from jumping it. And if you set up a chain system that threads through all the doors, that'll keep them from getting out when we're not here."

Bobby just shook his head. "Belle, they're wild animals. No matter what we do, if they want to get out, they're gonna get out."

Slapping her hand on the kitchen table, Annabelle screamed, "No, Bobby Macklemore! Don't you tell me this can't be done! You find a way!"

The shout shocked Clover awake, and a fierce baby wail followed. Then, rubbing his chin, Bobby stood, grabbed his ski-pole cane, and headed to the garage to find his tools.

Following Annabelle's suggestion, he reinforced the fencing, extended its height to six feet, and added a steel latch system that could be threaded with Grade 70 galvanized chain. By the time he was done, he was pretty sure he'd unofficially created a prison—one so bulletproof and impervious that it challenged San Quentin.

That night, proud and exhausted, Bobby smiled at Annabelle during dinner and played peekaboo with Clover, who was drunk on the discovery of her own laugh. His four glasses of bourbon and three cans of beer that night was a bit of overkill, but with Nanny A on one of her "tours" with Sheriff Dan Daley, he could, guiltfree, let it rip. Annabelle, thankful he'd finally followed her instructions, rewarded him that evening with some loving— even spreading her generosity wide enough to give him his first blow job of 1984.

Falling asleep that night, Bobby drifted into a haze of alpaca clouds and, for the first time since his mother's passing, floated down a river of peace.

The following morning, Bobby woke to a scream. Rolling over he saw Annabelle standing at the bedroom window, staring out at the alpaca pen. It was empty.

"Bobby!" she shouted. "What the fuck did you do?"

Rubbing crust from his eyes, Bobby answered, "Just what you told me to."

"Then where the hell are they, Bobby?"

"I told you." Bobby yawned. "They're wild creatures. If they wanna get out, they'll get out."

Leaning over him, Annabelle pointed her index finger at his face. "You are the biggest fucking waste of a human ever. I cannot believe I married you." Before the comment could land, Annabelle was out the door and in her car.

It did eventually land, though. It landed when Bobby sat on the toilet. Pulling a swab of toilet paper from the holder, he reached for a wipe and then stopped. A rush of emotion crashed over him, and with his hand wrapped in toilet paper, he wept and wept and wept, Annabelle's words echoing through his mind: *"You are the biggest fucking waste of a human ever. I cannot believe I married you."*

Driving through the valley, Annabelle had no recognition of the bomb she'd just dropped. All she could focus on was Paca Joe and its sandcastle blowing away in the wind. After touring every field possible, she accepted the only fate she could: animal control had found them. Turning her car back toward town, a storm of panic fell over her. Hyperventilating, she saw her future pass through the windshield: a life of boredom, bills, and wasted potential.

Fighting tears, she stumbled into the police station. When Sheriff Dan saw her, he knew immediately why she was there.

Grabbing her hand, he sat her on a waiting room chair. "I spoke with them," he said, trying to comfort her. "They got all ninety-eight of them." Relieved, Annabelle leaned back in her chair and thought to herself, *Ninety-eight . . . That means two are still missing!* About to share that information with Dan, she stopped and looked at her feet. *Good*, she thought. *Don't come back. Stay the fuck out there.*

The following days were harsh in a variety of ways. Arctic chills ran through the valley and Bobby and Annabelle's house. Annabelle was still livid—even after Bobby showed her where the alpacas had chewed through the tin backside of the pen. She was going to forgive him—in a week, probably—but in the meantime, she wanted him to suffer her silence.

Normally, the silent treatment technique wore Bobby down to a quiver, but something about this time was different. This time, Bobby didn't seem to care. He woke early, played with Clover, fed her, fed himself, did the dishes, and went into town. Then, he returned at sunset, played with Clover, fed her, fed himself, did the dishes, and went back into town.

When he got back, sometimes he would stumble into bed, and Annabelle would brush up against him, hoping to get some sign of engagement. Uninterested, he would just roll the other way and create space between them. As much as this behavior concerned her, Annabelle was even more worried about the fact that she needed Bobby to help get the alpacas from animal control—and if they were still in a fight, would he even help?

A few weeks after the incident, Annabelle woke early and asked Bobby if he wanted to go on a hike with her. It had been a while since they'd had any one-on-one time, and with the winter warming into spring, she thought it could be a promising way to start the day. They decided to head out toward Prescott Loop, Annabelle opting to sling Clover over her shoulder as they walked.

Starting up the path, Annabelle did her best to temper her nerves, but she wanted to know what Bobby was going to do about the alpacas—and until she asked about them, she wasn't sure she'd be able to enjoy the hike. So, she spat it out: "Bobby, what're you going to do about the alpacas?"

Throwing his hands in the air, he shot a look over his shoulder and said, "Why are you so obsessed with those fucking alpacas?"

Annabelle was shaken by his tone as well as confused by his question. "What do you mean? The alpacas are how we're going to make Paca Joe work. They're our core element."

Bobby laughed. "C'mon, Belle, nobody gives a fuck if it's alpaca wool or sheep's wool or cotton. If they buy it, it'll be because the colors and logo are cool."

Not even 9 a.m. yet, Annabelle realized at that moment that Bobby was not going to help. She also wondered if he was done with Paca Joe. He wasn't. But listening to her, all he could think was *Can't you just shut the hell up for once about this?* He didn't say this out loud, of course, but his eyes did, and the rest of the hike was spent in silence.

When they got home, Annabelle asked Bobby if he could at least watch Clover while she headed into town. After he gave her an annoyed nod yes, she then put on some makeup, grabbed her purse, and settled into her car. Driving Yeehaw Pass, a thousand different ways to plead her case ran through her mind, but considering she hadn't spoken to her father-in-law in almost three years, she really had no idea where to start.

She waited for twenty-seven minutes before the receptionist pointed her to Bill's office.

When she entered, Bill motioned for her to take a seat. He was on the phone, screaming into the receiver. Looking at his red face, spittle flying, a part of her considered getting up and leaving, but by the time she'd decided to do so, Bill slammed the phone on its base, rubbed his temples, fixed his hair, and handed Annabelle a warm handshake.

"Well, I'll be . . . this is quite a surprise," he began. "Can I get you anything? Water, or tea, or bourbon, maybe?"

"I'm okay," she responded, then feigned a smile as Bill sat in his chair.

"So," Bill added, "how can I help you?"

"I thought . . . well . . ." she started, only to pause. "It just seemed like we should catch up. A lot has happened over the years."

"So, I hear." Bill laughed. "How's Bobby doing? I hear he had a nasty fall out by Goldfinger."

"He did—shattered his kneecap and cracked his shoulder, but he's almost fully healed now. Just walking with a cane."

"That sounds about right." Bill nodded. "He was always like a rubber ball."

"Hah, yeah, that's Bobby," Annabelle replied, trying to force a chuckle at the end of her sentence. But nothing came, so she just shifted uncomfortably in her chair. "Oh," she sparked, "I'm sure you have heard, too, but we have a daughter now. Clover. She's three months old. Here, look." Annabelle pulled out her wallet and handed Bill a photo. He scanned it, smiled, and handed it back to her.

"Look at that—just what I imagined. Good hair. And she has your eyes."

Putting the picture back in her wallet, Annabelle grinned. "That's what people say . . . but she has Bobby's smile. It's big as day."

Bill nodded once again—and after noticing her nervous fingers pick at her wallet, he realized she was not here to reopen family ties. She was here for business. "So," he said. "Lemme guess—you want to talk alpacas."

"Huh, yeah, I guess . . . Is it that obvious?" She couldn't disguise that she was completely taken aback by his directness. "I was wondering . . . hoping, actually, that you knew someone in animal control who could help return them to us."

"Let me ask you a question, Annabelle. It's Annabelle, right?"

Annabelle nodded, her eyes widening.

Leaning in, Bill placed his elbows on his desk, clasped his hands, and said, "Why do you have a herd of alpacas?"

At this, she perked a bit. "To use for fabric. Bobby and I started an undergarment company that uses alpaca fabric. It's good for the environment, wicks well, and has a higher warmth factor per millimeter than merino wool."

"An undergarment company, huh? That's what you and Bobby have been working on?"

"Yes, sir," Annabelle answered proudly. "And your ex-wife, Suzanne, she was helping, as well."

"So, you come here after I haven't heard from you for years—after you have a child, whom I haven't seen or been invited to spend time with—and you ask me to help you get back your alpacas to use in a business you started with my dead ex-wife?"

"Umm, yes . . . Yes, sir, that's about right, I guess," Annabelle replied, her response somehow laced with optimism.

Bill looked at her, his pupils so large they almost overtook the blue in his eyes. "As far as I am concerned, those alpacas, and every alpaca in the world, can rot. And your undergarment company, which I have known about for the past year and a half, will never, as long as I'm walking this good green earth, see the light of day."

Annabelle took the statement in. It stung. It stung deep, so deep she felt knocked to a place without color or sound.

Returning to her senses, she grabbed her wallet, placed it in her purse, and stood up. Looking at the floor, she found a hole in the carpet. It exposed a decaying tear in its underpadding. Studying its decomposing edges, Annabelle lifted her head and looked at Bill. "You are a pathetic old man who is gonna die alone," she declared, then walked out.

Annabelle was able to hold on to her bravado until she arrived at her mom's. Landing on the doorstep, she pummeled the front door until Nanny A opened it, her hair a mess and blouse partially undone.

"Sweetie, sweetie, what's wrong?" Nanny A asked, her hand reaching out to hold her. Pushing her mother aside, Annabelle stormed into her house and slammed her purse on Nanny A's kitchen table.

"That man is pure evil! Pure goddamn evil!"

Annabelle watched as Nanny A entered the kitchen and sat at the table.

"Mom, he looked me right in the face and told me he would never let Paca Joe happen, ever!"

"That makes no sense," Nanny A responded, pulling her hair into a bun. "Bobby owns half of it."

"Not Bobby. His evil, pathetic, disgusting excuse for a father!"

"Wait," Nanny A said. Steadying herself in the chair, she looked at Annabelle, confused. "You spoke with Bill?"

Leaning her back against the kitchen sink, Annabelle looked at the ceiling, then ran her palms down her face. "I thought somehow, he could help us with the alpacas. I know, I know, it was stupid. But Bobby's his son. I never thought he would just be so heartless. I mean, just cruel. It was like he was counting the seconds to show me how much he hated us."

Looking at her mother, Annabelle's eyes could not help but tear. Her mother, looking back, stood from her chair and slammed a fist on the kitchen table. "Goddamn him!" Nanny A screamed.

"Goddamn that uneducated, inbred, wannabe dictator! He can go to hell! I promise you: I will find him and turn him into a goddam eunuch. A quivering, knee-crawling eunuch!"

Annabelle couldn't help but soften. Watching her mom with her fist raised, screaming at injustice was one of her favorite pastimes. "I swear on the existence of this hick, backward, racist town, we will take down that fascist piece of—"

"Abigail, is everything all right?" rang in from the hallway. Turning toward the question, Annabelle saw Sheriff Dan Daley enter the kitchen. He was buttoning his uniform top and combing his hair into place.

Embarrassed, they both quieted. Half filling a coffee mug, Sheriff Daley sat at the table next to Nanny A.

Waiting a beat, Nanny A looked at Annabelle, then back at Sheriff Dan. "Goddamn it, Dan, how can you work for that ingrate of a human?"

"I don't work for him, Abigail. I just enforce what passes for law around here," he said, tapping his spoon on the lip of the mug. "That said, not every place around here has to listen to what passes for law."

Studying him, Nanny grabbed his coffee mug and took a sip. "What the fuck does that mean, Dan?"

"Well," he said, licking his spoon, "it means the reservation functions with tribal sovereignty. Which means the tribal council has jurisdiction over their land—not the local or federal government. Which means, if you could get them to agree, they could house the alpacas without any threat besides Mother Nature herself."

# CHAPTER 27

## MAY 2002

On the to-do list of life, ketamine was not an item Clover ever expected to check off. She'd heard about it in school assemblies on drug prevention and had caught word of a snowflake from Seattle who was trading it for lift tickets, but she'd never expected to see it in person.

Or to be rolling up a ten-dollar bill and snorting it off Jesse Vanigan's desk.

But once she did, it did make sense as to why it was all she wanted to do. Ketamine was the one way she could completely disappear into a pocket of peaceful isolation. The whole world contracting to a pinhole where she would only have to focus on one specific thing. Sometimes that one specific thing was butter. Sometimes it was carpet threads. No matter how those specific fixations started, they would always end up on the same thing— cross-country skiing. The sound of a pole plant, a leg push, a foot land, an arm reach, the ketamine bringing her back to the singularity and simplicity of the pure, simple micro-moment.

This singularity, of course, came most alive during sex. When she could get lost in Jesse sucking her ear and tracing his tongue over her lobe and ossicle. His penis felt good, too, and at times, she was able to close the aperture of all sound and image and focus solely on the ticklish sensation of his shaft rubbing along her Skene's glands. Each thrust so determined, so definite, and so rhythmic, it synched with the memory of her pole plants and the pleasure she got from feeling their tips land squarely in the snow.

The aftermath of these moments was less rewarding. Jesse would roll over, plop a kiss on her forehead, and walk to the bathroom for a shockingly long piss. The walk and trip to the bathroom reminded her of those mornings, long ago, when she heard her father creak to the bathroom. She wondered if he would like Jesse. She wondered if he would like Jimmy. She wondered if she would like her father.

Nanny A, of course, was oblivious to the fact that half the time she saw Clover, she was in a K-hole—which was ironic, considering the onrush of ketamine in Fortooth was courtesy of the security guards Nanny A had hired to protect the Wolfe Mountain construction site. While the bombings that caused the avalanches had stopped the birth of Wolfe Mountain in utero, a side effect was that they also set off a frantic paranoia among the Fortoothians.

Fortunately, Grant did succeed in finding He Who Eats' foot and destroying any evidence that could've been traced to the Le'Echuwanna. And even more fortunately, he left behind a swatch of torn blue GORE-TEX that matched the jackets of the Glory Peak lift operators, which sent the investigators down a believable but inaccurate path.

Like the investigators, it was this piece of evidence that sent Nanny A into a mad twister. When Bill asked her if she wanted war, she naturally thought it was a business metaphor, but with this evidence, even though no forensics could connect it to a Glory Peak employee, his words became literal. And thanks to a brief stint she spent volunteering for the Black Panthers in '68, she believed she was ready for military action. Gunther, however, was not. But because of his Teutonic background, Fortooth citizens presumed he would mount an eventual countermeasure. In anticipation, Sheriff Dan Daley resourced bulletproof vests, SWAT gear, and for the first time ever, six MP5 submachine guns.

Bill, using his tactical military experience, organized a security team and set them up in alternating patrols around Glory Peak, the condominiums, the terrain park, and all planned future sites. The quiet battle that once waged between Bill and his family had now become valley visible.

This pleased He Who Eats, as he was now fully resigned to the *Rah-pah-no*, or, as he roughly translated to Grant and his warriors, the Great Clearing. In preparation, he painted his face white and sent chants to the Second World, asking it to create space for those he loved, those he hated, and those caught in-between. This behavior was, at first, acceptable to the tribe. But when he fashioned a peg leg from an elk metatarsal and tailored a union suit from a collection of bear pelts, the Elder Elders decided he was *in-cah-he-oh*—or lost beneath the field, which was a term that suggested he swam outside of reality.

To protect him, Grant offered to lead the meetings. Despite the failure of the attack, the tribe valued how his quick thinking not only saved He Who Eats' life but also saved them from investigation. With Grant now seen as a man of bark and bone, the Elder Elders were happy to let him assume chief-level duties and leadership—especially if that meant they had more time to discuss the benefits of day trading in AOL chat rooms.

Rounding out spring, most of the council meetings were of a basic bureaucratic nature: money updates, ceremony preparations, plumbing issues in the cafeteria, and so forth. But as the meetings moved into summer, construction started yet again at Wolfe Mountain and rendered their previous effort pointless. They had hoped to sabotage Wolfe Mountain permanently, but it became apparent that Wolfehaus had more money and determination than they'd imagined. To add to this, rumors spread of Glory Peak opening a new resort off Miner's Gasp.

As a result, the council began preparations for a groundbreaking, as well. That May, they voted to purchase 25,00 acres of land from the Seminole and apply for reservation status. Upon hearing this, He Who Eats flamed like a bushfire. *How could his tribe consider leaving their land, their way, their legacy, their future?* But after his initial eruption, he soon settled into a state of welcome relief. Though the tribe members talked of remaining where they were, and Squirreling Squirrel spoke of increasing the computer classes at the community center, He Who Eats knew there would be a great pilgrimage and that a majority of the Le'Echuwanna would move to South Florida. His goal now, as these tremors of change were felt, was to find space and patience for the Only One to remove all the obstacles that stood in the way of the Great Clearing.

As summer progressed and the contracts for the land purchase finalized, He Who Eats and Grant focused on persuading the tribe to move the New Breath Ceremony to the end of that summer. Normally, this ceremony accompanied the vernal and autumnal equinoxes, representing the birth and death of the seasons—but He Who Eats needed to stock his war party with as many Budding Elders as possible, and with a great pilgrimage on the horizon, he needed the promise of the tribe's financial dividends to attract some broke youngsters. Initially skeptical of the calendar change, Pouting Trout conceded that as the geographical range of the Le'Echuwanna adjusted, so, too, should its ceremonial calendar. With the unanimous support of the council, the New Breath Ceremony was now to occur at the end of August instead of November 2002.

For Clover, getting to August was a blur. More specifically, a K-holed blur that consisted of a mediocre effort in school, a foggy graduation day, and a senior prom that ended in an unconsummated attempt at a threesome with Jesse and his cousin, Scotty P.

The summer had been equally shrouded in hazy distortion. There were trips to Dave Matthews Band concerts, laser-sprinkled moments courtesy of a band called the Disco Biscuits, and a fond discovery of mescaline. It had been fun, Clover guessed, but none of it went deeper than her fifth layer of skin or lasted longer than the ecstasy or acid permitted. When she was sober, her chest was still hollow, and she wondered what she could do day or night to fill it. And when she did figure out how to fill it, the feeling had the staying power of a child's balloon—inflating to something near popping, then an hour later leaking its way back to an empty, flaccid flop.

Ten pounds lighter, hair living in a ponytail, it took the arrival of a nose ring and five piercings on Clover's right ear before Nanny A decided it was time to talk. Stumbling into the house late one morning, Clover was surprised to see Nanny A waiting at the kitchen table. She had a mug of yerba maté steaming and *Awakening Loving-Kindness* by Pema Chodron in her hand.

"Uh, hi . . . What's going on?" Clover asked as she rubbed her face, hoping the smell of cigarettes and alcohol could be sanded off.

"Not much," Nanny A peacefully responded. "Thought I'd take a little break from work today. Construction started up again, so not much to check on for a week or so." At this, she gave Clover a once-over that suggested Nanny A wasn't missing anything anymore. "How are you?"

"Good, good," Clover responded as she sat in the La-Z-Boy. "Had a fun night seeing the Allman Brothers Band at the Gorge."

"The Gorge?" asked Nanny A, not sure if that was a club or a planet.

"Yeah, it's an amphitheater, up in Quincy," Clover said. "Lotta cool bands play there. Place is gorgeous."

"Ah . . ." Nanny A smiled. "God, I can't even remember the last time I went to a concert. Or danced. Gunther wants to have a music festival to ring in the opening of the peak. He wants to have all the bands we've used for the soundtracks perform and have some sort of all-star jam."

"That sounds cool," Clover mumbled back. "Haven't really watched any of the latest videos, so not sure who's on them."

Taking a sip from her mug, Nanny A did her best to avoid the passive hostility she sensed at the corners of Clover's response.

"So," she went on, "I was thinking we'd spend the day together. Go on a hike or maybe take a drive out to Wanderer's Remorse. The river is always so peaceful this time of year."

Dubious, Clover scanned Nanny A—yerba maté out, Buddhist teachings in hand, a day off from work. She knew very well where this was going.

"Don't," Clover finally said, moving to leave.

"Don't what?" Nanny A asked innocently.

"Don't act like all of a sudden you care."

"What do you mean, all of a sudden? Clover, I always care. I love you."

"Bullshit," Clover barked. "You love Wolfehaus and Wolfe Mountain and all that Wolfe shit."

"Jesus, Clover, you gotta know why I bust my ass for it?"

"I don't care," Clover shot back.

"It's for us! It's for you! It's so we don't have to be beholden to that psychotic son of a bitch grandfather of yours!"

"I never asked for that! That was *your* decision!" Clover shrieked. "You did what you wanted to do because of whatever guilt you've got left over from Mom!"

Nanny A slammed a hand against the table, rattling her yerba maté.

"Take that back," she said bluntly—not with a yell, but with something guttural from the base of her larynx. Standing up, she walked to Clover, her eyes welling and body trembling. "You take that back right now."

Clover, purple with anger, looked into Nanny A's watering eyes. "No," she said. "It's true."

"Clover, please. Take that back," Nanny A whispered. She was shaking now, her lips barely able to mouth the words.

Staring at her, Clover opened her mouth and said, "No. I won't fucking take it back."

And then, it happened. Nanny A lunged for Clover, knocking her off the La-Z-Boy. And before Clover could move, Nanny A was on top of her, showering down a mess of open-handed slaps and half-hearted punches. It took a moment for Clover to understand what was happening, and when she did, she knocked Nanny A off her and scrambled to the kitchen wall.

Clearing a trail of spit from her mouth, Clover stomped to her room, pulled a duffel from her closet, filled it haphazardly with her essential belongings, and ran out the front door. Not once did she look at Nanny A, who was wailing on the ground—her body contorting in pain as she screamed and squeezed the life out of a throw pillow.

Jesse wasn't surprised to see Clover show up that night. He was, however, surprised to see the duffel bag she carried.

"It will only be for a bit," Clover assured him. "I'll find a place, I promise."

Trying to hide his surprise, Jesse grabbed the duffel and pulled her inside. "No worries at all, babe. We'll get you set up in the downstairs guest room."

And just like that, Clover was living with Jesse.

# CHAPTER 28

## JULY 1984

Getting a sit-down meeting with the Le'Echuwanna proved to be much more difficult than Annabelle imagined. Sheriff Dan Daley put in phone calls to Chief He Who Rubs the Staff, but the calls were not answered, and through a web of inquiries, he found out that He Who Rubs the Staff had recently been replaced by Chief He Who Eats Rabbit Tails—or, as the 1984 census reported, Fred Robert Charles.

The problem was, Sheriff Dan Daley would never approach Fred Robert Charles. His temper was notorious—having once chopped down an entire cedar grove when a root at its base tripped him during an elk chase. The wood did not go for naught, though—with it, he'd built the core of what eventually became his house.

Gathering this information from Sheriff Dan, Annabelle decided she needed to get in touch with He Who Eats. Animal control was holding the alpacas for one more week, and if a solution was not found, they would be euthanized by one of the local veterinarians. She'd tried to bring Bobby into the conversation multiple times, but instead he would turn a shoulder and take a hike.

Gunther, on the other hand, was supportive and would have been happy to join her, except every time he tried to approach the Le'Echuwanna, he was met with hostility. So much so that he once woke to a large assortment of elk organs on his picnic table and a piece of cardboard that read, Not Your Land.

With four days left to save her herd of alpacas, Annabelle decided she had to make an uninvited drive to the village. Waking early, she applied lipstick and mascara, then filled her purse with bear spray, a steak knife, and most importantly, her checkbook. Not knowing when she'd be back, she arranged for Nanny A to babysit Clover with the simple instructions that if she wasn't home by sunset, Nanny A should call Sheriff Daley.

Her drive that morning fell in two parts. The familiar first part was down Yeehaw Pass, over a road she'd navigated a thousand and four times. The second part was completely the opposite—one filled with discovery. And nerves. And the strange feeling of being a prospector exploring a land she already called home. Turning right onto the village road, everything unfurled for the first time. The trees, the road, a field of rolling yellow along a bubbling blue river.

Watching through the windshield, Annabelle suddenly understood why the Le'Echuwanna wanted to keep this from every white face in the valley. It was a sliver of heaven, and in the blurry distance, she imagined the alpacas flourishing here like orchids in the Amazon.

After a forever drive of lulling turns and stomach-dropping ebbs, Annabelle came upon a mud-and-clay entry fence to the village. There were ornate iron and turquoise decorations fused into it, and beyond, a driveway lined with freshly painted rocks of alternating red, white, and black.

Annabelle felt all eyes on her as she plodded up the road and as she came to a stop at the village's roundabout, she saw the opposite of what she was expecting—prosperity. The community center was spanking clean, built from mud, glass, and steel that suggested Bauhaus by way of adobe. Kids frolicked on ornate jungle gyms, and tribe members dressed in a combination of Levi's, L.L. Bean, and tailored animal skins. *This is a sliver of heaven*, Annabelle again thought, and wished, somehow, that she and Clover could live here with the alpacas.

Uncertain of where to go, she stepped into the community center, where rows and rows of books and Le'Echuwannan artifacts were on display.

Shuffling back and forth amid the books she saw a bobbing head; it was Squirreling Squirrel.

Clearing her throat, Annabelle coughed and waved in his direction. "Um, excuse me—can you help me, please? I'm trying to find someone."

Squirreling Squirrel lifted his head from a book on south Florida fauna. His glasses rested at the tip of his nose, and he blinked at Annabelle in confusion. "Uh," he started, "are you lost?"

"No," Annabelle responded. "I just need to speak with your chief—or I think he is your chief. His name is He Who Eats Rabbit Tails."

Squinting back at her, Squirreling Squirrel placed the book on a table and repositioned his glasses on the bridge of his nose. He then approached Annabelle. "Does he know you are here? I mean, is he expecting you?"

"No, but this is very important. And time sensitive."

"Okay. But he is, well, I guess . . . the best way to put it is he doesn't like to be... ambushed."

"I understand," Annabelle replied. "But this matter means everything in the world to me. And my family."

Squirreling Squirrel nodded. Despite his overriding anxiety, he always had a strong undercurrent of compassion. Looking her up and down, it was impossible not to see the shine of genuine kindness in her eyes and decided to trust her. "Okay," he finally said. "You could probably find him at the *He-che-he*. If you follow the path by the seesaw, it will go into the forest and dead-end at a grove. If he's still around, he'll be there."

Annabelle nodded and shook Squirreling Squirrel's hand. Embarrassed, he returned to his books as she exited and walked toward the seesaw.

Her walk through the village was interesting. In the layout of the buildings, Annabelle noticed a delicate balance between the Le'Echuwanna's construction and their obvious attempts to leave the environment undisturbed. Each building had been built upon preexisting clearings, with their shape and size adjusted to coexist unobtrusively within the available space. Additionally, she realized, the path she followed rolled out diffusely— not a carved walkway through grass or land, or even sidewalk comprising concrete slabs, but a delineation made with lines of fallen tree branches and rocks. It was as if the winds had formed the paths themselves.

Following the path around the village, it dead-ended, just as Squirreling Squirrel said at the *He-che-he*—a glade of green that sat amid an arc of red cedars. Within it sat a firepit, and around it, a circle of broken tree trunks and small boulders for seats.

Tiptoeing in, Annabelle looked around, hoping to find a suggestion of the rumored tornado of a man known as He Who Eats Rabbit Tails. But there was nothing—only breeze, and leaves, and the rustle of wildlife. Enjoying the peace, she shuffled over to one of the boulders and sat.

"What the fuck-hell do you think you are doing?" a voice suddenly barked.

Frightened, Annabelle popped up and scanned the grove. There was nobody in sight, but the voice had sounded like it came from next to her.

"I said, what the hell do you think you are doing?"

Confused, Annabelle spoke to the largest tree, its limbs hovering over the firepit. "I, um, am here to speak with He Who Eats Rabbit Tails . . . My name is Annabelle Macklemore; I'm Bobby Mac's wife. We live just outside of town off Yeehaw Pass."

From behind her, a large shrub came to life. It unraveled like a roly-poly and came to a standing position, revealing two quiet babies in its arms. Through pine branches, a face, covered in dirt, yawned and stretched to life.

"Don't call me that," it said. "Just call me He Who Eats. That full name is a waste of breath."

Turning around, Annabelle realized the chief himself was lumbering toward a wide tree trunk. Sitting down, he placed the two babies on their naked bums by his feet.

Annabelle wasn't sure how to react.

"What? I wasn't burying them, ya sick shit," He Who Eats said. "Just some *Na-ta-ho*. It's what we do to keep our newborns connected to the earth—its rhythm, ya know? As chief, I gotta burrow with them so they can learn what it's like to be dirt."

Annabelle's confusion shifted to a smile. Before she could think, she sputtered, "I-I-I—I *like* that. Pretty incredible, actually."

"Eh, who fucking knows?" He Who Eats said, swatting his hand through the air dismissively. "It's tradition . . . but sometimes I end up swallowing a rock and shit crooked for a week."

Once again, before she could measure a response, Annabelle released a laugh. Feeling surprisingly welcomed, she returned to her stone seat and clasped her hands. "What are their names?" she asked, pointing at the babies, who now stood strong by He Who Eats' calves.

"This little crap here is Chasing Wolf. Name fits cause he is constantly running around like a loose turd. This one here is Fancy Glove."

"Fancy Glove?" Annabelle asked, surprised.

"Yeah, his mom gave birth to him during that Michael Jackson Motown special. Did you see it? We got a VHS of it in the library. Fucking moonwalk! Goddamn magic! Skinny little shit sure can dance."

"I didn't." Annabelle smiled back. "I heard about it. And I like that song, 'Billie Jean.'"

"Aargh, that song sucks. Nothing but a Rick James rip-off," He Who Eats snarled.

"Rick James?"

"Yeah, Rick fucking James. You know, 'Mary Jane,' 'Give It to Me Baby'?"

Annabelle stared back at him, eyes wide, clearly not registering any of his references. Waving his hand at her, He Who Eats rocked back on his tree trunk. "Eh, who cares? I'm sure you didn't hike up here to discuss the almighty father of punk funk. You probably just want to talk alpacas."

Annabelle chuckled to herself. "How'd you know?"

"Because I see things. And you seem way too focused to want weed or shrooms. It's the only other time you white tips look for us—you think we got some line on drugs."

"I'm sorry. That must feel real shitty when that happens."

He Who Eats took in her words for a moment and studied her face. There was an earnestness to it, a transparency, which allowed him to see her strong but sad heart. "You know they're wild, right? You can do what you want to keep 'em, but they're just gonna go their way."

Annabelle chuckled again to herself.

"What's so funny?" He Who Eats asked, for the first time flashing a hint of insecurity. "That wasn't a joke."

"I know," Annabelle responded. "Bobby Mac said the same thing, and he ended up being right."

He Who Eats studied her again. This time, he studied her hard—almost in the hopes of finding something that would preclude the conclusion he was walking toward. But he didn't find what he was looking for. Instead, he found an honest-looking woman who was married to the guy whose father ruled Fortooth.

"Fucking Bobby Mac," he said. "That guy's like the Fortooth Spider-Man. He used to ski all over the valley with Fancy Glove's father, Snow Feather. Climbing up and down every damn mountain like a real ninja goat. That guy really likes being outside, huh?"

"Yes," Annabelle said with a half-smile. "And he respects it. A lot," she added, nodding at the wilderness around them. "Like, he respects it with everything he has. The alpaca thing . . . that's just us trying to do something that will give us some purpose, I guess. Create something good in all this. And give his dad a real *fuck you*."

He Who Eats snorted. "That's a lot of pressure to put on an alpaca."

Looking up at him, Chasing Wolf mimicked his snort and, like a drunk otter, crawled toward the firepit. Her maternal instinct kicking in, Annabelle reached out and grabbed him before he fell into the rock pile. Holding him under his armpits, she placed the oblivious Chasing Wolf next to He Who Eats.

Rubbing his forehead, He Who Eats tried to push the vision he was having back to the Second World. He did not want to see alpacas on his land. He did not want to watch furry little wannabe llamas fornicate in his valley or on his ridges. But with every rub, the image just further crystalized, until he saw a herd of one hundred alpacas scattered across the mountainside. Maybe this was how it was supposed to be. The Le'Echuwanna were still the keepers of the bighorn sheep, but for hundreds of years, there had been no sheep.

Change, as ever, was a constant in the valley, and the Le'Echuwanna would still need a totem to pray to. And though these creatures did not come with thirty-pound horns, they still could patrol the mountaintops like an army of proud four-legged cliff crawlers.

Accepting this was now written, He Who Eats guffawed and said, "We're not gonna fence them, okay? They get free range up in here. And the tribe gets 2 percent of all sales. Gross."

Annabelle swung a double take at He Who Eats. *How did he know about Paca Joe?*

But before she could ask, he added, "Like I said—I see things. And I hear things, too. Sheriff Daley can't keep a secret for piss."

That was just the Fortooth way. There were no secrets here, just everyone pretending there were. Someone was always telling someone something that shouldn't be shared. Then, they'd swear that someone to secrecy so that they wouldn't feel guilty for telling them.

That was how Bill found Bobby Mac. One day after he heard Annabelle had met with the Le'Echuwanna to house the alpacas, he handed Tubby $250 to find out where Bobby was spending his summer. Reluctantly, Tubby shared the info and followed it with, "Please, let's just keep this, ya know, between us."

Bill happily agreed, and by that afternoon was waiting at the entrance to the Boneyard in his red Land Rover. When Bobby saw him, he was relieved to finally face the inevitable. As much as he was proud of himself for storming off at their last meeting and not speaking to him in the intervening two years, he knew they would meet again—not because of some sort of cosmic alignment but because the town was small and his dad was still alive.

Smiling at the sight of his son coming over the hill, Bill pulled his aviator sunglasses from his shirt pocket and put them on. There was no way he was going to betray a milligram of emotion. This was business. And Bobby, seeing Bill behind his mirrored glasses, knew the conversation he was about to enter, so he pulled his Revo sunglasses from his jacket and did the same. At first, there was nothing but awkward silence, both doing their best to hide the actual happiness they felt. Finally, after a squawking crow chased down a tangle of earthworms, Bobby spoke.

"Figured you'd show up," he said.

"It's a small town," Bill countered, "and we do have some new family in common."

"You heard about that, huh?"

"Of course. I heard the day she was born. Then Annabelle came to the office to tell me all about her. Showed me some pictures, too. Kid is cute as hell."

From the tremble at the side of his mouth, Bill knew Annabelle didn't tell Bobby she'd visited him. Sensing an edge, he dug deeper. "She also told me about the business you want to start. Paca Joe? Sounds promising. Good market with not much competition."

"Yep. Annabelle's done a pretty amazing job getting it up and putting the team together. We'll be turning a nice profit by year's end, with lots of room for growth," Bobby answered, his voice weaker than when the conversation had started.

"You got room for investors? I can carry it in all our shops. We get good sales—I could also call Jesse Jewel over at REI, get her to shake up some orders."

Bobby's lips flattened at the edges. "So, this is how you think you are gonna do it, huh?"

"Not sure what you mean—but if you're talking about my offer, it'll help get your company off the ground, and you'd have someone who could mentor and advise you on the business side of things. Clover could have a grandfather," he added. "Lots of wins here."

"Yeah, lots of wins—until I want to do what I fucking want!" Bobby Mac shot back, ripping off his sunglasses. "Then it'll become us versus you, and I am tired of that stupid fucking game."

Bill shook his head and dropped his gaze at his boots. *This kid does not fucking get it*, he thought.

"Why do you hate me so much?" he asked, the slightest sense of sadness in his words.

"Because this all means nothing to you," Bobby answered. "Me, Belle, Clover. Mom. All fucking nothing."

Somehow, this landed, and Bill felt a cold sting to his right forearm. Leaning over to catch his breath, he walked to the driver's side door.

"You think that if you want. But this offer's not lasting out the week. And if you pass, then you become my competition, and there is no way in hell I am letting any competition do business in this valley."

With a slam, he was in the car, and with a spray of gravel, barreling back toward town.

"Yep," Bobby said out loud, even though there was nobody there to hear him. "That went just about as expected."

That night, Bobby fumbled through dinner, trying everything he could to not bring up his meeting with his father. Fortunately, Annabelle was on cloud eleven and only wanted to talk about her meeting with He Who Eats.

"Gunther offered to help," she shared. "He still has access to the horse trailers we used to get them here, and he said he could get two of the rock climbers using water on his property to help move them to the backside of the village. Can you believe this? We'll have a safe space for them. And they are just-just-just going to love it! The grass is so gorgeous, and there is so much space for them to roam. It's absolutely perfect."

Ladling out some black beans, Nanny A nodded. "I knew they would be receptive. The Indigenous are always in tune with the true nature of things. They knew what had to happen. And I'm sure getting some crow under Bill's nails must have felt pretty good, too."

Annabelle smiled. "Exactly, Mom, exactly. You should have seen the place. It was like one giant conversation with nature—everything they did was out of respect for not ruining the harmony of what was already there. When you're done with your leave, you should teach a course about their social systems back at Boulder. The kids would love it."

Nanny A nodded silently and poured a spoonful of beans into Clover's plastic bowl. Meanwhile, Bobby was still lost in a replay of his earlier exchange with his father. The memory turning him nauseous, he shoveled the rest of his dinner back into the clay serving dish and planted a kiss on Clover's head.

"Congratulations," he said to Annabelle, squeezing her shoulder, and with that, he headed to the door. "I've got some errands to run in town. I'll be back."

Before anybody could argue, he was out the door—and when the sound of the car driving off fell silent, Nanny A leaned back in her chair and gave her daughter a direct and pointed look.

"What?" Annabelle asked, but she knew what was coming.

"How can you still think he's not messing around, Belle."

Annabelle had to steady her hand to avoid dropping her fork.

"Every night, he goes into town, and when he comes home, it's at two a.m., and he reeks of cigarettes and bathroom soap."

"Because that is just not his style, Mom. Yes, he's immature. And yes, he's bad at communicating—but he loves me. And Clove."

"I have no doubt about that, sweetie, but he is a man," answered Nanny A. "And when they feel shitty, the only thing that can make them feel better is either killing something or getting a woman to look gooey at them. And when that happens, an injection switch flips, and they get a thousand times dumber than they already are."

"Well, Bobby is not average, Mom. And yes, he is a man, but he also knows how close we are to getting Paca Joe going, and he would never screw that up."

Nanny A sat back in her chair and looked at her daughter. She had been cheated on herself—by Annabelle's father—and the pattern she was witnessing in Bobby's behavior was almost identical. But she also remembered what it was like to face the possibility that her husband was messing around on her when they just had their child.

Yes, Bobby was a loving man—but if Nanny A had to place a bet, she'd place the odds of Annabelle being wrong about his fidelity at about 140 percent.

Friday came quickly for everyone—and despite not contributing to the recent success with rehoming the alpacas, Bobby was happy for Annabelle. He thought about helping and almost offered to drive the horse trailers, but that would have kept him from doing what he was in the process of doing—

selling Danu's to Clarence Samuel McClintock Jr., the second-generation owner of McClintock's Guns, Ammo, and Other Utilities.

Since Suzanne's passing, McClintock had made it known he was eager to purchase Danu's. Bobby, now knowing his father was on a path of brutal retaliation, felt it was necessary to create a nest egg for his family—and Danu's required a lot more attention than he expected. With McClintock offering good hard cash, Bobby figured, "Why not?" and closed the deal.

So, while Annabelle loaded ninety-eight alpacas into eight large horse trailers with a smiling Gunther, Bobby Mac took a cashier's check for $995,000 from Clarence Samuel McClintock Jr. and deposited it into their joint checking account.

Walking back from the bank, he was nothing but that ten-thousand-watt grin. He now had options laid out before him—giant, magnificent options that afforded any future his family wanted. Staring at the setting sun, one magnificent thought ricocheted through his heart: *Now, I can lead us to happiness.*

Across the valley, as the same sun set with the same warm golden shine, ninety-eight alpacas found their footing along Hangman's Rock. They were anxious at first, now unfortunately used to the cold presence of iron blocking their ability to roam. So, with hesitance, they stepped off the trailers.

Standing there, no fence or armed officer in sight, it took them a couple of minutes to realize they had a horizon and mountain to explore. But when they did, they took off on their two-toed feet and spread like fingers along the hills, inhaling their first pure breath of freedom since leaving Peru. Annabelle watched as they hopped and climbed, sure-footed, toward the sun, one single thought ricocheting through her heart: *Now, I can lead us to happiness.*

When she returned home that evening, it was to a house lit by candle and a bouquet of roses, which Bobby Mac handed her as soon as she walked through the front door.

"Clover's spending the night at Nanny A's," he told her, leaning in to give her a kiss. Annabelle was speechless, unable to imagine a more perfect welcome. Then Bobby picked her up and spun her in his arms, and they started giggling like it was their fourth date.

"Bobby . . . Bobby, we did it!" she said, radiating. "You should have been there! It was so gorgeous, I can't even explain!"

"I believe you, I believe you, I believe you," Bobby shined back. "But wait, just give me one second, and then you can tell me everything."

Before Annabelle could respond, Bobby was at the kitchen island, grabbing a piece of paper and handing it to her. It was a bank deposit slip. Holding it in her hands, Annabelle studied the $995,000 figure written on the paper. *This has to be fake*, she thought, but the bank account number on the slip matched that of their joint account.

"Oh my God, Bobby," she gasped. "What is this?"

"Nine-hundred and ninety-five thousand dollars!" Bobby exclaimed.

"What?" shrieked Annabelle, dumbfounded. Purely, blindly, dizzyingly dumbfounded.

"I sold Danu's to Bill McClintock. He's been bothering me about it since Mom's funeral, and I got him to pay cash for it in one lump sum!"

It took a long moment for this to sink in. Annabelle was confused by so much—most of all by her very own reaction to Bobby's announcement. Why did it feel like suddenly she had a hatchet in her chest?

"Wait—," she said at last. "What do you mean you sold Danu's?"

"I mean, I sold it. The store, the inventory, the building—everything."

Annabelle took a breath. It wasn't big or dramatic, but it filled her lungs and left her still, and it was enough to tip Bobby off that she wasn't half as thrilled as he expected.

Reaching out his hand, he touched her arm. "Wait—what's wrong? You're holding a deposit slip for nine-hundred and ninety-five thousand dollars—that's enough for us to get a new house, level up Paca Joe, or put Clover through college twenty times."

Annabelle just shook her head. "Oh, Bobby," she said. "What did you do?"

"What do you mean what did I do?" Standing now, Bobby began to pace back and forth. "I got us almost a million dollars in cash!"

"Don't you get it?" Annabelle asked, suddenly infuriated by Bobby's pacing. "Or has it not sunk into your thick fucking head?"

This got Bobby's attention. Real fast.

"We needed Danu's," Annabelle insisted. "That was our main buyer for the year."

"So?" Bobby responded. "We can afford to get a new buyer. Shit, we can afford to open a store and just stock the line."

"Jesus, Bobby," Annabelle exclaimed. "You didn't pay attention at any of the meetings, did you? It wasn't just that Danu's was our first customer—we were piggybacking on their PO process, using their delivery services and insurance, and even using their employees to help us package and inventory everything. Danu's was our anchor!"

Bobby turned and collapsed into a chair across from Annabelle. Slumped over, hands on his thighs, he had absolutely no idea how to respond.

Across the kitchen, Annabelle shook her head, tears rolling silent down her cheeks.

"You killed us, Bobby," she whispered. "You destroyed the single thing beyond Clover I care about."

Bobby reeled back in his chair. Not knowing what to do next, he rubbed his thighs, stood, and circled the kitchen. Annabelle, oblivious, was lost in her own daze. It took the sound of his fist crashing through the kitchen cabinet to snap her back to reality, and by the time she realized what had just happened, Bobby Mac was gone. On his way to town. To drink brown liquor and find Lindsey Jessups—the woman he had been having an affair with for the last six months.

Where he was going was of no interest or concern to Annabelle—not now, after everything that had just transpired. Walking to the kitchen table she blew out the candles, swept up the shards of wood from the broken cabinet, and got into her car.

At first, she wasn't sure where she was going, but she found herself four miles down Yeehaw Pass on Crow's Nest Lane. In minutes, she'd be at Gunther's trading post. And after a moment of thought, she realized that was the only place she could imagine going.

To her dismay, Gunther wasn't there, but she had an idea where he could be—Punishment Lake. Loading his fishing gear into the cab of his car, Gunther was pleased to see Annabelle pull her Subaru next to his Volkswagen and park. He was also pleased when she pulled him to her lips and kissed him long and soft. He was, however, very surprised when she led him to his car and pulled off his jacket and shirt.

Meanwhile, just over a mile from Punishment Lake, Nanny A sat at her kitchen table. In front of her, next to a candle and a glass of merlot, was a shoebox filled with old letters. They were from Annabelle's father, and in them were cursive lines about voracious biting, gut-wrenching I-miss-you-so-much-I-could-die loneliness, and the hardest to revisit, a promise of being "buried in a Lincoln Continental" so they could "spend eternity driving the amber highway together."

Love, once promised and lived madly, was all over those pages. And now, in her daily life, it meant nothing. These words were just cracks left on the vase she'd repaired when the love she held in it for her ex-husband fell and shattered on the floor.

But, looking at the letters, she was heartbroken all over again. And this time, not for herself, but for her daughter. Because she had the knowledge that one day, the love Annabelle held so tight would become nothing but worn pages in a shoebox kept as a reminder to never fall in love again. It was an unbearable feeling—and the pain she was feeling would have been unbearable, too, if not for one thing.

"Nananananananana!" squeaked Clover. Pulling herself from her letters, Nanny A looked left at her granddaughter who held a plastic bowl in her hand and smiled as she tapped it against the tabletop of her highchair.

She wanted more black beans. Now.

# CHAPTER 29

## AUGUST 2002

It had been years since Nanny A had been in one of her shoeboxes. This one had Annabelle written on top, and in it was a collection of letters she'd sent while on her summer of '75 teen tour. She was hating it. She was loving it. She had crushes. She had enemies. She had ideas about what she wanted to do next summer. She had requests for more money and new underwear.

Nanny A smiled as she reread them. This was the closest reminder of what she loved—what she *truly* loved—and it had nothing to do with Wolfehaus, or Gunther, or even Clover. It had only to do with the two of them. Their secrets. Their thoughts. Their forever connection. As she read them, the tears did not come as they did in the past. In their place, instead, was the tingling assurance that came when someone was about to do the right thing.

In this case, the right thing she was about to do concerned Clover. Since their fight, Clover had not spoken to her, been by the house, reached out to anyone she knew, or taken a single dollar from her checking account. As far as she knew, Clover could have been another fraying letter in her shoebox. Or just the thing to remind her to return to herself.

The Wolfehaus employees quickly recognized there was something different about Nanny A. She no longer joked with them about girlfriends or Myspace postings or threw cupcakes at them when they climbed the rock wall. Her time, instead, was spent alone, in her office, on the computer, printing out a variety of documents and assembling what she knew as her "get the fuck outta Wolfehaus plan." Her aim was to create a self-sustaining infrastructure, finalize an easy-to-execute production model, and then transfer all her assets and ownership to Clover. It would be placed in a trust, and from afar, she could watch Wolfehaus hum along as she finished what Annabelle had started: the journey of turning a young girl into a strong independent woman.

A couple of weeks into her submersion, Gunther knocked on her office door to check in. It had been months since they'd spent time together, and months more since they were physical with one another. Out of respect, he didn't find other people to fulfill his needs for intimacy, as he still pictured her soft hips and fierce riding when he masturbated.

"I just heard back from the foreman. They're a week ahead of schedule with the foundation. And the first six lifts will be done by the end of August," he offered, hoping this news would warm a response.

"That's wonderful, G," Nanny A responded, her eyes still locked on her computer screen.

Smiling, Gunther took a trepidatious step into her office. "And guess what else, Abigail? The council approved our permits for the concert. We can officially combine the Snow Ball with the opening of Wolfe Mountain."

For a moment, a nearly dead ember sparked in Nanny A's chest from this news. She turned toward Gunther and offered a warm smile. "I am so happy for you, Gunther. You must be so proud."

Gunther smiled but also shrunk. He didn't know why, but in hearing the comment, a flush of anxiety ran through him. He was initially puzzled, but then he realized, it was in her use of pronouns. *You* not *we*.

She never before used pronouns that were not inclusive. Ones that were not about *us* or *our* or *ours*. Even when she spoke with the Spanish-speaking employees, she used *nuestros* or *nosotros*. Because for her, Wolfehaus was all about the us. The family.

"Abigail, I have been thinking," Gunther said, his voice soft but sweet. "I know I have been preoccupied with the construction, and the Snow Ball, and the opening—and that's all well and good, but I haven't made dinner for you in some time. I would like to, very much, again."

Nanny A smiled back at Gunther. She knew that meant sex, and with the amount of time since they'd last had it, this most likely meant a night filled with multiple exchanges in multiple positions. It was tempting, as was the promise of his schnitzel. Looking into Gunther's eyes, something told Nanny A that this dinner was the same thing for him—a much-needed physical release and a way to say a final goodbye.

Grabbing her reading glasses off her head, Nanny A touched a temple tip to her mouth and thought on it. "You know what, G, I'd enjoy that. How about this Saturday?"

Gunther's face lit up. "Ah, perfect," he exclaimed. "Perfect! I will see you then, *mein fraulein. Auf wiedersehen*, and peace out."

Glowing, he left her office. Also glowing, Nanny A returned to her Excel spreadsheet and imagined, in its columns, shadings of Saturday night. She looked forward to a touch, and as she imagined Gunther going down on her, she had a flash of Jack Dempsey Florence-Schwartzberg and hoped he finally learned how to give oral.

The following morning, Nanny A did the now atypical act of stopping at Lola's Diner. Unlike in the past, it wasn't for blueberry pancakes or a thermos full of coffee—it was to see Sheriff Dan Daley.

Walking into the aluminum building, she found him in the back, nursing a hot tea and reading the *Fortooth Daily*. Grinning at her, he leaned his head left and pushed a chair out for her to sit. Nanny A slid into it and realized just how easy it was to grin back.

"I thought you weren't talking to me," Sheriff Dan Daley said as Nanny A reached for his mug and helped herself to a sip.

"I thought *you* weren't talking to *me*," she said, wincing at the taste. The sheriff laughed a little at that.

"Chinese herbs," he said and gestured at the mug. "Stopped drinking coffee a while ago. It was affecting my cortisol levels. This keeps my adrenal glands balanced." He leaned in closer, as if to share a secret. "And it's doing miracle work on my colon."

"Your colon, huh?" Nanny A chuckled. "If I remember correctly, Jesus himself wouldn't be capable of producing a miracle necessary to rectify that level of chaos."

"Which is exactly why I gave up his teachings for Buddhism," Sheriff Dan quipped, raising his salt-and-pepper brows. He gave her a quick wink, which Nanny A returned.

*This is flirting. This is what it feels like to flirt again*, she thought.

Collecting herself, she turned toward Sheriff Dan and pulled a manila envelope from her jacket.

"I need a favor, Dan," she said, placing the package on the table.

"Finally, getting in the ol' drug game, huh?"

"I wish. Be a lot less work, probably."

"I shouldn't be worried about anything here, should I?" Sheriff Dan asked, sipping on his Chinese herbs and eyeing the manila envelope.

"No, of course not. And don't be an ass," Nanny A answered. "I just need someone to hold on to these docs. They're backups of my assets. Just been getting my things in order and . . . I don't know, I guess I figured you'd be a safe place to keep copies."

"Well, considering how much trouble I've had saying no to your assets in the past, there's no reason I can think of to start now."

"Jesus," Nanny A said, laughing. "You need to find some Chinese herbs to help you with those jokes."

"And if I do, will you grab some supper with me?" Sheriff Dan asked, hiding his hope behind a swig from his mug.

Nanny A looked him up and down. He was grayer than when they met, but his too-thick mustache was thankfully gone, and he still had those hands . . . and she couldn't help but love those hands.

"How about Sunday?" she said, knowing full well she'd be meeting with Gunther the night before. "I'll cook for you. Rice and beans. And if I am feeling it, some lomo saltado."

Sheriff Dan grabbed the manila envelope and placed it in his briefcase. He tried to fight it, but he sure did have a big smile.

## JUNE 2002, TWO MONTHS EARLIER

"Aw, come on!" Clover shrieked, giggling. "You know I'm not that stupid!" She really wasn't, but Jacques—the security guard who sat with her in an unmarked black Jeep Wrangler—thought she was. Pulling on a joint, he coughed up a laugh.

"Maybe, maybe not. I don't fucking know, but there is no way I am letting you take this for less than five hundred."

"Dude, come on! How am I supposed to squeeze anything out of that? I won't even clear a nickel," Clover answered in a purr.

"Holy shit, did you see that?" Jacques yelled as he took another hit of the joint, pointing through the window at a squiggle in the landscape. "That tree just popped up from the ground, holy shit!"

Looking at the field, Clover saw six bamboo spears sway back and forth in the wind—each one with a bulbous swell at top. They were the town's namesake.

"Hah, yeah, those are Fortooths—rattlesnakes that stand straight like that when they're getting ready to hunt. If they bite you, boom," Clover said, turning her hand into a gun and pointing it at Jacques. "You're dead as dirt. No savin' ya."

"Holy fuck, dude. And they are all around here? Shit, I gotta get steel toe boots, right?"

"No, not at all. They don't bother us. You have to literally fall on one for it to bite you. Or piss it off so badly, it has other reasons to want to bite you. Listen, Jacques, look at me." Eyes bloodred and dry as dust, Jacques turned his high-as-fuck face to Clover. "Let's do this. You give me this ounce for four hundred. If I can sell it all in a week, I come back here and buy one a week or more from you for the remainder of the summer. If I don't, I'll buy it for seven fifty and pay you the remainder over the next three weeks."

"Seven fifty?" coughed Jacques. "I was only asking for six hundred—"

"I know," interjected Clover. "And that's why this is a beautiful deal for you. You either make a big profit on one buy or have a steady profit for the next ten weeks."

Jacques smiled and took another hit off the joint as one of the straight-as-a-spear Fortooths leaped at a field mouse. Caught in its inch-long set of double fangs, the mouse tried to wiggle away but was stuck, in a viselike trap, absorbing a paralytic venom. Fifteen seconds later, it was dead, and two minutes later, Clover began her first job as a ketamine dealer.

And that's how her summer went. She'd get product from Jacques on Monday, then spend all of Monday night turning one ounce into three, with the addition of sugar and cornstarch. Then all of Tuesday through Sunday, she sold it in town.

As expected, business was good. In a town as small as Fortooth, excitement was always at a premium, and when a new toy came around, everyone wanted to play with it. Also, being who she was, she was listened to. And feared. First for her grandfather's name and second for her grandmother's. Outside of the cartel, it would be difficult to imagine a dealer moving with more impunity than Clover Dolores Macklemore.

Inheriting the entrepreneurial instinct of his always traveling father, Jesse was aroused by the small business Clover had built. Soon, there was talk of her moving with him to Providence when he started college. There, she could continue her work, providing liberal minds with an excuse to spend their parents' money and pretend they were sucking some lost temporal fume off the Electric Kool-Aid Acid Test. Clover, at first, was hesitant to nibble on this. Their relationship was about sex, music, drugs, alcohol, or whatever else could be glorified through the tingle. But one night, after a rabid session in Jesse's hot tub that ended with one of the most glorious ecstasy-induced orgasms he'd ever had, he told Clover he loved her. "Not just 'cause you're hot," he'd said. "Or 'cause you know how to make me come harder than anyone I've been with. You just *get* me."

Truth was, Clover didn't love Jesse outside of the sex. She didn't even understand how he liked Widespread Panic or The String Cheese Incident. But she loved the sex. And if that was the currency it took to get out of Fortooth Bend, she began to think that was something worth capitalizing on.

In about eleven weeks Clover was able, despite tapping into a few generous dollops from her supply, to amass $36,411. By her expectations, she would be close to $50,000 at summer's end, and from the research she'd done online, that was plenty to rent a place in Providence for two years.

By that time, she figured she would either still be with Jesse or broken up and dating someone who owned a restaurant. The truth was, she'd never intended to stay with Jesse past summer, let alone fall in love with him. But as their sex kept up, she'd noticed herself getting jealous and possessive.

Maybe there would be a breakthrough of some kind—one that would lead to the invisible, psychic-like connection she'd had with Jimmy, where he could tap into every volume change of her frequency and counter with an intuitive response that needed no words, touch, or look. Maybe as the orgasms increased and the regularity with which he screamed "I love you!" multiplied, Jesse could learn to read her like, well . . . like Jimmy.

With August coming to an end, Clover began preparations for her move to Providence. Throughout the month, she would spend her mornings waiting until Nanny A left and then she would sneak into the house and raid it for whatever she needed. Outside of clothes, there wasn't much. Mostly just photographs of her parents; the Paca Joe samples she still had in plastic bags; notes her mom kept in some sort of business journal; Dingus McGee, the giraffe her father gave her on her second Valentine's Day; and a fanny pack of her mother's from her time in Peru. It held loose ends of an audiotape, and a tusk or fang of some animal wrapped in what looked like snakeskin.

Intrigued, she packed it, but she still wrestled about whether she would pack her skis. Even though every visit ended with her in the basement, sanding their edges and waxing their base, it had been almost nine months since she last skied, and the whispers of those mornings were becoming harder to ignore.

A week before she planned on leaving, she decided to take one set of skis, poles, and boots because, as she said to Jesse, "Providence gets snow, right?"

Not surprisingly, Jesse's father did not come home before Jesse left for school. But he did arrange for a shipping company to send his stuff east, and deposited all the money Jesse would need to get him through the move and first semester. His mother talked of visiting him in early October, when she got back from her honeymoon in Kenya and after she finished setting up her new brownstone in SoHo. So, the end of August was perfect, as it allowed them to spend the last few nights they had in Fortooth doing essentially whatever the fuck they wanted. For Jesse, this meant seeing as many people as possible; for Clover, this meant nights wandering the town and saying her goodbyes through half-shuttered windows to the people who populated the last eighteen years of her life.

Two nights before her departure, she decided to take one of her most practiced nighttime routes. Starting at the center of town, she moved her way outward, toward the quiet perimeter streets. Turning off Main Street to Road Runner Lane, she saw Principal Janks bake ziti and spin his girlfriend to Captain & Tennille. Clarence Samuel McClintock Jr. taking pictures with his wife of handmade pastel dioramas they staged with stuffed animals. Then, as she crept farther out of town, there was Sheriff Dan Daley, practicing Beatles songs on a Casio keyboard, and Baby Tubbs in his boxers, cigarette dangling from his mouth, cleaning trout in his kitchen sink.

And finally, there was Jimmy's old ranch house, the paint peeling from the window frames and the rooms empty and dark. It had been six weeks since his father killed himself, many wondering if it was from the loss of his job due to Glory Peak buying up all the municipal land or the fact that his brain had run too many miles. Clover had tried several times to contact Jimmy when she'd heard, but each time, his location got lost in the quagmire of navy bureaucracy. Seeing the house now, a shiver ran through her. She missed Jimmy. Terribly. And she would miss everyone else, too. Watching them that night, it was impossible to deny the cellular level at which each one had melded to her. It was beyond nuclei, cytoplasm, and membranes. They were part of the ribosomes and mitochondria that fed her breath and body. They carried the source of life, not just for her but the entire Farangotta Valley.

By the time Clover made it onto Marie Major Drive, she was nothing but a floating fog of sadness. This confused and annoyed her. She thought she had come to hate Fortooth. The people, the food, the baggage, the sound of her last name—which she planned on changing when she moved to Providence.

But now, taking her last walk through its streets, she swore to herself that she would never forget a face or a name.

As the houses turned in for the night, Clover found herself at the end of a cul-de-sac, where a prairie-style house sat behind a wooden fence. The house itself was nothing special. The only thing even somewhat special about it was that Cathy Porter lived there—a fellow graduate of the Prescott S. Norville Elementary and High School class of 2002 and voted most likely to become a regular on *Friends*. She had friends, so many, and a boyfriend who was vice president of the student council, and a dentist father who'd built up a loyal following by offering discounts on retainers and teeth whitening.

For most, Cathy's life was pedestrian. Family dinners at six, a younger brother whose greatest hope was to be the captain of the debate team, and a mother with a compulsion for puzzles featuring flora of the Pacific Northwest. But for Clover, Cathy's pedestrian life was pure, unadulterated exoticness.

In fact, it was magnificent exoticness—and knowing this magnificent exoticness would elude her, somehow always within sight but out of reach, Clover was intent on having one last gulp of it.

Normally, there was a Lexus in the driveway and a family sharing baked chicken in the kitchen. But tonight, the driveway sat empty, and the house was in darkness. Walking the perimeter, she looked through the windows and took in the slate counter of the kitchen table. Then the black-and-white cow paintings that hung on every living room wall, and finally, the worn leather sofa taking up too much space in an overstuffed study. Circling to the back, Clover imagined Cathy's parents lying in bed, David Letterman glowing from their wall-mounted TV as they snuggled into the latest Tom Clancy novel. But instead, there was nothing. Just drawn shades and a lone light illuminating a bedroom at the north end of the house. Hoping to see Cathy's brother clicking through a video game or bootleg copy of some R-rated film, she decided to creep closer to the window for a peak.

Through the drawn shade, it was difficult to make out an image, but she was able to hear the growing moans of a woman enjoying the attention of a lover. *Bootleg movie*, Clover laughed to herself. *Or maybe her brother is with his girlfriend.*

Clover had never witnessed anyone other than herself have sex before. Curious, she moved to the window and arched her eyes toward an opening at its base.

It was still difficult to see into the room. But through the flashes of light the TV cast, she was able to make out something squirming on the bed. Sound, however, was perfectly clear. And as she tiptoed closer, her vantage point revealed that behind the partially opened blinds, the window was wide open.

Giving up on seeing anything of importance, Clover closed her eyes and decided to just focus on the audio. As a chorus of moaning built and layered toward a crescendo, she was certain about two things: First, this wasn't porn, but two people indeed having sex. And second, she could recognize that male voice. A heartbeat later, as though to confirm her suspicions, she heard the voice of none other than Jesse fucking Vanigan say, "I love you."

A wash of acid rose up her throat. Sweeping the blinds open, Clover got a front-row seat to a show she never wanted to see: her boyfriend, Jesse, cheating on her with a sweaty Cathy Porter, his penis partially still inside her. And then came static. Red, scratchy static.

Clover screamed—or something like that—and before she could stop, she lifted a garden hose off the ground and whipped it through the glass, shattering it. Enraged, she kept whipping the hose at the toothy windowpane, realizing belatedly that the hose was on and attached to a sprinkler, that released a corolla-like spray throughout the room.

Shocked by the gushing hose, Clover stumbled back and watched Jesse and Cathy scramble for their clothes. Aflame with anger, Clover felt her body heat rise to such a peak, she expected to explode. Instead, all her pain allowed her to do was run. And run.

By the time she got to Nanny A's—or her former house, or her parents' former house—her breathing was so convoluted and abrupt, it was impossible to hear her sobbing. Incapable of standing, Clover fell through the front door and screamed, "Nanny A, are you here?"

Silence answered, and realizing the lights were off and there was no car in the driveway, Clover wondered where she could be. It was Saturday, eight o'clock—and considering she wasn't talking to Sheriff Dan Daley, there was only one place she could be: Gunther's.

By the time she got to Gunther's, the wheezing of her lungs had given over to the yelps of her cries. Careening to the porch, she collected her breath and wiped her face with the sleeve of her shirt. Her pulse finally slowing, she took three calming breaths and reached for the doorknob. But it was already open and swaying in the night.

Unsure of what to do, Clover entered—and what she discovered was a house in romance mode. Candles burned in bronze holders, a half-empty bottle of wine rested on the counter, Nina Simone cooed "I Loves You, Porgy" from speakers.

Hoping to find proof of Nanny A, she crept farther into the living room. But there was none.

That was, until she spotted the master bedroom door ajar. Already, this was feeling a little too much like the scene she'd just witnessed at Cathy's house. Stopping to ask herself if she wanted to know more, Clover bit her lip, clenched her fist, and approached the door. Behind it, came a soft whimper and the accordion-like breath of rhythmic gasping. As she took another step forward, the whimpering stopped, and what followed was the rapid thudding of what sounded like a dog tail wagging against the floor. Then came Gunther's voice, "Abigail? ABIGAIL?"

Hand shaking, Clover opened the door to find a fully naked Gunther Wolfe pushing rhythmically on Nanny A's exposed chest—trying to administer a frenzied form of CPR.

When he looked up and spotted Clover standing in the doorway, he shouted, "Call 911!"

Clover sprinted to the nearest phone, and as she dialed, she knew the image of her dead grandmother and Gunther's uncircumcised penis would be tattooed to her mind forever.

Clover did not speak for two weeks following the death of Nanny A. From the moment they pronounced her dead at the hospital, through the funeral, through the nondenominational grieving ceremony, through the tribal cremation her former students threw, Clover did not utter a single word. Or make eye contact with anyone.

She tried to catch Sheriff Dan Daley's eyes once, whom she assumed would be heartbroken by this event. But from what she could tell, he wasn't—because he knew, from the 911 call, Nanny A had a heart attack in the middle of sex with Gunther. And he knew Nanny A was supposed to have dinner with him the following night. Refusing to mourn, Sheriff Dan Daley was officially done with any love he had left and instead replaced it with a more active feeling—hate.

So, with no one left for Clover to grieve with, she sat in silence. Or stood in silence. Eyes on the floor and face blank as people hugged her, kissed her dry cheek, and whispered condolences.

Nanny A sure had touched a lot of people. Flowers arrived in countless bouquets—so many, they could have inventoried a flower shop on their own—and letters came long, handwritten, and plagued with phrases like *life-changing*. There was also one person, a man in his mid-thirties, in a high-quality suit, who wept for two hours during her viewing. His name was a strange amalgamation of Irish and Jewish, something like Jack O'Florence Schwartz-something. He told Clover that Nanny A was his teacher and that he planned on endowing a scholarship in her honor at the University of Colorado Boulder for minority women in the social sciences. But Clover did not care. She did not care about any of this.

She was, however, curious about one thing. Gunther. He was here. He was there. He was everywhere. Waiting in the eaves, his body always seeming to be half cast in shadow. But he never approached her. He just watched her. Out of the corner of his eye, through reflected surfaces, across rooms and streets. Unlike Jesse Vanigan's quiet stares, these did not bother her because Clover knew they did not sum her up as prey. They were the looks of a newborn cub searching for his lost mother but finding instead another adult female he hoped would keep him warm. For once, she did not hate his weakness or the desperation it carried. But still, it was not enough to bring words to her mouth.

Two weeks and one day after Nanny A's heart gave out—and only three days after the funeral and other proceedings came to a close—Clover heard a knock on her door. At first, she thought it was just the wind tapping the oak of a loose doorframe, but after several seconds, it repeated, the sound steady like a drum. When she turned the corner and drifted down the hallway to the front door, she realized it wasn't the wind but something else. Some*body* else.

Standing behind the door was Gunther Wolfe. He held a strudel, a canteen of coffee, and a bag. Intrigued, Clover pulled her hair into a ponytail, opened the door, and stood to the side so that Gunther could walk in. Which he did. Over to the kitchen table, where he rested the strudel and pulled up a chair.

Silence followed. A lot of it.

Listening to the second hand of the grandfather clock click in the kitchen, Clover felt Gunther try to pull her eyes to him, but she refused. Instead, she sat on the arm of the sofa, her back slumped and ponytail aimed at him. Accepting that a conversation wasn't going to happen, Gunther breathed in the hum of the refrigerator, rose, positioned the chair back against the kitchen table, and left.

When the sound of Gunther's car faded into the night, Clover moved to a seat on the sofa. Scanning the room, she saw nothing and everything. Brown walls and photos of her parents. Nanny A's purple fleece, the bar her father built from Danu's soda counter. Whether she wanted to admit it or not, around her were the remnants of two generations of death. Totems of past dreams, material proof that said, "Yes, I once traveled" or "Yes, I once took an art class" or "Yes, I could use my hands for more than just masturbation." She realized that this house, like the shoeboxes Nanny A kept in the attic, was just a big container to hold memories of something that no longer existed.

Accepting this, Clover decided there was only one thing to do: get fucked up. And this was why Clover loved ketamine—it was the fastest, most effective way to disappear into a pinhole. A thick, coarse bump would make her eyes twitch. But a long rail of eight inches would kick her head to the ceiling, throb her temples, and dilute her pupils down to an atom.

Walking into her former room, she disappeared into her closet and pulled a section of a floorboard up. In it, wrapped in a purple sarong, was a patinated bronze box shaped like a peacock.

Returning to the kitchen table, she opened it and pulled out a sandwich-size Ziploc. Fourteen grams of ketamine sat in the bag. Dumping the contents on the table, Clover took a playing card from her wallet and separated out a small pile of the powder. The queen of hearts staring at her from her hand, she slid the pile back and forth in elongated strokes that spread the powder into a thin ten-inch line of ketamine.

Grabbing her wallet again, she took out a ten-dollar bill. It already had the curved impression of being rolled up many times and was easy for Clover to twist into a straw. She then placed it over the line, took a giant inhale, and felt the powder shoot through her nose and land, tart, in the back of the throat. She coughed. Then a smile began to form, and before the feeling of helium rising took over her brain, she cut another line.

Clover did nine lines that night. And partnered with a bottle of Nanny A's sixteen-year-old Lagavulin single malt scotch, her temples shot to a gallop. A loud gallop. So loud and fierce, she could not hear anything but the pumping of her blood or see anything but a blast of white. Stumbling through the living room, she was simultaneously numb and on fire. Nothing she grabbed had any weight, and everything she touched sent her skin crawling, as if a million spear-holding soldiers were stabbing their sharpened tips into every one of her gasping pores.

Soon, the only thing she could feel, or see, was flame. The popping, crackling, color-changing chameleon of white and orange that sprouted from a BIC lighter she always kept on her in case someone needed to spark a bowl. Clamping down on it, she clicked it off and on. And in the process turned her fingertips black, unaware that her skin was charring and melting into a waxy blend of epidermal goo with every spark of the lighter. Immune to the pain, Clover wondered what would happen if the flame of the lighter touched the wick of the living room candles.

Not much, she discovered. The candle flames were just another jumping, flickering manifestation of oxygen and flame that became very boring. Out of drugs and out of whiskey, Clover needed something else to remind her body to pulse. Looking through a living room window, she saw something that did. The blurry, milky mass of cheese hanging in the night sky. She was going outside. But first, she walked to the pantry and grabbed a long extension cord from the shelf.

Despite how zonked she was, Clover understood the implications of her decision. She wasn't just going outside; she was going on a stumbling, vision-impaired trek into the heart of the Farangotta. Putting eighteen years of memory to the test, she staggered blindly through the nightscape and gave her body over to the unexpected dagger of rocks, brush, and trees.

Somehow, she avoided all major obstacles and leaned into a ketamine-powered autopilot that directed her on a lopsided hike up Jade Ridge. Bloodied and filled with splinters of slate, she slipped on broken shale and fought for balance with outstretched arms. Unaware of the large, cold raindrops that began to fall from the sky and unaware of why she even bothered to trundle forward, she fell to the base of a pine tree that stood alone at the top of Jade Peak.

Across the valley, if Clover's eyes functioned, she would have seen eleven young women and men scattered along a variety of ridge lines. They were halfway through the *Oh-sah-cha-me*, each one hoping to find the connection that brought everything together in one sharable breath.

But she was, by all accounts, blind now. And also, felt nothing. Not even the rain, which had increased to a storming torrent of top and side drops. Pulling herself up the tree to a fat branch, she sat on it, oblivious to a collection of cairns, each balanced two feet high at the tree's roots below. Illogically, they defied the pummel of the storm, while above them, Clover illogically steadied herself to a stand. Pulling the extension cord from her shirt, she wrapped the plug around the branch. *This is going to feel good,* she thought, and then she wound the cord around her neck and whispered, "Thank you God, thank you, you stupid piece of shit."

A lightning bolt streaked next, sparking a flame in her throat that danced like the tip of her BIC lighter. It gave her sight again. And with clear eyes, she saw her mother, father, grandmother, and Dingus McGee—her stuffed animal giraffe—holding sparklers and spinning in slow motion. They motioned for her to come. Each one smiling, each one with their arms out, each one floating in clothes that billowed in slow-motion ripples. *Now I can be happy*, Clover thought, as she stepped off the branch and reached for her mother's wide-open arms.

# PART 4

"The Rabbit will eat," said the Fox.
"But only if there are carrots in the ceiling of his den."

—As excerpted from the Le'Echuwanna guide
to edible plants and healing fungi, courtesy of the University of Colorado,
Boulder, *Introduction to Cultural Studies of Ethnic Groups
within the Pacific Northwest of the United States*,
Revised Edition, 2010

# CHAPTER 30

**FEBRUARY 10, 1988**

It is with water that all change in the Farangotta Valley takes place. Sometimes, storms will sweep in, violent and ruthless, and chip a chunk off a mountain or a sliver of shale from a peak. But those moments stand few and far between. It is, however, with the rain, and the melted snow that collects in the valley, once it has fallen from clouds and settles en masse, that change truly happens. Waterfalls cascading over cliffs, creaks filling and rushing in steady gushes, carrying dirt down hills into sludgy formations that aerate, fortify, and mix the topsoil. And then, there is the leaking—the water that seeps through the rocks, trees, and dirt of the valley, that fills the cracks and crevices where air has snuck and feeds the plants and flowers that bloom in spring.

Following a single drop of this water would be to follow a path through millions of years of the geological activity that gave birth, then form, then shading to the Farangotta. Following a drop as it slinked through earth, down hair-thick cracks into the dense depths of a mountain, it was conceivable that, over time, this drop could bore its way through all terra and collect in the ceiling of a mineshaft. And eventually, after fifty years of collecting, reach such saturation it could bore a tiny hole and drip onto the floor of a mineshaft.

Or in this case, onto Annabelle as she lay on a cot in the mineshaft. This, of course, was possible, but it was also possible that the storm was so magnificent that the shaft, and the rock, and the mountain that shielded them were too weak to protect them much longer. And after eight minutes of water dripping onto the side of Annabelle's temple, she had to accept it did not come from sitting under the Peruvian waterfall she dreamed of. It came from a far worse reality: the ceiling was peeing on her.

Placing a hand over her face, she blocked the drips, rolled over, and arced her neck awake. Across from her, Bobby snored, the miner's lamp flickering faint as water trickled from the wall.

"B-Bobby," she sputtered. "Bobby, wake up—please." Nothing but a mumble came back. Grabbing a moldy burlap bag of coffee from under her pillow, she threw it at him. It landed in a thud and shocked open his eyes.

"What-what?" he growled, initially, like Annabelle, forgetting where he was. Looking around, the unfortunate reality returned. "Shit, I must've been dreaming. I thought I was by the Napo. You remember that river where we swam with the pink dolphins in Ecuador? Fuck, I was so nervous a piranha was gonna bite my pecker off."

Annabelle smiled, even though she didn't want to. But she did. Then, she sat up, pulled her hair into a ponytail, and rubbed her face. Now fully awake, she needed movement.

"Okay, Bobby," she said, "we need a plan."

"I hear you, babe, but right now, I don't know what more we can do. Based on that leaking, we either got one of the most brutal storms going on above us, or there's been a shift somewhere and snow is melting through. This is a recipe for an avalanche if there ever was one."

"I don't care, Bobby," Annabelle pushed back. "We have to find a solution."

Invigorated, Annabelle stood from the cot and investigated the mine. Pushing on barely finished corners and the worn four-by-four beams that held the shaft intact, she started searching once again for a new compartment. Watching her, Bobby shook his head. "Belle, I don't think you should be pushing on stuff right now with everything so loosened up."

"Listen, Bobby, we've got to find a way to the top or bottom! We've been down here for I don't know how many hours, and I'm not gonna fucking die here." Annabelle looked at the ceiling, then what she thought could be the front of the shaft room. "There's gotta be a path or something else they used to build this place."

"It didn't work that way, babe," Bobby answered. "The rail tracks weren't built to here. These rooms were just side parts part of a bigger system that came from the base of the mountain—not the top or middle."

"Fine, then how do we get to the main track system? Jesus, Bobby, just freaking help me," Annabelle snapped.

Bobby craned his neck back and looked at her. "What?"

"What, what?" she responded, annoyed.

"Just say it," he shot back.

"Say what?" Annabelle replied.

"You think this is my fault."

"I never said that," Annabelle countered, still examining the rock and walls.

"Yes, you do!" Bobby screamed back. "You were fine going on the Wobble Trail. I asked you before we went! You said okay. And then you said we should take Miner's Gasp."

"Okay, Bobby, I am not blaming you. Let's just get out of—"

"Yes, you fucking are!" Bobby interrupted. "You are always blaming me for everything!"

Annabelle turned to face Bobby. "Of course, I am blaming you. You're the reason we're here! Everything that got us fucking here! You fucking around, you selling Danu's, you drinking every goddamn night—every stupid thing you've ever fucking done is what's led us to this point!"

"Whoa, wait a second—I wasn't the only one who was fucking around. You and Gunther have been going at it for at least the last year!"

Shocked, Annabelle staggered back and grabbed her stomach. She didn't realize Bobby had so much as a clue about her affair with Gunther, but that wasn't even what surprised her most. It was the look in his eyes—he was hurt. Scratching behind her left ear, Annabelle searched for an answer.

"Bobby, I—I, uh—"

"Don't," interrupted Bobby. "You sit here on your fucking high horse, acting like I am a piece of shit, but you know what? *You're* the piece of shit! You're the piece of shit, and I wish I never fucking went into that restaurant or fucking married you! All you care about is your fucking bullshit! You think I got it easy—you think coming back here and living here was easy for me?"

Annabelle grabbed her stomach tighter and retreated to her cot. Shell-shocked, she sat down and stared at the ground when an earth-shifting jolt rang through the mine and sent Bobby into a wall and Annabelle to the ground. Dust clouded around them, and when it finally cleared, a large gush of water fell from the ceiling.

"Oh my God, Bobby, was that an earthquake?" Annabelle asked, coughing.

"No. Someone is blasting. They're trying to dynamite their way to us."

## SEPTEMBER 2002

When Clover woke up, it was to a king-size bed under a collection of elk skins and wool blankets. She was also in new clothes: an oversize Eddie Bauer waffle shirt with holes in the sleeves and a worn pair of red adidas track pants.

Shockingly, she was dry and warm— in a house she'd never been to before. Sitting up, she scanned the living room and saw a group of teenagers covered in a variety of animal pelts, devouring hot bowls of stew and passing blunts. Rubbing her eyes, she then saw three large flat-screen TVs all playing the same rerun of *Deep Space Nine* and watched He Who Eats maneuver through the kitchen on a peg leg attached to a roller skate. Not sure what do, Clover stood and leaned against the fireplace crackling through its last log.

He Who Eats spotted her and rolled to a stop. Raising his arms to the sky, he shouted, "Cowabunga, y'all, she's alive. The white devil is alive!"

Everyone turned around, all glowing in a way that suggested they recently accomplished something transcendent. A marathon maybe, or an epic climb. Watching them, Clover had no idea she was looking at the latest graduating class of the *Oh-sah-cha-me*. And the newest Elder Elders of the Le'Echuwanna, now a population of 106. Sensing her fear, He Who Eats walked to his stove and ladled out a bowl of stew.

"Come on, pull up a chair—we got food for you even though your grandfather is that wampum-chasing prick, Bill Fuckface Macklemore."

The tribespeople shifted their chairs to make room for Clover. He Who Eats then handed her the bowl and said, "This is some of the best goddamn elk you'll ever try."

Clover wasn't a fan of elk, but she was starving. And besides, it smelled great. Spooning a bite of stew into her mouth, she almost gasped at the burst of flavor. It was like she swallowed the freshest garden ever—sage, rosemary, garlic, all combining in a velvety sauce that hinted of carrots and chipotle.

"Looks like Sleeping Beauty likes our squirrel nut soup," He Who Eats bellowed as Clover shoveled the stew into her mouth. Moments later, she was scraping the bowl. "Princess want another serving?"

Clover nodded and as she did, a jolt bolted up her neck. Surprised at the pain, she scanned the kitchen and caught her reflection in a windowpane. Even though her image was muggy, she could see something wrapped around her throat. Her blood chilled at its sight and went even colder when she reached her hand under her ponytail and felt a damp buckskin dressing bandaged around her neck. Touching it, she throbbed with pain.

Laughing, He Who Eats handed her a fresh bowl. "That's from the *Me-oh-watch-oh*—the four-legged furry fuckers."

Clover coughed into her bowl. "What did you just say?"

Fancy Glove leaned forward and placed his bowl on the kitchen table. "He said the four-legged furry fuckers." Before Clover could respond, he offered his hand to shake. "My birth name is Fancy Glove, but you can call me Grant."

Clover nodded dully, still distracted by the bandage on her neck. "I'm Clover—"

"We know," Grant said.

Slowly, Clover turned her face toward Grant. His skin was smooth, a sun-kissed light red, that barely showed the trace of a fresh shave.

"But did he . . .? What did he just say?"

"*Me-oh-watch-oh*, the four-legged furry fuckers. They're alpacas. You probably didn't know it, but the *Me-oh-watch-oh* is one of the offshoots of the alpacas your family brought to the valley. Two were lost when they got rustled up back in the day by animal control. They've been living separate from the rest of the herd. Not just on our land but roaming the whole valley."

"And they bred—a lot. Like, a lot, a lot, a lot," a young girl, who Clover would learn was named Lapping Pearl, shared. "They're on Jade Ridge mostly—that's how they found you."

"Found me?" Clover asked, confused. "*You* didn't find me?"

"Hell no, Princess," said He Who Eats. "All of these guys were in ceremony chasing the new breath. One of the *Me-oh-watch-oh* found you. Grabbed you by the back of your neck and dragged your lanky ass down to Tear Cup Lake—and then we found you."

"C'mon," Clover challenged with a half laugh. "There is no way an alpaca is that strong."

"Normal alpacas aren't," He Who Eats answered. "But these alpacas been roaming and living off the primal nectar of the land. So now they're juiced. Like Schwarzenegger in *Conan*. They've been training on the wheel. 'Could crush a mustang if it came running."

Clover had no idea how to respond to this. Not smiling but not serious, she looked around the room as everyone looked back at her. Now trembling, she reached for the bowl and stood up.

"Uh, um. Mr. He Who Eats . . . uh, thank you for everything. It was real good, and I appreciate it. I think I'm going to head back home now and get some rest."

"Home?" He Who Eats cackled. "You don't got no home. It burned down two days ago."

Clover collapsed in the chair. Two days ago? Now it was all adding up. The bandage tight around her throat. Her fingertips sore, scars, pink and flaking across them. A memory next played before her—her holding a BIC lighter to her fingers, the flame melting them like wax. She was so high; she couldn't even feel it. And those candles she'd lit . . .

Watching Clover's face fall white, Grant cleared his throat and said, "I think it's time we filled you in on a few things."

Between Grant and He Who Eats, Clover learned that when they found her, she was near hypothermic and covered in a crusty combination of blood and mud. Her hair was plastered in a scabby clump to her cheek, and her fingers were scalded black from some type of fire. They would have taken her to the hospital, but Clover kept mumbling, "Fuck Glory Peak," so they thought it was safer to bring her to He Who Eats to recover. Over two days, she mostly slept, but she woke up twice—once to ask for "Dingus" and once to let them know she "burned a mother down." Not long after that, He Who Eats learned from Fortooth gossip that Clover's home had gone to ash in a fire, and she was considered missing.

Rubbing her head, all Clover could think was, *Jesus, what fucking drama. When will all this bullshit end?*

As Clover digested their recap, He Who Eats walked into the living room and fell into his La-Z-Boy. Pulling a joint from behind his ear, he grabbed a remote, about to scan his TVs for some *Seinfeld* reruns when he noticed a scrunch of wrinkles on Clover's brows. Sighing, he muted the television and turned to her.

"Listen," he said, "you can stay here as long as you want. Whether you get it or don't, you spent a night facing the screaming winds and got through it—the way I see it now, you passed the *Oh-sah-cha-me*. So, if you want to bunk up and help us prepare for the *Rah-pah-no*, I got plenty of food and ammo."

"The *Rah-pah-no*?" Clover asked. "What's that?"

"The great clearing," he said.

"The great clearing?" Clover asked. Not sure how serious to be, she curled a half smile and asked, "Okay, and what's that?" He Who Eats took a deep hit of his joint and sent a side-eye her way. "Nothing much—just something we're training to do in December when we'll wipe your grandpa and Nanny's companies from all things air and earth."

vv2

## DECEMBER 2002

As far as Bill Macklemore was concerned, he was already at war, and he had been for a while—with Wolfehaus, the rebellious spirit of his granddaughter, the still-missing bodies of his son and daughter-in-law, a wandering herd of overgrown alpacas, and the ghosts of his wife, Nanny A, and eight German soldiers.

The Le'Echuwanna, at least, were nowhere on this list, as he had recently made a deal to purchase a large swath of land they owned out beyond Punishment Lake. And from what he heard, most of them were relocating to Florida to enjoy warm weather and no income tax. So now, it was about attacking the challenges of constructing a new Wild West–style resort that represented the manifest destiny of the 1800s and managing the intractable shadow of guilt and familial specter that warped his days.

Most would equate this warping to paranoia and some, even, to early-onset dementia—but Bill saw it all as one thing: his family trying to take away Glory Peak. At first, he was able to contain these moments, but as fall blew into winter and the snow once again dusted the valley white, these shadowy ghosts began to find him in public and without a hint of when they would arrive. The initial visits were no doubt inspired by the now seven-week disappearance of his granddaughter—and on one early morning, while he was walking the future site of his latest real estate development, Glory Sky, with his foreman and CFO, he abruptly stopped and yanked off his aviator glasses.

"What's that?" he asked, pointing to a brown speck in the distance. Seeing nothing, the foreman and CFO craned their necks to look for whatever he was signaling.

"Is that Clover? Is she skiing? I think that's Clover!" Ecstatic, he ran for his red Land Rover, but by the time he'd spun it on and aimed it at the spot in the distance, he realized there was nothing but old snow. Turning the car off, he returned to the foreman and CFO, who rubbed their faces in confusion—and growing concern for Bill's mental health.

From that moment forward, the visions were more regular. Some mornings, he saw Bobby climbing the Goldfinger with a pair of telemark skis; other times, he saw his daughter-in-law draining the water from his hot tub. Sometimes, he saw the disfigured faces of German soldiers staring at him through windows, ice melting off their half-shot skulls. Unable to look at their faces, his would shift to the Nazi Eagle embroidered on the breast of their uniforms, its talons clutching a swastika—and then, in a blink of an eye, they'd be blown to confetti by heavy artillery.

Over time, he thought that maybe he'd get used to those faces—that maybe he'd forget the earth-moving shake of that artillery or the weight of a loaded M1 Garand in his grip. But those faces only got bigger and brighter with each pass of night. And Bill feared them, like how someone with a chronic foot injury feared standing or walking, knowing that just by doing what was needed to get through the day, pain would inevitably come.

In time, the Glory Peak employees recognized something was off with Bill. It first came with the appearance of stubble on his face. In the history of his existence in Fortooth Bend, Bill had never gone one day without presenting the softest, most perfectly shaven face in the valley. During his early years, he would keep his army-issued Gillette safety razor with him so that he could disappear into any nearby bathroom to keep his stubble baby-soft tight. Later, he would travel with a triple-head Norelco shaver in his briefcase and, in his glove compartment, a bottle of the Proraso aftershave he discovered while stationed in Turin. Most recently, it was a battery-powered Braun he powered up in the middle of phone calls or meetings. But regardless of the instrument, he made sure his face was like all the intermediate runs on his mountain: immaculately groomed.

Until now. Now, it was splotchy, with a five o'clock shadow and glades of overgrowth. A beard never fully formed, but the hair was there—long, short, inconsistent in height and density—and it was enough to cause a quiet alarm in those around him.

The second example was in the tiptoeing he did from one location to another. Like a child sneaking to the refrigerator at night, he would tiptoe to a doorway, pause for a moment, check to see if anyone was around, then tiptoe down a hallway to his next destination.

To combat the awkwardness of this behavior, Bill's secretary started scheduling his meetings fifteen minutes early so he would already be seated by the time everyone arrived. And then, as they departed, she would present him with some papers to sign so that he wouldn't have to rise and leave. Under normal circumstances, this may have been manageable, as Fortooth was filled with all sorts of eccentrics, but with winter on its way and a land war with Wolfehaus in motion, it was the worst time ever for Bill to begin to lose his mind. Especially as the most ambitious expansion in Glory Peak's existence—and not just from a construction standpoint—was about to begin.

Glory Peak was going to host the XL Games, and for the first time in the history of extreme snow sports, NBC was going to broadcast the event. And not just broadcast it, but broadcast it right from Bill's Mountain. For years, Bill lobbied for these rights, and as he was the first in North America to install a full-on terrain park with Bobby's Bandido Bowl, it made sense that, as extreme winter sports went primetime, it would happen from Glory Peak. Sensing the opportunity, Bill planned on using the broadcast to show the world Glory Peak's unrivaled magic and, in doing so, planned on ending the XL Games with the Huevos Rancheros Stampedo. Then, there would be a ceremonial first shoveling of construction on Glory Sky, the soon-to-be preeminent ski destination in the Americas, and the world could finally see the mythical Farangotta Valley and North American ski life as one singular thing: William Jefferson Macklemore.

The hope from the Glory Peak board was that they would be able to get through this event with the reputation of said mythical founder intact—and this was, despite appearances, Bill's hope, as well. He was self-aware enough to understand this opportunity was the great summation of what he'd worked his entire life for, but not self-aware enough to realize how close his behavior was to blowing it away.

The truth was Bill was more unaware than he was aware about anything. But one thing that he was certain of was that being alone brought horror. No longer were his sleepless nights about anxious denial; they were now tangible chess games against ghosts. To survive them, he turned to the loaded comfort of his army-issued Colt M1911A1 pistol, hidden in the worn brown leather of the briefcase he carried in public. He knew the Colt wouldn't actually help him with ghosts, but he found comfort in it regardless. Just like how, in the privacy of his home, he brought the Thompson M1A1 submachine gun he carried through his service out of storage. He would hold it at night, in his living room, and stare out the ceiling-high windows with a tumbler of Cherry Heering on the arm of his large leather sofa. Sometimes, during an extreme bout of fear, he would place it on the passenger seat of his Land Rover as he drove the streets at night.

Inevitably, on these trips, he would end up at one place: the charred house that, once upon a time, belonged to his son. Then to Nanny A, and then to Clover—and now, to nobody, as it been reduced to ash and stone.

Eyeing it through the window of his car, he would spy the remnants of the porch and, beyond it, a brick fireplace standing in a living room with one wall and no floor. The second floor was gone, having collapsed into the cement of the basement, and the alpaca pen—that fucking alpaca pen— was now charred and tattered. But it stood, taunting him with dangling chains, a trough of snow, and footprints. The two-toed footprints of those curly-haired aliens.

"Fuckers probably still came here looking for food," he'd said out loud to himself. "Those fucking fuckers!"

Then, on one visit in December, at 3:11 a.m., the imagined taunting, spitting, and turd-dropping of the alpacas got so bad, Bill loaded his Thompson and emptied a full cartridge on the pen. Unable to withstand the forty rounds, the pen collapsed in a crash of timber. "Where you gonna go now, you hairy shitheels?" Bill screamed at the surrounding mountains. Turning toward Jade Ridge, he raised the machine gun and yelled, "I'll find you—I will find each one of you!"

True to his word, he tried and spent his nights tiptoeing through the Farangotta mountainside. Always in his hands was the Thompson submachine gun, and on his body, his white 10th Infantry army-issued winter fatigues. And always in the distance was Glory Peak. Its lights twinkling and hazing their way up and down the resort. He would smile at the construction of the spectator area, the additional half-pipes and concession stands being erected in anticipation of the crowds.

And he would think, *This is going to be Glory Peak's greatest year yet.*

If, he could only keep it from those dirty Peruvian monsters. Unable to find them on these midnight recon missions, he was, however, able to always find something in the radiance of the moon—Bobby.

# CHAPTER 32

## FEBRUARY 1985

I t took several moments for Bobby to realize he did not wake up in his house. First, the sun hit him from the right side of his head, not the left side of his face. Second, he was fully naked, a sign that he'd fallen asleep after sex, which he hadn't had with Annabelle for months. And third, there was no alpaca blanket rubbing up against his chin.

Rolling over, he did see an immaculate room with shelves of books filled with color-coded binders, a denim sofa with two layers of throw pillows, and a closet door, three inches open and revealing a perfectly organized selection of pants, sweaters, socks, and the most highly regarded collection of unmentionables in town.

Beyond having what was considered the snazziest interior design business in Fortooth, Lindsey Jessups was known for her proclivity for silk and lace. Not that she advertised it with a flippant attitude toward intimacy. She was very selective about whom she brought into her home. Having spent most of her twenties married to a former stockbroker who was now in jail for embezzlement, Lindsey decided to move to Fortooth hoping to get away from the snickers of the Upper West Side. Initially, she'd only visited with her former husband, who'd never failed to plan high-end trips there dripping with unnecessary expense. This, according to the locals placed her on the Gucci Pad side of the mountain. But when she'd officially moved to town, it was discovered she was the product of a Vermont farming family from just outside of Jay Peak. So, at her core, she had the heart of a snowflake and the liver of a townie, which allowed her to keep up with the generous pours of Cherry Heering and wake at sunrise for fresh powder.

Unlike everyone else in town, Bobby did not notice her until one early afternoon when he saw someone make a clean zipper line through the back bumps of Balls and Sacks, a difficult to access mini-canyon that shot onto a cul-de-sac at the backside of the mountain. Bobby was not normally impressed by other skiers, but there was something about watching this specific run that struck him as good. He liked its simplicity. How there was no exaggeration of movement—how the speed was consistent, how the skis moved through its turns without an unnecessary spread of snow. Watching each tight arc, made in perfect metronome, he imagined the staccato scrape of the ski's edges taking, then releasing their turn. Curious as to who operated the teal Rossignols, Bobby pulled his car to the end of the run and waited at the base. Assuming it was a man, Bobby flashed his ten-thousand-watt grin when he realized it wasn't a man but Lindsey Jessups. Before she could even pop out of her bindings, Bobby was in conversation.

"You made that look easy," he said.

Looking back at the run, Lindsey planted her poles, took off her gloves, and said, quite matter-of-factly, "It was."

"Hah," Bobby responded. "I know half the skiers in town would disagree with you."

"Well, clearly, they didn't grow up skiing sheets of ice where you basically had to use an ax to hold an edge."

"So, you didn't grow up skiing the greatest champagne pow in the West?"

"God, I hate that term—*pow*. Why does every meathead skier have to make up a cool expression for every part of the sport?"

"Hey, I didn't come up with it."

"I know." Lindsey smiled. "Just trying to minimize your meathead, Bobby Mac."

For the first few weeks, they just skied together, Bobby showing her his favorite backcountry runs, then introducing her to Tubby and his snowcat. Like fire, it spread through town that Bobby was skiing with Lindsey, a woman who was a lot of things—but most certainly not his wife. Normally, gossip of this nature would find its way, on an eastbound wind, straight to the wife's doorstep—but Bobby was royalty, Annabelle still an interloper, and every local understood they had to protect their prince's business. Even if it meant keeping it from his wife. And mother-in-law.

But when Bobby spent his first night at Lindsey's, this protection melted in the midday sun. She liked Bobby; he was an unbelievable skier and had one of the most generous smiles she ever saw. The sex was good, too—a bit too selfish to win a gold, but it consistently placed silver, no matter the time of day or location.

As she brought him a warm cup of coffee, Bobby noticed she was dressed, her hair blown out, and her turtleneck tucked into her jeans.

"Listen," she started. "I don't want to get into anything complicated. This is going to open a lot of grief for you. You take the time you need, and when things are sorted, why don't you come find me again, and we can reevaluate?"

Bobby took the coffee and sipped. "You thought about this, huh?"

"No. It's just obvious what needs to be done. And I don't want to move." Rising, she handed him his pants off the sofa. "You've got five minutes to get ready," she added, then headed downstairs.

Arriving home, he was surprised to see Nanny A waiting. She was folding laundry and sterilizing canning jars when he entered. Five cups of yerba maté in, she moved at a ferocious speed. As he tried to creep undetected toward the stairs, Nanny A slammed the laundry basket on the kitchen table and shouted, "Don't you dare!"

Stopping, he turned and walked to the sofa.

"You got some fucking nerve, I tell you, some fucking nerve!" she screamed across the living room.

Leaning back into the sofa, Bobby steadied himself. "It's not what you think . . ."

"Not what I think? Not what I think? Are you kidding me? It's *exactly* what I think. I think it is a spoiled fucking man-child destroying his family because he can't come to terms with his daddy issues and how small his pecker is!"

"That's not the situation, Abigail," Bobby responded.

"Really, Bobby? Little Bobby doesn't think that is the situation. You think you are unique here? This story is as old as time, buddy boy. Greeks wrote about it, and now the little prince of a Podunk, piece-of-shit ski town that no one in the world gives two craps about is gonna pretend it's somehow different?"

"I don't know, Abigail. Is it any different than a professor getting kicked off the faculty for screwing one of her students?"

Nanny A stopped in her tracks. The air sucked dry from her throat, she placed her hands on her hips and shook her head at the ceiling. Finally, she said, "Fuuuuuck," pulled up a kitchen chair, and grabbed her maté gourd. "You didn't tell Annabelle, did you?"

"No," Bobby responded. "Because it is none of her business. Just like this is none of your business."

Nanny A slammed her gourd on the kitchen table. Pointing her index finger at him, she said, "Listen, you little shit—don't you dare tell me this is none of my business. You are talking about my daughter and granddaughter here. They are every bit my business. And if I see you around here one more time, I will break your fucking pecker off and use it as alpaca feed."

Bobby took a beat to let the statement settle. He hadn't slept well. He didn't smell great, and four weeks straight of whiskey binging was beginning to challenge his ability to think rationally. The truth was that he *was* cheating on his wife, who was taking care of his daughter—so as much as he'd love to throw Nanny A's history with her college student in her face, he couldn't deny that in this situation he was the villain.

But still, something about this whole exchange made him angry. Like when a crappy skier cuts in front of you when you're connecting a perfect stretch of turns. So, Bobby stood and did something he'd never done before. He looked Nanny A straight in the eyes and said, "Abigail, you hypocritical piece of shit. Go fuck yourself."

Before Nanny A could so much as release a shocked laugh, Bobby was out the door and headed back to town.

For the next three weeks, Bobby found himself on Baby Tubbs and Lou Paul Ginger's sofa. They were perfectly happy to host, as it came with free drinks at the Horned Pony and weed Bobby got from a Le'Echuwannan named He Who Eats Rabbit Tails.

Bobby tried many times to see Annabelle during this period, but every attempt was thwarted by Nanny A, who would stop him on the porch and tell him, "Belle's not here." And she usually wasn't—as Annabelle was either having sex at Gunther's or planning a way to resurrect Paca Joe. And then sometimes when Bobby swung by and Nanny A was babysitting Clover, she would intercept him at the door with Clover in her stroller. At first, Bobby had difficulty figuring out how to entertain her, but he found out fast that she was happy as long as she was in motion. Flat hikes were the simple start, which somehow led to her in a sling over his shoulder as he did slow loops on his cross-country skis around Punishment Lake. These were the moments he discovered she liked best, and sometimes, he swore he could hear what sounded like faint giggles when he connected long glides. Over time, these became the most intimate moments they shared. Her bouncing body one with his back, flowing up and down, forward, and back—his spine and lungs the only things keeping his heart from touching hers.

Bill, very early on, had heard about Lindsey and Bobby Mac. He'd found out the day after they first had sex out by Tear Cup Lake—and he knew a year later when he spent his first night at her house.

Baby Tubbs and Lou Paul Ginger liked cash, mountain food, and ski passes, so it was easy for him to track Bobby's actions through these negligible payments. What was more difficult was finding Bobby. Bobby still had this cosmic ability to somehow remain invisible in a town with a population under 2,100. But Bill needed to find him—and talk to him alone—because there was something of great importance to discuss.

After weeks of searching, Bill finally found his son pissing by a grove of aspens out by Peckerwood Pass, his skis planted next to him, his pole straps hanging off their tips.

Bobby was surprised to see him out there, even though Bill knew the terrain of Farangotta as well as any white man could—and with his Land Rover lifted an additional four inches, he was capable of traversing almost every one of its gullies.

"Holy fuck," Bobby said when he turned and saw him.

"Holy fuck," Bill responded, smiling. "You taking turns on Peacock or Minehole?"

Zipping his pants, Bobby grabbed his skis. "Peacock. Minehole has too much rock exposure. Wanted to hit Tootsie Roll, but the way the wind's blowing wasn't worth it."

"Yeah, well, this weather's all over the place. Surprised we haven't gotten more calls out here about avalanches. But then again, you are the only one crazy enough to ski those ridges solo."

Bobby laughed to himself. *Yeah, maybe*, he thought. *But so was Snow Feather.*

Then, Bobby's laugh skidded to a stop. Remembering who he was talking to, he grabbed his skis and turned down the path to the park entrance.

"Where you going?" asked Bill.

"Don't worry about it," Bobby responded.

"I can give you a ride."

"It's okay."

"No, I am serious," Bill insisted. "Please, it's important. I've been looking for you. There's something we've got to discuss."

Bobby, twenty feet ahead of Bill, stopped. He'd never had anything important to talk about with his father before.

Pulling his goggles off his head, he turned to face him. "Where'd you park the car?"

Driving back to town, Bobby did a double take. His father's vehicle was almost identical to his previous Land Rover, with the exception of a red paint job and reinforced steel on the floor and dashboard. Looking at his father, he couldn't help but dissolve into an episode of some familiar but scrambled ABC melodrama from twenty years back. It was almost as though he'd fallen through a rip in the fabric of space-time, tumbling back to 1968. Bill's hair still blond, but the Land Rover, instead, a heritage green, and Bobby, 108 pounds of teenager. Staring into the passenger-side mirror, Bobby saw something he hadn't thought about in forever, youth.

"So," Bill started, "I heard about you and Annabelle."

Jolted back to reality, the passenger mirror now reflected the present. Bobby unshaven, his hairline sneaking back, and wide raccoon circles around his eyes. It was no doubt a version of hell.

"Yeah," he answered. "Things aren't great right now."

"I'd imagine." Bill nodded, eyes fixed on the road. "Not a great place to be . . . Been there myself, as you know."

Unsure of how to respond, Bobby decided to bring the conversation to topic. "So, what's so important?"

Bill pressed his lips into a thin line. "Well, I just want you to know I am here if you need me. It doesn't have to be this way. I know Annabelle doesn't like me, and with things the way they are right now, maybe it can mean more time for us."

"More time for us? Okay, William. Not quite sure what that means."

"Well, Robert," Bill snarked back, "it means you can spend some time up on the mountain. Get back in the swing of the peak. I know that Paca Joe thing is having some trouble getting up and running. It could be a way to make some cash and get you back on a nine-to-five schedule."

Bobby shook his head. "So, this important thing you wanted so badly to talk to me about is actually just offering me a job I didn't ask for?"

"You've always had a job with me, son; I just wanted to talk to you about finally showing up for it."

Bobby unrolled the window, allowing for a gust of near-freezing wind to rush over his face. *It would be so easy*, he thought. He had money, courtesy of the Danu's sale, so that wasn't the issue. The issue was movement. And the constant sense of free fall he felt. To tread water for a beat. To just sit, or stand, or lie down and do nothing for a moment. For several moments. That could be a win. Maybe.

"Listen, I know it might be a problem now, but Annabelle . . . she'll get over it. And she'll find someone else . . . someone better suited for her."

Bobby's eyes snapped open. He turned toward his father. "What the hell does that mean?"

"I just meant, Bobby, she's . . ." He sighed, shrugging. "Well, you can do better."

"What are you talking about? We're here because of me. She tried to get me to rein it back—I didn't. I mean, yeah, she's got this crazy hard-on for the Paca Joe thing, but that's only because of . . ." Bobby looked at his father.

"Listen, I get it." Bill laughed. "You were trying to get your own thing going. Get away from the ol' pain-in-the-ass dad. Make your bones. It's a normal thing to want to do. Shit, I had to enlist to get away from my asshole father. But it didn't work out. Annabelle couldn't hack it. You know the mother—you've seen the stock she's coming from."

Bobby glared back at his father. "Listen," Bobby said, tone clipped, "the reason it didn't work had nothing to do with Annabelle. She busted her ass. It wasn't easy, and there was a ton of bad luck. And then I—"

"Why are you defending her?" Bill interrupted. "She's no angel. Let me tell you, she shouldn't be calling a kettle any color, if you hear me."

"No, I don't, William. What the hell are you saying?"

"Hey, son, I don't know why you are getting riled with me. You have a problem, ask your wife. Or ask that Kraut fellow she seems to be spending her days with."

Bobby reached down to the floorboard for his ski gloves. "Let me out," he ordered.

"Come on, son, let's just dial it back a bit—"

"Don't call me that," Bobby snapped back.

"B, let's just—"

"I said, *let me out!*"

Bill slammed the brakes, skidding the Land Rover toward a snowbank on the side of the road.

"What the hell, Bobby? You scared the lunch out of me!" Bill screamed. But Bobby couldn't hear him. He was already out of the car, grabbing his skis, and running toward a small pitch along the road. As Bill placed the gearshift in park and opened his door, Bobby was already skiing down the escarpment, nothing but shadow in his wake.

When Bobby got back to Baby Tubbs's place, he spat, barked, and phantom-punched a full round of anger. "Fucking Bill! That dickface is always trying to fuck with me!"

Dipping into the Rumple Minze, it took no more than three swigs before he decided to get in his car and drive to Gunther's. Turning off Yeehaw Pass, he could see his house in the distance. Driving faster, a million confrontations tumbled through his mind. He would break things. He would stomp. He would throw chairs through windows. He would release a roaring monster of a fit that would shake the clouds and split the grounds.

Turning onto Gunther's road, Armageddon rode shotgun in Bobby's over-revving car. But then, a hundred feet from Gunther's driveway, he saw it: Annabelle's Subaru. And then he pulled his foot off the gas and shifted into a melancholy neutral. Looking at the assortment of stickers that covered her rear bumper, Bobby's eyes swelled. Visualize Whirled Peas. Feed the World. Beam Me Up, Scotty, There's No Intelligent Life Down Here.

They weren't on the bumper when they bought the car from Principal Janks four years ago. Each one was applied on a trip they took during spring, when they stopped just past the county line at Custard's Last Fruit Stand and Feed Store to fill up on unleaded. Each one carried a memory, usually of laughs and giggles when they both couldn't believe they became bumper sticker people. But it was the newest bumper sticker, the one Bobby had added one morning while Annabelle was sleeping, that stared back at him, fresh and still vibrant. Its goal was to make Annabelle smile and maybe even one day describe a happy memory they shared. But now seeing it, it just increased the churn inside Bobby. If the Van Is A 'rocking, Don't Come A 'knocking.

Eyes red, Bobby burst into tears and sputtered strings of phlegm. And then he turned rabid, hunched over his steering wheel, and released a storm of punches at the AC vents. Yanking the gearshift into reverse, Bobby pulled back, made a jerky lunge forward, and plowed back down the road. The speedometer hitting fifty, Bobby had one thought that screamed above all the others: *Fuck you, whirled peas, fuck you!*

# CHAPTER 33

**DECEMBER 2002**

Having spent pretty much every day of her eighteen years in Fortooth and the outback of the Farangotta Valley, it seemed inconceivable to Clover that there was a location within this region she didn't already know. But now, having spent several months with He Who Eats and his fellow Le'Echuwanna warriors, she learned that when it came to the rhythm of the valley, she knew jack nothing.

They woke early, which she was used to from her ski training days but, because of her ketamine vacation, had not practiced as of late, and next they outfitted themselves based on what they learned by performing the *Mah-he-oh-ha*—the air drink. Believing the early-morning wind held directions for the day, they would wake, still in their pajamas, and crane their head out a window. It was a fascinating sight to see. Their eyes closed, necks extending like a turtle's as they flared their nostrils and pulled the scents and temperatures over their cilia and into their sinuses. Watching from the house, Clover wished she, too, could swallow deep breaths of air and hold it until the oxygen disappeared in her bloodstream and revealed the morning's design. But she couldn't, so she waited for them in the kitchen, and ate a breakfast of beans and eggs.

He Who Eats didn't speak much in the morning, as his vocal cords didn't seem to come alive until after twelve o'clock, so he just grunted, pointed, and filled plates with hot food, then left them for his warriors to clear.

Finishing their breakfast, they would file out to long, thin branches of pine planted in the ground. These were markers where below them, hidden in the snow, were skis. The first time Clover saw this, she was dumbstruck. In all her time in Fortooth, she never had seen a Le'Echuwannan on skis. Annoyed by Clover's aghast expression, He Who Eats broke his silence one morning and whispered, "What, you think you invented skiing? How the fuck do you think we got around here the past three hundred years?"

"No, it's just—"

He Who Eats raised his paw-like hand. "Just don't. I barely like you as it is. I don't want you saying something dumb as falcon shit to make me hate you. Just grab your skis by the fern over there."

Clover looked at He Who Eats as he saddled into a telemark binding and a chunky ski with a gradual taper in the middle. She then walked to the fern and dug her hand in the snow. After the sting of the cold stopped, she felt something familiar, the plastic front of her Salomon bindings. Lips arcing upward, she lifted them from the snow.

They were her skis, all right—and since she knew their weight so well, she instantly recognized them despite what appeared to be a fresh coat of white paint. Confused, she turned to the rest of the Le'Echuwanna, who were clicking into their bindings. Their skis were white, too. Understanding what the paint job now meant, she placed her skis on the ground, pulled two poles from the snow, and buckled in. Ready, she looked at He Who Eats, who motioned her to take position at the tail end of the line. Then, with what seemed to be silence, Clover watched He Who Eats turn his skis downhill and disappear into its tree-speckled face.

Clover had trouble keeping up. Downhill was not her specialty, but she'd logged enough time on steep runs to become adept at alpine skiing. Another problem was that she did not know the winds' recipe, so she followed blindly, unaware when to dip her shoulder to avoid an oncoming gust or stand her body straight to maintain better balance through a crust of mixed snow. She had so much to learn about this world, and for the first time, she felt like a foreigner in her own home.

When she caught up to the team, they already had their skis and poles buried in the snow with their marking branches staked in the ground. Having forgotten to bring hers, Clover scurried around and found a thin fan of pine, then stuck it by her skis. Not knowing what to do next, she chose to shadow Lapping Pearl, the young girl with the large appetite.

When she found Lapping Pearl, she was lying on her stomach, attaching large swatches of bark to her backside. Now camouflaged, she wiggled deeper into the snow and pulled a .30-06 rifle from her side and pointed its tip at the valley. Clover did her best to mimic this—and dug herself a hole beside Lapping Pearl, even though she didn't have a rifle or bark. Spreading snow over her appendages, she held a deep breath and tried to become a rotting tree under a wash of fresh powder.

Watching her from afar, He Who Eats couldn't help himself from smiling—both because Clover very much looked like a fool but also because Clover, somehow, was fitting right in.

As the morning began to take shape under a yellow sky, it became apparent to Clover that each warrior was assuming a different state of being. They were humans, yes, Le'Echuwannans further, but as they practiced their morning routine, it was clear they each channeled a specific animal.

She had heard of the idea of spirit animals before but had never seen a human attempt to actually transform into one. It was humorous at first, but then it morphed into something elegant, graceful—a regal rendering of modern dance feathered by nature's hand.

*What animal am I?* she thought. *What furry valley friend am I supposed to be?*

Watching the warriors move through their practice, Clover attempted to identify which animal each warrior embodied. It was apparent Lapping Pearl was a squirrel, and Clover loved watching her nervous dances from tree to tree. He Who Likes Oaks was an elk, which she suspected was at least in part due to his broad size and gangly limbs. Clover watched him, covered in pelts and crowned by a twelve-point rack of horns, as he moseyed through the snow, on occasion bending his head to search for hidden grass. Slippery Tongue, a particularly fierce young woman who had an affection for giving everyone the finger, took on the role of a bighorn sheep. She wore tailored skins and a helmet of horns, and on occasion, she'd go so far as to headbutt the base of a tree.

Clover's gaze then drifted to He Who Eats, who, well, based on his size and temperament, was obviously a grizzly bear. But what was not obvious, based on his size and temperament, was the grace and delicacy he brought to the role. His grizzly was not the ornery grizzly who just woke from hibernation. It was the gentle, nurturing grizzly—the one who protected his cubs from the elements and shared the salmon he pulled from the river.

But of all the warrior animals Clover observed, it was Grant's wolf that intrigued her the most. He'd used Velcro to fasten a pelt of silver gray to his jacket and painted his face in swirls of black and white. His look was a virtual knockout of power and sinuous cool, but the way he moved—that was what truly struck Clover. He took stealthy, controlled steps; patiently rested by tree trunks; and made powerful leaps when he decided to give chase or run. He was everything Clover loved about winter—quiet, monochromatic, a resting mass of power that could act with brutal efficiency if it chose to. Watching him, Clover knew she wanted to be a wolf. A regal, composed, vicious, voracious wolf.

When they returned to He Who Eats' house, Clover was determined to find a way to officially join the young party of warriors. It was a weird detour on her life path. Only a week ago, she was supposed to be moving to Providence on a nest egg built with drug money. She even thought she'd be in love with Jesse by then, or at least entertaining the idea of it while Nanny A continued to live on, worshipping Wolfehaus.

But now she was here. In a living room with three TVs and a group of people resolved to destroy what her grandfather and grandmother built. She hated her grandparents. She also loved them. She also hated herself for ever trusting Jesse and loved that she could name her favorite Nusrat Fateh Ali Khan album thanks to Nanny A. The Nanny A who she was an unforgivable asshole to right before her heart gave out.

And yet, there she was just outside of He Who Eats' upstairs office, watching him through the doorframe. He was rocking back and forth at his desk, humming along to a Funkadelic album that scratched on a record player. When she heard the album side come to an end, she opened the door and took a step in. Now she could see he was stringing beads to the seam of a pouch. Blue and red ones oscillating back and forth along its edge. Taking a step closer, she pocketed her thumbs in her pants and stood just behind his chair. He Who Eats said nothing so after a deep breath and quiet cough, Clover said, "Chief, I want to become a warrior."

Off her words, He Who Eats released a throaty, wet laugh. "Okay, okay, White Princess, let's settle down. You can share our food and go on our morning patrols—'cause I sure as shit know you like the workout—but come on, you ain't no warrior chow."

"But I survived the *Oh-sah-cha-me*. You said it yourself."

"Survived? I was being generous. You luckily survived what was probably a fucking suicide attempt, knowing how you white tips deal with your shit. Just enjoy the stew till you figure out what you want to do."

"I've figured it out. I want to help."

"Help?" He Who Eats chortled. "Do you realize that means attacking your grandfather and your nanny's business she probably killed herself trying to build? They're your kin. You're not attacking your kin."

"My kin is dead," Clover answered.

He Who Eats placed the pouch he was beading on his desk, then turned toward Clover. Her eyes held a vast sadness and he knew what happened to people like this—people who lost their anchor and were left to waves they had no idea how to bob through. He also knew if Bobby Mac or Annabelle were alive, they would hate with all their might what was happening to the valley.

"Okay, Princess," he relented. "You ready to go on a war party tonight with Slippery Tongue? They're attacking chairlift two on Bobby's Bandido Bowl."

Clover took in the ask, but the delay in her response said everything.

"That's what I thought, Princess." He Who Eats released a soft chuckle. "Listen," he said, picking the pouch back up from the desk. "You're in the river right now. And you don't know which riverbank to swim to. And we sure as rain ain't gonna force you to swim to ours. But I'll make you a deal: if you ever do want to swim to ours, you let me know. Or you know what? You let Grant know. He's the general out there. If he says you're good, I'll give you some war paint."

For some reason, approaching He Who Eats was easier than approaching Grant. It was always nerve-racking for Clover to talk with people her age, and after watching Grant stalk the base of Cupping Palm Gorge, she was in fresh awe. It took her several minutes to find him and when she did, he was outside, crouched behind a two-foot-high bank of plowed snow holding a snowball. Unaware of what was happening, Clover walked over and stood on the other side of the snowplow. Acting the gentleman, he rose and placed the snowball on the bank. But before she could open her mouth, He Who Likes Oaks and Slippery Tongue emerged from behind a group of pines and rifled a round of snowballs at them.

Covered in snow, Clover jumped over the snowbank. Hiding behind it was Grant who handed her an armful of fresh snowballs. Rearing up, they fired as many as they could. Clover had no idea what she was aiming for and saw nothing as a spray of snow came back at her. Soon, the melee devolved into laughter and mouthfuls of slushy shrapnel. When the laughter subsided and Clover was able to wipe the snowy pulp from her eyes, she caught a glance of He Who Likes Oaks limping from an ice ball he took to his testicles. And Slippery Tongue cackling about how she "Got you, hookers!"

Grant seemed as if he was just back from a spa. Totally relaxed, his faced wiped dry, he was already placing fresh snowballs on the snowbank in anticipation of the next onslaught. Unaware of the pink oval on her forehead from a snowball she took to the face, Clover walked over to Grant and grabbed a handful of snow. Hard pressing it into a sphere, she placed it on the snowbank and released a surprising giggle. Grant giggled back then placed a final snowball on the snowbank.

"You want to talk?" Grant asked.

Clover nodded and wiped the last few pieces of snow from her face.

"Hey," Grant said, turning toward Slippery Tongue and He Who Likes Oaks. "I'm gonna hang with Clover."

He Who Likes Oaks smiled and launched the snowball he carried deep into the forest. "Cool, cool. Slippery T, you wanna hit some *Madden*?"

Slippery Tongue looked at Clover and Grant. Annoyed, she threw the snowball in her hand at the ground, then raised two middle fingers from her waist like a gunfighter. "Fuck you guys—I'm gonna play Mickey's *World of Illusion*. The new *Madden* sucks."

Grant smiled and turned toward Clover. "You ready?"

"Where are we going?" Clover asked, unsure.

"I don't know. Figure west will work." Reaching down into the snowbank, Grant pulled a pair of poles and snowshoes buried in front of a staked aspen branch. Scanning the property, Clover found another aspen branch at the end of the driveway. Excited, she walked toward it and dug out a set of snowshoes.


West was a good call for the hike. It was flat and open and allowed them to hug the top edge of China Cup Canyon, which provided an unobstructed view of Jade Ridge and Hangman's Rock.

At first, Grant seemed unsure what to say, so he just pointed at objects and gave abridged breakdowns of what the landmarks meant in Le'Echuwannan lore. Clover, absorbing the mythology, stomped, listened, and breathed. She took in how the lines of grays and white in the limestone of Jade Ridge were considered different plains where previous Elder Elders went to sleep. How Olathe corn powered the golden Lahontan cutthroat trout in some sort of amphetamine high down the Sad Sack River into the freshwater pool of Punishment Lake. How the nighttime clouds were tobacco puffs released by mother moon during her dinner smoke.

For the first time, the valley came together as one story, even down to the red iron dust that sprinkled its way along Hangman's Cliff. That was from the shavings of the *La'Mamanuh*—the maternal overseer of the valley who carved bowls from the redwoods for the bears and Fortooths to sleep in during winter. It was a schooling, and as the hike curved along a south-facing ledge, it became a history lesson that ended with the valley's greatest intrusion: Glory Peak resort.

Clover wasn't sure what to say. Every negative impact on the land and environment was always traced back to not only a single organization but a single man. She hated that they were connected by name. Hated that DNA connected them by form and hated that he was the only person left in her family. If she could, she would have burrowed into the ground and hid till she turned to stone, a speck in the limestone, a forgotten fossil with no connection to the Macklemore family. But Grant was sharing too much and now, as a warrior to be, she needed this information.

"You know, at first, we didn't hate the resort," Grant said, sidestepping the slate shards poking through the snow.

"But he started taking the land. Not just land that was for sale but land that never had an owner. Never saw fence. And when your grandmother, I mean, Wolfehaus, began buying it, too . . ."

Grant paused and looked at Clover. His look was a lot to take in. Sincere, measured, mature. Many years beyond what she was used to seeing in Jesse Vanigan's eyes. There was also something else she saw in his eyes—integrity.

"It's been tough for the rest of the tribe. They don't see why we need to fight. Or want to. They think us doing this is *me-ko-de*."

Clover leaned forward, her eyes pinched, hoping to find a hint to understanding the word he just said.

"Sorry," Grant said and stopped. "It means like when a drunk wants to be a bird. Like a fool's—"

"Errand?" Clover interrupted.

"Exactly. I mean, we've been attacking the Glory Sky and Wolfe Mountain construction sites for almost seven months now. So that's definitely more than an errand."

"Wait," Clover said. "I thought the construction issues were from environmental problems, like dams breaking or gas releasing. Sheriff Dan said a lot of the quakes and mudslides were from a weak infrastructure left from the mining days."

Grant smiled. Clover, realizing what he was saying with the smile, leaned back and placed her arms on her hips. "So, all this training isn't for something you *might* do?"

"Partly. But we've also been hitting both sides since June. Then leaving some *ching-ga-te-oh*, you know, hints the other party was responsible—that way, Wolfehaus and Glory Peak would get riled up against each other. Lapping Pearl came up with that idea."

"Jesus," Clover whispered, her lower jaw dropping as this reality ping-ponged against the rumors she'd heard over the summer. There was no talk of land wars or hidden battles fought from moon till sun with mercenaries and shadow activists.

"So that explosion earlier last summer . . . was you?" Clover guessed.

"Yes," Grant confirmed, going quiet for a moment. "And it did not go as planned."

Clover took it in. *No shit* she thought. She then said, "So is that what happened to He Who Eats' leg?"

"Yeah, it happened when . . ." Grant stopped and pointed his ski poles at the herd of alpacas on the horizon. "Look!" He beamed at Clover, "Can you see them?"

Clover followed his gaze to the snow-cloaked face of Jade Ridge. Dotted across the rock summit was a herd of alpacas. Large alpacas. Disproportionately massive alpacas, lumbering along moss-covered slabs of limestone.

Clover stood there in awe. These were the *Me-oh-watch-oh*—the colossal offshoot herd that spawned from the two missing alpacas from her mother's original herd. These were the ones who had supposedly saved her life by dragging her to safety.

Smiling like a five-year-old at Disney World, Grant shuffled closer to the edge.

"Aren't they incredible? I mean, look at that hair! They're like a bunch of Rastas on Blue Mountain. *Yeah, mon!*"

Clover watched as they lowered their long necks toward the moss on the ground. Their chews were slow and deliberate, each bite sending a signal across the valley to an unspoken receiver on the back of her neck. The vibration she received seemed small compared to the scale of their heads and mouths, but the faster they chewed, the faster her neck pulsed. And when they raised their heads, she mirrored them with an arc of her own. It was like a game of telephone—a tin can game of telephone, going from one set of brains to another, in this case, alpaca to Clover, on a line strung invisible across the valley.

    *No*, Clover thought. *I'm not going to be a wolf. I'm going to be a* Me-oh-watch-oh—*a four-legged furry fucker.*

# CHAPTER 34

**DECEMBER 2002**

"The mountain either loves you or not. And when it does, you make magic."

These words of narration ran shallow in Gunther's ears. He was sitting in an edit bay, watching selects from Wolfehaus' latest film, *Powder Nightmares, Powder Dreams*, and preparing notes for the editors. They had two weeks to lock picture, color correct, and sound mix the film for its premiere at the grand opening of Wolfe Mountain and the 2002 Snow Ball Music Festival. He was nervous about the opening and about securing the final permits needed for the concert, but most of all, he was sad. He had lost his second Charters woman, and the gaping hole in his heart reduced him to nothing but a thin outline of a man, rendered in the black ink of a 1920s cartoon. But he was not Mickey Mouse whistling on a steamship—he was Gunther Wolfe, and he was fighting a steady stream of melancholy.

To this day, Gunther still remembered the conversation he'd had with his grandfather that laid his understanding for this unavoidable feeling. It was when he was six that the old man nudged his glasses up the bridge of his nose and sat Gunther next to a fireplace active with heat and flames.

"Gunther," he'd said, "I know you're young, but there's something that has shadowed your mother, me, my father, and my grandfather all these years and I think it's time I shared this with you."

Gunther remembered looking up at his grandfather, confused. A beat earlier, he was licking melted chocolate off his fingers in his grandparents' kitchen. Now he felt like he was being reprimanded in school. Watching his grandfather take the glasses off his face, Gunther was confused by his heavy eyes.

"Gunther, we are haunted by a word that is not only innate to the Bavarian way but innate to the Wolfe family line. One that describes how life is merely an amalgamation of tragic, sorrowful, miserable, heartbreaking events."

Like it was happening in the present, Gunther remembered how cold his grandfather's hand was when he reached for it and how he thought it would make his grandfather smile to hold his. It didn't.

"You must protect very firmly the boundary of your heart and mind. For this word, my sweet Gunther . . . it stands for an illness that's like a cockroach. And like the cockroach you will at first not know it's there, but then one day, you will see one, and next you will find thousands in the walls, waiting to get out." Pausing just long enough for the fire to crackle and spit in the gap between his words, Gunther's grandfather said, "Always, please always, protect against the cockroaches, or you will find your walls filled with the weltschmerz."

Presently, it was impossible for Gunther to protect his walls. And not only was it impossible to protect them, he was also somehow reveling in the warmth that the cockroaches swarming his body provided. Covering him in a tomb-like swaddle of clicking feet and swiveling antennae, Gunther drank in the heavy syrup of his despair. His beautiful, wooly despair, keeping him snug and safe under an undulating blanket of weltschmertz.

The Wolfehaus crew understood his heartbreak and sorrow. They felt it, too. While Nanny A may have traded in her maternity card with Clover, she didn't at work, and used it with every employee, skier, camera person, and yes, even snowboarder who came through their doors. Overcome by a company-wide depression, the team struggled to come up with the appropriate tribute to honor her. But Gunther wouldn't hear any of them. He didn't want to be reminded of what he called "her disappearance"—which was how he referred to it, as if it were possible for her to reappear one morning at Lola's, and order blueberry pancakes and scalding hot water for her maté.

He did make one concession, a minor one. When they decided to go from a numeric to letter naming system for the ski lifts, he allowed them to change the name of the main quad lift from the Wolfeberg A lift to the Nanny A lift. And not explaining why to the team, he also decided to rename the east bowl Annabelle's Bowl. Truth be told, only Mountain Girl, the VP of marketing, cared about what anything was called, and if they agreed not to call the mini valley next to Logan's Run "the Slit," she agreed to put all naming arguments aside and focus on making sure Wolfe Mountain opened by New Year's.

Which was still in question. Because despite the additional security, the attacks on the Wolfe Mountain chalet were increasing. First, there was the clipping of the electric breakers that powered the septic systems. Then, there was the near destruction of the windows in the chalet, which proved to be worse than the actual destruction of them, when, one morning, tiny pellet holes had been discovered in the corners of all the windows, creating large spiderweb-like cracks. This was a frustrating state for window repair because if the windows were shattered, all one would have to do was clean up the shards of glass and remove the pieces still anchored to the window frame. But in this case, they had to first shatter each window before replacing them, which created additional days of work and a nightmare for the lawyers investigating workers' compensation issues in case any of the shattered glass splintered into employees' hands.

Next, holes were drilled into the water mains, and most recently, human feces had been found in the display cases of what was to be the new location of Gunther's former chocolate shop. Every time one of these acts of vandalism were discovered, Mountain Girl would call and inform Gunther. And every time, his response would be the same: "Well, I suspect we must hire more guards—just make sure they are clean and of good countenance."

Mountain Girl, herself guilty of suspect cleanliness, always responded with, "Dude, don't sweat it. MG is on it."

And he wouldn't "sweat it," for it was a much comfier existence to gaze out the window surrounded by billowy clouds of weltschmertz and wonder why Clover never reached out to him regarding the paperwork Nanny A left assigning her ownership of Wolfe Mountain.

∿

Bill, however, was not gazing out windows or exercising comfier existences. He was exercising unruly existences. Loud, unpredictable, confusing existences. For example, when the cables were cut on the Prospector chairlift, Bill took it upon himself to boot out and spearhead the investigations. Arriving at the scene, he got on hand and knee and examined the base of the lift where the cables were splintered.

Talking to his head of security, a theory was presented of vandals, wire cutters, and a blowtorch. Bill, however, had a different hypothesis altogether, and upon inspection, he noticed the cable broken in a variety of places. He also saw a cloverleaf trail of prints in the snow and a fresh collection of scat under the terminal towers.

*This was an attack, all right,* he realized. *But not one by the lazy weed-heads of Wolfehaus. It was by one of those vicious, varmint-like abominations.*

Pulling the head security guard aside, Bill explained his theory. "Sergeant John," he said.

"Umm, sir, I am not a sergeant—I'm just here from Pinkerton Security," the head guard replied.

"Listen now, Sergeant," Bill continued, undeterred. "What I need here is a complete biological examination of the area right by where that cable was snapped. You see, what we have here is an act of warfare. And I'll bet you ten thousand clean dollars, you examine that tear, and you'll see that the 'pacas did it."

"Excuse me, sir, I'm not quite sure I heard you right. The 'pacas?"

"You heard me damn clear, Sergeant. Those fucking 'pacas, that have been circumnavigating the hills near twenty years now. Watching us. Camouflaging themselves during the day, biding their time. They know what's happening next week; they know what's at stake."

"I'm sorry, sir," the head guard answered, pulling his orange-tinted Oakley sunglasses from his face. "I think . . . I am a bit behind you on this. What is a 'paca?"

"A 'paca, ya shitheel, is an alpaca. One of those Peruvian turd droppers that were put on the planet for two things: to piss sweaters and piss me off."

"Wait, sir—I am still a bit confused—you have alpacas here?"

"Hells yes, we do, Sergeant! Up in the hills, breeding like dogs. Probably have formed a vicious pack by now, and from the look of things, they got razor blades for teeth."

The head security guard put his Oakley sunglasses back on his face. Nodding slowly, he patted Bill on his shoulder and said, "Okay, sir, I hear you. We will make sure to look for the 'pacas."

"Good." Bill nodded. "Now, let's get some forensics on that wire."

Stomping back to his car, Bill knew, sure as snowmelt, that the head of security was not 10th Infantry material. He also knew containment needed to be achieved before the XL Games. And furthermore, that there was no one in the Glory Peak organization capable of this task. So, as usual, it would be up to William Jefferson Macklemore to protect the Glory.

His solution came in the form of Fortooth lore, Greek mythos, and a well-documented Byzantine history of twenty-nine emperors dying from poison. During his time in Italy, Bill learned of a particular recipe, cultivated from a certain perennial that bloomed dark-purple petals in the form of cylindrical helmets. In Italy, it was known as monkshood; in Greece, wolfsbane; and in Fortooth, the Widow's Kiss. And it grew in swatches along the northern fork of the Sad Sack River.

For decades Bill traveled the Sad Sack, having once hoped to turn an area along its banks into a summer fishing lodge. But when the geological report came back highlighting the danger of the Widow's Kiss, Bill was advised against moving forward. But that didn't mean he stopped visiting these banks. No matter the season, he visited them often. They were one of the few places in the valley where he could find complete isolation, and when he wanted to disappear into memories of peeping salamanders and choruses of ribbits, this is where he went.

With five days left until the arrival of NBC, the official groundbreaking of Glory Sky, and the XL Games, Bill woke early on a Wednesday to walk the Sad Sack River. And as much as he'd hoped otherwise, he was not alone. The spirit of his ex-wife, Suzanne, accompanied him and so did a German soldier with his lower intestine trailing from his stomach. At first, they revealed themselves in the back of Bill's Land Rover, where they sat silently and took in the drive through the bug-splattered blur of Bill's windshield. And then, in the reflection of the river water where they followed Bill by foot—Suzanne's weathered visage further muddied by an assortment of ripples drawn by the morning flies.

The snow was soft here and as untouched as any in the Farangotta, and for a moment, Bill was transported back to that instant when he first crossed the valley into the giant reveal of Hangman's Cliff. It was a quick moment, interrupted when a trout surfaced with a breakfast splash. Then, remembering why he was there, Bill searched the banks until he saw it in the distance—a long green stem with a trumpet of cascading purple petals falling down its spine. Getting closer, he pulled a pair of gloves from his pocket and a rusty bayonet, which caused the ghost of the German solider to release a painful death wail. Spinning to address him, Bill watched as the soldier dissolved into the clear glass of the water. Stepping into his place, Suzanne pulled, long and silent, on a Virginia Slim. Her skin sizzled, embers hissing through her cheeks, as ash fell from her forehead. Her eyes, nothing but coals, fixed blank on Bill.

"What? What do you want?" Bill screamed at her.

Suzanne said nothing and just exhaled smoke as Bill put on his gloves, clipped the flowers, and placed them in a plastic bag.

Across town, Clover craned her head out of He Who Eats' upstairs window. Inhaling the crisp morning air, she thought about which set of Paca Joe samples she would wear during this morning's exercise. She had yet to partake in one of the actions, but she was diligent in her training, and because of her focus and physical stamina, she had earned a place of respect among the warriors.

She hadn't quite mastered the art of gaining directions from the morning wind, but she was getting an idea of how to read the weather and let the breeze and humidity give her a sense of what the day would bring. That morning, she sensed snow would fall in the afternoon, then it would be blue-sky sunny, but late-December cold, which meant Grant would be playing sprinting wolf—her favorite of his wolves.

Taking a perimeter position along a ridge of rocks that looked down on the trees bordering Tear Cup Lake, Clover watched Grant, and the warriors slide into position for a raid on an imagined group of security guards. From her vantage, she saw Grant's wolf sprint back and forth, playfully swatting at an imagined butterfly. With his hands cupped like a pup's paws, Grant swiped with a canine-esque conviction that reminded her of the sincerity Jimmy brought to his pre-navy training. She wondered, then, where he was, and for the first time since he'd left, was reminded what simple goodness looked like.

Hopping in playful ups and downs to a lone pine, Clover watched Grant remove a 9mm Sig Sauer from his pelt when a jolt of pain shot through her spine.

Immediately, she keeled over and shut her eyes as inexplicable bolts of yellow and green flashed on her lids. Confused and gasping for air, Clover inspected her body. She wasn't hurt, but when she reached for the pain on the back of her neck—it was bloody.

Throughout the day, she received several more of these unexpected jolts. Fortunately, they mostly occurred when she was alone and out of sight of the other warriors. She didn't want to seem weak in front of them, and the one time she felt the stabbing while the others were around, she bit her lip until it bled.

This went unnoticed by everyone but Grant, who, not wanting to embarrass Clover, acted like he hadn't noticed anything. But later that night, when it woke her for the third time, Clover decided it was time to ask for help.

Ghosting through the house, she found Grant asleep in one of the downstairs bedrooms and woke him. Quiet, she asked him if they could speak in the kitchen, and when he said yes, she told him of the jarring pains in her neck.

Listening to her story between long pulls of Northern Lights, Grant nodded and let dense clouds of worm-shaped smoke crawl from his nose. When she finished, he emptied the ash in his pipe and walked to the coat rack. Handing her a jacket and hat, he led her out the door.

As Clover expected from her morning read of the weather, it was snowing—a light, large-flaked sort of snowfall that would make every skier in town wake up early.

Heading toward the snowbank, Grant reached a pair of pine swatches staked in the ground. Digging out two pairs of snowshoes, Grant clicked in and started down He Who Eats' backyard toward Jade Ridge.

"Where are we going?" Clover whispered as the snow collected like falling ash on her face.

"We gotta find the *Me-oh-watch-ohs*. I hope not, but I think something has happened to them."

Clover's heart thumped at the sound of his words. "Grant, what do you mean?"

"I'm not sure," Grant replied. "But I saw something last night when I slept."

What Grant saw was a neon-green haze spread like melting wax over the valley. He was nude, walking in the snow but somehow warm. And around him, splayed on shaven pine trees, were the bloodied pelts of alpacas.

Hiking up the crest of Jade Ridge, his fear was that they would stumble upon the mutilated corpses of the alpaca herd. Getting closer to the ridge, he saw something more serene—a herd of alpacas lying on the rocks in some sort of deep sleep. A layer of snow dusted their fur, and in the glow of the moon, they had a slightly angelic and slightly cosmic look. Panicked, Grant trudged to one draped over a small hump of rock. Kneeling beside it, he saw frozen black eyes—fogged over and matte with pupils the size of acorns. Reaching for its neck, Grant felt its cold, limp body. Before he could turn around to warn Clover, he heard a wounded no and the distinct crunch of snowshoes running toward him. Kneeling, Clover grabbed for the alpaca's head and released large rapid breaths. "Grant, what... what... what can we do?" she stuttered.

Grant rested his hand on her shoulder, trying to calm her rising screams.

"Please, please, we have to help them!"

"Clover, you must let them go," Grant replied.

"No, we must save them! We must help them!"

"It's their time, Clover. They're on their next journey."

"No!" Clover wept, her head resting on the neck of the dead alpaca. Around them, twenty-six others were all on their next journey.

Eyes fogged over from crying; Clover pressed her cheek along the soft, cloudlike hair of the alpaca's snout. She watched as its nose glistened from the snowflakes melting on its tip and did not notice when a pair of black combat boots stepped in front of her. But then, she heard a voice: "It is okay, Clover, it's where they're supposed to be."

Slowly, she raised her head and saw, backlit by a three-quarter moon, Jimmy.

# CHAPTER 35

**FEBRUARY 10, 1988**

T he moment in between rumbles was interminable. Bobby was right: they were using dynamite somewhere above them—and not that far away. The question now was whether this dynamite was being used to get to them or if it was a precaution to prevent future avalanches.

Looking at Annabelle hunched on the ground, covered in a spray of dust, Bobby wished there was some way to correct a situation that could only be described as "deeply and irreversibly fucked." To find a way out on their own would be mathematically impossible, so survival would come down to the not-so-simple matter of staying alive long enough for a rescue.

"Do you think they're going to blow again?" Annabelle asked, still covering her head with folded arms.

"Maybe . . . I hope," he said. "They still haven't found us, so I hope they'll keep blasting."

"It's loud," Annabelle followed. "I don't know what is freaking me out more, the last explosion or waiting for the next one."

Bobby understood what she meant. The explosion rattled the bones and thumped the eardrums, but the waiting—the in-between when they were left with nothing but their nerves—that caused a peak of anxiety so acute, only another shocking, bass-rattling explosion could stop it.

"I have no idea how we got here," Annabelle said, shaking her head. "It's all so fucking absurd. The fucking morning of our divorce—and now we're stuck in a mineshaft under a thousand feet of snow."

"Yeah," Bobby agreed, "it is all so fucking absurd."

Annabelle leaned against the base of her makeshift bed and looked at Bobby. "I just don't get it. Why did you not care? What the fuck did I do that made you stop caring?"

"I could ask you the same question," he said. "It's not like I was the only one who checked out. Everything I did . . . it just didn't make a difference after a while. You just hated me."

"I didn't at all, Bobby. I just wanted to feel like you cared about me. About us. Anything. Anything that proved you were happy, but you never gave me that."

"That's bullshit, Belle. I tried. I tried to do whatever you wanted. You wanted to move back here and homestead. You wanted to build a life back on the range. You remember, right? I'm not making this shit up."

Annabelle turned her stare from Bobby to her boots. He *was* right. She wanted all those things, and he had done them—but more than anything, she'd wanted to have a family. One with a partner who gave her a sense of security she'd never felt growing up without a father. Yes, Bobby was male, and he could do all the classic things an American male was supposed to. Fix things, move things, pay for things—hunt things, even, if needed. But also, like a very large selection of American males, Bobby did not understand that what Annabelle really wanted in a partner was someone who would hold her when the logic and weight of daily life bore through her shoulders. Someone who could just look her in the eyes and tell her, "It will all be okay."

Looking at Bobby, Annabelle said, "You know, Bobby, you had a choice. You didn't have to stay if you weren't happy. You didn't have to do any of it. Go to Ecuador, move back here, start Paca Joe—fuck whoever you fucked. You're an adult, for Christ's sake. You could have made a different choice in all of it."

Bobby stared at Annabelle. "You had the same choices, Belle. You could have—"

A quake rang through the mineshaft. Brutal, it sent Bobby against a wall and launched Annabelle three feet into the air. Arms flailing, she landed on the edge of the cot, then tumbled to the floor. It took her a moment to come to, and when she did, she saw Bobby face down on the floor, unconscious.

"Bobby . . . Bobby," she sputtered. "Bobby, get up. I need you to get up." Grabbing his arm, she tried to move toward him, but the pain in her back was too much. Wincing, she rolled onto her back when Bobby finally stirred.

"Ah, thank God, Bobby," she whispered. Her eyes scrunched and locked on the ceiling.

"Listen B, you gotta help me up, baby, I think I fucked up my back." Reaching for him, she saw him rise just beyond her fingertips. He was dazed and barely held his head, but his lips were somehow arched to reveal teeth, and that stupid ten-thousand-watt grin of his.

Trying to stand, he shifted onto his hip when a large drop of water fell on his face. Several more followed, and then a stream flowed from the ceiling. Looking up, he saw a small waterfall leak down on him. It felt good—but when he turned toward Annabelle, he didn't get a chance to see the stream transform from a waterfall to a rockslide.

The ceiling, once strong, had crumbled to nothing—and covered Bobby in a pile of earth.

## AUGUST 1986

Annabelle stared out over the valley floor. It had been a while since she went for a hike, and a while since she'd spent any true alone time outside the house. Instinctually, she did not want to. Instinctually, she wanted to spend her time with Clover—or kill her pain with Gunther.

Anything else she did was only because daily maintenance required it. And even then, she pushed those requirements to their brink. Her armpit hair was somehow always a six-day stubble, and her pubic hair had grown to such length that her trim V-shaped underwear could not cover the wiry strands. Her hair, normally clean, was seldom brushed and hidden, for the most part, under an alpaca beanie. Her nails, also normally honed, were chipped and dirty—a by-product of far too much chewing and too little washing. Meeting her for the first time, one would think she may have just finished hiking the Pacific Coast Trail. But if you knew her and saw her now, it would be obvious she was depressed. Depressed as a water-caged dolphin.

Nanny A tried to reach her many times during these days. Mostly, these attempts were met with "not now," or "leave me alone," or the most predictably mundane, "I just don't wanna talk about it."

She knew Annabelle was sleeping with Gunther, and not being one to argue the medicinal value of a good orgasm, she tried to focus the conversation instead on what she needed to do about her marriage. And more importantly, Clover. Unwilling to be avoided anymore, one Monday morning, Nanny A forced her way into Annabelle's house and cornered her in the laundry room.

"Belle," Nanny A started. "You have to think of Clover and what's next. The boy is not coming back. Everyone in town knows it. He's gone beyond screwing that tacky designer lady, and now he's on to all the vacation girls. And the drinking. Rumor has it he's going through three, four bottles of the red stuff—what is it called?"

"Cherry Heering," Annabelle answered flatly.

"Yeah, well, he's on it. Whatever that is, and from what I hear, it's like a Scandinavian Spanish fly—gives you a hard-on for days and makes you think you're part Casanova and part Bruce Lee."

"Yeah, it can have that effect," Annabelle said, closing her eyes. From then on, the conversation turned to gobbledygook. Like when Charlie Brown or any of the Peanuts spoke to an adult. Annabelle listened, but all she could hear was "Wah-wah-wah-wah-wah." And instead of words communicating an idea or plan, she saw visions. Clear, pristine visions. Of her. And Bobby. And Clover. A unit of three laughing on sleigh rides, laughing on hikes, laughing in movies, and at weddings. And then crying in their later years at the miraculous birth of Clover's child.

*Yes,* Annabelle thought. *I am fucking Gunther, and it is good. And Bobby is fucking whoever, and it is quick and bad—but we are going to get back together, so Nanny A and everyone else in town can go fuck themselves.*

Gunther had suspected this was how Annabelle felt. That she was still, very much, not over Bobby. Outside of the sex, their communication had grown lopsided. When they first connected, their time was brought to life by Annabelle sharing every dream and thought that percolated through her mind. Now, it was all about Gunther sharing every dream and thought that percolated through his. This did not initially bother Gunther, as the attention and companionship were more important than the intention. But as the disconnect became impossible to shake, he tried desperately to pull her back to where they'd started.

His first effort came in the shape of a ceramic bowl after a particularly unintimate exchange of intimacy.

"What is this?" she asked, confused.

"It's a bowl," Gunther responded proud.

"Um, okay. But why are you giving me a bowl?"

"For two reasons," Gunther replied, a smile broad on his face. "One, to hold your dreams. And two, to use when you eat your mushroom barley stew. That way, you don't have to always eat it out of your thermos."

Annabelle smiled and looked up at Gunther. She wanted to appreciate the gesture—it was sweet and considerate in a way that Bobby never was— but in the end, it just made her thoughts return to Bobby, and that wasn't what either of them wanted.

Nanny A was right about some stuff though, Bobby was on a fucking tear. He also was not done with the "tacky designer," as Annabelle discovered one night when she followed the two of them to her place after a night of binge drinking at the Horned Pony. He also wasn't drinking Cherry Heering. He was drinking something far more insidious and mood altering—gin from the bottle.

Before they met to officially discuss their divorce, Annabelle had tried everything she could to find time to talk with Bobby. She approached him at Baby Tubbs's house, and he'd told her it wasn't the time. She approached him at Diggity's, and he told her to find him later at Baby Tubbs's place. She even tried once to broach it at the Horned Pony during après ski, and he responded by saying, "Only if you do twelve shots of Heering." Angry and embarrassed, Annabelle stomped out of the bar, swearing never to go back there again. But somehow, despite Bobby's evasions, she still resolved to save their marriage.

Which was why, on December 5th, 1987, Annabelle was relieved to find Bobby knocking at their front door, hopefully ready to talk. She wasn't expecting him and felt a rush of inadequacy when she realized she hadn't showered and didn't have any makeup on. Nervous, she welcomed him in, then excused herself to their master bathroom to brush her hair and apply a quick coat of mascara and lip gloss.

After pulling on a fresh pair of Levi's, she sprinted back downstairs to see Bobby pouring a cup of coffee in the kitchen.

Turning toward the stairs, Bobby let out a sheepish smile. He recognized Annabelle had just gussied herself up and saw the glow that lit her eyes when she was happy. Sipping his coffee, he sat on the La-Z-Boy he inherited from his mother. Annabelle, a jumble of electric nerves, sat across from him on the sofa and pulled her ponytail apart, allowing her curls to drape shiny and wild on her shoulders. Blowing on his coffee, Bobby placed the mug on a side table and rocked forward in the La-Z-Boy until it stood straight like a normal chair.

"How have you been?" he asked.

"Good, busy, I guess. We got the first round of samples in—from that first batch of fur we loomed. There's some imperfections in the fabric—but Mom says they're just spirit lines."

"Spirit lines?" Bobby asked, skeptical of anything that came from Nanny A's mouth.

"Yeah, you know, like in Navajo rugs, when you see that one line of thread that looks like a mistake. She says they're actually put there on purpose by the artist to help the weaver's spirit exit their body and separate the rug from any harmful thoughts that could have been translated when it was made."

"That's great, Annabelle. I am really happy for you," Bobby answered—saying all that was necessary with that simple, monosyllabic pronoun. *You. You*, the singular. *You*, the individual. The single, solitary *you*, which was decidedly and definitely no longer the *we* or the *us*.

Annabelle folded her hands on her lap and took a deep breath.

"Why are you here, Bobby?" she asked, knowing exactly where the conversation was going. Rubbing his head, Bobby reclined in the La-Z-Boy, then shot back up and stood. Pacing across from Annabelle, he searched for words—any words that could soothe and soften the information he was about to share. Watching closely, Annabelle knew he was not going to look her in the eyes, or touch her hand, or tell her it was all going to be okay.

Grabbing her thighs, she whispered, "Just say it."

But Bobby couldn't speak. He could pace, rub his hands through his hair, and look at the floor, but he still couldn't bring himself to say anything.

"Bobby," Annabelle pleaded. "Just say it."

But still, there was nothing.

Finally, Annabelle snapped. "Just say it, Bobby!"

"Okay, okay!" Bobby whined back. "I want to get a divorce!"

Hearing this, Annabelle stood up and pulled her hair into a ponytail. She'd been expecting this for a long time, and some naive part of her had thought maybe she'd even come to prepare herself for this moment—but now that it was here, she didn't feel prepared at all.

Hands shaking, she asked, "Okay . . . but why now?"

"What do you mean why now?"

"Why do you want to divorce me now? I've let you do whatever you want. You go out and get drunk every night while I take care of Clover, and I don't raise hell, even though I'm fully aware you're fucking whoever you want—"

"Belle . . ."

"So, what is it, Bobby? Why now? Have I gotten too fat?" she asked, slapping her thighs, which weren't fat at all. "Is it because I'm too lazy? Am I too lazy, Bobby?"

Bobby only stared back at her, at a loss for words. Then, he weakly said, "No, Belle. It's not you, it's just that—"

"Bullshit," Annabelle interrupted. "Don't give me that. Don't tell me it's not me. What did I do wrong? What don't you like about me? Is it my mother? Is it the alpacas?"

"No, Belle, I told you—it's none of that. It's all me, I just—"

"Just tell me, you stupid, fat, lazy, worthless piece of shit! Just fucking tell me!" Annabelle screamed.

Bobby stopped his pacing and looked at Annabelle. "It's that! It's the way you talk to me! You treat me like I'm nothing, and I'm fucking done with it!"

"Okay, okay," Annabelle responded, face going white. "Please, forgive me. I'm so sorry, Bobby. I didn't mean any of that. I'm just mad and angry and hurt and—"

"Don't you get it?" Bobby interrupted. "I don't love you anymore. I actually fucking hate you and every fucking part of you!"

Annabelle collapsed on the sofa. Around her, all sound turned to warble, and all color drained. The world had stop rotating and nothing was in focus. So, she did not see when Bobby turned to leave or hear when Bobby turned the engine over and speed into town. All she could do was feel the pain of that moment and the throbbing of the same question as she sat numb on the sofa: *Is this my fault?*

In many ways, after that moment, it felt like she'd never gotten off that sofa. The days would pass, but Annabelle wasn't there to see them. Or Nanny A when she showed up to force-feed her a meal, bully her into a shower, or tell her something crazy she'd heard from Sheriff Daley.

That apparently, on December 5th, 1987, Bobby Mac was hired as VP of client relations by William Jefferson Macklemore and the Glory Peak Mountain Resort and Vacation Club, LLC.

# CHAPTER 36

**DECEMBER 2002**

---

Clover, no doubt, had quite the summer and fall. In the months since graduation, she started and ended a torrid love affair, became a drug dealer, got addicted to Special K, lost her grandmother, burned down her house, attempted suicide, and was unofficially initiated into the Le'Echuwanna, who inspired her to attack two major ski resorts powered by the spirit of a herd of genetically exceptional alpacas. But none of that landed in her gut like it did when she saw Jimmy on top of Jade Ridge. All the heartbreak she accrued over the summer evaporated on the spot, and before she could notice the burned skin that covered the left side of his face, she engulfed him in a hug that made his kidneys wince.

Walking along the ridge crest, it was difficult for Clover not to assault Jimmy with a cavalcade of questions or provide a cavalcade of stories about what she'd been up to since he left. But instead, under the moon, she allowed for silence. She knew he would disapprove of her actions, but she also knew he would not place judgment on what they meant. They were beyond trivial things, and as such, their sins were nothing but words.

As she looked at him, Jimmy tried his best to hide the scalelike damage done to his chin, cheek, and temple. There were stories in his scars, each one carrying a memory of what he had been up to for the past six months in Iraq.

Pained by the mere thought of the acts he likely committed, Clover walked and wondered and wiped the tears filling her eyes.

Grant, being Grant, was in tune with Clover's energy. Clover, heel after toe, was managing a long, anxious gait, each step cycling through a powerful combination of emotions. Surprise, longing, guilt, lust, love, curiosity, frustration, confusion, and everything that lived between. He was impressed that she somehow hadn't ignited and launched, missile-like, into the ether. He sensed the history between her and Jimmy and didn't want to overstep their connection by complimenting her composure or offering her a high-five. Nor did he want to jeopardize the world-changing *Rah-pah-no* they were training for—because what Clover didn't yet know was that Jimmy was an integral part of it.

By the time they got to Jimmy's tent, a military issued one, staked under a rock indentation at the south side of Jade Ridge, Clover still had no idea where to begin. She didn't know what to ask, or what to tell, or how she was going to find a reason to touch him. But she did know all three things would happen.

Taking her snowshoes off at his door, she was surprised to see Grant make no effort to do the same.

"Are you going back?" Clover asked.

Grant nodded, then shot a confirmation at Jimmy. Jimmy returned a nod and gave a muted, near-invisible salute. Shaking the snow from his skis, Grant turned toward the front side of Jade Ridge and planted his poles.

"Wait," Clover said. "You don't have to go. You can stay."

"I know." Grant smiled. "But you have a lot to catch up on. Just take the east side down, it's the fastest. I'll see you in the morning."

Clover watched as Grant disappeared soundlessly into the night, then she followed Jimmy into his tent.

As with most things Jimmy did, the tent was an example of simplicity and creative maximization. The bed was sculpted from hay and dirt and covered in perfect pleats by green army blankets and sleeping bags. Shelves and a small table were built out of foraged wood, and a firepit was dug in the center. Above it sat a metal grate that could be used for cooking, and even farther above it, the ceiling peaked to a cone, with a small hole cut in the top to let smoke disappear into the sky. Stacked to the left of the bed was a collection of books, and next to that, a collection of military boxes with faint stenciling. A cooler that Clover figured was for food waited by the door, and four lanterns hung from hooks, swaying in the direction of the winds.

Watching Jimmy light the lanterns, Clover looked for a place to sit and found one on a military trunk adjacent to the glowing firepit.

Jimmy then sat across from Clover, on his bed. As the lanterns pulsed in soft gold, they looked at each other in short passes and with each lock of eyes, a smile would overcome their glance, then turn them away, bashful and childlike. It wasn't flirting—it was something purer. But it was an extension of a powerful, familiar, and intense feeling.

Finally, Jimmy got up and walked over to the firepit. Lighting some aspen, he placed it in bed of ash and sat at the far end of the trunk.

This was all Clover needed to finally speak.

"I'm sorry about your father," she said at last.

Tracking a spark that popped from the dry log, Jimmy watched it drift and fall to nothing on the dirt floor. "Thanks. I was worried he would have trouble when he lost his job. He always needed that to ground him."

Clover nodded, then cleared a small tadpole forming in the back of her throat. "I tried to find you when he passed, but they wouldn't tell me where you were stationed."

"That sounds about right," Jimmy answered, his voice barely audible over the crackling fire.

Sliding closer to him, Clover traced her thumb over her index finger. "When did you get back?" she asked in whisper.

"August. First week."

"And you didn't find me? Ah, Jimmy . . . Why? I would have died to see you."

"I did. I saw you. Around town. Going to Jesse's. Leaving Jesse's. At Nanny A's funeral. All those things."

Clover took a deep breath. So, he knew about Jesse. He knew of the dark, stupid feeling that came with Jesse. Maybe this was a sin Jimmy could not forgive.

"I thought you knew I was back. I was leaving rocks around to let you know. Maybe a phone call would have been better."

Clover looked around the tent; there was no electricity and, without a doubt, no phone. "You don't look like you have one," she said, smiling.

"I don't," Jimmy said as he poked the fire, lost in the red warmth of the white bark turning to flame. Clover, watching, sensed he was someplace else—and that it wasn't the someplace else he lost himself to a year earlier. This was the someplace else that came with violent change. It was the hollow place one carves out for themselves, deep inside, so that they could hide from the world.

"Listen, Jimmy," Clover said, "that Jesse thing . . . it wasn't what you think. Actually, I don't know what you think, but it—well, it wasn't real."

Jimmy pulled the poker from the fire and rested it on the ground. "You don't owe me an explanation. It's your life. I just . . . well, I'm sorry I didn't call you, is all. I should have called you."

He held Clover's eyes for a long time. There wasn't romance in the look, but there was genuine love there. "Please forgive me, Clove."

Clover looked at him, a rush of emotion rising like a barrel wave above her heart. Unable to avoid it, she let it crash over her, then grabbed Jimmy and hugged him tight. Jimmy, sensitive to the brush of anything on his face, angled his head to avoid her shoulder and found himself resting his right cheek in the warm spot above her bosom and below her clavicle. It was real here, and it was safe, and it was a place without an atom of sexuality. Despite their history, both were happy to be back—not with their lover but their best friend.

Walking back to He Who Eats' place, Clover studied the ground. She could see clear as the early morn traded sky with the setting moon and revealed every crumble of earth that made up the puzzle of ground below her. It wasn't hers; it wasn't Jimmy's. Or even Grant's. It was not even its own. It was fate's. It was time's. And just by walking on it, it changed. And just by being there, it changed. Rocks dislodged, snow displaced dirt, wind carved veiny rivulets that weakened the earth, and it all became something different than it was that morning. Or yesterday. Or before—and in spite of—who owned it.

Clover was not good at understanding meaning or coming up with metaphors, but there was something there—at least so she thought. And maybe one day, this abstract sense of change and narrative would make sense. Just like maybe one day, it would make sense as to why Jimmy enlisted and why he would choose explosives as a specialty. And why, one evening, while he was sitting in a porta-potty in Kabul, a light bulb shorted and started the fire that scarred Jimmy's face and led to his honorable discharge. It made sense, in some ways, because it brought him back to Fortooth, and as she found out that evening, he would be using his explosive skills in their raid against Glory Peak and Wolfe Mountain.

But it didn't make sense that this was the route it'd required to get him back. One that, just with his presence, so many things, lives, and objects would be altered—including his own.

*Couldn't it just have been,* she wondered, *that Jimmy stayed in Fortooth, got to be friends with Grant, and didn't have to go halfway around the world and burn a third of his body to help them?*

The following day at He Who Eats' was marked with an unusual solemnity. The tribe didn't train that morning and instead prepared for something that had a greater sense of importance. When Clover asked what they were doing, everyone turned to He Who Eats to explain, but all he could say was, "We're just leveling the waters." Getting no further explanation, she asked if she could join, but He Who Eats firmly said no.

For the remainder of the day, Clover watched, in silence, as the tribe stitched together pelts and beaded them with ram horns and turquoise. Noticing she was tense from not knowing what was happening, Grant brought her to his bedroom. Sitting her on his bed, he told her they were preparing to say goodbye to the other Elder Elders, who were moving to Orlando to set up residence on land they bought from the Seminoles. He explained they were going to perform a sunset dance and return, by evening, to review the latest attack plans.

Appreciating the emotions speeding through her body, Grant asked if she could do her best to manage them until they returned. "Yes," she said, and when he thanked her and touched her wrist, all she could think about was his return.

Meanwhile, all He Who Eats could think about was getting to the community center.

When Sleeping Mouse told him they were selling the beautifully large and sacredly fertile *Pe-ah-eh-oh* to Glory Peak Mountain Resort and Vacation Club, LLC, He Who Eats knew the disintegration of the former incarnation of the keepers of the bighorn sheep, known by all as the Le'Echuwanna, was here. Because he knew with the money from the land sale would come the purchase of the Florida land. And with the purchase of the Florida land would come the hiring of an environmentally conscious architectural firm out of Miami-Dade County and the sale of the printing company in Farangotta. And with the sale of the printing company would come the decision, from 84 percent of the tribe, to relocate to the Everglades and create a trust for the land, buildings, and people deciding to stay in Fortooth.

And in this was the danger. There was plenty of money to survive in Fortooth forever—and to make sure the land and buildings would always be cared for—but if the Le'Echuwanna were no longer in Fortooth, was there anything worth caring for?

Unless, of course, there was. And, as He Who Eats always argued, it was not about the number of items at the all-you-can-eat buffet; it was about how good the chilled shrimp were. And as much as it removed three ventricles from his heart, burned them to ash, and blew those ashes to the corners of nothing, he was relieved to watch the wilted iceberg and rank raspberry vinaigrette of this buffet disappear to Florida. Because that meant, once those items were removed, the greatest, most spectacular chilled Le'Echuwannan shrimp would be left.

Arriving at the village, outlined in the burnt bronze of the setting sun, He Who Eats was at peace, knowing that he, finally, found the all-you-can-eat buffet of his dreams.

Looking in on the evening from the vantage of a third-party perspective, it would be difficult to argue its beauty. Driving into the village, the first thing of notice was the line of torches along the driveway and periphery of the buildings. In spring, it would have seemed as if the fireflies took a neon hold of the property, but being winter, the torches stood warm and sparkly, like candles on a birthday cake above a vanilla icing of snow.

Next were the outfits—and simply put, they were grand. Layer upon layer of fur draped under necklace upon necklace of crystal and stone. Colors ranged from lavender to indigo, to *morado*, to beryl red, to cerulean, and the most incredible shade of *xanthe* human eyes had ever seen. It wasn't easy to walk in this attire, but when the Elder Elders and the Budding Elders sat together in the former library of the community center, it was a genuine sartorial sight. One that made He Who Eats question the value of the tribe's splintering. There was history here—six hundred years of history, pulsing in every person, article, and word and flooding the Le'Echuwannan bloodline with oxygen-rich community.

This last night, that very oxygen flowed madly. Pouting Trout led the opening song with one of the greatest renditions of *Lah-ho-che-man*— or the "Hello Song," as translated to English—any generation of the Le'Echuwanna had ever heard. Grant's mother, Sacred Crow, performed the most gentle and wispy version of the Pollen dance in history, and Squirreling Squirrel's heartfelt chant of the "Shaking Tale and Tail" left no eye without moisture. Even He Who Eats was moved by the performance—so much so, he considered changing Squirreling Squirrel's name to Open Sparrow out of respect for the layered emotion he brought to each meditative syllable of the chant.

But if an Oscar was to be given to one performance—actually, one shared performance—it would've been to He Who Eats and Grant for the passage of the three sheep horn. This ceremony was conducted between an outgoing and incoming chief, and in its choreography was the great chronicle of life: birth to puberty, puberty to adulthood, adulthood to the age of the wise, and finally, the shedding of the pelt and ascension to the "new vessel." It was part dance, part drum, part song and meditation. And in the way that He Who Eats and Grant performed it, every spectator projected visions of their truth, past and future.

Sacred Crow wept with happiness as she watched her son perform birth—but watching Grant perform the shedding of the pelt made her weep with such tangible, unrivaled sadness, she swore she witnessed his death before her very eyes. He was truth. And the playful gravity he brought to the ascent to the adult self, confirmed to the Elder Elders that the Budding Elders would carry their traditions forward with grace. And swagger.

However, it was the moment in the ceremony when the cycle began anew and the spirit of the wise ascended to the next world that landed with the greatest breathlessness. This was channeled through the life force that was He Who Eats. Yes, he was an asshole. Yes, he was a bully. Yes, he was blunt, and stinky, and paranoid, and borderline psychotic, but in the history of the Le'Echuwanna, and possibly any post–Cro-Magnon race, he was the closest a human came to channeling the volcanic essence that imbued body, creature, plant, and protozoa with soul.

Falling to his knees, He Who Eats emulated a spirit shedding its human form. Then, pointing his arms to the sky, he floated to an imaginary alter-world where he injected himself into an alter-world egg, fertilized by alter-world sperm, only to be birthed back into the living world as a baby girl. Splayed on the ground, he whimpered and gurgled the soft, delicate hiccups of a newborn, his hands reaching for and holding gently the very essence of earth and life.

When He Who Eats finished his song and pulled a hollow sheep horn from his pelt to place at the feet of a seated Grant, the community held its breath and the beat of their hearts. This was real. The cycle was going to continue. And after twenty-three seconds of frozen biological silence, they let out a collective breath, not just for the rebirth of their chief, but for the rebirth of the Le'Echuwanna.

There was a brief after-party catered by Sleeping Mouse. Venison burgers, German sausages, and cold beer were served. It was good there was beer because it allowed for the open softness of a hoppy buzz and disallowed the anger that came with bourbon. It also allowed Squirreling Squirrel to approach He Who Eats and ask, "Can you please not die on your raid?" and it allowed Sacred Crow to tell He Who Eats that she "admired his blind strength." And most touching of all for He Who Eats, it allowed Pouting Trout to tell him he was "the spirit of the ancestors, the spirit of the breathing people, and the spirit of those yet to be."

As they departed that night, nothing but empty Solo cups and paper plates left as a reminder of the tribe that once was, He Who Eats, Grant, and the remaining warriors knew they were the only custodians left of what was now the old way.

When the tribe returned to He Who Eats' house on Sleeping Camel, Clover recognized a distinct change in their energy. He Who Eats was no longer the center of everyone's eyes or ears. Instead, everything circled around Grant. When they ate, He Who Likes Oaks made sure all food and water was first served to Grant, and as everyone chewed, they waited for him to review the raid plans. Sitting at the kitchen table, she also noticed a newfound peace embedded in Grant's actions, the sort of peace that came with knowing that whatever you said or did would be regarded with complete acceptance.

Eating a bowl of elk stew, Grant instructed Slippery Tongue to call for Jimmy. Putting down her food without her customary middle-finger salute, Slippery Tongue walked to the front yard and let out a bellowing owl hoot that flapped its way up Jade Ridge and into Jimmy's tent.

Twenty minutes later, Jimmy joined the war party around the fireplace, and Grant proceeded to discuss their plan of attack. It was to take place on the first of January at three o'clock in the afternoon, during the middle of the Huevos Rancheros Stampedo, the opening act of the first annual Snow Ball Festival, and medal ceremony for the XL Games. The night before, Jimmy and a soon-to-be-selected team would place the putty explosives in his tent on the crest of Bobby's Bandido Bowl, the construction site at *Pe-ah-eh-oh*, and the center ridge of Wolfe Mountain. The following day, they would dress as snowboarders and skiers, carry their weapons into the resorts via ski and snowboard bags, and proceed to take out chairlifts and buildings. There were instructions not to attack any civilians, but security was fair game, and extra tobacco would be gifted to anyone who could take out management.

When the meeting was over, everyone threw handfuls of sage into the fire and retired to their rooms. Jimmy, last to leave, paid tribute to the fire with a pack of Winston cigarettes. As he put on his jacket and gloves, Clover ran to his side.

"Wait, wait—I want to come with you," she said. Jimmy looked at her with the sort of wide-eyed silence that indicated he hadn't expected this offer—not because Jimmy had difficulty understanding that people had expectations based on shared histories but because it was apparent to him, and everyone, that they were no longer each other's. And that was okay. Though she had never said it out loud, everyone knew Clover's heart was now with Chief Grant.

# CHAPTER 37

## FEBRUARY 1988

It annoyed Bobby that his first few months following the Glory Peak work routine came with too much ease. He knew the mountain, knew the lodge, knew the people, and as much as he did not want to admit, knew his father, and the stubborn linearity of his mind. He was a bulldozer, so all and everything that sprouted from Glory Peak came from his father's bulldozer brain. If there was no snow, he would make it. If there was no fresh trout, he would fly it in. If there were no people on the slopes, he would give away free food and alcohol. Fortooth never had a chance against Bill, and now, Bobby realized, neither did he.

The recompense for Bobby's surrender was the genuine affection he received from the Glory Peak team. The lift operators, ski patrol, bartenders, comptrollers, and bus drivers—all were smitten by the vision of Bobby in a Glory Peak jacket and hat. They left him muffins on his desk, offered him rides on their golf carts or snowmobiles, tapped fresh kegs if he was at après ski. With his return to the mountain, Glory Peak was a flutter, like the Farangotta itself, which was experiencing one of its greatest snowfalls in years. The 1987-88 winter was shaping up to be a year of record powder, record attendance, and a record-happy Bill Macklemore.

Life was different across town. Nanny A was livid with Bobby, and Annabelle floated through her days in a tub of depression. She would meet

Gunther in the afternoon for short sessions of sex, then spend her evenings in small pockets of happiness playing with Clover. Nanny A did her best to fill in as much as possible—cleaning, cooking, ironing, and generally acting the part of mother and housekeeper. She also tried to remain silent about Annabelle and Bobby, but sometimes she just couldn't bring herself to lie to her daughter anymore and had to speak the truth: Annabelle and Bobby's marriage was over.

Those nights always ended in a screaming fight or silence.

The person who dealt with this the most was Sheriff Dan Daley, as he was a man and, therefore, the direct object of Nanny A's disdain. At night, she would drive to his house and spout a diatribe on the stupidity of his gender and their complete inability to earn the *man* in "human." Pacing in the kitchen, she would whip her hands like some Taekwondo demonstration and argue that the race should be called hu-woman and that all testicles should be removed and attached to turkey basters or large syringes.

Sheriff Dan Daley initially laughed when she made these comments, but when his chuckles began to further piss Nanny A off, she targeted him directly. Ad hominem attacks on his handlebar mustache; his part gaucho, part cowboy street clothes; his alphabetized collection of eight-track tapes. But when her tirades were thrown at his family and the settlers who came to Fortooth during the Gold Rush, Sheriff Dan Daley could take it no longer.

Finally, he fought back. And to his dismay, Nanny A responded with total shock. This was not the Sheriff Dan Daley she had come to know, but it was the *man* she had come to expect. After the shock of his explosion wore off, Nanny A rose from a seat at Sheriff Dan Daley's kitchen table and pointed her right index finger at him.

"You thick-dicked piece of whale shit. How dare you talk to me like that?" she began. "You think I care for one second about anything you think? Or do you think for one second that I need you beyond the eight minutes of erection you provide?"

Sheriff Dan Daley tried his best to pacify the situation. "Listen, Abigail," he started, rubbing the back of his neck. "You're misinterpreting what I am saying. I am just tired of sitting here and being torn apart by you."

"You're tired of that, huh?" Nanny A replied, running her hand through her hair. "Well, you know what? You sure as hell don't have to worry about that anymore, Dan. Sheriff Dan. Sheriff Daniel Daley! Because as far as I'm concerned, you and those stupid, fat, incisor-chomping Macklemore's can go fuck a barbwire fence."

Sheriff Dan rose to his feet, face completely red, ready to serve his own plate of vitriol—but only choked-up silence followed. Before he could find Nanny A's hand to ask her to stick around long enough to see reason, she had grabbed her purse and was out the door.

Melancholy fell over Sheriff Dan Daley. Matched only by the melancholy that was actively overtaking Bobby Mac. Unlike with Sheriff Dan Daley, it wasn't the melancholy of heartbreak but the melancholy of concession—the melancholy that arrived when you accepted the fact that you were going to settle in life. The moment when the daily will to fight was traded for a bear claw and Sanka.

Exhausted, Bobby wanted to hide. And he did, in the most unexpected of places: the Glory Peak financials.

As always, Bill's hope for Bobby did not meet the reality of Bobby. Bill hoped Bobby would walk the grounds, offer handshakes, pose for banners, lift kids, and sing to a wealth of après guests. What he got, instead, was a Bobby who spent his days locked in his office, reviewing costs, revenues, and cash-flow reports. It made no sense to Bill, especially as Bobby's social aptitude was as legendary as his backcountry expertise. But that was because there was one thing Bill did not account for—the power of Bobby's own shame. That alone kept him locked in his office.

But it also gave him an atom of hope.

As Bobby familiarized himself with this program named Microsoft Excel, he learned how to track costs, interest, and to account for this new term he learned called EBITDA. None of this was useful on a ski slope, but maybe, he thought, just maybe, all this could find its way back to Paca Joe. Though he couldn't yet admit it, he hoped to approach his father about investing in Paca Joe. And he hoped that when he did, Bill would say yes, not as a way to further establish his control over Bobby, but because he saw before him a brilliant business opportunity.

Hoping to gain a greater understanding of business, Bobby dug deeper into the growth of the company and researched its land purchases and loans—and what he discovered was surprising. All the land was assigned to a trust, SJD Trust and Principal, and for whatever reason, he couldn't find any paperwork regarding ownership of the trust.

Bringing it up with the CFO, he was met with an awkward explanation about how "it was just a dummy corporation set up in case of lawsuits." Fine, if that was the case—but the company had money owed to it because it leased the land to the construction company Bill created to handle the building of the hotels, time-shares, and condos. Disinterested in finding the extra energy needed to search for the ownership papers, Bobby chose to return to the giant margins in concessions and liquor. But then, one day, his craving for chili became too much.

This happened often in ski towns. Usually, it happened after logging four hours of morning turns when something warm, hearty, and full of protein was needed to fuel you up for the back end of the day. And that was what almost happened to Bobby as, one day, he looked out his office window and saw a bushy-blond teen shred down Columbus Alley—a double black run riddled with waist-high moguls. The sight of this kid suturing his way down the mountain triggered something of a Pavlovian response in Bobby. It wasn't a trigger that made him want to ski— even though he saw the ski's edge, heard the snow crunch, and felt the warm burn in his upper thighs with each arc. No, this trigger was for what happened after he would have done all that. It was for chili.

Those days, it was rare for Bobby to take lunch in the cafeteria of the main lodge, as too many high-fives were thrown his way. But that was where the best chili was, and needing to quench this craving quickly, he knew it was the only place to go. The guests, fortunately, had no idea who he was, but the employees took notice, and as he grabbed his lunch tray and stepped into line, two bowls were handed to him. Embarrassed by the attention, Bobby nodded his thank-you and walked to the cashier, who waved him by as he tried to pay.

Settling into a chair, Bobby was halfway through his first bowl when he realized how long it had been since he'd spent time in the main lodge. It was larger than when he was younger, and there were more sponsorship signs and poster promotions than he remembered, but it still had the old, rustic, log cabin flavor from when it was first built. And it still had that cinnamon smell of winter drinks and that nose-tingling rush of burning pine logs. And shockingly, it still had the installation of photos and historical items from the original Glory Peak around the fireplace. Aged pickaxes, the timing belt of the old Ford that powered the first ski lift, photos of Bill chopping down trees, skiing shirtless, and laughing next to the first keg installed in Glory Peak. And even more shockingly, next to that was a photo that stopped Bobby cold.

It was a picture of him as a child, riding on Bill's shoulders with Suzanne smiling next to them, the couple, both on skis. It had been a while since he'd seen a photograph of his mother, and looking at her in the photo, he realized it had been even longer since he'd seen her smile. Dead or alive.

Taking in her eyes, a jolt shot to his heart, and pulled by a slow-moving rope, he took measured steps toward the picture. The tears came next, but not full-blown sobbing—just tears tracing a transparent trail down his cheeks. He couldn't help but look at this picture and realize that *this* was what it was like for his mother to be in love. That this was what it was like for Bobby to love his father. That this was what it was like to be a family.

Reaching for the dusty glass of the picture frame, Bobby hoped his fingers could pass through it into an alternate, three-dimensional world where he could touch his mother's hand and hug her leg—but they stopped on the glass and left nothing but a fingerprint.

Shocked at the size of his fingerprint, Bobby rubbed it away, revealing a caption under the photo that read, December 18, 1966. Founder William J. Macklemore; his son, Robert Butler Macklemore; and his wife, Suzanne Joanne Macklemore, formally Suzanne Joanne Dempsey, heir to local department store Danu's.

It took a second for Bobby to take it all in.

Then, it took a few more seconds for Bobby to take in something else. His mother's name.

Staring at it, Bobby saw two versions. "Suzanne Joanne Macklemore" and "formally Suzanne Joanne Dempsey." Or possibly, quite possibly, and most likely, formally SJD. Dropping his hand from the pane, Bobby bolted out the door.

When Bobby arrived at Bill's office, he was surprised to see him in shorts and a fur hat. He was underlining Flying Burrito Brothers at the top right corner of his whiteboard and held a tumbler of scotch. Smiling at the sight of Bobby, he put the cap back on his felt marker and walked to his desk.

"Bobby, what a nice surprise! How you doing, son?" Bill asked.

Bobby wasn't sure what to say, and it took a couple of tentative steps forward, then back, and then forward again for him to point at the whiteboard and say, "What's that?"

"That . . ." Bill paused to spin the ice in his tumbler. "Well, that, son, is the master plan."

Bobby, confused, took two steps closer and examined it. Scribbles of Bobby and rebuild and Lindsey Jessups and Olympics and Joe Namath and Cadillac stamped themselves across the board. Nothing but a tangle of letters, it seemed every word in the dictionary sat black and red on the board. Every word but two. Clover and Annabelle.

Trying to decipher this cacophony of chicken scratches, Bobby turned to his father.

"Why is Lindsey Jessups' name up here?" he asked.

"Well, I'm going to hire her to redo the lodge. Fine lady, good taste, and did you know she's very well-connected to investment money in New York? Truly a remarkable woman, I tell you."

Bobby, still weighed down by what he'd seen in the main lodge cafeteria, shuffled to one of the chairs across from Bill's desk and slumped into it.

"You okay, son?" Bill asked, surprised Bobby was so sullen. "I was planning on reviewing all this with you. Like I told you when you signed up, all decisions will be made jointly moving forward."

Bobby had no response.

All he could do was sit there and fight the drowning feeling that filled his skull with the throbbing goo of a head cold. But then, Bill moved closer, sat on the corner of his desk, and slapped Bobby proudly on the knee. Bill thought this would engender some camaraderie, but instead, it woke Bobby from his daze.

"What is SJD Trust and Principal?" Bobby asked, his voice solid.

"Excuse me, son, what are you talking about?" Bill asked, sliding up from the desk and walking to the whiteboard.

"SJD Trust and Principal. It's the trust that owns the land Glory Peak sits on."

"I-I, uh, don't know," Bill stammered. Bobby had never seen his father stammer before. It made him uncomfortable; it also gave him a shot of courage.

"I think it's one of the companies the accountants set up to handle liability on the mountain. You know how that goes with accidents," Bill continued.

"I do know how it goes with accidents. But under whose name was it set up?"

Bill paused behind the chair at his desk. "Well, Bobby, now that I think about it . . . it was something I believe I did with your mother, back in the day. She was concerned if something happened, they could come after me. So, she thought it was more, you know, prudent to set up a trust under her name for better protection. Legally."

"Protect us? Or you?" Bobby responded coldly.

"Well, all of us . . . Bobby, see, your mother was practically royalty back in the day here, and nothing would have happened to her if something went, um, south. See, it made sense to make her the liable one. That's how business works, son, you need—"

Bobby raised an open hand and converted it into an index finger. Pointing it at Bill, he pursed his lips. About to speak, he instead lifted a crystal ashtray from his desk and threw it a foot from Bills's head. It shattered against the wall, and sent Bill ducking to the ground, where he saw Bobby's feet stomp out of the office and down the stairs.

For Bobby, the next few hours blended into a lump of alcohol-glazed confusion. There was drinking, and there were phone calls, and finally, one of the phone calls was answered by Annabelle. Her excitement to hear his voice gave way to disappointment when his drunk slurring and tearful pleas morphed into verbal confusion. She did, however, agree to meet him the following morning at Prescott Loop, and he did, despite the copious amounts of Cherry Heering he had consumed, set an alarm for 6 a.m. But what he did that was most impressive in his intoxicated state was find the original paperwork for SJD Trust in his mother's personal papers. And just as he hoped, the trust had been set up in her name.

# CHAPTER 38

**FEBRUARY 10, 1988**

When Annabelle got through the layer of rock and dirt to get to Bobby, she discovered what looked like a rookie fighter who spent four rounds too many with the champ. His nose was flattened and cut broadly across the bridge. His right eye was swollen and bled from the tear duct. And his hair hid a large gash that sent a trail of blood down his forehead to his temples. Dazed, Bobby was barely able to form a word, let alone a sentence, but like that rookie boxer who was fighting with all heart, he didn't lose himself to unconsciousness.

There was, unfortunately, a rocking, seasick sort of wave that swelled over him in rhythmic pulses, and dragged him in and out of reality. And in those moments, he felt Annabelle wipe his face and wrap his head in the waffle pattern of her long-sleeve shirt. He sensed she was crying—not just soft, rumpled tears but heaving, panicked sobs that skirted the edge of hysteria. When the float of unconsciousness receded from his wobbly head and he reentered the steady legs of reality, Bobby saw Annabelle over him, cleaning the dirt off his face.

"Holy fuck, Bobby, thank God! Thank God, thank God!" she squealed, part amazed, part relieved, and part confused by the reliability of Bobby's good luck.

"I don't feel good," Bobby replied with cracked lips.

"I know, baby, I know," she said. "The dynamite blew out the top of the mineshaft. It's all falling apart."

Bobby turned his head and took in the mineshaft. He had forgotten, for a moment, where they were, thinking, in his unconscious state, he was in the South Pacific chasing an octopus along the ocean floor.

Coughing, he shifted his tender body to a seat. Wiping the iron dust from his face, he tried to formulate a plan. But just as the first promising idea formed, a rib-shaking earthquake ran through the tunnel, raining large pieces of ceiling on the far end of the cavity.

It took a few minutes for the dust to dissipate and for Annabelle and Bobby to cough out the cloud around them. When they did, they were able to find each other's hands. And each other's eyes, which they locked on to with such strength, they felt their optic nerves tug from their brains to their hearts.

Not knowing what to say or if words were even necessary, Bobby moved toward Annabelle's lips until their mouths touched. As they kissed, he felt every bit of her warm breath release fast and heavy into his mouth. After a few seconds, he leaned back to see her, a smile forming on her lips. And then he saw it. Right behind her, at the base of the shaft—a small opening with light shining from it.

"Belle—Belle, *look*!" Bobby shouted.

Spinning around, Annabelle saw what drove Bobby's exclamation. Then, sprinting toward the opening, Annabelle bent down to see if she could fit.

"Bobby, there's enough room here for us! It worked, they split open the mine!" Turning toward him, relief ran across her dust-covered face. There was pink in her cheeks, light in her eyes. Rolling onto fours, Bobby crawled toward her.

"Okay, okay, pea," Bobby coughed. "I'm with you. You ready?"

Smiling, Annabelle waited till he reached her, then grabbed his scuffed and bloody hand, and led them down the opening.

## JANUARY 1, 2003

From his balcony, Bill saw the outline of the XL Games superpipe at the base of Bobby's Bandido Bowl. Its giant twenty-two-foot-high walls were outlined by the rise of the morning sun as it stretched its head above the tree line. In front of it, taking form on foot and by car, was an assortment of news reporters preparing for the afternoon's broadcast.

Bill's nerves, still tense with worry over how the day might go, slightly lightened when he heard from Park Service that twenty-seven alpacas were found dead along Jade Ridge. But even though his assault had quieted their numbers, Bill knew the war was not over. So, he prepared for the inevitable: the retaliation of the alpacas.

Inch by inch, Bill filled his Land Rover with every weapon and piece of gear he used in the 10th Mountain Division. There was his white one-piece, full-body ski suit, his thin wooden skis and skins, his 1911 Colt .45, his Thompson submachine gun, ten fully stocked clips, ski boots with rubber-cleated soles, ski poles with leather handles, and ski goggles—green-lensed and polished to perfection. As Bill struggled to get into his now overstuffed car, he was so focused on the oncoming melee that he refused to let the sight of his ex-wife's ghost in the passenger seat, or the two German soldiers in back, deter him from his assignment.

Across town, Gunther had his own assignments to deal with. A mile-long list of assignments, in fact, which he chose to ignore as he lay in bed and floated on clouds of weltschmerz. Peeking his left eye out from under an alpaca blanket, he saw the final-stage preparations for the first annual Snow Ball Music Festival through his window. Anticipating a flurry of phone calls, he turned his BlackBerry off and pulled the landline from the wall. No matter how inviting this all should be, no matter how proud he should have felt in finding a bucket of gold at the end of his entrepreneurial rainbow, Gunther chose to engage in two sentiments: "Eh" and "Weltschmerz!"

Because, he realized, none of it really mattered, anyway. One day, it would all be gone. One day, the sun would explode, and every trace of Earth and human existence would be annihilated, and so in the truest sense of the word, this all would really be *gone*.

Actually, it was already gone. It was gone the day Nanny A died and left everything to a girl with a ketamine addiction and an affection for setting house fires.

*If only I could taste Nanny A*, Gunther thought. *If only I could smell the back of her neck, then maybe there would be a reason to get out of bed.* Reaching his hand down his pants, he found his penis, flaccid and ice cold. In a pointless attempt to resuscitate it, he squeezed it tight, hoping blood would flow through its corpus cavernosum and wake back to life. But nothing happened, and like a stack of gummy worms, it continued to lay lifeless in his hand. Relieved, Gunther released his penis and pulled the comforter fully over him. Through the white patches in the fabric, the outline of trees swayed just outside his windows.

Closing his eyes, Gunther wondered why God thought trees would be a good delivery system for oxygen and began to imagine a world where rocks were what turned carbon dioxide into oxygen. These thoughts had stoner-level appeal, until a streak of shadows crossed the outline of the trees. Confused by what he'd just seen, Gunther lowered the comforter, rose from the bed, and walked toward his window.

Through it, he spied twelve Le'Echuwannan teenagers trekking silently down the slope toward Bobby's Bandido Bowl. Or maybe Wolfe Peak. Or maybe both. Based on what he saw, it was difficult to know which direction they were going.

And based on what he felt, it was even more difficult to care because, "Weltschmerz."

Which was the opposite of how He Who Eats woke up. He Who Eats woke up a single, vibrating spinal cord of energy. He was neon gas, his large six-foot-five body the only thing strong and fortified enough to contain what had been bubbling like a geyser for years. This was the day of the *Rah-pah-no*, the final battle, the cleansing battle, the battle to end all battles—and despite the dangers, He Who Eats was ecstatic to commence "a nuclear shit bomb." So, he got up early, before the sun rose, and walked to the pair of chairs up the hill from his house to think.

For He Who Eats, this time was not about vision. It was about sound and feeling and breeze and temperature. He wanted to inhale the valley, to allow any scent, nutrient, or element into his widening nostrils, then to careen down his throat and disappear into his bloodstream. He wanted the valley to power his body with its history, its essence, its wisdom to overtake any trace of his ego and guide him forward as an instrument of the *Rah-pah-no*. An invisible instrument of the *Rah-pah-no*. An airy instrument of the *Rah-pah-no*. The ultimate instrument of the *Rah-pah-no*.

Walking back home, he saw Grant and his fellow warriors stirring with the same intention. Each one held their head out a window, eyes closed, allowing the morning to wash over them. The wind was warm and steady, which meant that for the most part, the day's recipe was going to be glorious, clear, and what the skiers called bluebird—which meant no clouds, just bright sun and blue skies. But there was also a jarring dip in the temperature. Which meant that come noon, they could be greeted by nothing or everything. And that come noon, it could very well, be a different day.

The idea that the day could take an unexpected turn did not sit well with Clover. She liked knowing how the night would fall and how the afternoon would unfold and if two or one pair of socks were needed when she left the house. Accepting the bluebird part of the day was no problem but accepting that she did not know how today would end was torturous.

Grant sensed her apprehension, when after breakfast, as they sat in the living room and passed the elk pipe, he felt a run of electricity shoot off Clover's fingers. *Maybe this is too much of us to expect from her*, Grant thought, as he watched Clover take a slow pull off the pipe. *Maybe she should sit back and tend the fires*. But he knew that even if she was in over her head, she'd never allow for that. Grant knew from the moment he first watched her cross-country ski at Punishment Lake that Clover was somehow always preparing for the *Rah-pah-no*.

Even Jimmy's arrival didn't settle her nerves. But then again, the Jimmy who walked into He Who Eats' house was not operating on the same frequency as the Jimmy who left a year earlier. His wires conducted differently now, his previously controlled current now replaced with a scattered start and stop energy.

Clover tried to catch his eyes but was only met with shifting glances and a rejection of the elk pipe. When the ceremony finished and they retired to their rooms to dress, Grant intercepted Clover and drew her out to the front porch. She felt relief when he touched her forearm, and before she could even digest the intention, she wrapped her arms around his waist and rested her head on his shoulder. Grant's hair smelled of pine and weed—two smells she had trouble accepting, but being close to his neck, his pulse provided the tranquilizer she needed. After several beats and breaths, Clover leaned back and nodded. Grant then leaned forward and pressed his lips against her cheek. There was no sound, no soft smack of release, just the warm presence of his lips on her skin.

"All you have to do is ask," he said. "If it's too much, I will stop it. This is your home, too."

Clover didn't respond; she just measured her breath against his and thought about her mother.

Arriving at the base of Bobby's Bandido Bowl, Bill decided to wear his old pair of Cébé sunglasses instead of his normal Ray-Ban aviators. The Cébé's were navy blue, fully mirrored, and had leather side shields that protected his eyes not only from the glare that bounced off the snow but from anyone who wanted to see them—which Bill needed because if he was going to stay alert for intruders, he had to hide the near-frantic scan of his eyes.

This would not be easy, as there was a larger-than-normal number of faces he would have to interact with. He had the XL executives, the NBC executives, as well as the snowboard brands and energy drink executives. In what was going to be one of his most visible days in the history of Glory Peak, Bill had his greatest need for anonymity.

Thankfully, he was a well-practiced politician. And thankfully, his choice of sunglasses did the trick in masking his eyes as he shook hands, flashed grins, and pretended to be present with people whose names he immediately forgot. He was still able to take in the compliments regarding the greatness of the mountain, the professionalism of the staff, and the surprising quality of food for a ski resort, but underneath his genial facade, he was eager for one thing—a reason to deploy his Colt 1911.

Eager to get to the viewing booth he built to have a clear vantage of Bobby's Bandido Bowl, Bill ushered everyone—the execs, Lindsey Jessups, the newly appointed decorator on all Glory Peak properties, and his CFO, Tobias Clifton—up the stairs, where a buffet of ribs, Caesar salad, and trout was waiting. As he hoped, several binoculars had been placed on stands, masquerading as viewing aids for the event. Only Bill knew their true purpose was as a tool for recon. He needed to scan the mountain for potential enemy assaults or suspicious behavior, and, with the exception of the backside of the mountain, he now saw everything on Bobby's Bandido Bowl.

The problem was Bill didn't know what to look for. Was it a rogue platoon of German soldiers, a posse of rabid monster-size alpacas, or the chain-smoking ghost of his ex-wife? Keeping a set of binoculars practically glued to his face, Bill scanned everything. And everyone was a suspect. Everyone but an innocuous group of local teens with rifles in their ski bags who had pre-planted C-4 on the mountain. One local, however, did catch his attention. Limping through the parking lot on an elk-bone peg leg with a pair of Oakley ski goggles stretched across his forehead. No boots, no poles, no skis—he did not look like he was here for the runs or to watch the snowboard half-pipe event that was about to start.

Bill himself was not a fan of the snowboard, even though Glory Peak was one of the first mountains to allow it. And as all the young visitors were choosing it over skiing, he had no choice but to accept it on his slopes, but as for the sport itself—which was nothing more than skateboarding on a winter hill or surfing on frozen water—it violated every element of adventure he'd associated with the off-piste training of the 10th Mountain Division. His team and employees knew how he felt about snowboarding, so it was no surprise to them that as contestants launched off the half-pipe and strung together beef curtains, rusty trombones, Korean bacons, and lando-rolls, that Bill's attention was not on the half-pipe, but on the spectators. One very specific spectator.

As the Burton representatives hollered and the NBC executives gorged on trout, all Bill thought was, *Why is He Who Eats here? And who is that skinny white boy he's talking to at the coffee stand?* If his mental faculties had been intact, Bill would have noticed, beneath the large burn scar on his face, that the skinny white boy he'd just referenced was none other than Jimmy Harriman, Clover's former best friend and boyfriend. But his mental faculties were frayed and running on the dry steam of near-empty adrenal glands. So, as Bill looked through his binoculars at, He Who Eats, it was not Jimmy he saw, but a ghost. A new ghost. Another ghost; seared and decaying at the base of his mountain. *Finally*, he thought, *a rebel.*

Interestingly enough, Bill wasn't wrong. Jimmy had spent the previous night planting C-4 all over the Bobby's Bandido Bowl and Wolfe Mountain. But unbeknownst to Bill, He Who Eats, and the war party, Jimmy had taken it upon himself to plant additional C-4 under Bill's fire-engine red Land Rover. The reason for this was that Jimmy knew Bill was the sort of man who, once the first round of explosives detonated and drew attention, would play hero, jump in his car, and drive up the mountain to the main chairlift to help the injured—or at least pretend to for the sake of saving his business.

If Jimmy was correct, it would be easy to suggest the car got caught in the shrapnel of the explosions and was not specifically targeted in the attack. Which, based on the briefing He Who Eats just finished having with Jimmy at the coffee stand, would start in twenty minutes.

Staring through the binoculars, Bill watched He Who Eats extend his large, paw-like hand, then pull Jimmy close to him and lift him in a hug filled with tears. Bill then watched him put Jimmy back on the metal stairs of the lodge, grab a long white ski bag, and hop to the gondola.

Tracking He Who Eats as he peg-legged through the morning mass of skiers, Bill wondered, *Why the hell would this gimp with one leg be skiing?* The ski bag he'd just collected showed no sign of containing the sit-down ski setup used by paraplegics or amputees and looked damn near brand-new and probably just purchased.

Watching him step onto the gondola just a hundred yards from the coffee stand, Bill felt a sudden sting of adrenaline in his back. He had felt this only twice before: the morning Bobby disappeared and the moment before the 10th Mountain Division's final attack on the Germans.

*It's a sign*, Bill thought and waved over the head security guard, who was picking through the baby back ribs on the buffet.

"Sergeant John," Bill whispered into the man's ear. "Sergeant John, I need you to walkie the receiving soldiers at the peak end of the gondola and tell them a subject has been identified."

Rib still in his mouth, the head security guard placed it on the viewing stand rail and wiped his face with the back of his jacketed arm.

"Um, sir, just a reminder—my name's Carter," the head security guard responded.

"Okay, okay—Sergeant Carter," Bill responded with a smile. "Walkie in the suspect. He's six-foot-five, looks like a mountain, and goes by the name He Who Eats."

"He Who Eats, sir?" the head security guard answered, confused.

"Yes, Sergeant. And to be honest, your questions are beginning to rile me up—I don't have time for fat, ugly, and stupid on my shift. He's a Native. The gondola operator will understand."

The head security guard fumbled for his walkie on his side belt, waiting a beat for Bill to maybe step away and let him off the hook. But Bill didn't move, so the security guard radioed, "Hey, uh . . . Carter, here. Carter to the head gondola operator. Come in, gondola—"

"What's up, Carter?" the other security guard asked casually.

"I-I've got Mr. Macklemore—"

"Colonel," Bill interrupted.

"Uh, yes . . . I'm sorry, sir," Carter said, returning his mouth to the walkie. "I have Colonel Macklemore here asking if you can identify a large, six-foot-five Native man who goes by the name He Who Eats and—"

"Detain him!" Bill interjected, ripping the walkie out of Carter's hand and talking directly to the gondola security guard. "Detain him, and I will personally come and get him. Do you understand my orders?"

After a moment of silence, the gondola security guard said, "Yeah, sure, Mr. Macklemore."

"Next time, you're to respond with Lima Charlie," Bill replied curtly and handed the walkie-talkie back to Carter, who placed it back on his belt.

Bill then grabbed Carter by the back of his neck and pulled him in. "I need you and your platoon to set up a perimeter around Upper Potato Head Way. Make sure you cut off all other ski trails and just leave that trail open. I will meet you at the bottom of the catwalk, where it becomes Shamrock Loop. I will be in my winter fatigues. You will not see me, but keep your earbud in, and I will walkie you my coordinates." Carter merely blinked back at him, completely bewildered by every aspect of this entire exchange.

Bill then reached for the half-eaten rib on the railing, handed it back to him, waved goodbye to the executives, and stomped down the stairs of the viewing stand to his red Land Rover.

Scanning the gondola landing, the gondola operator didn't see any evidence of a six-foot-five Native man who looked like he went by the name He Who Eats. And that's because He Who Eats was already off the gondola when the operator received the call and hiking toward a small rock ridge that hooked like a talon above the landing.

While on the gondola, He Who Eats had removed white coyote pelts from the ski bag and affixed a long shrub to his back. When he got off, he had transformed—now half polar bear and half ponderosa pine. Moving on all fours, he advanced up a small incline and settled under the ridge in a prone sniper position. Removing the ski bag from his shoulder, he pulled out a Remington Model 700 hunting rifle painted white and rested it on the snow.

Through the scope, he saw a young snowboarder launch above the half-pipe and spin a 720 back down its lip. Then, in silence, he saw the crowd cheer and raise their hands in fist-pumping flurries. Scanning the scene, he spotted high-fives and hips dancing, but no matter where he pointed the scope, he didn't see Bill or the red bob of Jimmy's wool hat.

Concerned, he inched forward, the snow cold on his belly, and pulled a small mirror from his pocket. Pointing it west across the peak, he flashed a glare toward a rock ledge on the other side of the gondola. Immediately, a glare shot back from a swatch of short pines, hiding an already-in-position Grant. Grant had been stationed there since the chairlift opened, making sure no one discovered the C-4 or disrupted the line of sight needed for the remote detonators.

Below them both and sitting outside the small cafeteria at the mountain base was Clover. On her back she carried a North Face daypack filled with additional munitions and backup detonators. Planted at her side was a pair of skis and poles in case she needed to relay the detonators to Jimmy. Eyes on the mountain, she saw the volley of mirror flashes between He Who Eats and Grant. Grabbing her stomach, she understood the countdown had begun.

There was just thirty seconds until the *Rah-pah-no*. Thirty seconds until the battle to end the war was about to commence.

Panning across her surroundings, Clover took in the world she was about to forever change. Six-year-olds scampered below ski school signs, fur-rimmed hoods pulled tight over their heads with just enough room to let their eyes and nose touch the cold morning air. Tourists lined up in bunches of six, locked their arms together and flashed grins that were multiple months in the making. Locals blew on the boiling top of a cup of coffee, the steam massaging their upper lips, then splitting in half and sliding past their cheeks and pink ears. Looking at these faces, these forms, these bodies upholstered in three-ply GORE-TEX and fleece, a single consistent element glowed from every person Clover studied. Happiness. Innocent, genuine, happiness.

*This was a playground*, she realized. This was chocolate-covered raspberries. This was something people squirreled 10 percent of their paychecks away for and had likely spent all their PTO on. This was her family—her father's DNA, her mother's DNA, her grandparents' alchemic result of faith, love, and purpose.

And she was about to destroy it. All of it.

With five seconds left and four volleys of mirrors to go, Clover dropped the North Face bag and stood up. Cupping her hands around her mouth, she screamed a long, drawn-out "Noooooo!" A loud, booming no that might have come from the singular pain caused by a mineshaft dug in the heart of the Farangotta. A no, so loud and booming, it knocked He Who Eats off his scope, like a gunshot to the chest, and Grant back against the snow—and Bill into the steering wheel of his car.

And then, something else happened. Something Clover did not expect, or anyone else: the arrival of the second indecipherable part of the day. The one that brewed in rising gusts of wind along the flaky layer of top snow that covered Bobby's Bandido Bowl. These were a combination of warm and cold gusts, each carrying a varying spectrum of temperature, speed, and information. Some suggested a cold swell from the east, others, a warm spell from the west, and when they collided, they spun into a mini-tornado that rushed toward the sky like a mushroom blast, sending the clouds in every direction. From his prone position, He Who Eats watched a light layer of fresh snowfall twirl and spin in arcs along the mountain crust. It was drunk, it was nimble, it was graceful, and it was unpredictable. Watching this dance and taking in the bipolar hot-and-cold wind that carried it in loop-de-loops, He Who Eats realized what was about to happen—the *Pay-ah-eh-ah-poe*.

"Holy fuck," he huffed to himself. "The *Rah-pah-no* happening with a *Pay-ah-eh-ah-poe*. The universe has lightning in its balls. This is gonna be the great motherfucking divide!"

And then it started. Large, butterfly-size flakes of snow fell from the sky. They were sparse at first—rare hummingbirds of floating white. But soon, they got thicker, a large, thick swarm of flakes that fell so fast, looking at the landscape felt like looking through a screen of cheesecloth.

Hoping to create a sight line down to the mountain's base, He Who Eats stood and rested his hand over his eyes, but he couldn't see anything. Not even a foot in front of him. But he could hear. And in the distance, he heard an announcer get on a loudspeaker and share that the Extreme XL Games were temporarily suspended. He also heard the announcer follow up with, "Due to poor visibility, all lifts on Bobby's Bandido Bowl are also now suspended."

Raising his arms toward the sky, He Who Eats let out a primal, guttural wail that spoke to every gram of pain, love, and joy inside him. "Bring it to me, Wise One! Let me feel your loins on my face and your seed on us ants. I want it, you bonkers bolt of life. I want to taste it all!"

And just like that, He Who Eats got it all. A large sheet of snow unleashed itself from its firm grip on the peak above Bobby's Bandido Bowl, and in a rumbling rush, catapulted itself down the mountain toward the half-pipe and lodge. Watching the rolling mass thunder its way toward the spectators, a giant hole burned through He Who Eats' chest. "No," he said, intending for it to come out as a scream, only for the words to come out as breath. Then, before his eyes, the avalanche swallowed up hundreds of people too awestruck to get out of the way.

"Grant!" He Who Eats shouted. "Abort, abort! We need to get the people!"

Grant barely heard He Who Eats' voice above the screams and roaring crashes of glass and buildings being bulldozed by snow. But he knew what he was saying. Fast, he dug his hands in the snow and pulled out his skis. Clipping in, he darted off the rock ledge toward Clover.

The snow was still falling, thick and heavy, and as he skied through the flakes, his face turned red from their lashings. Just when he was about to kneel into a crouching position to protect his face, a beacon of neon pink ski pants came at him. About to crash into it, Grant slid to a stop, inches from Clover's face.

"We need to go down, Clover—we need to abort! He Who Eats is going to signal everyone else. Can you make it down?"

"Yeah, I think so," she responded, blocking the snowflakes slapping at her face.

"Stay low—it will help you get through the snow. I'll see you down there," Grant said, the volume of his voice near a scream and yet still muffled by the howling wind.

Clover nodded and watched him fade into the whiteout. Clipping into her boots, she followed, near blind.

By the time she got down to the mountain base, visibility had worsened, and the distant aural effects echoing up the mountain were now eardrum scarring. Wails, cries, weeping, prayers—they tore through the lodge area in a deafening white noise. Unclipping from her skis, Clover stumbled into a lake-size mass of avalanche-caused destruction. The half-pipe was lying on its side, torn in two, its once steel sides now jagged wells of snow. Next to it lay the viewing tower, nothing but a knot of pipe and pine. And sticking through the snow mass, like the bent spokes of a bicycle wheel after a thunderous crash, were bodies. Armies and armies of bodies. Legs protruded at bizarre angles, heads fought for air just above the snow line, and arms thrashed like flags in the wind, attached to a person submerged, somewhere, fighting for breath and daylight. Running toward a lone hand, Clover dug manic till she found a young NBC production assistant who was blue in the face and gasping for air. Pulling him from the avalanche bank, she then turned and ran toward a woman in a pretzeled triangle, half swallowed by ice and snow. Her face was smeared in blood, and her ear hung by a thin flap of skin, torn from the avalanche's impact.

Gentle, Clover excavated her and, even more gentle, lifted her over her shoulder and in an adrenaline-charged burst, carried her to a bench at the far side of the mountain base. As she walked, she watched other members of the war party tend to skiers stuck or battered by the avalanche. Slippery Tongue offered water to a grandmother heaving dry coughs, and Grant dragged two dreadlocked snowboarders—snowboards still attached—to an open spot at the far end of the parking lot. Following just behind was He Who Likes Oaks, who steadied a woman with a ski pole impaled in her neck.

But it was in the distance that Clover saw the most upsetting sight of all: Jimmy sprinting through an open field, stopping every twenty yards to turn and fire a Beretta M9 at a charging Bill.

Pushing through the blinding snow, Clover tried to see where he was headed and saw, just ahead of him, the outline of what seemed like a snowmobile. Panicked, Clover released a "Jimmy, no!" but her voice got swallowed up by the storm. Only the lone, single-shot pow of his handgun, followed by the rat-a-tat of Bill's submachine gun, could be heard over the chaos.

When Clover reached the field, it was to the blurred image of Bill raising his gun and aiming at Jimmy. Holding steady, he squeezed off a full-auto burst, with one of the bullets lodging in Jimmy's lower back, knocking him to the ground inches from the snowmobile.

"No, Grandpa, noooo!" Clover shouted. Shocked by the sound of Clover's voice, Bill spun toward her with his machine gun raised.

"Stand down, soldier!" he screamed and released a warning round five feet from her. Sliding to a stop, Clover heaved as her grandfather pointed a steaming submachine gun at her. His face was white, his eyes swirling, his forehead shiny with sweat. "Grandpa, what are you doing? It's me, Clover!" she said, hoping the strength in her voice would slap him back to reality. And it did, for a moment—just long enough for Jimmy to reach the snowmobile, jump on, turn the ignition, and speed out of sight.

"No!" Bill wailed as he saw the snowmobile lumber toward the powdery ridges in the distance. Slinging the gun over his shoulder, he sprinted for his red Land Rover in the parking lot. Losing him in the storm, Clover waited breathless until she watched a box of red careen toward Yeehaw Pass.

It was the sound of the gunshots that eventually dragged Gunther out of bed. They were unmistakable and unique to any gunfire he'd had heard in the Farangotta. At first, they sounded playful, like party poppers finding their use on New Year's. But when he heard additional, full-auto volleys, it became apparent it was submachine gunfire.

Running to his closet, he pulled on a wool sweater and prepared to do something he hadn't done in weeks—go outside. Hobbling to the front door, his boots almost on, Gunther heard the roar of a snowmobile rev up his slope. As he arrived at his front porch, he then saw the passing image of the revving snowmobile. Riding it was a young man with a red wool hat, charging toward the base of Jade Ridge. And swerving behind him, was a fire-engine red Land Rover—Bill's fire-engine-red Land Rover—chasing the snowmobile as it swooshed through the fog-thick storm.

"*Scheisse*," Gunther huffed. "What is that pig of a man doing?" Watching the Land Rover slide left in the snow, Gunther felt the remaining blanket of weltschmerz fall off his back. Raising his hands to a cup around his mouth, Gunther screamed, "William, what are you doing?"

Watching the Land Rover spit snow at him as it powered up the hill was not the answer he hoped for.

Stomping back into the house, Gunther grabbed a jacket, scarf, and hat, then stormed his way toward the Mercedes G-Wagon in his driveway. *What is wrong with this man?* Gunther thought. *Why must he destroy everything? The contempt! It must stop!* Yanking open the driver's side of his G-Wagon,

Gunther spun the motor, engaged the clutch, drove down his driveway, and aimed at the red blur in the distance.

Meanwhile, He Who Eats followed the same red blur. He had chains on his tires to hold tread and steered his pickup down Yeehaw Pass deadlocked on Bill. Back at the main lodge, Clover, amid her frantic tears, had barely been able to spit out what she saw to him. But with none of the C-4 triggered and the distant sight of Bill swerving toward Jade Ridge, He Who Eats pieced together what happened.

Leaving Grant to nurse the survivors, He Who Eats grabbed Clover's shaking hands and looked her deep in the eyes. His breath was calm, his eyes settled, with none of the swirls they had of late, and said, "Princess, listen to me. I will bring Jimmy back."

Clover nodded slow as he spoke, hypnotized by the gentle cadence of his words. Releasing her hands, she watched He Who Eats hobble to his car, gas the engine, and chug after Jimmy. As she watched him accelerate up the hill toward Yeehaw Pass, Clover realized it would take too long to catch them by car. It was clear that the fastest way to catch them would be by cutting through the valley, then up the beginner trail of Jade Ridge.

Pulling her cross-country skis from her bag, she fastened into them and grabbed her poles. Aware the cars had a massive lead, she decided to take MacGregor's Ole Copper-Spoked Pass, knowing if she didn't break stride and endured the brutal burn that would come to her legs and lungs, she would make it there by the time Bill did.

The chase started slow, as her body forgot the metabolic output needed to power after them. But then, as she turned onto the entrance of MacGregor's Pass, she found the muscle memory of her pole plants and skates. With each lunge, she picked up speed, and giving herself over to the technique she and Jimmy honed just a year ago, she was soon on the trail to Jade Ridge—ahead of Jimmy's snowmobile in the distance.

Huffing a trail of black diesel into the white of the storm, the snowmobile ricocheted up and down snowbanks in tumults until a final lurch left sent it into a shallow crevasse, crashing its hood into a burst of powder.

Dazed, Jimmy staggered from the snowmobile and crawled toward the mountain base. The snow flurried in a dense, eye-level cloud around him, but through it, he could make out a red blur of metal coming toward him. He knew Bill wasn't going to stop and he knew Bill intended on weaponizing his Land Rover against him.

No option for escape, Jimmy grabbed the daypack from his shoulders, unzipped it, and pulled out a yellow handgrip trigger. Struggling to pull the antenna up with his frostbitten fingers, Jimmy pressed the trigger hard against his head—and tried to ignite the C-4 under Bill's car.

Nothing happened. Just the sound of Bill's squealing engine. And then, *boom*.

A bright-orange ball of fire exploded beneath the Land Rover and hurtled it crooked toward the mountain.

For the first time in a long time, the world was silent. The snow continued to dump from the sky and spin in cyclones of wind, but no scream of man or metal disrupted the valley. Nature was having its way. Almost unencumbered except for a bloodied William Jefferson Macklemore, who hung from his seat belt in his overturned Land Rover. Trying to free himself, Bill was talking, once again, to a ghost in his backseat.

"Bobby," he muttered, seeing his son before him. "Bobby, can you help me?" The ghost said nothing. It just dissolved into swirls of snowflakes as Bill reached his hand out, trying to keep it from leaving.

Concussed, bruised, and owning two cracked ribs, Bill thought about how lucky he was to insist on reinforcing the frame of his Land Rover after Suzanne's death. Half expecting her ghost to show up next, Bill unclipped his seat belt, reloaded his Colt, pushed opened his door, and limped after Jimmy.

Which was to Clover's complete shock. And Gunther's arriving surprise as he, too, saw Bill stagger up the slope. Watching Bill pinch off shots, Gunther's blood bubbled with a feeling he hadn't allowed for in years—rage. Slamming his G-Wagon to a stop, Gunther flung open the door and stomped after Bill.

"William, you imbecile, put that gun down!" he bellowed. But through the dense fabric of snow, only Clover could see or hear him.

Jimmy, on the other hand, was seeing in duplicate. Triplicate. The hole where the bullet struck had grown, and blood now soaked both sides of his flannel. Hoping he could make it to his tent with enough energy to reload his gun and have one last standoff, he inched his way toward the craggy ridge of the mountain. His tent was now close enough to be visible in the distance, but as Jimmy reached for a crown of limestone to steady himself, a large jolting pain ripped through his right leg and sent him crashing to the snow. Rolling onto his back, Jimmy saw a spray of red on his right and smelled the tang of iron that came when blood conversed with oxygen. Refusing to slow, he turned on his stomach and crawled forward when another jolt of heat ripped through his left leg.

Twisting over, he reached for the freshly singed hole in his thigh. Like a sponge, the white powder drank up the blood and turned the snow burgundy around him.

Blind with pain, Jimmy laid on his back and reached for the cool touch of the quarter-size flakes storming down. Their chill landed moist on his fingertips and sparked a rush of endorphins that overtook all the pain he was feeling. So much so, he did not notice when Bill stood above him and aimed his Colt at his head. There were three bullets left in his clip, and from this range, at least two would land and split his head open. Clicking one into the chamber, Bill pushed the barrel of the gun toward the euphoric unawareness of Jimmy's skull.

"You fucking Nazi scum," Bill hissed. "You'll never get my land."

Then, cocking his gun, Bill expertly placed his left hand in front of his face to shield himself from the inevitable spray of brain and bone. Except that never happened. Because Gunther finally caught up to them, and he was fervent, zealous, ardent. Pissed.

Lunging at Bill, he tackled him into the powder. It was a soft landing, one that dampened the force by which he was clotheslined. Shocked, Bill coughed up a few drops of blood from where he'd bit his tongue. Gunther, meanwhile, huddled over Jimmy, trying his best to slow his bleeding. Pressing against a hole in Jimmy's leg, Gunther was unaware that Bill was still conscious. He finally noticed when he heard the click of Bill's Colt pulling its hammer into place.

Turning toward the sound, he saw Bill wobble to a stand. His arm shook but it still had its sight on Jimmy. Gunther, prepared to take the bullet, stood in front of Jimmy. But it was unnecessary as a blur of hair, silky white, with necks preening tall, stampeded toward Bill.

The *Me-oh-watch-ohs*. The four-legged furry fuckers. There were only six of them left, but they galloped—angry, grunting, and honking spit— and collided directly into Bill's rib cage, sending him ten feet back onto the ground. A clean KO, the gun flew from his hand into the powder at the far end of the ridge.

Unsure of what had just happened, Gunther waved his hands through the flurries, hoping to see something that hinted at the blur that just blew through the storm. But there was nothing—just an unconscious Bill and a bleeding Jimmy.

Returning to Jimmy on the ground, Gunther pulled off his jacket and rested it under his head. Then, eyeing Bill, Gunther stomped over to him, grabbed him by his wild blond hair, and draped him between two narrow limestone spires. At this point, Clover reached the ridge. She was huffing, and the piercing wheeze of cold whistled through her nostrils and lungs. Seeing Gunther with Bill's limp body, she felt relief—but seeing Jimmy in a pool of burgundy slush, she felt fear.

Sprinting to him, she slid to his side and watched him grin and reach for the snowflakes. They turned to water in his hand, and as the drops slid along his fingers and tickled his knuckles, he smiled.

Watching him lie there, with his hand extended skyward, a sense of calm washed over Clover. Because in his eyes, that childlike focus she once depended on had returned. As she raised her hand to close his eyes and allow Jimmy to move into the next world, the out-of-breath roar of He Who Eats stopped her.

"What the hell are you doing, *kemo-wabi*?" he asked. Turning toward him, all Clover could do was take in the mountain-like silhouette of He Who Eats walking in snowfall. "You better settle that shit down—that little pecker's not ready to cross."

Confused, Clover looked back at Jimmy. He was surrounded by blood and seemed to be thigh-deep in whatever blissful afterlife everyone hoped for. But he was still breathing.

"He's going to be okay?" Clover asked, her hands now beginning to tremble.

"Of course, he's gonna be okay. Dreamt last night he had two kids, weird as shit, and was living up in Bozeman."

Hobbling on his antler leg, He Who Eats nudged Clover to the side, and with one sinewy move, he reached down and scooped Jimmy up from the snow. Placing him gently on his feet, He Who Eats stared Jimmy in the eyes and said, "Okay, twig, enough drama for today. We still got to get to the *Rah-pah-no*, and I don't have much more gimping in me."

Jimmy, still smiling, handed He Who Eats his daypack. Reaching inside, He Who Eats found the two remaining hand triggers. Extending their antennae, he powered them on, then, looking up ridge, saw Gunther standing beside Bill's splayed body.

"So, you're the German douchebag, eh?" He Who Eats shouted at Gunther, who turned around so fast, it was clear he hadn't seen them standing at the base of the ridge.

"Yeah, I am," Gunther responded proudly.

"Well, I guess, thanks for the alpacas." He Who Eats laughed.

"What do you mean? They're all gone," Gunther replied. He was dead serious.

"What do you mean, what do I mean? Don't you have no eyesight in Deutschland?" He Who Eats asked, aware that once the snowfall slowed and visibility returned, everyone would see the six alpacas on the ridge who bore witness to this all. Or maybe not. Their vision was not his concern, especially as he was finally face to face with Bill—the *Eh-Kar-loh*.

Grabbing him by the back of his 10th Infantry fatigues, He Who Eats stood Bill up. Bill tried his best to stand proud, but was too weak and filled with too much shame to look He Who Eats in the eyes—knowing that if he did, in them, he would see the corpses of twenty-seven alpacas, eight German soldiers, his former in-laws, and his former wife. And looking deeper into them, he would see the ghosts of Bobby and Annabelle. And the loss of his granddaughter, Clover.

Knowing this was too much for any man to bear, He Who Eats draped Bill's arm over his shoulder and walked him to the far end of Jade Ridge. Grabbing his face with his hand, he held Bill steady enough to ask one last thing.

"Are you ready?"

Bill, fully aware of what the question meant, shook his head a defiant no.

Digesting the response, He Who Eats let his lips swell, and a smile the size of December rolled over him. "Well, shit, *Eh-Kar-loh*, that's good enough for me," he said. And before Bill grasped what was happening, He Who Eats swaddled him in a bear-hug and jumped off Jade Ridge.

The fall seemed like an eternity. And as they closed their eyes and felt the warm and cold gusts of the *Pay-ah-eh-ah-poe*, Bill finally understood what it meant to be air, and He Who Eats finally understood what it meant to be nature. Powerful, unpredictable nature—capable of brutality and beauty on a whim. Then, as they both fell, hovering some place between heaven and earth, He Who Eats pressed down on the remote triggers and ignited the explosives on Bobby's Bandido Bowl and Wolfe Mountain.

The ensuing tremors were mind-boggling. Each explosive released an earthquake-size rattle that jiggled every object for a thousand miles and sent every memory in the valley into a jumbled twine of past and present. Rewind two hundred years here. Fast-forward eighty years there. Dirt, rock, and trees reformed in ways to deny all that had accrued over millennia.

The Farangotta was split open in earth and time, and somewhere, in the midst of it all, and fifteen years earlier, were Bobby Mac and Annabelle. They waited in a small tunnel with the promising flush of daylight above them as rounds and rounds of explosives blew, rattling every object for a thousand miles. Hoping to get to the slushy ice wall at the end of the tunnel, they soon found the bottom halves of their bodies covered in snow. Now unable to move, further blasts rained earth and ice on them, trapping them deeper in Miner's Gasp as the inevitable outcome of their lives became apparent. Relieved there was nothing left to fight, nothing left to try, and nothing left to do, Annabelle leaned tight into Bobby's body. Gently rubbing her temple, Bobby could only do one thing—because in the moment, Bobby could only feel one thing. Love.

With her ear near his lips and the snow and earth falling heavy over them, Bobby closed his eyes and whispered to Annabelle, again, and again. "It will all be okay," he said. "It will all be okay."

　　　　　　　　　　　　　〰

It took three days for the snow to stop falling and an additional four days to survey the damage caused by both the avalanche and C-4 explosives.

Wolfe Mountain was nothing but rubble, and Bobby's Bandido Bowl was nothing but a terrain park ghost town. But outside of the destruction of the man-made lodges and condominiums, a more fascinating turn of events occurred. The river that fed Punishment Lake had split in two and was already feeding a large tear-shaped gash in the bedrock, forming a new lake. Hangman's Cliff, which sat on an extended fault line, cracked into several layers and took on the singular geological appearance of a massive stone accordion. And Miner's Gasp shed its steep-sloped sides to reveal a near-perfect oval plateau outlined by rolling edges. Edges that Nanny A would have even described as feminine.

At its base was a crumble of copper, and on the west side of its base was an even greater discovery—the bodies of Robert and Annabelle Macklemore locked in a mummified embrace. Within a day of transferring their bodies to the coroner's, a piece of paper was discovered in a plastic bag in Bobby's jacket. It showed the transfer of Glory Peak, via a trust in the name of Suzanne Joanne Dempsey, to Robert Butler Macklemore, then to Clover Dolores Macklemore. Two days after that, Sheriff Dan Daley came forward with additional paperwork showing the transfer of Wolfehaus, and all its holdings, from Abigail Augusta Charters to Clover Dolores Macklemore.

At times in the future, when Clover sat quietly with Grant in the Elder Elders' hut, or alone in her downstairs office, going through things—with a necklace made of boar fang and coral snake around her neck—she would assess the effects of the *Rah-pah-no* on Fortooth and the greater Farangotta Valley.

It was different now, but somehow also the same. The same as it was before the Europeans settled, yet different now from the departure of the Elder Elders to Florida. Not knowing why, she was astounded it all fell under her ownership. And not knowing why, she wondered what her parents thought just before they made their great transition.

But just as she stuck her head in the morning air to discover the great recipe of the day, Clover had only to close her eyes to find the answer. And see that, because of all that happened, her father could die a happy man. And her mother a happy woman. And so they did.